A Flight of Saints

𝔄 𝔉𝔩𝔦𝔤𝔥𝔱 𝔬𝔣 𝔖𝔞𝔦𝔫𝔱𝔰

Elizabeth Braithwaite

PAMPERED PILGRIM PRESS

A Flight of Saints
Text and illustrations copyright © 2025 J.E. Braithwaite

All rights reserved. No part of this publication may be reproduced, stored in a retrieval system, distributed, or transmitted in any form or by any means—electronic, mechanical, photocopying, recording, or otherwise—without the prior written permission of the author, except in the case of brief quotations embodied in reviews.

Cover art © Haychley Webb
Cover designed by Stephanie Hofmann
Text designed and typeset by Dinah Drazin

Published by Pampered Pilgrim Press
www.janechristmas.ca

ISBN 9798300870607

I

The Feast of John the Baptist
Convent of Saint Agatha, Trento
1179

Little Fey was in the refectory when I arrived. Her name was Sister Fey but I called her Little Fey because she was small. She was also round and pale, like a sweet bun, but it would not do to call her Round Fey. Not to her face. Not to the face I was desperate to avoid that morning.

I entered the room to begin our chores, eyes averted, and hurried to the other side of the long table. For once I was grateful for our convent's strict rule. Ever since Saint Agatha's came under the Great Silence we had been forbidden to speak. Those who did were beaten, though that rarely hushed Little Fey, who was never punished. Besides, she didn't always require words; a simple change in manner could alert her that something was up; that some morsel of news or twaddle was being withheld from her. The Great

Silence heightened her sensitivity so that a slight hesitation in my eyes or in my step would subject me to a full and immediate interrogation that would not let up until I broke. I swear she could tell I held news or rumour by the set of my mouth. She was not easy to be around.

This time, I could not give myself away. I hardened my heart before I entered the room, softened my movements and bearing so she could not read my face, so she would be none the wiser as to what swirled in my head and heart. But as soon as I was in her presence mastery failed me: My hands turned damp, I felt my cheeks rising red, my belly felt like fish were swimming in it. I turned my head; admonished myself. *Restrain yourself or she will know you are hiding something.*

It is not my nature to lie or hold secrets. It is an acquired, necessary talent. Little Fey and I were the dearest of friends. We slept side by side. Together, we had grown, chattered, laughed, played, and sang as much as we had prayed, chanted, and learned our catechism. Such was our bond that we knew one another's habits and humours; we knew the other so well that if we were in different rooms, even under the wrap of this new and unwelcome cloak of silence, we could hear one another's soul cry. The blink of eyes, the pace of breath, the quiver of a lip—these spoke as loudly as any voice. But now, my lips, eyes, breath were betraying me, giving hint about the visitor from the night just past who had said the best words I have heard in all my fourteen winters; words that could spell freedom from this awful place as easily as they could spell my death.

My breath became fast, ragged. I pinched my arm to snuff

it. Had she noticed? I looked. She had. Her blue eyes were wide. She tilted her head.

I looked down to the flags.

Quick, put a new thought into your head! Act as if all is well!

But I couldn't find a new thought. I made my way down my side of the table, my movements jerky, my gait in spasm. All this twitching made me look like one possessed. She'd be full curious now, wanting to wheedle out my secret, to demand. account for my tossing-turning last night. I didn't need to look at her to know this; I could feel the heat from her questioning eyes.

The whiff of bread reminded me that I was hungry. I looked down the length of the refectory table where morning had sprawled across it, casting honeyed light on the remains of eggs and bread. Butter and jam, too. Well, it was a feast day; still even when our beloved Mother Elena was in charge, we never knew such extravagance. Now, with the fast broken, the sisters were back in their cells, possibly to pray, more likely to gossip and titter with Mother Clothilde in her rooms.

Steadier now, I set my jaw, put a countenance upon my face that made me appear as if there was nothing odd about feeling fish swimming in my belly, and proceeded with my task. I boldly looked at Little Fey.

To see her you would think her the holiest among us: tunic neat; hands constantly pressed in prayer; flaxen hair framing her head like a halo; eyes the colour of the Virgin's robes. As if God Himself had dropped her into the midst and said, 'This is how my bride should look.' It was like staring into the sun. I felt holier just being near her. She had that effect on people, and she knew it and used it to advantage. But she had a secret, too, and it was worse than mine.

She stood now in her cultivated pose: hands clasped in front of her chest, head tipped, the small smile affecting the manner of holy patience as she waited for my usual sigh of surrender. She knew I was weak and would give up any twaddle in the flick of a bird's feather.

No, Little Fey. Not this time. You can try to crack me open like a walnut and devour what is inside, but I will not break. Nay, I refuse to break. Refuse to break. Refuse to break!

Even as I thought it, my resolve sheered away, eager to satiate her hunger. It was like being at war with myself.

You are older than her; pull yourself together. I stood straighter, glared at her and jerked my head toward the dirty trenchers to say, *Come. Where is your duty?*

I hustled along my side of the refectory table, the model of efficiency, and gathered the riffraff. Busyness was my friend. A thick smear of drying yolk glistened on the rim of a trencher. I lifted it to my face and licked it off the wood. Leftover crusts went into my pocket.

When next my eyes slid toward Little Fey, piety had left her face, replaced by a look of fiery demand: *Tell me what is in your head!*

It only tightened my will. Besides, what fool is she? Why would I spill my heart right here with the ever-present fear of prying ears and eyes?

She coughed for my attention. I paid no mind. My finger swept up a slick of butter and found my mouth. She could give pout all she wanted.

Psst.

I shook my head; denied her my eye.

She began to whimper like a dog. A foolish risk. If Mother heard, then it would be me who took the whip. Mother wouldn't touch Little Fey, but she'd gladly beat me for the both of us. Was that Little Fey's game—my secret in exchange for being spared punishment?

I stacked the trenchers in the crook of my arm, collected cups and forks.

The faint sound of rasping caught my ears. My eyes darted toward it; toward her. She glowered as she scraped her palms against the raw edge of the refectory table. Back and forth.

I matched her glare, made my eyes large and angry, set my mouth tight. *Naughty Fey! Stop!* If she didn't—and she wouldn't—her hands would be full of splinters that I would have to pluck, and if Mother Clothilde found out, her fury would land on me.

Little Fey returned my opprobrium with a sneer: *Only if you tell me.*

Refuse to break!

I spun round, and carried the dirty tableware to the kitchen. A fork slipped from my grasp and clanged on the flags. Little Fey picked it up and followed me to the washboard. She stuck her face up against mine, held the fork in a manner that suggested violence.

I grabbed it, waved it back at her. *Not now! Leave me be.*

But why? Her eyes and mouth fell to a sulk.

This was our language: Forbidden to use our voices, we spoke with eyes and hands. It had been this way for nearly a year, a year since Mother Elena had been taken from this place and replaced by one who was cruel and cold of heart. Saint Agatha's was once the joyous place I called home; now I lived in fear of my life every day.

Suddenly, Sister Bettina barrelled in, balancing rounds of bread dough on two trays. We parted for her as she made for the oven and slid them in. Without acknowledging us, she groped in a side nook of the oven, drew out two sweet buns and immediately dropped them on the floor.

Her hands flew to her face in feigned dismay: 'Spoiled now.'

One of the dogs bounded for them but Sister Bettina was quick with her foot. She picked up the buns, winked at us, and stuffed them in our pockets. The bun was warm against my leg.

'Quick,' she whispered, steering us toward the door. Then, in a loud, stern voice: 'Both of you, make haste to the garden and fetch me four fennel bulbs, some sorrel and thyme. And only the best ones.' She waved her arms like a flustered goose and shooed us forth.

Sister Bettina was allowed to speak because she was the cook and the cellarer. It was only us younger ones that Mother Clothilde despised and silenced. Most of the older sisters, eager to earn her favour, had turned against us the moment she stepped over the threshold, awed by her refinement, her heeled shoes, her alabaster skin, the perfection of her clean fingernails; the type who bathes in milk. When Mother Elena was our superior, these same sisters cheerfully worked alongside us, indoors and out, so that we all had sun-darkened skin and hands that showed our labours. Not so long ago they had been fussy in their devotion to us, always kind, never tattling. Now everyone was a traitor. They were all in milk baths now. Except Sister Bettina. She alone remained loyal to us.

Little Fey and I made for the furthest patch behind the washhouse where fennel and sorrel grew, where Sister Bettina knew we would not be seen. We crouched next to the water barrel and ripped our buns in half: I saved half for Sister Gretchen; Little Fey saved her half for Fat Val. Then we stuffed the bread into our mouths and stifled moans of pleasure as the cinnamon hit our tongues. We once ate like ladies; now we ate like wolves.

'Tell me,' Little Fey pressed.

'*Ne sis pestis.* The more you do the more I won't tell.' I was not above doling out my own measure of petulance. Then, remorseful for my unkind spirit, I whispered, 'Maybe tonight.' I needed time to muster the thoughts and ideas crowding my head, and to draw them into coherence before I spoke them.

She was good as gold after that; kept her distance, even in chapel when she sat apart from me, knowing my preference for solitude when I prayed.

But it wasn't prayer that was in my heart; it was escape.

The secret I held, that had in short time become as much a part of me as breath itself, came from a strange encounter the previous night. But before I tell it, I must first confess to the shameful state I was in. My body was sore from toil and fear; my belly cramped with hunger; and my spirit was gone from me, beyond hope, beyond solace. I could no longer endure my life at Saint Agatha's, and desperation pointed in only one direction.

It was not always thus. Saint Agatha's once shone with all that was good and right in Creation. Life had been merry when we were in the care of Mother Elena. She loved us fiercely and was never unkind. She let us chatter and laugh. Although we were cloistered, I felt free and fortunate, and whenever I think back to those times all I hear is birdsong and the laughter of my sisters. Not that we were idle. Far from it. We were taught our letters, our numbers, and how to read. We were instructed in matters of medicine and assisted Mother Elena when she tended to the sick both inside and outside the convent. We worked in the gardens, and shared the bounty of our crops with the poor of Trento, of which there are many. We gained skill with needle and cloth, with chant and singing. I had been given instruction in manuscript illumination, taken under the wings of the patient sisters who worked in the scriptorium (the same who now shunned me) and who taught me the art of penmanship, and how to make large letters using vermilion. Under their guidance I learned how to grind orchil, soot, roots, and leaves and to mix them with yolk, sap, and water to make various inks. I learned to draw petals and leaves to embellish my simple letters. I watched in awe as the older, experienced sisters used crushed gold, which we obtained from the monks, to make their work glitter on the parchment. The scriptorium was where I was happiest; it was my chapel. I did not always feel close to God but I felt closest to Him there.

All that ended when Mother Clothilde flounced into our midst. She limited our making of medicines, put a stop to our gifts of food to the poor. She shut down our scriptorium. In doing so, my faith dried. When she decreed an end to speech and singing, it was as if the world itself had ceased to beat. We could no longer greet one another and curtsey as was our custom; we were only to dip to our haughty new superior. Those who did not heed her edicts—and who could remember all her edicts?—were punished. The smallest transgression earned you a week cleaning the privy pit and, depending on her mood, sleeping beside it until the Sabbath.

We were plunged into cruel silence that was broken only by the wails and pleas of sisters being whipped for straying from Mother's grim decrees; and by their muffled cries as they coddled bruised wounds, lacerated skin, and broken bones alone in their pallets. It was a nightmare.

So it was on that night of which I tell, shattered in body and spirit, that I made the decision—one that makes me shiver and cross myself with a sinner's disgrace—to end my life. *Mea culpa, mea culpa.*

My terrible desire was magnified by an uncommonly vicious storm, as if Heaven had taken umbrage at my plight and my private oath. Wind whipped our home and screamed through the passageways. The rains were torrential. It had been this way since Martius, and we were soon to enter the hay month, that is, Quintilis. There would be no threshing or reaping this year. Rain battered the land daily, and turned grain fields into lakes, and the kitchen and physick gardens into swamps. Still-born apples and figs clung to sodden boughs; normally plump and plenteous blackberry yielded fruit as hard as a nut; spring furrows were washed clean of their seeds. No one could remember a time like it. I wanted to be brave like Noah and build a boat, or at least suggest we salvage some crops and replant them in the *giardini botanici*. Mother Elena would have rejoiced at the idea, but under Mother Clothilde, enterprise, like speech, was silenced. We were doomed. Like my sisters, I succumbed to the prevailing woe of death by drowning or starvation. Not Mother Clothilde: Her furs and rich kin would save her.

That night, my duty was to stay alert for travellers, difficult as it was to imagine anyone out on such a violent night. I pondered my miserable state as thunder cracked and wind bellowed, as the flags beneath my feet trembled; or maybe it was my feet that trembled, the flags being of steadier foundation than I.

I had been stoking the fire, watching log after log die in the roaring flames, when one of the big logs inexplicably rolled from the grate and threw out a starburst of sparks, some of which landed upon my tunic. Rather than brush them off, I stared in grim fascination as they nibbled my thin fabric of tow. An epiphany struck, an exhilaration not unlike that which comes from finally gleaning meaning from a dense piece of Scripture. For I saw in that moment how perfectly, how easily I could free myself from misery; that the answer to my wretched life was a quick death. I could be ash by Compline.

Delirious with morbid excitement I coaxed and fanned the hungry embers: *Feast away.*

Thread by thread, it gnawed my garment until it had eaten a hole in it and looked poised to gorge on the rest. There was a burst of flame, one with substance, and I closed my eyes, made the sign of the Holy Cross, and awaited the *whoosh!* that would ignite and consume me whole.

And then, nothing. I opened my eyes to gauge the flame's tardy progress, only to discover that there were no sparks, no flame. A phantom hand had snuffed my one hope for eternal freedom!

Insulted and angry, I moved closer to the maw of the fire, offering it my hem. *Come, do your fiery worst.* But it, too, rebuffed my garment. *Ungrateful fire!* I knelt closer. I was almost fully inside the grate's cavity when a mighty rumble from the storm caused me to lose my balance, and I fell over and hit my head on the stone.

I scrambled to my feet. Another boom unsteadied me. The storm's fury had increased to a terrifying intensity. Rain pelted the shutters like gravel; wind screamed through the hall and threatened to extinguish the wall torches. The abbey's walls quaked. If I couldn't die by my own hand, perhaps the storm would bring down the walls of this vile place and finish me.

At that moment, one of the choir sisters scurried by, whimpering into her beads, on her way to ring the bell for Compline. My shoulders slumped. My chance with Death had passed because the Compline bell marked the time that I was to leave my post.

In glum defeat, I secured the fire, and took the torches

from their sconces and doused them. I left one alight as I made my way to the door to bolt it. As I approached, the door began to shake violently. I jumped back. Surely, the Devil! The pounding continued, rapid, urgent, until eventually fear abated and reason arrived, assuring me that it was not demon, but human.

I wiped my sooty hands on my apron and opened the door; the wind almost took it from my hand. Standing on the threshold was a man with a white, bearded face, partially hidden beneath a cowl.

I drew him inside, and he fell against the wall, panting like a horse pursued. I searched for a blanket to dry him. Gaining his breath, he pushed back his cowl. I recognised him immediately and bent the knee. It was Father Volmar, a monk-priest from Saint Disibod who had visited us many times when Mother Elena was our superior. Did he know of our new superior?

I helped him remove his sodden cloak.

The commotion had brought Mother Clothilde scurrying into the hall. She had a penchant for Eastern garb: colourful kirtles, salvars, and woven slippers. This, I guessed, was to give the impression that she'd just arrived from the Holy Land, as if she had kinship with the desert mothers and fathers. Her thick yellow braid, unveiled (for shame!), was coiled like a cobra over her shoulder. Her lips held the coy smile she kept for noble visitors, but as soon as she laid eyes on this new visitor, it dropped and returned to its regular scowl.

Meanwhile, the monk's body had inflated like bellows, ready for the warm greeting he normally received here, but

Mother's withering look blew his air right out. Not for her Benedict's rule of hospitality.

'Forgive this sudden arrival,' he had blubbered loudly. 'I had paused under a tree on the far side of the field, and must have fallen asleep. A crack of lightning woke me, and before I knew it the elements were fully upon me. Such ferocious wind! Praise God for your house. May His blessing be on it.'

Not for him Saint Agatha's severe rule of silence. I hid my mirth while Mother stared at him.

'I am Father Volmar from the house of Saint Disibod. I am on my way to Rome.'

Her demeanour changed. She hollered to Sister Bettina, 'Food!' To me she hissed: 'Why do you thand like thtone, Thithter Luthia? Get the theepthkin for poor Father.'

Her childlike voice lacked a facility with sibilants. Whether this was the style of her home-language or an affliction of her mouth I did not know.

By the time I returned from her bidding, two fine glasses glittered with ruby wine.

I shook the fleece over Father's lap so it hung to the floor and covered his bare legs.

'You carry a message for His Holiness?' Her tone was cloying.

'I do,' said Father Volmar. His eyes fell on the bowl of warm meat soup Sister Bettina placed into his hands.

'Pray, what?' said Mother.

The monk paused before he tipped the bowl to his mouth. 'It is a confidence I carry, and thus I must deliver it in confidence.'

'Come now. We are all sisters and brothers in Christ, sworn to the same vows.' Her fingernails played against the glass.

'Indeed, and I uphold those vows now.'

She gave him a tight smile. She did not like being bested.

'As you wish. What news from Saint Disibod? I have not been Mother here long. Being from Savoia I am not au fait with affairs in… Swabia, is it?'

'Rheinpfalz, Mother. Ours is a brotherhood of nineteen, including our abbot. I am humbled to say that it was in our home that a young Hildegard was raised to godly nature.'

One of her hands balled into a fist until its knuckles were white as goose down; her face took on a rictus.

'The same who is a great abbess now,' he taunted.

This was too good to miss: I began to tend the fire unnecessarily. As I reached for a log, I saw Father Volmar's eyes twinkle above the rim of his bowl, watching her.

'Our work seeks to end Church corruption and vanity. By the grace of God, we are guided by the prayerful example of Abbess Hildegard.'

I turned for the iron and risked a look at Mother: Her eyes were shut to effect impatience. She disliked the great Abbess. I had overheard her prattle to the choir sisters that Hildegard was a charlatan; that only a harlot reaped praise from men.

'That woman is more witch than wise woman,' she said, setting down her glass.

Father lowered his bowl. 'You would speak ill of one of your sex; one with the courage of David to preach in piazzas and pulpits? Who attracts the faithful and the curious and turns the curious into the faithful? What of her benefit to religious life? Never has a nunnery had so many acolytes. And then there are the many souls she cures…'

'Cures what?' Mother's raised voice made me jump. 'She grinds a few herbs, and is hailed healer of the world. She says God speaks to her, but does He not speak to us all, Father? Why do men listen to her? Her gift, if you can call it that, is not in healing but in bewitching. I hear she has a fair face. Seems to be all it takes these days to fetch interest from Rome.'

She stood abruptly and picked up the decanter. I braced. She was known to throw things. 'Her sorcery falls afoul of many in the Church who see through this pretender. If she is so wise, she would do well to silence her tongue and watch her back. Now, if you will excuse me; God awaits my humble prayers.'

The cold followed her out of the room.

I turned to Father Volmar, slumped in his chair. A watery line had made a furrow on his hairy cheek.

'Are you not well? Shall I take you to your cell?' Mother's decree of silence granted exception if it appeared that a guest or visitor was in crisis. I decided Father was in crisis.

He shook his head. His tears shone.

'Child,' he said. Not sister, but child. My heart leapt; I had almost forgotten how it felt to be addressed with kindness. 'It is not for myself that I weep, but for you. God has seen your faith and your labour, and He, too, weeps for you. Your habit is torn, your wimple is stained from your tears, your hands are raw from lengthy toil. I see, too, that your wrist blooms with the colour of harm, and it looks to me that the welt on your cheek is fresh. What monster would strike a child of God?'

His words threw me, for he had accurately read my day. That very afternoon I had been running between garden and grate, collecting wet sticks and laying them near the fireplaces to dry. I had already emptied ash from all eight grates, swept them clean and laid new fires. On my way to the woodpile, I had paused at the barrel for a ladle of water just as Mother Clothilde rounded the corner. Seeing me, she grabbed my wrist. The ladle flew out of my hand and fell on her foot. Up went her other hand and down it came against my face. 'How dare you waste time on yourself when you should be at your chores.'

I had run back to my toil, but tears got the better of me and I dropped to my knees in the mud, holding my burning cheek, weeping without control.

As I sat at Father's feet, I was ashamed that he was seeing me in my woeful state, but I was also glad he was seeing me as I was. No one seemed to know, or cared to know of our suffering inside Saint Agatha's.

Before I could beg his help, he said:

'My days frequently find me in the presence of one of the purest people ever created. A woman I serve as humbly and as lovingly as I would my own mother, were she still alive, may God preserve her soul.'

Now warm and dry, he sat erect, eyes bright, and lively in manner and gesture. The fire mimicked his effervescence; its flames leapt like a dog greeting its master.

'All she writes—music, sermons, letters—comes directly

from Heaven. Even her remedies are inspired by what God tells her.'

Mother Elena had taught us all about Hildegard, this brave, audacious nun. We worshipped her as devoutly as we did the Heavenly Father.

'Mother Elena made up her remedies and medicines in our apothecarium.' I had felt it necessary to show my knowledge so he might recognise my quality, prideful as that may seem. 'We always included the Abbess and her community—and yours, Father—in our prayers.'

'I heard she left this place, your Mother Elena.'

A stab of grief.

'Not willingly.' I bowed my head, as memory flared of horses and cart clattering up to the convent doors; of large men in bishop's livery seizing her, binding her wrists like a criminal; her screams and pleas as they dragged her away.

I shook my head to remove the scene, and returned mind and speech to Father.

'How does she—the Abbess—make room for all who yearn to join her house?'

'She builds more cells! She built Rupertsberg, and when that was full, she built another house in Bingen. She does not dither. By my soul, the woman is pure action.'

How I wished to be pure action.

He tapped his satchel, leaned forward and whispered, 'Her new work, *Ordo Virtutum*, for His Holiness. God's Word descends on her like a fire and burns its message into her. I have seen it with my own eyes. Indeed, it is my job to record it.'

With those words, my soul a milkweed pod of tightly

packed anxiety burst, and its transfigured filaments of hope seemed to fly all the way to Bingen, and there I saw myself in the black tunic of the community, with white coif and veil, praying in a place of labour and light. In that moment, I changed. I glimpsed promise and prospect. I knew I deserved better.

I should have been ashamed of my hubris, my greedy pride, but the battered, the abused do not know hubris, only desperation.

Father's eyes darted between me and the door. Again, he leaned forward.

'Abbess Hildegard would weep to have one like you in her house.' He looked back at the door. 'She would welcome you like a long-lost member of her family, and parade you among the others, singing your gifts.'

My heart lit up with a thousand candles.

'She treats everyone with equal joy. She believes with heart and soul what Christ told his disciples in Jericho, the words that Matthew tells in his Gospel: 'Whosoever will be great among you, will be your servant.'

He took my hands in his large, heavy ones; hands I could trust.

'Servants we all must be, but not slaves. Your faith will shatter if you allow yourself to be broken. Do not let this come to pass.'

I was without coherence in thought or tongue. I was about to cry out, 'Save me!' but he spoke first.

'Lucia, there is more I must say.' His face turned grave. 'Mother Elena was waiting for the right time to tell you, but as she is gone, it must fall to me.'

The thousand candles sputtered.

At first, he spoke the nonsense-blather of one whose mouth and mind are out of harmony, but after another glance at the door it came: 'This is hard to hear but say it I must: The one you called mother before you came to live here is not the one who birthed you.'

I drew back, astonished.

'Father, my mother is long dead. Your news is meant for another.'

He shook his head.

'Your father was hand-fasted to one who had a change of heart, who chose a life with God, but who then found herself with child.'

'Without marriage?' I crossed myself.

'Without marriage. It happens.' He shrugged. 'She was sent away until her birthing time. Your father demanded the babe as reparation, for he claimed to have had a vision that the child would be a boy, which he wanted very much. Your mother gave consent. The child was born, weaned, and handed to your father. He was not well pleased to receive a girl. He wed your mother's sister and it was she who raised you as her own.'

How did he know this, and why hadn't Mother Elena told me herself?

'And what of the one who birthed me?'

'She duly made her vows. I know her story because I took her confession. Your true mother is at Bingen.'

I gasped, but he read my face wrong.

'Do not worry about the taint of shame. Only she, Abbess Hildegard, me, and now you know of it,' he said hurriedly. 'It will go no further.'

He was wrong about feeling shame; that's not what I felt. I felt opportunity.

I put on a false face and nodded gravely, as a plan mounted in me.

'What is she like, this mother I don't know?'

'A good woman. Quiet, industrious. I have not had reason to speak to her since her confession, but I see her now and again when I am at the community. Do not disparage her for her sin, child. We all fall prey to our passions and must be forgiven.'

I wanted to laugh in his face: What care have I for propriety when Providence is charging toward me! My mind, which moments earlier had been clogged with the rot of helplessness, began to spin fresh thinking and weave a scheme: I could go to Bingen and be reunited with my mother, but more importantly I could go to Bingen and pledge life and limb to Abbess Hildegard!

I opened my mouth to ask Father how to accomplish this—daring to suggest that he take me with him when he left in the morning—when I saw Mother Clothilde standing in the door.

I stood up.

Her suspicious eyes narrowed on me.

Turning to Father she said: 'We break the fatht after Laudth. Unleth you plan to leave before then.'

'I shall leave after the Pater Noster. If your kitchen will

spare a bit of bread, I will take that with me on my way.'

She looked at me again. 'Off with you, Luthia. I thall thow Father to hith thell.'

I made my face a picture of humility and penitence, curtseyed to them both, and hurried bedward. So great was my excitement that I vowed to stay awake and ruminate on Father Volmar's words, and make a plan of escape. As soon as I reached my pallet and my swollen cheek had touched the straw, I dropped into slumber. At some point during the night, however, I awoke, restless and anxious in my tossing.

It made no difference. Come morning, his words and the dangerous seed he had planted were alive in me. The rejuvenating properties of opportunity and adventure ran in my veins. I stumbled into my tunic, threw cold water on my face three times—*Patris, Filius, Spiritus Sanctus*—and scurried down the stairwell to begin my daily chores.

Passing a window, I noticed the rain had stopped, the sun was out. *Deus laudetur!*

At the bottom of the stairwell, I composed myself to a sober, plain demeanour, not wanting anyone to detect the excitement hammering inside me. But when I walked into the refectory the storm cloud of suspicion was already gathering in Little Fey's eyes.

'Swear you will tell no one.'

'I swear. Touch wood.' Little Fey tapped the cross of olive wood that hung from her neck.

Moonlight spilled between gaps in the rafters and lit her face. Her eyes were full upon me, waiting. I listened for the sleep-snuffle of the other novices in the room. All was quiet except for Sister Gretchen's whimpers. She had taken the whip after Nones for speaking aloud to God. Like Little Fey, Gretchen was my friend. Her agony was therefore my agony. It was true that her head was too much in the clouds and she was forgetful of rules, but she didn't deserve a beating. None of us did. I longed to reach across to her, for she slept on the pallet next to Little Fey, but I dared not risk being caught and beaten myself.

Abed, we faced one another on the pallet we shared, noses almost touching. Little Fey's breath was not sweet, but then most of the time neither was she. Yet, in spite of her goading, her petulance, the way she often berated me for not being as pious as she, I loved her. I was the only one she treated callously, and in an odd way it felt a privilege. She was one way with others, but she was herself with me. And yes, even despite her terrible secret, I loved her.

She nudged me with her foot.

Certain that everyone was asleep, I told her all. Father Volmar. Bingen. Abbess Hildegard. Almost all. I did not mention what he had said about my mother.

She closed her eyes, nodded her head, committed all to memory. She was silent throughout my telling, but at the word 'escape,' her breath caught.

'I can't live here anymore,' I said. 'I am terrified every day. Mother does not care if we live or die. But Abbess Hildegard may give me sanctuary.'

'Do you know the way?'

'Most of it.' My voice faltered because this was not true. 'Besides, God will guide me.'

'When?'

'When He wills it.' By which I meant, *When chance arises*, for I had my doubts about God. He was as guilty as anyone for our dire circumstances.

'I will come with you,' she said.

'You can't. The journey will be a great trial, far across the great mountains.'

'Still, I *will* come.' There was just enough light to make out the obstinate line of her mouth. 'You swore to care for me always, remember?'

'As I do now. Mother fears you and will not touch you; you are safest here.'

'And yet, I shall come. You can't stop me.'

She turned her face and rolled away.

11

The Feast of Processus and Martinianus, Martyrs
Convent of Saint Agatha, Trento

The following afternoon Sister Gretchen and I were on our knees in the wet garden. Our task was to remove flotsam around the tender plants that had survived the relentless rains and that now, even in their battered state, stretched on determined stems toward the sun.

Sister Gretchen had been first to befriend me when I arrived at Saint Agatha's. She was prone to silliness and made me laugh. She once dropped a small vial of ink into the laundry water, and as our white coifs, veils, and pinafores turned pale blue, she claimed the Virgin had touched the water with her robe. Her playfulness was balanced by her devotion, particularly to the stories of the saints, which stirred her imagination. Beyond the classroom, she would frequently test us on our knowledge of them, scolding us for our ignorance. Since Mother Clothilde's arrival, her impishness and tendency to brabble and question found no favour, and she took the whip more than any of us.

Yesterday's beating had been especially harsh. Shivering despite the heat, she knelt, hunched, beside the garden, as frail as the plants we were trying to save. Her long curly hair, red as a berry, had been hacked to the scalp. Earlier, as we dressed for the day, I saw patches of bare skin and dried blood on her head. Her coif now covered most of it, but it didn't conceal the scratches and harm-colours on her face.

I glanced at her hands, swollen and blue-black, and offered to do the garden work.

Without warning, she put a finger in the muddy earth and scribed, *I'm coming.*

My heart sprang into my throat. How did she know of my plan to escape? My hand swiftly brushed away her words.

How? I scribed back tentatively.

Fey.

'She was sworn to secrecy.' I spoke into my hand as it scratched my nose. Eyes were everywhere at Saint Agatha's.

'I beg you. If I stay, Mother will kill me.'

'If you come and we are caught, we will all be killed.'

I stared at the earth. If I planted myself, could I grow into something that wasn't punished or frightened all the time?

Sister Gretchen gently rolled back her sleeves. Purple and yellow coloured her arms. 'Nothing to lose, then.'

I loved her like I loved Little Fey. I could not leave her behind.

'Fine, you shall come. But swear you will not speak of it to anyone.'

'I swear.'

How foolish we were to dream this, never mind attempting it. My heart thumped with terror. We would surely be caught. But what choice did we have? Stay and be beaten to death; or flee, risk capture and be beaten to death? It was death by bludgeon either way.

So now we were three.

But no sooner was I settled to three than we were four!

As the sun dipped toward Vespers, and my daily labours were almost at an end, I carried the last ash bucket to empty behind the barn. There was Fat Val, dumping the kitchen slop. She was named Sister Valentina but in my head she was Fat Val because she was. Whereas Sister Gretchen was slender as thread, Fat Val was taller than the pole of a bread paddle, and as lumpy as a loaf that sat on it. Slovenly, too: Her pallet was always unkempt, her tunic stained and twisted—sometimes she wore it the wrong way round—and her coif was always skew-whiff; everything about her was, from her unruly dark eyebrows to her tangle of pale hair. She never paid heed in the classroom, either. It had annoyed Mother Elena. I would offer to help her with her lessons, but she'd refuse or be listless when I tried to get her to count on the abacus.

She drew her hand across her nose to wipe away the snot and a collection of crumbs on her upper lip. She was always eating.

'I'm coming, too,' she mumbled.

I stumbled back, and would have landed in the slop had she not been quick to pull me back.

'But…?'

'Little Fey. And Sister Gretchen.'

'But...?'

'I don't care. Besides, you need me. I'm strong.'

Strong? Hale, that she was, but what of her spirit, her perseverance? She had a complaining demeanour, and did we need that on such a journey? Could she even run, for I daresay there would be plenty of that. I glanced at the hill that rose behind Saint Agatha's, the direction of our escape. Could she manage that? Her slovenliness didn't much concern me; we'd be living amid forests and fauna, but when I looked at her oafish shape, I couldn't imagine she'd have the fortitude or the will for a long trek. My mind's eye drew up the sight of three of us running ahead and her dragging herself far behind.

'There will be mountains to climb,' I said. I hadn't mentioned this to the others; it had only entered my thoughts now. Could Fat Val climb a mountain?

'I know mountains,' she said. 'I was born among them.'

She, too, had been at Saint Agatha's when I arrived, and while I had never questioned her or anyone about their birthplace, this was certainly not the time to do so.

I emptied my bucket.

'Mind the slop.' She grabbed my sleeve. 'You might slip again.'

Despite her faults, I loved Fat Val. Like Little Fey and Gretchen, we had grown up together. We were as close to one another as blood kin. I could not refuse her. But this had to stop.

'If any more are told, the plan will be foiled.'

'Tell that to Sister Fey before she informs the whole house.' She picked a rotting apple out of the heap and began to eat it.

'And Sister Mea,' I hissed, 'must not get wind of this. Do not risk trouble with her.'

Sister Mea was our foe. She had arrived recently at Saint Agatha's during the ides of Iulius, close to the Feast of the Apostle Barnabas. No explanation was given about who she was or why she had come. She was aloof in manner and bearing, and spent much time tending her hair. Mother Clothilde made sure our hair was shorn; but not so for Sister Mea. Her frequent to-ing and fro-ing from Mother's office turned the air noisy with silent curiosity. Was she a spy? I often caught her watching us. But her worst crime was when she brazenly took the empty pallet between Sister Gretchen and Fat Val. This inflamed Fat Val, who preferred her distance from Sister Gretchen on account of Sister Gretchen's night noises, and because she desired privacy. This abrupt, unwanted change to the sleeping arrangements caused an animus between her and Sister Mea. Out of sight of Mother Clothilde, they fought like snakes.

I couldn't think of Sister Mea now; I had to find Little Fey. Pious and holy, who gossips like a fishwife. All my thinking, all my hope, would be for naught because of her prattle. She would ruin everything.

I found her in chapel, saying her beads. *Ever the charlatan.*

I knelt behind her on the uneven flags while my nose adapted to the musk of incense, and my eyes searched the cave-like dark for lurkers.

'Praying for a more restrained tongue?'

She turned, scowled at my words.

What? my eyes screamed. *It is all your fault. Stop talking about our escape!*

She dug her nails into her palms and began to scratch.

As a result of the silence imposed on us by Mother Clothilde, we created a silent language all our own. That is how we four plotted our escape. We pointed with our eyes, spoke with our hands, summoned attention with the tap of a foot or a surreptitious nudge of elbow. We drew necessary words and directions on dusty floors and window ledges, and, as Sister Gretchen had done, in the earth when our chores took us outside.

There were seven other novices in our dormitorium, younger than us and more inclined to obedience and tattle to Mother Clothilde. We avoided them as assiduously as we avoided Sister Mea and her flinty scrutiny of us. One day, I caught her watching me from across the garden as I tended to my relief. Utterly without heed for another sister's modesty!

Little Fey, Sister Gretchen, Fat Val, and I worked in pairs to relay or gather information concerning our escape. It was easier that way since chores were often undertaken in pairs, and while we were seldom paired the way we would have liked, we managed hasty meetings at the privy or the slop pile. At night, it was easy for me to confer with Little Fey since we slept next to one another; not so easy for Fat Val and Sister Gretchen with Sister Mea between them.

First and foremost, we promised one another that we would only flee together, not separately. As Sister Gretchen said—by way of running two fingers down her cheeks and one finger to infer a slash across her heart—we would be bereft without companionship, and our survival would suffer.

Second, we practised silent manoeuvres.

I would alert them with a quiet *hem-hem*, and they would observe me as I leaped from my pallet, threw on my tunic, and grabbed my bundle all within the blink of an eye. They practised my movements so they, too, could be quick.

Like players on a stage, we rehearsed how to be fleet of foot on the stairs from the dormitorium to the kitchen, which was a challenge for Fat Val on account of her bulk, though she made progress daily; or how to leave our pallets without rustling the straw. We practised how to run like rabbits from the back door to the salix fence at the far end of the kitchen garden without tripping. We practised speed and stealth during chores or in the rare, spare moments of the day and evening, and in all elements. I never gave mind to risk because to consider the consequences would have dashed my courage entirely.

Each day we became more adept, more daring. One day, Fat Val and I, arms laden with firewood, entered a room where Mother Clothilde was reading. Her back was to us, and we managed to lay down our burden without disturbing her. We even stuck out our tongues at her behind her back. She only noticed us when another sister came into the room and alerted her, and then it was all: 'How dare you enter my presence without announcing yourselves.'

We both received the whip, but we agreed it was worth it as it proved our furtiveness. I knew then that we had a chance.

But when Fat Val resumed hostilities with Sister Mea; when I spied Little Fey whispering conspiratorially to one of the younger novices (was she enticing her to join us?); when I caught Sister Gretchen dozing at her chores, I began to think it would be better to flee on my own. If they were unthinking now, how would they be when we were free?

Prayer was on my lips and in my heart constantly. With only God to rely on, I made myself into the most devout soul in Christendom. I prayed for strength, for courage, for my sisters to be more vigilant; I prayed for a sign: *And not a weak sign, dear Lord, but one that is plain and clear, for I am no good with subtlety.*

Soon, we were as prepared as could be. We had a route of escape, we had practised going up and down the stairwell without making a sound, and we had begun to gather food for our journey and hoard it deep in the straw of our pallets so not even the mice could find it.

Eager and ready, our problem was with God. He was not forthcoming with a sign. Such is His way. No ear can hear his coming. He never tells us when His summons might arrive or when His beneficence will shine on us. He only teaches us to be attentive and expeditious when called. But as time went on, as Sun and Moon transited across Heaven, as day rolled into night with nary a sign, I began to feast on the bread of anxiety. *How can this be?*, my distressed eyes asked my sisters. *Has God abandoned us? Where are the angels to deliver us from our torment?*

These questions were with me each night as I prepared for bed, and all day as I listened to the screams of my sisters being punished. I cursed Father Volmar for daring me to hold a dream, for telling me things about my mother, and about Bingen, for leading me astray with prideful ambition. And I cursed God who promised to be steadfast, but whose gaze was not on us, but elsewhere.

If God is our heavenly father, and the Pope is our earthly father, and we are all born from fathers, then it is right to expect some diligence toward our care, but as I waited and waited for help in our escape, I began to wonder about the purpose and faithfulness of fathers. My own had been an example of dereliction.

He was a cobbler, a man of few emotions and fewer words, who never wondered at the moon and stars, or admired a spring flower, or returned the affectionate muzzle of our donkey Padre. I remember his cold attendance at the bedside of my mother—that is, the woman I knew to be my mother—the night she died. Her pale, damp skin glistening in the candlelight as she thrashed on the straw; the vivid red that gushed from her. When my brother slipped out of her and into the world, I saw one life arrive and another depart; by dawn, he was gone, too. I was four winters old.

When my mother died, my father bemoaned not the loss of her, but the loss of her care of him. How was he to work and raise a child, a girl-child at that, he lamented to the world.

Denied his comfort and care, he seemed to refuse out of spite to offer it to his child. I wanted to love him but we did not rub along well. After a time, he was in my way, and I was in his.

I was too curious for his liking; he was too cold for my liking. He would order me outside to play, but when I ventured into the woods behind our house or taught myself to float in the stream, he grew cross when he had to come and get me, saying next time he would let me drown or be eaten by wolves.

Indoors, I was more of a burden.

'Please, Papa, what is this?' I would say, picking up a long-handled tool from his work table.

'What?'

'And this, Papa; what are these?'

'Put that down! Do not touch anything!'

'Will you teach me to use it?'

'No! You are a girl! There is nothing for you to learn except how to cook and be quiet.'

'I *can* learn. I *want* to learn.' I stomped my feet.

'Lucia, I am trying to work. Why must you pester me? Go outside. Play with the other children.'

'I don't want to play. I want to learn.'

I stomped so hard that his tray of tiny nails jumped off the table.

I was in the way. Soon I would be on my way.

Early one morning, Papa announced we were going for a ride. I thought it a sign that his grief had lifted, that he was ready to love me. I did a little dance around the cart to show my joy while he tethered it to Padre.

We left before dawn, the world all shadow and outline until glorious sun broke across the wide sky in fiery streaks of orange and blue. I was in awe of the beauty. This was the world! How big it was! How full of grass, flowers, trees, and hills! In the fields, oxen and sheep raised their heads to stare at us and it made me laugh. When I looked back, they were still staring.

Our cart rumbled over dry, rocky soil, across velvet meadows, and over hills as rounded and hunched as my father's shoulders. When the ground rose, I could see forever; when it dipped, large, wind-blown stacks of hay tumbled past as if we were flying through clouds.

On the far side of a vast yellow field, I watched a building rise from the ground. At first, it looked like a long animal ready to pounce, tail erect. It had my complete attention. But the closer we got the more it revealed itself until the tail became a campanile, and the body a sprawling grey building furred with lichen. Small curved windows peered like watchful eyes; the broad arch across the wooden front door like a frown. I was not frightened; I was enchanted.

I would have thought it a castle had my father not said, '*Cè. Il convento.*' I did not know why we had come to a convent.

He tied Padre to a stone post, took my hand in his hard, calloused one, and walked me to the door.

A woman opened it before he had time to lift the knocker. She was tall, slender, young. A breeze found her and ruffled her brown tunic and white veil.

She looked unhappily at my father. Then, seeing me, she bent down, hands on her knees, face as bright as a candle.

Her chin trembled, and she looked close to tears. I wondered if I had frightened her.

'I am,' she sputtered out, 'Mother Elena. I look after everyone at Saint Agatha's.'

I loosened my grip of Papa's hand as she drew us out of the baking sun and led us through the big doors.

Inside, my head wheeled around the soaring entrance while Papa and Mother Elena spoke in hushed voices. The air was cool and smelled of lemons and lavender. The floors were laid with large flags, a contrast to the earth floor of our home. Sunlight wrapped around columns as thick and tall as the trees I played among. And doors. So many! I began to count them, *Uno, due, tre, quattro...* A trickle of childish laughter came to me from somewhere. I turned toward it.

'Lucia.' Papa tugged my hand.

I looked up at him.

'Mother Elena will look after you now. She will teach you to pray and to read. God be with you.'

Without another word, without waiting for a word from me, he passed my small hand to her warm, smooth one, turned, and walked out the door. He walked through the gate, untied Padre, climbed into the cart, and shook the reins. Only Padre looked back at me.

I did not know what to do, whether to cry or call out to him.

'You will be known as Sister Lucia now,' said Mother Elena. 'Come, your new sisters are excited to meet you.' It seemed my arrival had been expected.

Still bewildered and ashamed that my father could so easily discard me, I walked beside her down the corridor. The laughter drew closer. She pushed open a door, and a new world spread before me. A large courtyard with pillars covered in thickets of white roses, and fruit trees and flowers; a small fountain plashed like the sound of the tiny nails on father's work table. Little girls like me ran and chattered. Older ones, like Mother Elena, played alongside them or read to them in a circle on the ground.

'Mother Elena.' I pointed to a girl who held a book. 'When will I learn to read?'

She laughed. 'As soon as you want.'

I adapted to life at Saint Agatha's as if born into it. The order, the routine, the shared tasks, the utter happiness of the place; it was like the Garden of Eden. It did not take long for me to forget my father.

Beyond daily chores, lessons, and chapel, I wandered and explored my new home. Corridors leading this way and that. Straight steps, twisting steps, stone steps, wooden steps. Doors that led to chambers with doors to other chambers; doors that led to the cellar with its store of preserves and oils, hooks of bloody flesh, barrels of ale, wheat sheaves, and sacks of broomcorn and foxtail millet. Next to it was my favourite room, the scriptorium. Whenever I entered, I did so with the same reverence I accorded the chapel, except here reverence sprang alive with colour: drawings, paintings, and parchment richly illuminated with figures, creatures, flowers, and climbing plants.

The chapel was on the main floor next to the chapter house, which was next to the front door and receiving hall. It was long and dark, like a cave, but a cave perfumed with incense. Off the receiving hall were two guest cells, a small sitting room, the kitchen, and the refectory. At the back of the kitchen a long set of steps wound up to a dormitorium where we younger ones slept. The cells of the choir sisters were one floor beneath, as was Mother's cell and office. It also had an open, galleried area that served as our bibliotheca.

A map of all this lived behind my eyes, and it served me well. Because I knew the place so well, I was often asked to fetch something from the maze of rooms and I was able to run the errand with haste. My wanderings through the convent also enabled me to discover signs of egress and damage by creatures who had burrowed or nibbled their way into the food stores.

'What if Sister Lucia had not found this?' the choir sisters cried when I reported my discoveries. 'Our grain would be ruined. We would be without bread.'

They embraced me with their gratitude, and I blossomed under the glow of appreciation and encouragement.

With no mother of my own, Mother Elena became my mother. With no siblings, Gretchen, Valentina, and Fey became my blood. It was the first time I had friends.

Little Fey, youngest among us, had arrived as a foundling at Eastertide, the year following my arrival. I was the one who discovered her.

It happened one morning after the fast was broken. A mewling sound had drifted in on a warm breeze, and because one of the convent cats had given birth we assumed it was her kittens. But later, when I opened the back door to empty the food waste, there was a baby, without basket or swaddling, writhing in the grass; small and white as a new lamb.

I had lifted her up and held her close to still her cries. *There, there. I will look after you. I will not leave you.*

Mother Elena accepted the babe as she had accepted all of us, as gifts from God. We never learned who had left the baby, nor the name of her family, or from where she hailed. It was as if the child had dropped from the sky.

'We will name her Sister Fey,' said Mother Elena. She called all of us 'sister' regardless of rank or age. 'Our Lord did not make distinctions between people, and so neither shall we,' she explained. 'He embraced the tax collector as warmly as He did His disciples.'

She surprised us by what she said next: 'Sister Lucia will be in charge of her care.'

It did not mean I was solely responsible, it meant that Mother Elena was trying to raise me out of the unexplained sadness that wandered in me. It wasn't a sadness of sorrow, but of loss, emptiness; a desire for purpose.

Little Fey—as I called her—gave me purpose. I bathed her, rocked her to sleep. Once she was weaned, I fed her. Thus, we grew together, and in time our souls blended like two tears.

When she was five springs old, an elderly sister noticed marks on Little Fey's palms, and declared them to be the wounds of Christ. I knew it wasn't true. So much of what we are taught or told is given and received on faith, but as much as the Church works to turn doubters into believers, it can also turn believers into doubters. There is God's hand

and then there is Lucifer's hand, and not everyone can tell one from the other. My mind would not accept stigmata on anyone except He who bore them first. It was sinful to think otherwise, and part of that thinking sprung from a desire to protect Fey from this burden. The other part sprung from seeing a shadow pass Mother Elena's eyes at the old nun's declaration. Yet she said nothing; did nothing. She certainly didn't stop the steady arrival of folk who began arriving at Saint Agatha's to see the blessèd child for themselves, and, for a coin, touch her hem. Our coffers swelled.

I should have asked Mother about doubt and miracles and perhaps also about my own loose attachment to God. Hadn't she taught us the importance of listening to the voice that spoke from our hearts rather than the one that spoke in our heads? To not let stern words from the pulpit be our only guide? And yet I couldn't. I was afraid of losing her affection. My heart swelled when she singled me out in front of others for something clever I had done, or when I caught her smiling at me. I'd never known such love, and I wasn't going to lose that. If keeping Little Fey's secret assured me of Mother Elena's devotion, so be it. Love is not always pure in purpose or reason: It is as much a force of Pride as it is of Providence. Faith and love make sinners of us all.

While I was in thrall of Mother Elena, she was in thrall of the courageous Abbess named Hildegard, of the Holy houses at Rupertsberg and Bingen. She called her *stupor mundi*, the wonder of the world. When the Disibod monks such as Father Volmar stopped at Saint Agatha's to share new potions and healing remedies from the Abbess's table,

Mother would rush to our apothecarium and grind the herbs and mix the oils and tinctures that would conjure these new medicines. The monks also brought us chants that Hildegard had newly written, and we practised these, our voices soaring in the small chapel. Everything that Hildegard devised or pronounced was distilled into our learning.

Unsurprisingly, we all became acolytes of the Bingen abbess. Our toil, prayer, and duty seemed to exist for she who had the ear of popes, kings, and emperors; who preached in the piazza. Sometimes I imagined living in her community, though I never yearned to leave Saint Agatha's; I was as devoted to Mother Elena as she was to us.

One day, I stepped into her office while she was writing a letter. She wrote many, and they accumulated like flocks on her desk to be dispatched like birds into the world beyond our stone nest, beyond Trento, beyond even the icy wall of the great mountains.

'Why do you write, Mother?'

'My words speak what I wish to ask the person to whom I write.'

'What person?'

'Sisters and brothers in other communities.'

'Why do you not wait until you see them to talk to them?'

'Because I do not always have opportunity to see them. It is important to act quickly upon questions that arise within you so that you may know the answers and grow in wisdom.'

'Why not ask your questions to God?'

'God directs me to those on earth who can answer my questions. Today, I am writing to Father Volmar. He is spiritual guide to Abbess Hildegard. He visited us at Christmastide. Do you remember? He brought us spelt with which to make our bread because Hildegard believes it is a kinder, softer wheat that brings joy to the heart. I am thanking him for it.'

'What else?' I stood on tiptoe to get a better look, though I was far from being able to read.

She laughed. 'Our words are sometimes private matters. What is important is to converse with all, to make friends.'

She set aside her parchment and pushed toward me a scrap and a quill.

'Would you like to try?'

She guided my hand as she showed me how to dip the nib in the small pot of black ink. My chubby hand clutched the quill awkwardly and scrawled across the page; wild scrolling circles at first and, as my mind gained sway over my movements, more controlled ones. I drew a line that rose and dipped across the page, and scratched small dots and crosses above it.

'These are stars above the mountains,' I said.

Mother clapped with delight.

'Such imagination, Sister Lucia. Shall I ask one of the choir sisters to teach you your letters?'

That is how I began my education in the scriptorium, my new chapel. God was there in clearer form. Prayerful contemplation became prayerful concentration. Instead of incense, the comingled aroma of resins, dyes, inks, skins, and feathers was ever-present. I learned how to cure swan, crow, hawk, and goose feathers by hanging or by soaking, and to roll them in hot sand. In time, I made my own quills, scraping the calamus with a knife, and paring and slitting the nib to draw up the ink.

I began with simple texts and pieces of Scripture to accustom my hand to reed and quill. I already knew my letters, but here I could practise their distinct shapes and give each a soul. Letter B was a fat man, proud of chest and greedy of belly; N was a broomstick leaning across the frame of an opened door. By my tenth winter, I was allowed to rubricate short passages with red ink. My fingers became gloriously stained.

My instruction came from Sister Julietta, who had the gift of artistry. Small worlds grew inside the letters she drew: C, D, O, Q came alive with grape vines, flowers, saints, the Holy Family. She drew a monkey hanging by its tail from letter J, which made me laugh. From letter S she made two spiny-tailed fishes. The voids around the text she filled with wonders that bloomed across the page like roses across a wall. Fools and urchins peeked from leafy arabesques, angels hovered over the shoulders of saints, wild beasts strode majestically around the page. She did not heed boundaries, and of all she taught me it's what I remember most: Straying beyond borders opens one's spirit and art.

When I lamented my childish hand, she counselled patience.

'Do not despair, Sister Lucia. I have been doing this since I was a girl; you have been doing this since the last new moon. You have all the time in the world to learn.'

But we did not have all the time in the world. The Great Disruption was charging toward the convent doors.

The next day, without herald or reason, the bishop's men

arrived. They bound Mother Elena's wrists, bundled her into a cart, and whisked her away.

Her abrupt absence was like falling into cold water and scrambling to the surface for air. I stumbled through the days, mouth agape, under the spell of sorrow. My tears watered the garden, flavoured my food, cleaned the chapel floor. We tried to continue her work, but to no avail. Our home had lost its mooring, and we were oarless boats, tossed on seas of grief and bewilderment without hope of harbour.

At night, face down on my straw, I sobbed, 'Oh, Hildegard, Hildegard. Help us.'

III

The Feast of Peter in Chains
Convent of Saint Agatha, Trento

A full moon had passed since Father Volmar's visit. The same moon that had witnessed the monk-priest's words of hope that had kindled in me the fire of escape. But as the days went on, and our terrible trials and agony continued, hope drained. Were we ever to leave this place? What more could we do? My sisters and I continued to rehearse our flight but our efforts were lacklustre. We were prepared beyond preparedness. Poised to flee. Alert to opportunity. But where was our sign? Where was God?

It was the night before the Feast of Peter in Chains. I should have been contemplating the Apostle's wretchedness in captivity, but my mind would not stick to it. I could only think of my own wretchedness. I burrowed my face deep into the nest of my pallet to stifle my piteous sobs so as not to distress Little Fey. But she knew. Her small hand fell on my back to console me.

Eventually I turned over. Tears would not save us. There had to be another way, another plan.

A bird flew into the dormitorium. I watched its tiny shape flit through the moonbeam, back and forth, back and forth, until the flutter of its wings calmed me toward sleep. But while mind and body craved sleep, neither would yield to it. Instead, sleep brushed me like ragged wind, and I began to flit like the bird I had observed, from one side of the pallet to the other. My toss-turning would surely wake Little Fey, but when I stilled myself and heard her breath, slow and even, I knew she was deep in slumber.

The Vigil bell's dull clang jerked me. I stared into the black listening to the groan and creak of the floorboards beneath our dormitorium as the choir sisters shuffled in their sleepwalk to chapel. The air became still again, and the tease of sweet sleep resumed its drift until I was jolted awake again by the scurry of those same feet returning to their cells. *Deus, da mihi patientiam!*

Once again, slumber rolled over me like morning fog. Night was in its liminal phase, when Moon wanes and Sun stirs; when God summons angels from starry beds to do His bidding. But tonight I did not want the bother of angels; only the mercy of sleep.

Something nudged me. I turned onto my stomach thinking Little Fey's leg had knocked me. But no. Another nudge came, sharper this time, like a farmer prodding swine. *Mother Clothilde?* It couldn't be. She'd have sent one of the nuns to fetch me, and I would have heard her coming up the stairs.

Then my foot flinched, as if a feather was being drawn

across it. Annoyed, I lifted my head to catch the culprit. But there was no one. Perhaps a spider in the straw, or the graze of a feather dropped from the little bird? My ears and eyes keened to the grainy darkness. The dormitorium was still as death, save for the slumber-speak of my sisters.

A floorboard creaked at the foot of my pallet. And again. I held my breath. The air stirred with an otherworldly perfume, followed by the fan-like folding and unfolding of wings.

Angels.

I could not see them but they were there. Not cherubs, plump in flesh and mischief, the kind who frolicked in the margins of the texts I once illuminated before quill and quire were silenced. These were older, graver angels; the kind who bear tidings.

An eerie glow had filled the room. I sat up. My eyes were drawn to the small window across from me, and the view beyond. A familiar one, of the far-off range of black hills rippling against the jagged line of the Alpes. I often wondered what lived beyond them: People who spoke in different tongues? Strange animals? Ogres and dragons? But now a curious radiance lit the scene, and a thin, fiery arc pulsed insistently behind the hills. It looked wrong; it was definitely too early for sunrise. Then my hand flew to my mouth: the arc was rising *between* the hills and the mountain peaks when it should be rising *behind* the peaks! I looked at my sisters, anxious for their witness, but on they slept.

The sliver of sun continued to beat, but now it was louder so that it filled my ears, and a voice called to me, as if from the other side of Heaven. *God? Saint Peter? Abbess Hildegard?*

I cupped both my ears, leaned forward.

A breath entered my ears: *Arise. It is time. Go.*

Was this the Divine sign? Had my ceaseless prayers finally arrived like a trumpet blast to God's ears? I shook my head in disbelief. I was fourteen winters old; my prayers were child's play to Our Lord, sweet in passion but short on gravitas. Surely He did not attend the likes of me. But at the same time, why dither and doubt like Saint Thomas? How more timely or clearer could this sign be? And on this of all days, the Feast of Peter in Chains. God had chosen me, Sister Lucia of Trento, as He had chosen the Apostle, and was freeing me from my fetters.

Go.

I reached across to Little Fey, mindful of straw crunching, alerting others. She was curled like a tiny ammonite. I shook her gently and leaned over her ear. 'It is time. Wake Sister Gretchen but caution her to silence.'

Her eyes sprang. She rolled and cupped one hand over Sister Gretchen's mouth because Sister Gretchen was given to loud yawning. I half expected her to cry and thrash, but when she saw who gripped her, she relaxed. Little Fey, her back to me, would half mouth, half whisper: 'Shhh. Today.' As we had rehearsed.

But what happened next had not been rehearsed. Sister Gretchen was to get up and wake Fat Val who slept one pallet beyond her—the pallet between them occupied by sinister Sister Mea. As Sister Gretchen eased off her pallet like a sylph, she was suddenly grabbed by Sister Mea who then kicked Fat Val, who was sleeping on her stomach. My mouth dropped; my heart stopped. *Please God, not this.*

Fat Val rose from her straw like a serpent, eyes ablaze, tongue poised to spew rebuke, but as soon as Sister Mea cocked her head toward the stairwell Fat Val recovered herself, scrambled from her pallet and into her tunic.

Then, I scarce believed my eyes: Sister Mea climbed off her pallet, threw on her tunic, and grabbed her bundle. As if she had practised alongside us! As if she was part of our plan! She had not been invited to escape with us. How did she know of it?

Nothing could be done about it now. We had to make haste.

Our movements were swift, nimble. I glanced at the window where the sun had now resumed its normal ascension behind the mountains. Soon the golden arc would break above the peaks and cast bright rays upon our gamble. I looked at my pallet, a large white feather upon it.

I hurried on tip-toe to the dormitorium stairs to join Little Fey, Fat Val, Sister Gretchen, and—improbably—Sister Mea. Ignoring my eyes, she jerked her head for me to go.

We descended one behind the other into the black spiral well. During our practice, we had noted the squeaky treads, the curve of the wall, but now, hooded by the dark, terror flew into me. What if we are caught? Or the cock rouses? Or the Matins bell rings before its time? My mouth went dry; my heart thumped with a ferocity I was certain could be heard throughout the house. My trembling fingers pressed into the cold stone walls on either side, and I prayed my nerve would hold. Down I circled: down and around, down and around.

A Flight of Saints

A blade of dawn leapt from a nearby window onto the floor, lighting the last step.

We skittered like mice across the kitchen flags toward the back door. The room was a cluster-storm of breads, dried figs, apples, and cooked meats, the result of Sister Bettina's flurried preparations for the Apostle's feast day. She would soon arrive to resume her work. The lingering smell of ash and rich grease made me hungry. We grabbed anything that was at hand. I plunged my hand through a sunbeam that hovered above a plate of gristle—flies busy upon it—and pocketed the remains. There was a bun: I grabbed that, too. An egg as well, but I put it down. I could not see it surviving intact for long in my pocket: I had kept my tunic clean in preparation for our flight.

At the door, knees knocking, something behind us moved. One of Mother's greyhounds, awakened by our presence, got up to greet us. If its thick tail slapped against the copper, it would give us up to its cruel mistress.

Little Fey stepped forward. She raised her scabby palm at the dog, and it immediately laid down and lolled its head onto the slate. My mouth dropped, but I dared not say anything.

Fat Val lifted the latch, and we filed into the garden. The stench of vegetable rot and slurry rushed at me and made me gag. I lifted the neck of my tunic to cover my nose and mouth against it.

Last out, I pulled the old oak after me, mindful not to let it go too far and scream on its hinges. Doors are much like people; their humours alter depending on the night just passed; docile one day, choleric the next. When I was a child, I pretended that this weathered door was the face of a kind knight scarred by many battles; its iron pull ring his earring. I put away childish thoughts, found the mark I had secretly gouged into the flags as the stop point, then eased the door across the threshold before my courage ran out.

All of a sudden it jerked from my hand! Sister Bettina, face as pale as a gutted cod, eyes bleary with sleep, drew in her breath; her mouth opened as she prepared to alert the house.

'Hush.'

The word slipped through my lips and pulled back as a gasp. She and I were both startled by my boldness. As I scrambled for a reason to explain our stealth, she apologised.

'I did not know it was you, *cara*. I heard…'

But I was already into my lie.

'We must away, dear Sister, to fetch a surprise for Mother.'

All eyes turned to me. We hadn't thought of suitable surprises.

'For the Feast of the Virgin,' Fat Val blurted.

From the corner of my eye, I saw Sister Gretchen's shoulders twitch, and her mouth ready to correct Fat Val. My elbow nudged her to silence. She would brabble: 'It is not the Feast of the Virgin; it is the Feast of Peter in Chains.' Fat Val always jargogled the feasts; Sister Gretchen knew them by heart.

It didn't matter. Sister Bettina was already nodding. Like Fat Val, she was not quick when it came to feast days. Some of the choir sisters tittered behind their hands at the simpleness of Sister Bettina: 'She is touched,' they'd say. But woe to those who mock the cook: I saw what she slipped into their bowls.

As we continued our lie, guilt pricked me. Sister Bettina had always been kind to me.

'We are making a special presentation to Mother,' cooed Sister Mea. Our heads lurched: It was only the second time we had ever heard her speak. 'To honour her and Our Lord's Mother.'

'Yes,' I vouched.

Sister Bettina's brow furrowed, perhaps curious at this sudden felicity between Sister Mea and me; perhaps questioning why we would countenance any surprise or gift for a Mother who was cruel to us. Still, she parleyed.

'Must you all go?'

We nodded as one.

'Because it is heavy,' said Fat Val.

'And large. As big as a cow. You will see.' Sister Gretchen was as expert in lies as she was in her ken of the saints.

Our ruse swelled, along with Sister Bettina's trust.

'I will say nothing.' She put a finger to her lips, excited to be gathered into our confidence. She glanced at Mother's open window. 'Then make speed, but quietly.'

I looked into her face. 'Pray, leave the door unlatched so we need not knock when we return.'

She read the falseness of my words on my quivering lip. Her eyes turned moist. She pinched my cheeks.

'Of course, *cara*. May God protect you.'

There was a clatter behind her. She spun me around to face the garden.

'Go! Go,' she whispered. She shooed us away, glancing again at the open window. 'Before Mother wakes.'

We walked briskly, side-stepping the crunchy gravel, traipsing on the decayed timbers around the vegetable patch. My eyes locked on the salix fence at the end of the garden and the hill of impenetrable scrub behind it. It looked as far away as the moon.

I looked back at Sister Bettina, but she was gone, the door closed, and in that brief moment of turning my head, my foot caught and I fell into a tangle of desiccated zucchini stems. A small cry escaped my lips. I clamped my mouth: *Did Mother hear?*

Sister Gretchen looked at me with panic on her face. Suddenly she started back toward the house. I jumped up, grabbed her arm and pulled her after me.

We ran for our lives.

Sound and thought were drowned out by the hammering of my heart, rising, rising until it was thunder in my ears. I clawed through the brittle rails of the salix fence. Sister Gretchen shook off my hand and charged ahead; up through the bracken and brambles, feet snagging in long clumpy grass, stubbing toes against hidden rocks and fallen trees. I charged after her like a boar through thorny thickets. My coif slipped over my eyes. I ripped it off, stuffed it in my pocket. My hair, grown since its last shearing, flew out and clung to my damp face.

At the top of the hill, we collapsed behind a tree and rubbed the nettle stings and thorn scratches that covered our arms and legs.

'We did it,' breathed Sister Gretchen, eyes wide with surprise.

'Come!' I said, 'We must keep going.'

Little Fey grabbed my sleeve.

'Not before we have prayed for those we have left behind.'

Pray? There was no time for prayer, but if I didn't, I'd never hear the end of it from Little Fey.

We rolled onto our knees. Five heads bowed, eyes closed, bloodied palms came together, fingers steepled. I opened my eyes, glanced at the others. Little Fey nodded for me to begin. What to say? I hated Saint Agatha's. I had lost all kinship with the place, my home these eleven years. But hate was a sin that loosened communion with God, and I was in need of Him right now, and perhaps in the days ahead.

'Hurry,' hissed Sister Mea.

My words spat out: 'Our Father and Blessèd Mary, we humble maids beg Your Divine forgiveness…'

'Not forgiveness,' snapped Fat Val. Her coif was skewed as if pulled back from her head; a twig was lodged in her hair, and her freckled face was splattered with earth. 'Give thanks for freeing us from the devil Clothilde.'

I continued, words stumbling one after another: 'And we give heartfelt thanks for Your Divine summons to take leave'— a glance at Sister Valentina who rolled her eyes—'of our tormentors. Protect those we have left behind, soften those in charge of their care. Guide us onward to Bingen. *In nomine Patris, et Filii, et Spiritus Sancti, Amen.*'

'And bless Sister Bettina for not telling,' added Little Fey as we crossed ourselves and leapt to our feet.

'Andiamo,' I said.

We ran like hares sprung from a snare.

My legs pumped furiously; my bundle, lashed to my waist, slammed against my body. A madness tore through me as if all the fear and rage I had contained was at last being expelled as fire. My throat stung; there was no moisture in it.

The world rushed by in a blur of green and blue. My entire life had been spent inside the convent gates, and I had no idea how I was to parley with this other world.

We flew across grassy meadows, through woods of soaring slender pines. We stopped for the briefest of moments to catch our breath, then we were off again. We ran alongside streams, through gullies, over hillocks, across broad fields. The sky was a patch of white and grey clouds, like wild horses, galloping above me. I ran harder so they wouldn't overtake me.

My thoughts wheeled like a startled flock; coherence and order lost in a blizzard of memory, threat, obedience. But one thought arose above all the others: If Mother Clothilde catches us, she will kill us.

Faster, faster.

IV

The Feast of Saint Hyacinth of Caesarea

Along the Adige River

We ran for two days, following the Adige River. We did not stop the first night or the second. Not to rest or sleep. What we had taken from the convent kitchen was gone so we fed ourselves on apples, pears, and figs grabbed from the trees we passed, or put them in our bundles to eat later when we were hidden among the bushes.

At night, the bright, tufa-stone moon made our watery path shimmer like stars, and when we slipped through black forests and across the wide, silent meadows, the moon was still there for us, a lamp for our feet.

I should have been relieved at being free of Saint Agatha's, but instead I was prickled by the thorn of fear. Freedom did not hold the comfort I sought. It exposed my ignorance, left me unprotected. The cloister walls had been my armour despite the terror and restraint they imposed when I was within them.

Outside those walls, on open land, life was unpredictable and dangerous. I had traded the known horror of Saint Agatha's for the unknown horror of the wilderness. Wolves, bears, and other beasts roamed these parts. Adders, too.

On the third day, as light fell out of the afternoon and long shadows fingered land and river, I was out of breath and my body ached. There was a forest not far from the river and I directed my sisters toward its sanctuary.

Sister Gretchen and I, first to reach it, fell against a larch clutching the stitch in our stomachs. The others, one by one, faces red with exertion, fell to the ground and stretched their bodies beneath a huge cedar whose boughs flared like an empress's gown.

'Do you think she's sent folk to find us?'

The panic on Sister Gretchen's face when I had fallen in the kitchen garden was still fresh in my mind; her reconsideration of our gamble. No good would come from frightening her further. I straightened my back and affected a confidence I did not possess.

'I cannot say I know her mind.' A stupid thing to say: We knew her mind perfectly well, which was why we had fled. But I found myself adding: 'If she despised and beat us, why send people after us? Why would she want us back?'

Still panting from exhaustion, she stood up. 'I am going to the river to refill the gourd. If I sit, I shall not be able to get up.'

I looked ahead at the waves of grass that stretched between where we would shelter that night and the river. I had no strength left in me.

A Flight of Saints

I wished Sister Mea would go and fill the gourd so I could ask the others why she was with us, and which one of them had recklessly divulged our plan to her. I looked over to where she sat, apart from us, on a cool nest of ferns, shielded by her pride, looking like one accustomed to getting her way. Her presence rattled me, but I lacked the nerve and energy to confront her, and I knew the others were too spent to give me support.

'Do not be long,' I said, looking at the sky. 'It will be dark soon. I will be your watch.'

I sat on the ground and followed Sister Gretchen with my eyes, watched her thread through the twilit grass until she slipped into the void where green and black merged. Again, I thought of her face in the kitchen garden: *Will she take advantage of the dark and leave us?*

The others by now had rallied. Little Fey was on her knees praying; Fat Val was slumped against the cedar, head buried in her hands.

From my earliest days I had prayed, eaten, slept, and played with them. I knew them and loved them as my blood. But in this untamed world, sans cloistered manners, routine, and busyness, they appeared different to me. True, we had been forced into estrangement for more than a year, not permitted to speak or to freely share our day as we had before. Now that we were away from that godless place, able to speak, they were unnaturally quiet and prickly. Yes, we were tired, frightened, but for now, we were free. Maybe it was me needing to fill the terrible silence with the chatter of a plan: How do we survive? How shall we be among folk we encounter? Do we need a ruse? Yes, we need a ruse! Then, what shall it be?

Inexplicably, my roaming thoughts turned to Father Volmar and what he had said about my true mother. Why had she left me with my father? Was it so easy for a mother to give up a child? The monk's words had stirred unwelcome memories about my beginnings and how I had come to be at Saint Agatha's; thoughts I hadn't pondered for some time so that I could almost convince myself they had never existed. Thoughts that stirred shame and anger at having been discarded by my kin, left behind, deemed inconvenient.

I shook my head to dislodge the memories, and returned my thinking to my sisters. We had been carefree girls when Mother Elena was taken from us; and now in that dark year under Mother Clothilde, we were changed; older, wary. Once-happy natures had turned serious. There was more to them than I had known. What and who had brought them to Saint Agatha's? We had all arrived at young ages, so it was obviously not by choice. Did my sisters mourn the families who had brought them into the world? I wasn't sure I mourned mine. Why had we never spoken of this? Why didn't I know more about them? I knew everything about Adam and Eve, about Moses leading his people, about Elijah's travails, about Joseph and his brothers. I knew about Abbess Hildegard, the Pope and the pretender pope, and the cruel emperor. I knew about the clever fox and the mighty lion. But I did not know the stories of my sisters. And I didn't know why I didn't know those stories.

'My legs will not stop trembling,' Little Fey whimpered. She lifted her tunic. Blotches of red bloomed across her chubby, juddering legs. She was an elfin thing; it was wonder enough that she had kept pace with us.

'My own are similar.' I rubbed her legs. 'They will soon calm.'

My attention returned to Sister Gretchen. The river was not far and she was not one to dawdle. I imagined her movements—how long for her to reach the river; how long to fill the gourd; how long to splash water on her face (for I would have done that if it had been me filling the gourd); how long to climb the riverbank and return to us.

'Sister Gretchen is not back. I must go and see if she has come to harm.'

The others turned toward the pitch.

'I will go,' said Fat Val. She struggled to get up but only made it to her knees.

'Stay,' I said. 'I saw the direction she took.'

I walked out of the woods toward the river. It was fully dark now with only a band of moonlight to guide me. I could barely see in front of me. Long grass pushed like a tide against my legs and tunic. I tilted my head to the stars massed across the blue-black sky, searched for one as bright as that which led the kings to the stable. The hair on my arms stood up. I stomped the ground to scare away my fear and any crawling creatures that might lurk nearby. I kept walking until I smelled a change in the air; and felt the land slope and heard the trickle of water over stone.

'Sister Gretchen,' I whispered.

No answer.

My bare feet groped the ground and soon the warm mud

of the riverbank squished between my toes.

'Sister Gretchen.'

Has she fled? Has she drowned?

Above the tinkling of the river, I heard snuffling close by.

'I am here,' a voice trembled.

I heard the reeds swish; a hand touched my leg. I moved my hand to it and clutched it.

'I was worried about you.'

'I filled the gourd, but sorrow found me and I could not return right away. I did not want anyone to see my tears, but oh, Sister Lucia, I have never been so full of fright.'

I eased myself onto damp ground, pulled my tunic above my knees. The cool waters of the Adige swam around my hot, swollen feet. I kept hold of Sister Gretchen's hand.

'I am, too. I have put us all in danger. It was my idea to flee, and if we are caught, all of us will suffer, not only me.'

'I want to return to Saint Agatha's.'

'You cannot. She will kill you.'

'If I throw myself at her mercy and promise to restrain my character, she might spare me. I was a good worker.' She began to sob. 'She needs the likes of me. But if she does not spare my life, that, too, shall be relief. Out here, danger is everywhere.'

The river lapped at my feet.

'The day you came into the dormitorium, bloodied from Mother's beating. Do you remember? Your hands like claws; your hair shorn to your skull; the bruises and broken skin?' My voice caught. I saw it all in my mind's eye, and felt the rage that had stirred me then and had not abated. 'I wept for you that day, for all of us. God gave us life. He does not want our death. Not that way.'

Her tears dripped on my hands.

More words gathered in my mouth, words that would say, *Remember when Mother did that to you, or when she did this to you?* But I did not speak them because I did not think it kind to force my thinking on her, and have her feel that my words were undermining those I knew she had spoken with great difficulty from her heart. Instead, I reached for her hand, and caressed it with my thumb to show that I understood her fear, and that I felt as she did.

'Come,' I said. 'Back to the others. Do not fret about crying. We all have unwept tears. We are tired and frightened, but do not let Fear hasten you to a bad choice.'

I helped her up. 'I love you, Gretchen. Do not leave. You are the only one who cheers me.'

We climbed the riverbank, hand in hand, and treaded through the cool grass toward the black woods.

Someone said my name.

We stopped.

'It is I. Sister Valentina.'

'Where are you?'

I thrust an arm blindly into the dark and, finding hers, I clasped it, and let her lead us back to the forest.

Beneath the shelter of the cedar, we sat in silence. The moon had thrown an eerie blue light onto us that made us appear as ghostly versions of ourselves. I imagined this was what we would look like dead.

'Let us sit close together,' said Fat Val. 'We cannot light

a fire lest it betray us to others, but we can partake of one another's heat.'

We shuffled on our backsides. My belly groaned, but it was not the only one.

'I feel like Saint Hyacinth,' said Sister Gretchen. 'He was our age, and he starved to death in prison. May God spare us.'

Her tears had stopped, and I hoped she would not mention her desire to return to Saint Agatha's. It might tempt the others. I needed to capture her loyalty.

'You know all the saints, Sister Gretchen,' I said. 'On our way to Bingen you must give us a saint each day so that we remain faithful to our calling and our courage. But let us make it different from what we know: Since we are fair and young, tell us only of saints who are of our sex, or who are children, like Saint Hyacinth.'

Another thought seized me: 'Remember how Mother Elena referred to someone as a saint or blessèd when the Church had not yet decreed the person so? Let us do likewise. We will make our own feast days, our own saints; we alone will decide who to honour.'

'That is heresy, Sister Lucia,' said Little Fey.

'So? The Church teaches us to care for one another, but the Church did not care for us. It knew our suffering, but deemed us unworthy of rescue. I think *that's* heresy. Mother Clothilde forced us to flee like dogs and live wild lives. We shall therefore be wild in our faith.'

'The Church tells us to honour thy mother and thy father,' she continued. Her prissy goodness grated me.

'I refuse to honour her. And I would not be ashamed to say

so before God.'

In the blue glow, I saw Sister Gretchen smile. 'I shall make a calendar of saints worthy of us.'

'Then let us celebrate Saint Hyacinth as our first saint and honour him with a feast,' said Fat Val.

From her pocket she withdrew a parcel wrapped in cloth. We recognised it by aroma—a small loaf of fruit bread. We dove on it, tearing it and stuffing pieces into our mouths.

'Where did you get it?' My words fought with the bread in my maw.

'The kitchen. It was on the table as we left.'

'Thou shalt not steal,' said Sister Fey, nibbling the edge of her portion. I wanted to slap her.

'Then we should have taken more, for we were owed more,' said Sister Gretchen.

Yes. Be the rebel.

'It wasn't stealing. It was owed us,' said Fat Val. Crumbs spewed from her lips; she caught them in her hand and stuffed them back in.

'And you saved it for three days? To share?' I am not sure I would have been as thoughtful. The scraps of gristle I had plucked from the kitchen were long gone, eaten as I ran, not shared. Gristle. I would kill for gristle.

'I knew we would be low and in need of comfort and a treat.'

The fruit bread was all that, but it did not sate me. My stomach moaned for more.

'How will we eat on our journey?' said Little Fey. She leaned against my shoulder.

'We will rely on the garden God has provided for us.

Remember the magi: Their journey was long and unknown and God provided for them. A star was their guide; ours will be the Adige and the great Alpes.'

I cringed at my cheerful, hollow words as I held my belly and rocked away the pangs. Stars, rivers, mountains could not abate hunger.

'How far is it to Bingen?' said Fat Val.

'I am not certain,' I said, unthinking.

'Surely you have a plan.' Sister Mea's voice was like a snapped twig. I had half-forgotten her; she had only moved close to us when Fat Val produced the bread.

I tossed my head. 'We shall speak of it on the morrow for I am weary, and sleep bears down on me.'

No one challenged me; instead they followed my lead, pawed the ground and made prickly beds from ferns, moss, and cedar.

Sleep came slowly. Days of constant running refused to leave my bones and quiet my body. My legs twitched.

My mind was agitated, too, not from running but from guilt. For here was a terrible truth: I did not know the way to Bingen. No map, no direction, save for what I had overheard from travellers who stopped at Saint Agatha's on their way to and from the north country. Fragments such as: 'Keep the Adige River to your left,' and 'Botzen is a fair place to stop for rest,' and 'Hooligans roam the Via Imperii,' and 'It is a scandal what the merchants in Brixen charge for *melanzane*,' and 'Why are the roads not made wider for our carts?' That was all I knew. How to reach Botzen or how far to Brixen, let alone to Bingen, was beyond my ken. It hadn't concerned me

A Flight of Saints

when I plotted our escape because, truly, I could not think beyond it. If our escape was successful then I figured that we would find our way, or that the way would find us.

I tried to sleep but I was afraid to close my eyes and face Mother Clothilde in my dreams. She appeared nonetheless, a human Vesuvius with fiery water walls streaming from her opened mouth when told of our escape; the convent walls quaking, the pillars in the hall crashing like Jerusalem's temple; the remaining sisters screaming and cowering amid the wrath and destruction. Would I ever be free of the nightmare of Mother Clothilde?

My dream moved on to Sister Bettina, kneading dough in the kitchen. I remembered her red-ringed eyes at the kitchen door, her quivering jaw. She knew we would not return. I said a prayer for her, but the words that came were: *Save us, save us.*

V

The Feast of Saint Ruth
In the Valley of the Adige

I slept the sleep of the dead. At sunrise, I awoke with the dread of the living. My stomach lurched and tumbled. Terror stretched in me anew.

I counted my sleeping sisters. All were there. Even Sister Mea.

I peeked through the cedar fronds to see if Mother Clothilde's men were about. They were not. Oh, how she must feel the absence of five strong labourers. She would have to recruit the choir sisters to take on our chores, and they would not be pleased at having their indolence disturbed, and their clean, white hands stained once again with dirt.

My sisters stirred.

'Quiet,' I whispered, cautioning Sister Gretchen not to give a loud yawn.

Though I had not seen men-at-arms nearby that did not mean they weren't there. I listened to the air and to the ground. When my soul was satisfied that all was well, I said, *'Andiamo,'* and we dashed to the river to perform our ablutions. I threw cold water on my face: once, twice, three times—*Patris, Filii, Spiritus Sanctus*—and refilled the gourd. Thus, did our day begin.

We skulked along the Adige's shore shielded by reeds that lined the banks like a palisade, and by trees so laden with the Augustus heat that their thirsty boughs bent low into the river for drink. A flock of geese shattered the air, but our short time in the open world had taught us vigilance, and to heed the signals of the wild creatures. We hunkered in the reeds and held our breath as three barges sailed past with their noisy crew.

Over the past year, when on my pallet at Saint Agatha's waiting for sleep to take me from my fear, or watching a swift flit among the rafters, I would contemplate freedom, and my mind's eye would conjure a door opening onto sunlight. But it wasn't like that, or didn't feel like it. Freedom was a burden that came with a constant tide of caution. As I waited in the reeds for the barges and cobs to pass, I felt as captive as I had been under the thumb of Mother Clothilde.

Our silence made it worse. Although we knew to be silent so as not to give away our presence, there were many times when we were utterly alone, when it was safe to speak. And yet it seemed my sisters continued to languish under the spell of Mother Clothilde, mute in their fear. I wanted us to speak and laugh, to shirk fear and the weight of our predicament, but the only voice seemed to be mine, telling them this way or that, or when to hush their footsteps, or when to stop and rest. All around us there was sound: The birds had their chirrup, water its splash, leaves their rustle; Nature's voice rang out, but my sisters had lost theirs.

'Why do you not speak?' I asked. I could barely disguise my petulance. We stood at the edge of forest, another vast, empty plain before us, but still in sight of the Adige.

They shrugged.

'Are you afraid Mother Clothilde will hear you?'

I had meant it as a jest, but they looked at me crossly.

'Then speak. We have been taught to speak only after the fast is broken and the versicle spoken, but if you hadn't noticed we have been well beyond the convent gate for days, and besides we have no food with which to break the fast. Which means we can speak whenever we choose.'

They ignored me.

'You cling to a life that is no longer ours,' I goaded. 'We are away from our troubles…'

'And have possibly exchanged it for worse ones,' muttered Fat Val.

'Worse? You were whipped for the sin of an untidy pallet, and you consider this'— I waved my arms at the meadows, the mountains, the sunlit air—'worse penance? I think you all suffer from a loss of gratitude. Would you rather be back at Saint Agatha's?'

I immediately regretted my words lest Sister Gretchen chirp, 'Yes, and I shall return there forthwith.'

But she did not. Instead, Sister Mea moved in front of me and narrowed her eyes.

'Do you expect us to treat this as some kind of *passeggiata* around the piazza?'

It was the first time I had really taken her in. Before, I would watch her from afar, but now she was right in front of me, and there was no other place to look. She was taller than me, but not by much, and slenderer, but not by much. But her face was unmistakably beautiful. There was no other way to describe it. Her features were even and defined, as if painted by an artist on a smooth surface of golden bronze. Her green eyes were fierce but at odds with their shape, which reminded me of perfectly formed leaves lifted upwards at their outer corners. Her mouth protruded slightly, and coupled with the permanent uplift of her chin she gave the impression of looking down at you with distinct disapproval.

I swallowed hard despite my attempt to appear unruffled, and then Pride rescued me: *How dare she!* Everything in me was poised to ask her, there and then, why she was with us, how she had come to know of our escape… and yet I did not. I was afraid of Sister Mea. Not as afraid as I was of Mother Clothilde, but afraid of the shield of confidence she wore so easily. I was aware, too, that aside from Little Fey, Sister Mea was the only one among us who was fully professed. Fair to say, she had been professed with uncommon—scandalously uncommon, I'd say—swiftness, and I doubted it was due to her holiness, which I had yet to glimpse. I noticed that she had discarded much of her habit during our journey, but while the nun's weeds had given heft to her air of suspicion, the reduction of it now gave an air of unpredictability, perhaps even violence. *Like a snake shedding its skin*, I thought.

I quickly excused myself, saying I had to tend to my relief. I didn't want to engage with her any more than I had to, lest she asked me again about how we planned to get to Bingen, and I certainly had no answer to that.

When I returned, my sisters were scattered on the ground, lost to private thoughts. Without a word, I walked past them, and continued through the grass and toward the Adige. I knew they would follow.

They did not know where we were going, that is to say, our route. And I daresay that some part of them did not care so long as it was far away from Saint Agatha's. But their blind faith and preference for silence had begun to worry me far more than it irritated. As children, we never had secrets; we spoke freely and laughed. But the abrupt plunge into enforced silence, the cruel isolation had damaged us; had bred lazy compliance and necessary retreat, the nature of sheep, that convinced us that we could survive misery if we lived in our heads, in a world of our own making. And that's the land we could not escape, the sanctuary of imagined thoughts.

Us? We?

At first, I scoffed at the notion, yet why should I consider myself different? I had lived in the same place as them, through the same tortures as them. I, too, had found comfort in my head. Were it not for my dreams and hopes, I don't know if I would have survived. And now, I was still captive to my dreams, somewhat. I mean, right now, here I was thinking all this, not sharing it with others. The awareness drew me up short: I had fallen into the same trap. I was living in my head more than I was living in communion with others. Our terrible year with Mother Clothilde had stunted confidence and enterprise. It had changed us irretrievably. And I did not know what to do.

Toward the mountains and the greater, icy peaks beyond them, the Adige unfurled. The sun, fully upon it, made its limpid skin appear as if on fire. It flowed north, toward Bavaria and Germania, that much I had gleaned from listening to travellers at Saint Agatha's. As long as I kept the river in my sight, we were going the right way.

At midday, we drifted away from the river, from emerald dragonflies and silver fishes, toward meadow and woods; to blue butterflies, black birds, and brown hares. I longed to lie on the soft grass and watch the clouds, to look at something that would divert my thoughts from the tremble in my soul, but to stop was to tempt capture. We had to keep moving.

Mere days ago, we had moved from chapel to chore in obedient repetition: 'Seven times daily' as the psalmist proclaims; in a steady rhythm parcelled out with prayer and duty. I yearned for the same rhythm and variety in the wild world. Without it, we had nothing to brace the day's beginning and end save the waxing and waning of sun and moon. No eggs to collect from the henhouse, no flags to scrub, no potatoes or apples to peel, no tunics or crockery to mend or wash, no firewood to gather, no grates to sweep and fires to stoke, no cows or sheep to milk. I should have been grateful, filled with relief that I had no eggs to collect, or flags to scrub, or grates to sweep, but in truth, the unchained life was strange, unnatural. Without bells to mark the hours and chores to occupy us I feared we would become like cats, resistant to rule, deaf to command. I missed the way we once chanted, when our communal voices sent our song soaring to Heaven. Those were the times when I felt I belonged. Surely the rhythmic solace of chant could hush away our fear now and at least deliver lyrical courage.

I looked at the wide, open emptiness before us, and tilting back my head I sang: *'Domine labia mea aperies, Et os meum annunciabit laudem tuam.'*

My sisters spun round and glared.

'What? I am breaking the fast. Someone has to.'

'It is custom to break the fast with food, and unless you are Jesus, I doubt you can produce any,' said Sister Mea.

Sister Gretchen said, 'I didn't bring any scripture.'

Little Fey's face reddened with shame. 'I never thought to do so.'

Fat Val said, 'I can't remember any prayers.'

Sister Mea tossed her hair and continued walking.

'A sad situation, isn't it?' I said. 'How will it look if we are caught? Five in Holy orders and not one in possession of a scrap of Holy words. We will be deemed as bad as gyrovague monks, unworthy and unfit for a house of God.'

But then another thought brightened me: 'It is good that we have no written prayers with us, for if men-at-arms are hunting five nuns, they will expect to find the trappings of religion on us.'

'And what, pray, will they think of five girls wandering without a chaperone?' Little Fey's voice was surprisingly tart.

Any clever retort was cut short by the worry that bloomed across Fat Val's face. 'I can't remember the Pater Noster. How does it begin?'

'The same is true for me,' gasped Sister Gretchen. 'I knew my prayers by heart, but maybe it was false capability, that in fact I was prompted by the voices of others in chapel.'

It was good to hear them speak, even if it was worried speak.

'In chapel, I could not concentrate with Mother Clothilde there,' I said, encouraging the chatter. 'I was too scared to pray. Did you feel likewise? I have tried to recall psalms and prayers since we left Saint Agatha's but can only summon fragments. The versicle I spoke is all I know. How is it possible to lose words we spoke daily, all our lives?'

Fat Val twisted the front of her tunic. 'The Devil has stolen our words and cast us into this wilderness.'

'Ruth thought likewise,' said Sister Gretchen. She took Fat Val by the arm. 'Saint Ruth, as she will be known to us today'—she winked at me—'is the first female saint we will honour. Like us, Ruth was sad and frightened when she had to leave her land after her husband was taken to Heaven. Her mother-in-law Naomi urged Ruth to return to her blood family, but Ruth stayed with Naomi, and travelled with her, and laboured in the fields of a strange land to keep her fed. Loss and grief did not diminish her.'

I smiled back at Sister Gretchen. I hoped she would stay as loyal as Ruth.

'Of course, it helped that Ruth lured Boaz into her nest on the threshing floor, and proceeded to ride him…'

'Sister Gretchen!'

'Don't scold me. You said that we are out in the world and can now speak freely, and that is what I am doing now.'

I sputtered my words. 'But why be profane? You never spoke like that before.'

She shrugged. *Shrugged!*

'We were not able to speak for a year, so I spoke to myself and learned many things.'

I didn't want to know what those 'many things' were. I looked at the others to gauge their offense but they had moved on.

'Let us chant!' I said to change the subject. 'Mother Clothilde forbade us to sing and chant so let us defy her. We can surely summon one psalm.'

'The one about the shepherd,' said Little Fey. 'It was my favourite.'

The air came alive with her voice:
Our Lord governs me, and nothing shall I lack;
in place of pasture there he hath set me…

We joined in. Our singing was better than birdsong. And then, as if our voices were a prompt to some mysterious inner instruction, we drew into formation, and processed on the goat path as we had done on the chapel flags. Fat Val was out in front, singing and swaying, ignorant of pace or pattern, unheeding of our orderly line. Her slovenly way was a joy to see.

He hath brought me forth up on the water of respite;
he comforted my…

Suddenly she whirled around. 'Down! Be quick.'

Without thought or question, we dropped into the long grass, face down, and rolled away from the path. She began to sing: 'A rider approaches. He has seen me but not you. Stay low.'

I raised my head.

'Hide yourself.'

'No,' she said. 'I shall face this.'

My belly knotted. I shook my head. This could not end well. *Oh, Fat Val, impudence is your confidence. You are bold but not bright. You do not heed reason. You did not listen during your lessons at Saint Agatha's, and now you ignore my caution. And pray tell where you got the pinafore that now suddenly girds your waist?* It looked suspiciously like one belonging to Sister Bettina.

The meadow floor trembled; the rider closed in. I heard Fat Val hum, and when I peeked through the grass, she was swishing through it, away from us, fingertips sweeping idly along the tops. *Like a simpleton!* I hoped the rider would be in a great hurry and ride on.

'Maid!'

My eyes closed. I shuffled on my belly toward a boulder to better hear and see.

Fat Val ignored the man's call.

There was heat in his voice as he called a second time, 'Maid! Halt!'

She turned casually toward him and gave a lazy curtsey. The rider was dressed in a tunic of emerald silk tied with a thick tasselled belt; his black boots showed dubbin on the heel. One gloved hand held the reins, the other sat heavy in his lap.

I watched Fat Val approach his horse and stroke its flank. I saw her parley with the man, and point in the direction from which we had come, and gesture toward some distant, unknown road. I heard only fragments: '… at the fence yonder';

'... to Trento'; '... the market on Wednesday'; '... the wash house... women and their endless work.' On she went, blabbing like a washerwoman, not heeding the danger in front of her. Why did she tarry? *Silly girl!* I immediately regretted her being with us on our journey.

The rider began to show impatience, and tugged the reins. His horse was restless, too.

As she spoke, the man looked Fat Val over, as if appraising a cow at market. I did not catch what he said, but Fat Val shook her head.

He spoke loudly and grand: 'Then why are you alone? Who is your master?'

She said something, then waved to someone in the forest. The rider turned, craned his neck to see to whom she waved. I, too, was moved to crane my neck, but saw no one.

Abruptly, she slapped the horse's flank and said, 'My lord, you must away for the wind has changed, and the sky looks given to rain. There remain many miles to Saint Agatha's.'

She curtseyed, turned and waved again to someone unknown in the forest and hurried in that direction.

The rider watched her, snapped the reins, and the ground thundered.

When the sound of hooves abated, I heard an owl's hoot. I raised my head above the grass. It was Fat Val, at the edge of the wood, and she beckoned us. We flew to her.

I prepared my scold, but the others were first with their jabber.

'Who was he?'

'What did he ask?'

'What did you tell him?'

'Where did you find that pinafore?'

Reproach stayed still in my mouth because another question had begun to form: *Where did you get your courage?* At Saint Agatha's I often tittered at Fat Val's dishevelled appearance, her careless gait, her fatness. Now I was in awe of her bravery.

'He is going to the convent.' She gulped the air and fanned her face. 'Did you notice he had only one hand?'

'What takes him to Saint Agatha's?' Little Fey stroked Fat Val's arm to calm her.

'I do not know. I confess that my directions might have been wrong. And I told some lies.' She looked at us. 'He asked why I was alone and I told him I was looking for a lamb, and that my father was waiting in the wood. There is a small church far among the trees—can you see it? I decided that by "father" I could mean God. And when I spoke of a flock, it was of you, my sisters, that I referred. The one missing was me. I did not mean it to be a malicious lie. I will say seven Aves as penance.'

'Don't apologise,' gasped Sister Gretchen. 'You protected us. God's grace, not His punishment, will be upon you.'

'There is more,' said Fat Val. Her face coloured. She dug under the pinafore, reached into her tunic pocket and withdrew a dagger and a small pouch.

'Where did you get these?' I asked, voice at last finding me.

She handed me the pouch.

'I am so hungry. That accounts for my boldness. I thought he might have food in his satchel. My right hand kept him distracted with my directions while my left hand reached into the bag. Bad left hand!' She slapped her hand. 'All I managed to scrounge were these. The dagger may come in handy for our protection. The pouch may hold something we can trade for food.'

I upended the pouch into my palm. Our heads bent forward and just as quickly pulled back. A ruby the size of a plum, an emerald as big as a blackberry, and several small diamonds.

'Why would someone be going to Saint Agatha's with these?'

My question was meant for all of them, but my gaze landed on Sister Mea.

Her eyes, wide and green, met mine and slid away.

VI

The Feast of Saint Helena of Constantinople

Toward the Great Mountains

I counted off my fingers: five. I had seen the moon five times since we left Saint Agatha's.

We no longer ran; the journey was labour enough to walk. Every day brought steep hills to climb, vast valleys to cross. My legs ached. My feet were butchered meat: red and raw. My hands were stained with grime; the grooves around my fingernails filled with earth. I longed to bathe in the Adige, which we travelled alongside every day, but aside from three quick splashes on my face—*Patris, Filii, et Spiritus Sanctus*—to linger beyond that was a risk lest a barge sailed into view or a farmer came to the river for water.

My tunic hung loose and it smelled. My hands were constantly in its pockets searching for an errant scrap or crumb, but always came out empty. There were fruit trees and walnut trees along the way but I was sick of eating their fruit. My belly growled for meat and bread.

When we reached the top of a hill, I regarded the world like a great eagle, trained my eyes on the broad, verdant landscape we had covered and scrutinised it for pursuers. We hadn't encountered anyone since Fat Val had faced the rider bound for Saint Agatha's. I patted my bundle for the bag of jewels; still there. Enough jewels for a thousand feasts yet nowhere to exchange it for a heel of bread.

Always, after reviewing the distance we had come, I turned to face our onward direction. It could always be counted on to dampen my spirits. The massive, daunting land of never-ending undulations of green sloping off into other undulations, each darker than the one in front. Beyond them, the icy peaks of the Alpes. Below, the Adige's ruffled hem of shoreline that stretched to oblivion. There was no reprieve whichever way I looked. I was ashamed at my foolish thinking that I could navigate so large an unknown world. I didn't know whether to be mortified of my ignorance or proud of my courage.

'Where does it end?' Sister Gretchen's voice startled me. Her eyes, too, were on the Adige. The sun was high and had turned the river into a carpet of glitter as if Heaven had emptied its stars upon it. It threw such dazzling light back at us that we shielded our eyes.

'I do not know, only that it will see us to the pass that will take us into Bavaria and on to Germania.' That much I knew. *Please God, do not tempt her to ask me more.*

'We are like Saint Helena,' she sighed.

'Is she our saint today?'

She nodded. 'I know little about her except that she was

the mother of the mighty Emperor Constantine, that she was a great traveller, and that she found the tomb of Jesus.'

'Then we shall be travellers like Saint Helena. Perhaps she is guiding us,' I trilled, then privately cringed at my false enthusiasm. Still, I had to keep my sisters cheered, to lighten their worries, while my own heart kept wait for certain capture.

'Look,' I pointed below. 'A farm. Let us see what food we might find.'

The next day proceeded as the one before, as did the day after it. Still blindly following the Adige. Still faint with hunger. Still fearful of being found and returned to the hell from which we had escaped. Still wondering how or why Sister Mea was with us.

If there was anything to recommend our reckless adventure it was the endless Creation that surrounded us. When I worked in the scriptorium, I had embellished my pages with trailing vines, stars, and flowers because it was all that my mind held. All I knew or had seen had been within the cloister walls. Now the sum of Creation was before me, and it was wondrous with infinite inspiration, large and small: From snowy, billowy clouds that sailed with the grace of a fleet across the airy blue sea; to a single drop of dew rolling off the end of a drooping frond and falling in pearl-shaped iridescence, shattering upon a blade of grass, breaking into smaller pearls. Lowly ants scurrying with morsels into their tunnelled homes; bees alighting upon a bud and girding their legs with nectar; dragonflies zagging; butterflies dancing. And birds, everywhere birds: Birds on rocks, or hopping delicately on the chestnut brown mud of the riverbank, or darting from black forest to green meadow and back again. What I had illustrated in the scriptorium had been a pale render of this. God had led me out of a prison of misery and darkness, into a world of colour and variety.

I wiped the damp off my face with the hem of my tunic as we limped across a field toward a stand of trees. Once there, I slid to the ground, pulled a clump of wet moss from the earth and pressed the soft, cool sponge against my face and my feet. The others scavenged for grass and shoots to eat. The farms we passed had only small crops owing to the months of prolonged rain; some plants were still in infancy despite it already being the hay month. Having spied a chicken that had strayed from its flock, Fat Val—bravery be thy name—killed it with the stiletto. Our cheer was short: We had no way to cook it, and we knew we were not to eat raw flesh. Fat Val nonchalantly dumped it, feathers and all, in her bundle, unconcerned about the seeping blood or the flies that fought their way into it. A new horde had picked up the scent.

'At some point we will make a fire and roast it,' she said.

'By the morrow then,' said Sister Gretchen. 'After that it will reek and not be fit for a dog.'

It was too hot to eat anyway. Only then did I realise that I was munching the very moss I had used to cool my skin. *Meat. We need meat.*

Little Fey crawled toward me and dropped her head in

my lap. Unlike our browned faces, hers was pale as narcissus.

I took her hands in mine and looked at her palms. I had forgotten about her secret.

Little Fey's stigmata were false. It hurts to write those words but I was hurt that she allowed the claim to persist. Why others, older and wiser than I, did not examine the marks more fully, I cannot say. The desire for faith and belief can force us into false witness. But I saw it: Marks on the palms, but not on the top of the hands, nor the feet, nor the torso. Could it truly be stigmata without the necessary attributes? But no one believes a child. Had I spoken up, I would have been thought petty, even envious of the reverence she was being accorded. I would have been scolded for lacking belief in the mystery of our faith, and of the miracles so freely given by Our Lord and the Queen of Heaven. I wanted to say, 'Miracles? If you want a miracle then nail Little Fey to a cross and see if she is resurrected after three days.' But the voice that speaks inside me is infinitely braver and cleverer than what I utter aloud. Besides, I did not want them to crucify Little Fey. Had everyone known the truth they might have; and me as well for perpetuating the lie. My silence protected us both.

I had known of her lie a long time. It happened years ago, before her fifth Easter, so it was the atonement time of Lent. I had gone into the cloister garden to see if she wanted to play. She was sitting alone on the ground, her back to me, so absorbed in something that she didn't hear my approach. I thought to sneak up and surprise her but as I drew close, I saw it: She was gouging her palms with the end of a stick. I crept away and waited behind a door before calling out her name to let her know that I was near. By the time I came to her, the stick had been tossed to the side, and she was holding up her bloodied palms to me. I took her to the well and washed them clean. An older sister saw us, grabbed Little Fey's hands and declared hysterically that Saint Agatha's had been blessed with a miracle.

I had told no one what I had seen. I did not want to anger God or anyone at Saint Agatha's, nor did I want to question Mother Elena who surely would have known what to do. Most of all I didn't want to bring shame upon Little Fey. It was cowardly of me, yes, and I accept complicity.

As word spread of this so-called miracle, and our doors were flung open for folk to glimpse Little Fey's stigmata, our once-modest house was suddenly rich. That is, not very rich, but with enough coin to make repairs to the building, and to disperse the bounty to the poorest families. After Mother Elena's abrupt departure, the Divine wounds kept Little Fey protected. Mother Clothilde was genuinely frightened by them, and kept her distance—indeed shunned her, which, though cruel, at least spared my sister from harm.

Now, with her hands in mine I pretended to examine them. I assumed Little Fey knew that I knew, though neither of us had spoken of it. She eyed me now to determine what I might say.

'They are dark and raw,' I said, stating plainly what I saw. 'Does this augur weak humours?'

She turned her head from me and pulled away her hands, balled them into fists.

'It will not be long before we reach a town,' I assured her. 'We will stop there and rest so that you might regain your strength.'

She twisted and turned. Like a squirrel. She had always been this way. Never still. Always fidgeting.

'Let me plait your hair.'

That usually calmed her. I removed her coif, and her long hair, fine as gold silk, spilled over my knees.

'Remember your story about Father Volmar, who told you to flee to Bingen?' she said, head now turning to look at me precisely when I needed her to be still and her face turned away from me. I tugged her hair and she resettled. I separated her hair into three shafts.

'He did not tell me to flee; he surmised how I lived, said the words aloud to me, and from that I discerned what I must do.'

'Tell the story again. You won't have to whisper it this time.'

The others had only heard fragments of my encounter with Father Volmar. I had not been able to tell it all with Mother Clothilde or one in her coterie always seemingly within earshot.

I told it in full now, and when I was done, my sisters were amazed and appeared revived, thoughts of sore bodies and hunger far from their thoughts.

'It is too fantastic, like a dream,' said Fat Val.

'I have thought the same as well,' I said. 'Like a tale told by one who had imbibed heavily from the cup.'

'Had you?' said Sister Gretchen.

'I swear all to be true and sober. Besides, when have you seen me drink wine?'

'Then it was a miracle meeting,' she sighed. 'You said Father was old, but was he handsome? Maybe he and Hildegard are lovers.'

'Must your mind go to the marriage bed with every story?'

'Well, maybe it's true.'

I shook my head. I was beginning to worry about the foul thoughts that had taken up residence in her head.

'Father Volmar didn't tell you to bring us,' said Fat Val. 'Maybe there is no room for us at Bingen, or that we are ill-suited for such a place.'

'Don't say that, Sister. We are all suited. Besides, he told me the Abbess welcomes all.'

Privately, I felt myself more worthy for Bingen than the others. After all, it was me who the angels had visited; it was me to whom God had spoken; and it was I who had led our escape. At the same time, I had no doubt we would all be admitted. I trusted the word of Father Volmar.

That night, curled beneath a tree, my blanket a thick cluster of ferns, I thought again about the monk-priest who arrived in the storm. I still had not told my sisters of his words about my mother being at Bingen. I did not want them to think there was a selfish motive to our journey. Because there was none. Mother Elena had been more mother to me than any birth mother, and now in the silent night, her memory ebbed toward me and replaced that of Father Volmar. Every thought I had of her was always preceded by her leaving—the clatter of horses, the bounds on her wrist, the rough men pushing her toward the cart. It had been the greatest sorrow of my life. Mother Elena had loved chant and song and now there was no music to our lives. She had loved the garden and the sway of perfumed blooms on their tall stems, but the rains had battered them. There was no song or beauty after she left.

Still, why had she been taken? Like Abbess Hildegard, Mother Elena possessed an inner flowering of reason and perception. Had this special sensitivity been her undoing; had those with power seen in her a rival power they sought to silence? If true, why was she punished when one such as Hildegard was allowed to flourish?

A terrible pong woke me next morning. It was Fat Val's chicken. She had left her bundle near my head.

As I had done first thing each morning, I counted my sisters. Still there. Even Sister Mea. Still sleeping soundly. I seemed to be the only one who carried the burden of worry. By night, I dodged nightmares of Mother Clothilde; by day, I dodged my sisters' questions: 'How far to Bingen?' 'Where will we eat?' 'When will we eat?' 'My back is sore; what must I do?'

The question I wanted to ask them was: How do I draw you out of silence and into lively helpfulness? But that would inevitably lead to questions of a plan, of which I had none, followed by accusations of madness for leading them out into this wild world without one.

One thing I did know is that we needed to change our appearance. If Mother Clothilde had dispatched men to look for five nuns we needed a disguise.

I lay back down and tallied all the ways in which we had to change because we had to do more than alter garments. We needed to change our speech, bearing, conduct; the way we sought help. There was the vital matter of commerce: How does one conduct trade with a bag of stolen jewels? I had no familiarity with such things.

The breadth of my ignorance winded me. I had been one way inside the convent, now I must be another outside it, in the world, and I didn't know how to do it.

My heart began to quicken; I quickly tamped it down. No good would come from exposing my weakness. I had to be the exemplar, not the raving burden. Like my sisters, I was spending too much time in my head, and we would not get to Bingen with closed eyes and mouth. Father Volmar had urged me to be mistress of my life. God had breathed enough courage into me to muster escape. It was time to show wisdom with my newfound freedom.

But first, I had to stop pretending to be asleep.

I rolled onto my back. Dry leaves and twigs crunched beneath me.

I opened my eyes. I hadn't heard the others wake up.

VII

The Feast of Sarah the Matriarch

Near Botzen

They were sitting up. Watching me.

'Buongiorno.' I feigned lazy awakening; stretched my arms, gave a false yawn.

The air immediately burst alive with complaint.

'I am hungry and we have no food,' cried Little Fey.

'This flint won't catch; how will we boil nettles for tea?' said Fat Val.

'I don't like the woods,' said Sister Gretchen, gnawing an acorn that I guessed was a substitute for her fingernails, which she was trying not to chew. 'What howls were they last night? Wolf? Bear? Wolpertinger?'

Sister Mea, normally the silent one, thrust her chin at me.

'What is the plan, Sister Lucia? Where is the map? How are we to survive?'

Voices found, then.

I scrambled to my knees and rested on my heels. The bold words I had spoken to myself moments earlier vanished in the glare of attention. I blurted, 'I have a plan.'

I had no plan.

I had not thought beyond escaping the treacherous grip of Mother Clothilde. My spinning, wheeling mind could not conjure or fathom anything beyond the cost of capture. I was more surprised than all of them that our escape thus far had seen success.

But the glowering eyes of my sisters expected a plan. They expected much from me.

'Ha. No plan.' Sister Mea threw up her hands before I could speak.

My voice sputtered: 'I beg your patience, Sister Mea.'

Someone snorted. If there was anything we had learned about Sister Mea it was her lack of patience.

I had nothing for my defence except the question I could no longer contain.

'How have you come to be with us?'

She ignored the question and instead turned on me.

'Admit it; you don't have a plan. Never did. And *we're* following *you*? We must be mad! Have you any idea where we're going? Or are you leading us on some fantastical journey to oblivion?' She crossed her arms. Her jaw twitched, working up more wrath.

I didn't know what was more surprising, her sharp tone or her verbosity. Having begun, she couldn't seem to shut up.

Words and ideas tumbled around my head in search of a place to settle until I said:

'Here is the plan. We will make our way to Botzen; it should not be far. From there to Brixen, and onward to the Via Imperii. And across the Alpes.'

The surge of confidence relaxed me.

'The Via Imperii!' Sister Mea walked toward me. 'The road is rife with thieves, merchants, murderers! Do you aim to kill us?'

"Tis the only way into Bavaria. The quickest.'

'We shall risk it,' said Fat Val. She stood up from where she had slept and lumbered across to me. With a nod of approval to me, she folded her arms across her chest. One ally.

'After Bavaria…' Here, my words drifted. I did not know what came after Bavaria. Then again, would we even make it into Bavaria?

'How long before we are there?' Little Fey's fingers were stained from berries she had strung into prayer beads. Surely she wouldn't desert me. Two allies, perhaps?

'It is a long walk. But we must be prepared to wait and listen to God. Just as we waited at Saint Agatha's for His summons to flee. If He smiles on us, we will be in Bingen by the Feast of the Virgin's Nativity.'

The strain of perpetual cheer. I did not know how much longer I could keep the corners of my mouth turned up.

Sister Mea's eyes narrowed on me. 'How are you certain of the places you mention? You who have lived only at Saint Agatha's.'

'I heard them spoken by travellers to whom we gave hospitality.'

'You *heard*. But you did not ask them to improve your

knowledge.' Her cheeks puffed; she blew the air out of them.

Such conceit! My nostrils flared. My scorn was undisguised. 'Did you notice we weren't allowed to talk? Not with Mother circling. Or perhaps you were allowed; I confess I am not aware of the arrangement you kept with her. And why, why is this my fault? Why did *you* not seek direction? You who are so clever, so bold. You who have a voice. You who inserted yourself into our escape without our knowledge. How did you find out about it?'

'This was your idea,' she snarled, again ignoring the question we all wanted answered. 'You are the leader. Why are you unprepared?'

'How dare you…'

'Please!' Sister Gretchen raised her hands to halt our brabble. 'Someone will hear, and any plan will be futile. We'll be captured, tied up like pigs, and taken back to Mother Clothilde.' She turned to me. 'Sister Lucia, we need a disguise. To travel as nuns will raise suspicion.'

'Yes,' I said. 'I have considered…'

'*Allora*, here is the plan,' interjected Sister Mea, turning away from me. Was there no end to her superiority? 'I shall be a *duchessa*; you shall be my ladies.'

I couldn't believe it: scant on patience yet clearly abundant in audacious vanity.

She raised an arm to quell the chatter of the others. I saw the hollow under her arm; the lack of hair. Was she ill? I crossed my arms and surreptitiously cupped my hollows to make sure the downy tufts had not fallen off. Praise God, still there.

I spoke over her to regain my authority. 'Sister Gretchen is right. Our habits will bring attention. This is how it shall be. We will remove our coifs and arrange our veils in a less monastic manner or not wear them at all. Our attire must affect more worldly fashion.'

Sister Mea, hands on hips, laughed as if I had spoken in jest. 'And what do you know about worldly fashion?'

I ignored her—bravery was on my lips if not in my heart—and continued: 'And we shall no longer call one another "sister" for it alerts people to our vocation. Henceforth, Christian names only.'

The others, even Sister Mea, reared at this. Had I overstepped?

'But, Sister Lucia, I have been called this since birth.'

'Fey.' I said her name with emphasis; no more *Sister* Fey. 'Fey, we must change our appearance and manner to be safe.'

'I cannot do it, Sister Lucia. It will betray my vocation. God will see my unfaithfulness.'

I almost choked.

Do you not think He has seen through your ruse of a feigned stigmata and judged you on that? I'd say that's a fair bit of unfaithfulness right there.

'Lucia is right. God knows your heart already,' said Fat Val. She put an arm around Little Fey's shoulder. 'He knows us, whatever form we take.'

'We'll be like actors who assume costumes and countenances to play their parts,' said Gretchen, warming immediately to the plot. 'I like the idea of not being called sister. It feels wicked.'

At least it was another way to keep her with us.

'*Allora.*' Mea marched into the midst of our circle. She tossed her braid, shiny as crow feathers, over her shoulder, and spoke to us as if we were weak on comprehension. 'Like I said, this is who we will be. I will be Duchessa Bartolomea di Vicenza.'

I shook myself as if emerging from a wild dream. *You're what? So grand in your pretence!*

'You two'— she pointed to Gretchen and me—'will be my ladies. You'— she pointed to Fey—'will be my spiritual guide. You can keep your habit and we will still call you sister. And you'— she pointed to Fat Val—'you will be my cousin. If anyone asks, we will say we are on a pilgrimage.'

'We are walking in the opposite direction to Rome,' I sneered. She was obviously the kind who sought praise for her cleverness, and I was glad to call out her error.

'Not Rome,' she said. 'Santiago de Compostela.'

Gretchen clapped. 'Oh, a monsterful plan!'

My body was jangled by the betrayal. The idea to escape Saint Agatha's had been mine. The plan of how to escape had been mine. Yet Mea had turned heads and hearts away from me with a snap of her fingers: *You, you and you.*

'Must we jump whenever you snap?'

She came toward me and wagged a finger in my face.

'You are stubborn and above yourself, Lucia. Unless an idea comes from you it has no worth, and yet you are empty of ideas. We'll be killed in our sleep before you summon any sense, let alone a plan.'

I bit back my tears. 'Excuse me, I must tend to my relief.'

I turned and stomped as deep into the woods as I dared go, and let loose a silent scream.

As I squatted, fuming at her audaciousness, my mind travelled back to the day she arrived at Saint Agatha's. It had been another day of torrential rain. The choir sisters had finished their midday meal and were in their cells; we younger ones were clearing up after them. We had at first dismissed the sound of a cart, thinking it was the clatter of rain, but when we heard horses neigh, we looked out the window and saw a carriage approach. We rushed into the hall to find some industry so we might observe the event. I had grabbed a dusting rag. A choir sister rushed down the stairs from her cell to greet the visitors but before she had reached the door, three women burst through: Two appeared to be mother and daughter, the third, a lady's maid. The trio swept past in a cloud of perfume, mounted the stairs and barged into Mother's office. I had braced for Mother's scream of remonstrance, but there was no sound. Slowly, I worked my way up the stairs with the dusting rag, wiping the balustrade, and tried to overhear their business. But the office door was shut; the conversation whispered. When the bell rang for Nones, Mother's door was flung open. The mother and her maid skittered down the stairs, out the front door, not bothering to close it, and once in their litter they disappeared in a swoosh and spray of rain. The younger woman had remained in Mother's office. We did not see her again until after Compline when we retired to our dormitorium. There she stood between the row of pallets, arms crossed. Rain dripped from the rafters and made a noisy landing. Heedless of Mother's rule of silence, she had glared at us and said, 'This is worse than a stable,' and threw her bundle on the pallet between where Fat Val and Gretchen slept. And that was how things were left. Aside from the skirmishes between her and Fat Val, the rest of us had managed to avoid her.

Now, as I made my way through the copse back to the group, I thought of how she had cowed us. We had learned to read her, and knew when to give her space. We had indulged her long silences, her stares, aloof nature, her constant hair-brushing. But now I was done with her manner, done with being diminished by her. She had launched into our escape uninvited and refused to explain how and why. Well, she was going to answer me now.

I marched into the clearing. She was instructing the others on how not to be a nun. Like sheep, they followed her every word.

'*Allora*, when the religious walk, they dip their heads and look at the ground,' she was saying. 'Round shoulders, arms close to the body. We will not do that. You can, Sister Fey, but not the others. Understand? When you are spoken to, incline your heads but only a little to show you are paying attention, but do not let your face betray any expression or emotion. Gesture with small movements, as if to wave. Be poised but do not show too much humility, *sì*? Adopt the mien of noble ladies. As I do.'

I drew in my breath to chide her when a deep voice hollered: 'You, there. Stop!'

I whipped round. Three of them. One in a black cloak with the bishop's insignia. The other two, astride a pair of bays, dressed in poor leather. Clubs hung off their belts. My belly was a bag of cats. These were the bounty hunters dispatched by Mother Clothilde to find us.

My eyes turned back to the one in black; eyes shaded by the brim of a black velvet hood. His white Percheron pawed the ground twitchily.

'We seek five who fled the Convent of Saint Agatha,' he announced. His brow suddenly creased. 'Though I see but four of you. Still…'

I did my best to appear as if the remark did not surprise me, but as I glanced around I noticed our reduced numbers. Fat Val. Where was she?

I stepped forward and dipped. 'My lord.' My voice cracked: 'We do not know of who or what you speak.'

'I scarce believe you,' he scoffed. 'Every piazza in the Empire buzzes like a bee swarm with the news. We could bring back any number of girls and still get the reward.'

'Reward?' said Gretchen.

'Ten pieces of silver. A good amount for thieves.'

'Thieves?' Mea flashed outrage. 'How dare you…'

I interjected: 'You wound us with your insult. We are humble, honest maids.'

'So, which is it, nuns or thieves you seek, sir?' said Gretchen. She folded her arms to affect a position of challenge. 'Nuns would not steal.'

The three men roared.

'You are indeed simple if you believe that,' said the caped one. 'Do not be fooled by the monastic vow of poverty. The richest men I know are in Holy orders. But if you care to know, these nuns have taken food. I ask you, who would take food from a nunnery?'

Gretchen looked ready to do him harm. She did not like being called simple.

One of the dullards on either side of the caped man nodded at Little Fey.

'This one is surely a nun.'

I quickly moved to her side.

'She is, sire. A most holy one. She is the daughter of our lord and lady, and has…'

Suddenly, a shrill voice brayed and entered the clearing.

'You! Away from my women.'

Fat Val stormed in like a charging bull. We stepped back and gawked: Her appearance was greatly altered. Except for Little Fey, we had all abandoned our coifs, but Fat Val had gone further. The bodice of her habit was folded down to reveal a bosom with which we had not hitherto been acquainted, lifted and displayed like large apples. Her curly hair was twisted atop her head and held in place by a sprig of hawthorn berries. She looked rather comely. Around her midsection was a silk sash of shimmering persimmon. A sash that I had spied in Mea's bundle. I stole a glimpse at Mea: Her face had seen it and was as fiery as the hawthorn berries in Fat Val's hair.

I looked back to the riders. They were staring at Fat Val's bosom.

Fat Val paid no heed. Hands on hips she bellowed: 'Answer me now. Why do you tarry with my women?'

A smirk lifted the lips of the bishop's man; not the sort

who took the scold of women.

His tone turned syrupy. 'Forgive me, mistress, I thought they were runaways. I was querying them.'

'It is not your place to query them,' she yelled. 'They are collecting flora for the feast of Minervus and Eleazar. Ladies. *Andiamo.*'

'Are they now?' he said mildly. 'Another feast day. When we rode through Botzen yesterday they were making merry over the feast of Sarah the Matriarch. If not for the saints, how would we sinners revel?'

The men chuckled. We did not.

Gretchen whispered to me: 'She is wrong again. The martyrdom of Minervus and Eleazar comes after the Octave of the Assumption, and Saint Timothy…'

I elbowed her and hissed: 'Really? You fret about the saints in the midst of this?'

Fat Val's face remained dark. She clapped her hands at the men as if dismissing swine. 'Be gone.'

They did not move. One of the dullards dismounted and stood, legs and arms akimbo.

'If these maids are collecting flora, why is nothing in their arms?'

Her nostrils flared, she stomped her feet, her bosom bounced, she made ready her fists to fight. 'How dare you seek account of their work.'

Gretchen and I quickly restrained her.

She brushed off our hands and said to the men, 'I shall alert the master's dogs and men-at-arms at once. Women, come.'

She turned and stormed back into the woods. We filed after her obediently. When we were out of sight of the riders, she pushed us into the hollow of an enormous tree, its gaping trunk like the mouth of the great fish that swallowed Jonah.

'Oh, Valentina, again you saved us.' My hands pressed against the fear that pulsed in my belly and that rose to my ears.

'Give me back my sash,' said Mea.

'For shame, Sister Mea. You should kiss her, not admonish her,' said Little Fey.

A tree could grow from acorn to full height before Mea apologised. But I was surprised at the snap in Little Fey's voice. It was not like her to admonish anyone; she saved that honour for me.

'You are brave, Sister Valentina,' she continued. '*Deo gratias.*'

'How did you get your *tettes* so high and big?' said Gretchen, uncomfortably close to Fat Val's bosom.

'Give. Me. Back. My. Sash.' snarled Mea.

Fat Val untied the sash. Her bosom drooped. She reached into her bodice and pulled out our coifs, one after the other. *How had she got those?* Her bosom drooped further.

Suddenly, the ground rumbled; we huddled together inside the trunk.

'Shh! Don't move,' I said.

The damp of the trunk was cold against my back. I pressed an eye to a split in the wood, and saw the white Percheron and the two bays thunder past.

A Flight of Saints

That night, to ease our fright from our encounter with the bounty hunters, Gretchen told us about Sarah the Matriarch.

'When an angel appeared to Sarah, wife of Abraham, and told her she would have a child, she laughed. And why would she not, for she was in her tenth decade and childless. But in spite of her advanced years she trusted in God, and her faith was soon rewarded by the gift of a son. She named him Isaac, which means laughter. But not all was laughter with Sarah. Before Isaac was conceived, Sarah had given her servant Hagar to Abraham so that Hagar might bear him a child and continue his lineage. Hagar had given birth to Ishmael, which means God will hear. Abraham loved Ishmael, and he loved Hagar, but Sarah was jealous, and when Isaac was born, she made Abraham banish Hagar and Ishmael.'

'So, Sarah the Matriarch is also Sarah the Envious, or Sarah Who Casts Away Others,' said Fat Val. 'Not very saintly.'

'Yet, so it is told,' shrugged Gretchen.

'Why is she revered for bearing a child late in life and not disparaged for cruelly dispatching her friend?' I asked.

'Or the greater crime of asking her friend to bed an old man.' Gretchen shuddered.

There were many things I wished to ask the chroniclers of the Scriptures, but for now there was no room in my head. My only concern was how to evade those who hunted us.

VIII

The Feast of Saint Judith
Toward Botzen

'Ow!'
 My eyes shot open and adjusted to morning's light in time to see Mea, kneeling on her bed of twigs, hitting Fat Val; and Fat Val, defending herself by slapping Mea full on the face.

'That's for all the times you kicked me awake when you knew I couldn't complain.'

'Oaf!' Mea straddled Fat Val and rained blow after blow with her fists.

Fat Val grabbed Mea's hair. 'You're as cruel as Mother Clothilde. If I didn't know better, I'd say you were her daughter.'

'I had no choice but to kick you awake: With all that flesh you wouldn't have felt a nudge.'

'Sisters! For the love of God!'

I sat up and plucked the forest floor from my clothes and

hair. *What was that smell?* Fat Val's chicken; that thing had to go.

'She started it,' said Fat Val, punching back. No one disputed it. Mea had, for reasons unknown to any of us, tormented her since her arrival at Saint Agatha's.

"She started it," mimicked Mea. 'Are you a baby, too? A very fat baby, I would add. And this'— she punched Fat Val hard in the arm—'is for stealing my sash.'

Fat Val lunged at her anew.

Nam caritas Dei.

Rule Seventy in Blessèd Benedict's law forbade striking another; but what were Benedict's rules now? I picked up a small rock and threw it at them. It struck Mea on the bone of her wrist, and she cried out as she cradled it against her stomach.

I was already on my feet to apologise, but the look she gave made me step back. There was murder in her eyes. Her mouth was poised to rebuke me, but for once mine lashed first.

'Well done, sisters.' I didn't bother to mask my mockery. 'Where is your civility, your charity? We who are in service to God. Think how your actions and words pain Him. And you, Mea, the eldest of us, and a professed sister. For shame.'

I didn't know where this harsh voice came from, but I recognised it as the one I used in my dreams whenever I challenged the Devil or was being tempted by a palmer. I had never employed it aloud, even at my most exercised and angered; anything that came out had been watered and timid. Now, unleashed, my anger flew at all of them.

'Where is your gentleness, your kindness?' I jawed. The words spewed through my teeth. 'Why must you quarrel? Your energy would be better spent on ways to protect ourselves, or make easier our journey. But none of you seem to think. It's like you have left your brains back at Saint Agatha's. Given yesterday's narrow escape, how selfish you are to not contain your voices. I feel like Christ, burdened with a bunch of do-nothing, questioning apostles. What has become of you? Are you nuns or a circus of imbeciles? And someone get rid of that stinking chicken.'

I turned away, but not before a final snap: 'Gather your bundles. *Andiamo.*'

I swept up my things and stomped off. I was all out of patience. It's true, some of my anger was directed at myself for not being more prepared, for not having a defined route for this journey, for not being more knowledgeable about how to shift in this new realm. The world outside the convent was beating me and I felt myself tipping toward easy surrender. Then, too, there were my companions. Fractious and whinging. Slow to talk yet swift with complaint about my shortcomings, my lack of a plan. Did they offer anything? Of course not!

Even Little Fey irritated me. Hands always pressed together in prayer; tunic clean—how was that possible with air and ground so dusty that the rest of us had tunics and bodies the colour of mustard seeds? Last night, with our heads touching before our descent into slumber, I had told her that my only wish was to safely reach Bingen. She told me her only wish was to serve God and to go to Heaven. What a cloying simpleton. I watched her now, clutching her cross of holy twigs. Busy performing her piety while I fretted about our survival.

God, take this burden from me. I did not want to be leader, but who else to take it on? Little Fey was too young; Gretchen too flighty and unable to fix her mind on anything but men and the deeds done in the marriage bed. Fat Val showed bravery with the horsemen but was altogether too clumsy and unthinking. Mea pretended to be a leader but only wanted the authority, not the responsibility.

My vexations pushed me deeper into icy resentment until I began to think of ways to leave my sisters. How to do it? In the middle of the night while they slept; in daylight by saying I had to tend to my relief, and then slip from sight? Or by dropping silently into the tall grass and crawling toward the trees, then running into the forest where they would never find me? I would surely reach Bingen quicker. I didn't care what happened to them.

I surveyed the land and plotted the where and how. I wanted to hurt them, to make them regret taking me for granted. Let them fend for themselves. Yet, even as I craved this, I knew that to wander alone took more courage than I had, that the road of isolation and endurance required the fortitude of Moses. Even Elijah had been frightened when he fled Jezebel.

I looked at my sisters, lazy and desultory on their feet. I had thought we would be in Bingen by the Feast of the Virgin's Nativity, but at this pace I doubted we'd make it by Lent.

My feet scuffed the ground.

Little Fey turned round, stretched her hand to me.

'Pray, Sister Lucia; walk with me.'

I walked to her side, glumly took her hand.

She whispered, 'Do not leave us. Please.'

I felt my face flush.

'What makes you think I would?'

'I could hear your thoughts. I know we are difficult, but have patience. We are all too scared and unsure to do anything. You are our leader.'

We were in the mountains now. Every step we took was uphill. My legs ached and my tunic was damp from the labour of walking. The air was dry and hot. Large black birds circled above us. I yearned for the cooling sound of a stream or the splash of a waterfall, but all I heard were the groans of my sisters.

The path coiled around hills and mountains the way I once coiled my hair around my finger when I was anxious. What had made me anxious then? Whatever it was, this was a hundred times worse. This was suffering.

I trudged uphill under the glare of the sun, without breath, as if in a dream. I had lost count of how long it had been since we left Saint Agatha's. I shook the gourd; it was almost empty.

The path, such as there was, narrowed; the edges sheered away to dangerous depths. The ground of loose stones looked fresh; I looked up and wondered whether more would fall and stone us to death.

'What do you suppose happens when we die?'

Little Fey's question had been on my mind, too. I felt closer to Death than I did to Life.

'We return to the earth,' I said.

'Not to Heaven?'

'It feels like we are climbing to it,' huffed Fat Val. Her face was red as a beet.

'Don't you wish you could climb upon a cloud and let it take you wherever it was going?' said Gretchen. 'I think I should like to fly.'

Deus, da mihi fortitudinem. If I was guilty of living too much in my head, she was guilty of living in a dream, wrapped in imagination, inside her head.

She stretched her arms and began to twirl, like a simpleton, there on the mountainside; unheeding of the oblivion that was mere steps to the side of us.

Mea grabbed her by the arm just as Gretchen's foot slid over the side.

We shrieked and grabbed onto one another; I gripped the neck of Mea's tunic to prevent her from tumbling after Gretchen.

We pulled her from the edge and returned her to firmer ground. Had she gone over, there would have been nothing to break her fall.

'Why are you so reckless and stupid?' Mea erupted. 'You have no sense, absolutely none of it.' She dusted herself off, and with a final 'Idiot!' she stalked off.

Gretchen shrugged.

'Why do you shrug?' I scolded. 'She is right. Your carelessness could have cost us our lives.'

'Next time, we'll let you fall,' said Fat Val.

We rounded the hill and relief breathed out of me, for here the ground levelled, and the land was grassy..

My feet were hot with pain and it was not even midday.

Mea stalked further ahead. I kept my eyes on her. Her fuming silence, to which we were accustomed, filled the air around us and the valley beyond. It was wise to stay clear of her. Aside from my few attempts, no one had dared ask her how she had come to be with us. The mystery ate at me. And what was that look she had given me when we emptied the pouch of jewels that Fat Val stole from the first horseman? There was something Mea wasn't telling us.

Suddenly, I saw her veer from the path and scurry toward the woods. *Ah ha, this is it; this is where she will leave us.* I wouldn't have minded. Given all I had to think about on this long journey, I wouldn't miss her.

But what was this? She had stopped, turned to us, and beckoned.

By the time we reached her she was stretched on the ground.

'*Allora*, my limbs scream from pain, my stomach from hunger. Look at us. Our feet are swollen and covered in pustules, sore and oozing. Our skin is burned from the sun. We cannot continue like this. If we don't eat more than grass and water we will lose strength and die. I do not want to die. I beg you, Lucia, let us come to an agreement. Look at Fey. The little one never complains but it is plain that she is weak.'

Oh, Fey complains alright; you just can't hear her when you're wrapped in your thick cloak of selfishness.

A Flight of Saints

I looked at Little Fey, face glistening. Sullenly, protectively, I pulled her to me.

The others joined Mea on the ground. Gretchen passed the gourd. When it was empty and returned to her, she said, 'I can't go on like this. I am going to refill this, but when I return, I want to hear a plan. And someone else can carry this gourd. Why is it always me?'

'Fine,' I said to Mea. 'Let us take up your plan.'

Triumph spread across her face. *How like a true sinner.* The other two mumbled relief.

When Gretchen returned and saw me shedding my tunic she was full of excitement.

'There is a plan? Is it Mea's? What is my part?'

Mea barely looked at her. 'As I said before, you and Lucia are my ladies; Fey...'

'*Sister* Fey, if you please,' said Fey, tart of tone.

'Sister Fey will be my spiritual counsellor. Valentina'—she looked at her nemesis with a sort of grudging kindness—'Valentina will be my cousin.'

I braced for another outburst. Reading my wariness, Mea rolled her eyes. 'All will be well. *Allora*, empty your bundles so I can see what we can use.'

We tipped them out. We barely had anything save what we wore. My bundle held my coif, an under-shift that I didn't wear because it was too hot, and my shoes, which I wore infrequently to save wear; their soles were already thin. Aside from food, I had taken nothing from Saint Agatha's. I regretted that now; I could have used a second tunic.

'Sister Fey,' said Mea, 'You need not change a thing. I will give you my profession veil, to give you more authority. Now, do not take offence with what I am about to say, but your stigmata will help us. People will pay if you bless them...'

'I cannot sell what God has given me!' Little Fey wept into her clasped hands. *The tears of a player.*

I looked at Mea. *Seriously? The stigmata?* Hadn't she seen through this flimsy fraud? More to the point, her idea was reckless.

'Mother Clothilde has no doubt given the bounty hunters a full description of us, including the stigmata. Besides, we have jewels to pay our way.'

Mea thought for a moment, then nodded.. I felt a small breeze of victory.

'Sister Fey, disregard my words. Instead, rub earth on your hands to disguise your wounds. We must also disguise your origins. If asked, say you are from Vicenza, not Trento, and that I took you in. No, never mind. Remain silent. I will speak for you.'

Little Fey dried her tears.

Mea next turned to Gretchen and me, looked us up and down. If she was to play the haughty *duchessa*, she suited the part.

'You must look like ladies.' She rummaged in her bundle. 'Go to the water and wash completely, even your hair. Here is a piece of soap. Do not lose it or I will drown you. Leave your tunics here. I will clean them as best I can with the gourd water. Valentina and I will alter them.'

She dipped into her bundle again and this time extracted a small leather case that held needle and thread. She sighed.

A Flight of Saints

'Alas, no scissors.'

Valentina rummaged in her bundle and brought out the dagger. 'We can use this.'

I decided not to worry whether it was safe to leave them with a weapon.

Gretchen and I ran toward the pool, bare legs brushing against the grass. The sun was high and hot. We stepped into clear water, first on pebbles shining like watery jewels, then soft sand, until we slipped into the silk-like coolness.

Gretchen lifted the soap to her nose.

'It smells of olives. Where did she get this?'

'Must have brought it with her to Saint Agatha's. She kept a trunk in Mother's office. I saw it.'

'No wonder she always smells nice.'

'Have you noticed she has no hair under her arms?'

'Yes. Do you think she is ill?'

'I'm afraid to ask her. She is so strange. Why did you tell her of our plan to escape?'

I didn't believe she had asked Mea to join us but I couldn't think of another way into the conversation. If anyone knew anything it was Gretchen; she was one for twattle and rumour.

'Wasn't me. I thought it was you. I didn't know she was coming until we were standing at the stairwell. Why don't you ask her.'

'I haven't the courage. She takes umbrage with everything.'

'How long must we walk on tip-toes around her? It's exhausting. I can't wait to see how she will turn her habit into a gown befitting a *duchessa*.'

I rinsed the soap from my hair. It felt good to be clean. 'We are supposed to be on a humble pilgrimage. To dress grandly would betray us.'

Gretchen splashed and sang. She threw back her head in the water and let her hair fan like flames, then tipped forward and shook it back like a dog. I smiled at her joyful spirit. When we were younger, she would pile her red hair over her face, make small openings for the eyes and mouth, and say she was John the Baptist. That was before Mother Clothilde had arrived, before silence had turned Gretchen hard and crude. Now, as she frolicked in the glitter, this was her younger, purer self made manifest. It cheered me but also made me sad because I knew that once out of the water, she would return to what she had become. I wished we could stay in the water forever.

When we returned to the woods our tunics had been altered. I was not sure I could wear mine. It had been shortened to reveal my ankles, but it was the bodice that distressed me more: The sleeves were slashed, and the neckline, cut from shoulder to shoulder, exposed a large square of my flesh. Gretchen's neckline was more modest. There would be no mistaking us for those in Holy orders now. I shuddered to think what folk would make of us.

'Oh, I like it,' gasped Gretchen. *Of course you would.* She held her tunic to her chest. 'May I dress now?'

Mea nodded curtly. She glanced at me as she continued stitching, as if expecting similar praise. I was careful not to offend her but neither did I want to capitulate. I wished to ask whether our ruse could be amended so that I could join

Little Fey as a nun, but my poor tunic was beyond salvation.

'It is much changed from our custom,' I said. 'Our modesty is most...' I struggled for the correct word '... most reformed.'

'It is what women wear in the towns. We need to fit in.'

She said this without looking up, needle plunging into the remade bodice of Fat Val's tunic. She turned to Fat Val and held it up: 'How is this?'

The neckline had been opened like the letter V; the collar high against her long neck. It was regal and chaste. I wondered whether I had been given the harlot's dress as punishment for being slow to accept Mea's plan.

Fat Val smiled at Mea—a smile so wide I could see her teeth. 'Beautiful.'

What was this sudden felicity between these two?

Mea reached into her bundle and drew out two diaphanous lengths of fabric: one crimson; one blue. She held them out to me and Gretchen, and shook them impatiently when we did not take them instantly. Gretchen was busy twirling in her remade tunic.

'For each of you, to wear as headscarves. Or they can tuck into your bodice if you prefer. It does not matter which one you choose but the crimson is better suited to your brown hair, and the blue to Gretchen's red hair. I will show you later how to wear them.'

She pulled from her bundle the orange sash Fat Val had stolen from her the day just gone. How many of those did she have in there?

'This looked nice on you yesterday,' she said, handing it to her. 'That's what made me angry. The colour does not suit me, so you may have it. Wear it under your bosom as you did. We shall fashion a fine knot so the ends drape over your skirt. The brown and the orange will look beautiful together, yes?'

As she spoke, I noticed her bundle was tightly closed, whereas ours lay open on the ground.

'What is in your bundle for your disguise?' My words came out more challenge than curiosity.

'Some things. You shall see.'

'We freely showed the contents of ours at your request; why do you hold back with yours?'

Her eyes lowered. She pulled her bundle closer.

Gretchen continued to frolic in her remade dress, spinning so the skirt of her tunic flared a little. 'Yes, let's see what is in your lovely bundle.'

Her dancing became ever more careless, as only Gretchen's dancing could. If she didn't stop, she would make herself sick with dizziness. But on she twirled and hummed like a fool, until she came too close to Mea and caught her foot on Mea's bundle, and suddenly the contents spilled across the forest floor for all to see: A silk tunic as red as blood; scarves of indigo, gold, and violet; a tangle of pearl strands, too many to distinguish short from long, necklace from bracelet. There were also several small black pouches (contents unrevealed), but quickly forgotten because our eyes were drawn to something far more interesting.

Gretchen scrambled toward them. She held them up and stared in awe. 'What are they?'

Mea moved swiftly on her knees, gathering her scattered possessions and stuffing them back into her bundle. She snatched at Gretchen's hands, but Gretchen did not give them up.

'Shoes, of course. Are you blind?'

They were shoes that belonged to a world unknown to us. Gretchen began to push her dirty foot into one of them, but I grabbed them away.

'Don't,' I said. They were solid but had the lightness of a handful of flour. 'These are the work of an artist.'

My nose and the eye inside my head filled with scent and memory, of wood shavings and tawed leather, and a work table cluttered with awls, chisels, knives, and blocks of willow.

'My father was a cobbler,' I told them.

'Well, all praise to Crispian and Crispinian,' sneered Mea. Again, she snatched at the shoes but I held them away from her, turning them in my hand, admiring their beauty. The soles were leather but the upper parts were green silk, the green of mossy woodlands. The elongated toe box was decorated with tiny crystals and jewels arranged in a sunburst. The heel, alder I guessed, was as long as my thumb, and scooped slightly at the sides into a refined curve, and then covered in the same silk as the rest of the shoe. Green silk ribbons, fragile as dragonfly wings, would be laced around its wearer's ankle. None of the shoes my father made looked like these.

I was mesmerised as much by their elegance as by the kind of life its owner might have. For a moment I imagined myself as that owner, in a fine gown, stepping into a fine litter. My heart seized upon a life greatly different from the one I had, and I felt robbed, deceived. I looked at my bare feet streaked in earth and flotsam, and I yearned for more. Much more.

'Where are they from?' I asked.

Still gathering her things, Mea walked on her knees toward me, grabbed the shoes and held them to her breast. Embarrassment or guilt, I wasn't sure which, bloomed on her face.

'From someone.'

'What purpose do they have for a professed nun sworn to poverty?'

It felt good to use my tone of superiority, especially with her kneeling before me.

She was silent, her head hung low, and when she lifted it, she let loose a long, plaintive sigh. She sat back on her legs.

'*Allora*. I will tell you, but only when we are on our way.'

Never had we swept up our belongings with such haste.

My whirling thoughts returned to her strange arrival that day at Saint Agatha's with the woman and the maid. Aside from her spats with Fat Val, and her vanity, no mark could be laid against her, except that which I have already mentioned—that her hair was never sheared (nor was Mother Clothilde's, or Little Fey's on account of Mother's fear of her)—and that Mea had been professed with uncommon speed. The rule of silence had conveniently prevented questions from being asked, but now, at long last, they would be asked and answered.

We left the cool shade of the woods and returned to open meadow dressed in our disguises. Any discomfort or novelty about them vanished as we walked abreast, two on either side of Mea, waiting for her to speak.

She ran her palms nervously over her dark red tunic, the one that had fallen out of her bundle, and smoothed its creases against her body. With another great sigh she began: 'I was born in Vicenza. My father is the Duca di Vicenza. He is also podestà of the city, an important man. When my mother died, her title passed to me. So, in case you are in doubt of our ruse, I am truthfully Bartolomea, Duchessa di Vicenza.'

I interrupted: 'The women who brought you to Saint Agatha's...?'

'My stepmother. Awful woman. She wanted my title, and I had refused to give it up. Why should I? But she knew I would have to relinquish it when I married so she bided her time.

'I had been betrothed since birth to the son of the Duca di Padova. Domenico was his name. At first, I was indifferent to the marriage, but in time I grew to understand its necessity. Vicenza did not have many allies, and Padova was a vital one. But increasingly Padova also needed Vicenza. There was a time when both cities depended on the emperor for protection, but that is no longer the case. Barbarossa's cunning is as reliable as his treachery. So, I came to see the purpose of my marriage, that it would protect my family and our people. It also meant I could leave my stepmother. She made my life a misery.'

My mind raced to keep up with this litany of worldly concerns, a realm beyond my ken. I was given to believe that noble women outside the cloister were unschooled and spent all their time in grand homes with their needlework. Mea was different. She spoke like one who knew the ways of power, and who understood those who ruled us. She parleyed about the emperor as if she was acquainted with him.

'As for Domenico, when I came of age we were formally engaged and I fell in love. He was courteous, fair of face. I could have done worse. Everyone was happy for us. I was happy. But soon I discovered that Domenico had a lover—my cousin Isidora. I felt betrayed. Isidora and I had been like sisters; she was one of my closest friends. We told each other our secrets; she had obviously forgotten to tell me about her and Domenico. When my father learned of Isidora's and Domenico's deceit, his fury was so great that I thought it might lead to war, or at least a duel. But no. He bartered the insult for more land. Meanwhile, no one consoled me or cared that my heart and reputation were ruined.'

I was ashamed by how captivated I was by her tragedy. My sisters, too; their mouths agape.

'Did you share a bed with him?' Gretchen and her prurient eagerness. I gave her a sharp elbow.

To Mea I said: 'How unkind of your own blood to forsake you.'

'I was humiliated.'

'Of course,' we murmured as one.

'I felt marked a fool.'

'Naturally,' we concurred.

'Completely ruined, you understand.'

'We do,' we nodded.

'Then you understand why I killed him.'

We stopped walking; stopped nodding. I felt myself stop breathing. Fat Val clutched my arm and tightened her grip.

Oblivious to our reaction, Mea carried on: 'One day, a guard with whom I was friendly told me the lovers were at Isidora's villa. I went there and waited outside her rooms. When they came out, I ran at Domenico with a stiletto in my hand.'

Our hands flew to our cheeks.

Mea continued, sanguine. 'Why should I care? He disgraced me as well as my family. He deserved to die. I turned to plunge the stiletto into Isidora but she begged to be spared. She said she would give me anything. That is when I thought of the shoes. They had been made for her by a cordwainer she had seduced. Believe me, she really is a harlot. So, I accepted them in lieu of her life. A fair exchange.'

Sparing a thought for my sore feet and the thin, torn leather that encased them, I weighed the price of a lying swain's life against a pair of beautiful shoes, and decided, yes, a prudent trade. I was not proud of the thought but that was how it was.

'What did Domenico's family do when you murdered their son?' asked Little Fey. I was surprised she hadn't started to pray aloud. When she uttered the word 'murdered' it sent shudders through me. We had fled Saint Agatha's with a murderess!

'They were aflame with revenge,' Mea said with another shrug. 'They wanted my blood. I was afraid they might get it: My father was trying to see how much more land he could get in exchange for sending me to the gallows.'

'What happened next?' asked Fat Val.

'They agreed to spare my life on condition that I marry their other son Marcus, who is, in all honesty, an imbecile. More so than Domenico the philanderer. Well, I rephrase that: Marcus is not an idiot but he is pompous, entitled, extremely dull. However, I had no choice: It was marriage or the gallows. One is not so different from the other, is it not?'

She laughed at her jest. We did not.

'I accepted on condition that before the marriage I be permitted to be shrived of my sins at a convent. I let them choose the convent. My future mother-in-law hated me, and she took my stepmother's advice to choose Saint Agatha's: Clothilde is my stepmother's cousin, and so she knew the convent was lowly, and also knew of her cousin's penchant for cruelty. She saw it as double punishment. I did not care; I only needed a place to work on an escape.

'A few days after I arrived at Saint Agatha's, I told Clothilde I wanted to surrender my life to God. She's easily bribed by flattery and finery, and agreed to do it quickly. My family was paying her to house me, and I was paying her in exchange for professing me. Later, when I learned of your plot to flee both convent and country, well, things fell nicely into place for me.'

Setting aside the fact that she had confessed murder, this new revelation startled me. Was her profession a mere ploy, or had she truly, fully, given herself to God? The question was on my lips when Gretchen asked:

'How did you learn of our plot?'

'Ah, the language in a convent is not so different from the language at court. Noble men want to look at us but they

A Flight of Saints

do not want to hear us. However, we women are clever. We learn to speak with our eyes, our hands. We speak with our silence. I watched your gestures, your eye movements, the nod of the head, the tap of the foot, the countenance upon your faces, the lift of a finger, a cough, a whisper. You were most talkative.'

True. We had learned to read silence, smell silence, hear silence, like birds sensing danger. Day and night, screams for mercy had echoed throughout the convent as our fellow sisters were punished; the sheer terror of it forced our fluency and proficiency in silence. Our entire escape was connived this way. I marvelled at that now.

'And there was also Sister Fey,' said Mea.

My eyes turned to Little Fey, nervously twisting her berry beads.

'I only wanted to befriend her,' she said meekly.

'Why invite Mea when you knew how ill-disposed she was toward Valentina?'

'It was wiser to bring her with us than leave her to betray us. Besides, I thought that bringing her might make her grow fonder of Valentina.'

'Here you are mistaken, little one,' said Mea. She winked at Fat Val. 'Valentina and I fought only to avert attention. No one would suspect two sisters who hated one another of plotting an escape.'

'But the fights and arguments.' I was wide-eyed.

'Yes, some of it was true,' said Fal Val. 'Mea can be mean.'

'But mostly we are on good terms, are we not?' Mea put an arm around her.

It was a relief, and I hoped that with their felicity now revealed that I no longer had to contend with their arguments. But I was also hurt that their secret had been kept from me. I thought I had been aware of everything.

I steered Mea back to her story. 'When Valentina stole the jewels from the man the other day, your eyes betrayed you.'

'Yes. That was Marcus, brother of Domenico. My fiancé. It was a good thing he had not seen me or he would have seized me then and there. I am certain he was on his way to Saint Agatha's to bribe Mother Clothilde to release me into his arms. If we had not fled when we did, I do not know how I would have escaped him.' She laughed. 'Maybe I would have had to kill him, too.'

'You have done enough killing for one life,' murmured Fat Val.

'Lucky for him he only lost a hand.'

Once again, Mea's words stopped us cold.

What?

'It was an accident.' She pressed together her hands in a plea for us to understand the circumstances. 'When I killed Domenico, I was unaware that Marcus was there. While I was bartering for the shoes from Isidora, I heard a movement behind me, and I turned and lashed out too quickly. With the stiletto. Which struck his hand.'

'Joseph's staff! How much more violence is there to this story?' said Gretchen.

Little Fey said, 'Bless you, Mea. You behaved as Saint Judith did when she slew King Holofernes for deceiving her people.'

'What became of Isidora?' said Gretchen.

'I would not put it past her to have tricked Marcus into fetching me so that she could avenge Domenico's murder. And I daresay she wants her shoes back.'

She stopped and looked at us with pleading eyes. 'I had to join you. I can't be caught. I can't return home. Isidora wants my blood. Marcus wants revenge for the loss of his hand and for evading my promise to marry him. His family want revenge for the murder of one son, and my desertion of the other. My own family wants to punish me for the scandal I have caused. Clothilde fears the wrath of both families for allowing me to escape, and also imminent excommunication when it's discovered that she accepted my bribes in exchange for professing me. So you see, I am fleeing many people, not only Clothilde.'

If I am honest, if I were asked to swear an oath on the True Cross, none of what Mea said shocked me. Instead, I felt sympathy and admiration. I was in awe of her candour, for a confession like that would prompt most folk to hasten far from such a one as her. Not me. My regard for her changed significantly. My fear of her evaporated; I felt her equal for I recognised something feral in her that was also in me. Perhaps you expected a different reaction. If so, you expected a different person. Judge me as you will, but know this: I may be a bride of Christ, but I am also a handmaid of Satan.

IX

The Feast of Saint Mary of Magdala

Botzen

Late in the afternoon we approached the timbered palisade of Botzen. A great iron cross was mounted above the gate to keep out the Devil; a withered head was impaled on a spike to keep out the thieves. The catapults were manned.

The murderess's story had so transfixed me that I had not adequately prepared my wits for Botzen. In a blink, the cool, leafy refuge of the woods was gone and I was suddenly exposed to all and sundry.

I looked at my sisters in their disguises: a tall, raven-haired beauty in a red gown, a tiny blonde nun, and three tow-clad maids. I wore my sash as a shawl for modesty, but Gretchen wrapped hers around her head like an Arabian turban. She had stained her lips with berry as had Fat Val. We looked like we belonged in a carnival.

Apparently, the sentry thought likewise for he waved us through the gate without question. His attention was on lustier fare: A juggler was tossing oranges into the air, and the woman who retrieved those he (intentionally) dropped bent so low that her bosom tumbled free of her bodice. She feigned embarrassment, and kept stuffing her *tettes* back into their constraints only to let them fall out again. The sentry couldn't take his eyes off her.

Plain to everyone, except apparently the crowd and the sentry, was that the woman and the juggler were in collusion. While the woman preened and clumsily tried to cover her modesty I watched a boy—a third accomplice—run among the crowd and dip his hands into various pockets and purses. The distracted sentry, oblivious to this crime in stark daylight, ignored a second crime by admitting five escaped nuns into Botzen.

'Why are menfolk so beguiled by *tettes*?'

But my sisters did not hear me; their ears and eyes were captivated by a different scene.

I had never been to a town except on two occasions when I accompanied Mother Elena into Trento for birthings. Both were at night when merchants, palmers, and pardoners were at their gambling tables. Now, in daylight, I was agog at the energetic busyness around me. My lack of knowledge of how to get to Bingen was the least of my worries: How must I shift in this mayhem? What did I know of how to bargain or borrow, or how to behave? How were we to find food or bed? Was I to go from croft to croft knocking on doors to see who was kind, who might take pity on us, who would not question where we were from or where we were going? If I knocked on the wrong door and awakened one who would kill us, what then?

Only the murderess had lived in places with this kind of activity, and it showed: She weaved sinuously through the crowds as if nothing could possibly impede her while the rest of us walked as if we had been given new legs and eyes.

My simple senses were jangled. Men with black skin and white teeth stood in stalls selling spices and salt. Women with white skin and painted lips swayed importantly through the crowd. Some wore shoes with hard soles and their distinctive clomp marked them as important, confident. Many aromas came at me: Perfumes, but also the peppery pungency of ginger, the mint and anise scent of basil; the wet, salty smell of gutted fish. Jars of oils, and woven baskets of onions and garlic. Bowls, plates, and jugs of brightest brass. Women in black robes huddled behind turbaned men whose arms held out lengths of silk, chaisel, cotton, cloth of gold, skins, furs, and fat skeins of wool, fabrics I had only heard about. More colours than I had ever known passed before my eyes in glorious combinations: orange and indigo; blue and emerald; rose and dandelion. I was self-conscious in my brown tunic of tow. Elsewhere, stalls heaved with fruit and vegetables, an array like one might find upon the emperor's table—cauliflower, lemons, radicchio, carrots, aubergine, zucchini. A bright colour here, a glittering jewel there, the sight of a beautiful woman, a wealthy man. All manner of godly folk swirled before me, folk with intentions, purpose, ornament, and trade that had never entered my ken.

My eyes were everywhere and elsewhere. I walked into a flock of geese. I staggered through clouds of incense and found myself amid players performing the life of Mary Magdalene. Life rushed about me like a dance. Surely this was Babel, not Botzen.

Someone grabbed my arm and dragged me away from this. It was Mea, and her eyes were wide with opprobrium. She cocked her head for the others to follow and pulled me into a dank, narrow *vicolo* that smelled foul.

Against the wall she pinned me with her flinty glare.

'I thought Valentina was the clumsy one; what is the matter with you?'

'*Mi dispiace*,' I gulped. 'There is much to see and many people about. It has jargogled my movements.'

'Well, please continue;' she sneered, 'and we can count on being discovered and having our bodies flayed before supper.'

She shook her head and made gestures with her hands as if beseeching Our Lord.

Little Fey's fingers meanwhile were steepled; her lips moved.

'There she goes.' Fat Val rolled her eyes. 'Sweet-talking her way to Heaven.'

'What is it, Sister Fey?'

'I'm asking the Blessèd Virgin to take pity on us and deliver food.'

It had been ten days since we fled Saint Agatha's; ten days of running, walking, and hiding. Ten days with scant food. Our pockets were worn and stained from fingers rooting for errant crumbs. I had barely noticed hunger because fear pitched in me and filled the void, but now amid Botzen's abundance, my stomach all but leapt in want.

'You will eat soon and plenty,' said Mea. 'I will find lodgings.'

She looked at me, held out her palm. '*Allora*, the pouch.'

'It is safe with me,' I said. Would she take it and flee, leave us to the madness of this settlement? That was what a murderess would do.

She closed her eyes to steady her impatience. 'I have need of only one stone, Lucia; one of the diamonds will more than suffice.' Her face grew dark as a thunder cloud. 'Do you think I might abandon you?'

I handed her the pouch.

She pulled apart the drawstring, tipped the contents into her palm, plucked a diamond, put it into the pouch, and handed me the loose jewels. I put them in my pocket.

'Wait,' said Fat Val. From beneath her orange sash, she withdrew a small sack. 'Salt.'

I was relieved of Mea's scold.

'Did you steal this?'

She gave a chastened nod toward the crowded market.

Mea took the sack and smiled. 'Fine work, Valentina. The salt might suffice in a barter for lodgings, but I shall take the diamond in case. Sister Fey, come with me. The rest, stay here.' Then she held a warning finger to our faces. 'Do not move. Do not speak. Do not do anything.'

The sight of her long sharp fingernail made me think of the stiletto that had slayed Domenico, that had sliced off the hand of Marcus.

'Sometimes she is too high and mighty. Why don't we challenge her?' grumbled Fat Val as we watched Mea scurry off with Little Fey.

'She's your friend. Ask her. Then again, she has confessed to murder and dismemberment. I wouldn't try my chances,' said Gretchen.

'I thought we were friends, Valentina,' I said. 'You didn't tell me you were scheming with her.' She didn't reply.

We waited. People passed us or gawked at us from the entrance of the *vicolo*, then moved on awkwardly. I realised that the *vicolo* in which we stood was lined with piss gutters.

'Ignore the folk,' Gretchen said under her breath. 'It is the way in towns. The new, the foreign, are given wary treatment. Pay no mind.'

Before I could ask how she knew this, the murderess rushed back. Without Little Fey.

She answered my panicked eyes: 'I did not sell her. She is waiting at the taverna. Come. Do not say a word until we are in our rooms.'

Rooms?

At the taverna, we climbed the stairs to the top floor and closed the door behind us. I could scarce believe our situation. Two large chambers joined as one. Two windows at the front; one smaller one to the rear. The timbered ceiling was sloped and there were no holes in it. There was a wash area with ewer and bowl. And beds, not pallets but beds settled into frames with mattresses of straw and feather, and animal skins atop.

Mea arranged chairs around the table. She lifted the hem

of her tunic and wiped dust from a prie-dieu. Then, she walked over to me, reached into her pocket and handed me the diamond in its pouch. Her eyes showed a mixture of hurt and defiance.

Turning to the others she announced, '*Allora*, we are here for two nights. The bag of salt was worth that much to the innkeeper. We have Valentina to thank for that. I told him we were on a pilgrimage to Santiago de Compostela. At some point we will need to find a Templar to exchange the diamond for coin, but for now we do not need the jewels. I have arranged for hot water to be brought up so we might wash. Supper as well.'

She was much at ease with this life and its ways. Hot water. Food. Brought to us. Chambers with beds and linen. What world was this?

'It is more than we expected,' cooed Gretchen. 'I do not know what to say.'

'*Deo gratias*,' said Little Fey, who always summoned the right words.

By early evening, we were scrubbed, fed, and seated before a fire. Gretchen had remembered the recipe for sore feet—balm resin and honey—and having found the ingredients in the market she made up the unguent, which we smeared on our ruined feet.

Over the years, I had been told stories of the trials and fortitude of the desert fathers and mothers; how scarcity and solitude brought them closer to God, and that I, likewise, must take succour from them and not bemoan my poverty. Perhaps I had misheard the stories or misunderstood their meaning, because I had more fervour for God with a full belly than with an empty one. An empty belly made me think that God had forsaken me; a full one made me think God cared for me. What was this backward theology that glorified penury? Abundance did not weaken devotion to God; surely it strengthened it. For what was poverty but a sign of neglect and abandonment that hardened, rather than softened, the spirit?

I smiled at my sisters. I was ashamed of my earlier thoughts about fleeing them. Their companionship, their wiles and goodness were blessings. Even Mea the murderess. She had set us up in such pleasant rooms. And now I was clean, fed, safe. My only complaint was that my stomach was so full, so unaccustomed to food, that I required many visits to the privy pot.

Little Fey sat down next to me. I held her hand. How dark my skin was beside hers. We had all been coloured by the sun, but she was still pale as moonlight.

'How are they?' I stroked her palms with their false stigmata.

'They throb,' she said. 'In the past it has augured some effect or event. This time is different. I am like a filled pot that yearns to empty. My body is tired; my stomach hurts, too.'

I had seen her scratching her palms as we walked. I began to wonder whether it was more a means to quell her agitation, in the same way that Gretchen bit her nails, than a means to continue her fraud. Still, I played my part of sisterly concern.

'The stomach pain is from our sudden indulgence. My stomach hurts a little, too. You will sleep well tonight, and all day tomorrow if you like, for we have no need to venture out.'

But early next morning, we were awakened by persistent knocking at our door.

We leapt from our comfortable beds and dreams like fish from a stream. I looked at Mea. *Does the murderess have a plan?* But it was Fat Val who, again, was first to pounce.

'You.' She pointed to Mea. 'Get into bed. Sister Fey, kneel at the bedside and pray. You two'— she pointed to me and Gretchen—'hide.'

Gretchen threw a sheepskin over herself. I slid under the pallet where I could watch the door unseen.

'Who knocks?'

'It is I, the innkeeper.' The voice was urgent and whispered.

Fat Val opened the door. The man entered as if pursued.

'I beg pardon from you, mistresses, but I come to warn of three men of unchristian nature who are at this moment searching the taverna. They seek five who have fled a Holy house in Trento. I told them no such religious had been here, that those in Holy orders seek rest at Innichen Abbey, not in a taverna. They refused to believe me. Said they heard from some in this settlement that five young women had been seen. They are going room to room. I know not who you are but if you be those they seek, be warned. There is an empty room across the hall should you want to separate your numbers.'

Gretchen threw off the sheepskin. 'I will play the bawdy woman.'

'Always the lady,' I scowled, and gave her my eye.

'Maid, these are not men with whom to trifle. I would not be able to fight them off.'

A Flight of Saints

Mea sat up in bed. 'Thank you for your concern, good sir.'
When he left, I shimmied from under the bed.

'Stay where you are,' Mea said. I shimmied back. 'Gretchen, go to the other room and play the repentant pilgrim, *not* the bawdy woman. Do not trust them or entertain them. Call out if they molest you.'

Gretchen scrambled to her feet and fled with, so it seemed to me, a bit too much excitement. She loved a thrill, but this was no adventure.

'Sister Fey, stay on your knees,' continued Mea. 'Do not show your palms. Valentina, be as firm with them as you were with the men in the forest. Where is the dagger?'

Fat Val took it from her pocket and slid it along the floor. It skittered next to Sister Fey's knees, sharp side of the blade facing me. Mea reached down from the bed and picked it up. A shiver ran through me. I was as afraid now as the day we ran through the kitchen garden.

We waited in silence, keening for their footsteps. Perhaps I should have gone with Gretchen.

Suddenly, the door shook with such violent knocking that the table jumped and the shutters on the window shuddered. My head bumped against the underside of the bed. I saw Fat Val straighten her shoulders and compose herself for the encounter.

In strong voice she said to the door, 'What rude disturbance is this?'

'By order of the Principato Vescovile di Trento we are charged to search your rooms!'

I closed my eyes. I thought I might be sick.

My sister slid the bolt. Two men walked into the room. I saw only the lower part of the intruders: Black boots, brown leather tunics. Wooden clubs dangling from their belts. I dipped my head for a better look. Hard faces, flinty eyes. They were not the ones we had encountered in the forest, so they did not recognise Fat Val. She stood poised and dignified before them, a sheepskin wrapped around her like a shawl. She altered her voice to affect one who must summon reserves of patience to get through the day.

'State your business,' she said.

'You heard what we said,' said one.

'My mistress is unwell and cannot be disturbed.'

'What ails her?' The other man suddenly did not sound as brave as his knock.

'We are unsure, sir.' Her voice fell. 'She does perspire greatly, though. She took ill yesterday and it became necessary to secure these chambers when we arrived in town. It is why the nun prays at her bedside. Oh, woe to us if it is the Sweat.'

Both men covered their mouths. The shorter of the two spoke hurriedly: 'We seek five sisters who fled a convent in Trento.'

'Five *religious*?' Fat Val laughed the laugh of the court coquette. She tossed her head of curls. 'As you can see, we are only three. We are pilgrims on our way to be shrived from sinful lives. This Benedictine travels with us.'

'For what sin do you seek forgiveness?'

'Fornication.'

A small cry came from Little Fey.

'As you can see, our Holy companion is much disgraced

by us.'

At that moment, a third man clomped into the room. His cloak, which showed the bishop's insignia, was flung over his shoulder; his hands were busy adjusting his hose. Again, he was not one we had seen before. How many of these men were after us?

'The wench across the hall is not a sister. His voice rattled with catarrh. 'Checked her myself.' His chuckle turned into a gob of phlegm that he expelled onto the floor. He rubbed a dirty hand beneath his tunic. Cold air raced through my stomach.

'Sir, surely you did not molest her,' said Fat Val with as much breeze as she could muster.

'Surely I did, and more,' the man said with pride. He puffed his chest and altered his stance to improve upon his swagger.

Her voice remained steady. 'Then make haste to the apothecary, for though the girl travels with us she must sleep apart as she is contagious with the canker of lust.'

At this news the man wailed: 'She claimed herself clean.'

'She is, for she bathed a fortnight ago. But that is no cure for the pox, as you know.'

'The pox? I have been deceived!' he cried. He flailed his arms and gnashed his teeth. His agitation was so great that his alarmed companions hurried him away.

Fat Val closed the door after them. We heard their footsteps all the way to the street.

I slid from under the bed and flew to the window. The men were in the road, vainly consoling the wicked rogue who was still frantic, waving his arms and begging Our Lady to save him. I said a prayer: *May you die a horrible death.*

Mea sat up. Her face was ashen. We looked at one another not knowing what to say. She threw aside the sheepskin, and to Fat Val and me she mouthed: *Gretchen.*

To Little Fey, still on her knees, head bowed, I said aloud, 'Stay here, and do not cease praying.'

We crossed the hall to the room where Gretchen hid. She was on the bed, face crossed with tears, clutching the bedclothes. She was not in her tunic. She was not in anything.

We surrounded her with our arms and cooed succour as she sobbed. We knew what had happened.

'We told him you had the pox,' said Fat Val.

'He looked like one who might already have it,' said Mea, who drew Gretchen to her tightly. I had not seen such care in her before, or concern. 'You must clean your privy parts immediately. Come, I will help.'

But Gretchen did not move. She looked at me. 'I need to confess.'

'Dear Gretchen.' I sunk into her neck 'There is no need. The evildoer disgraced…'

'Hush. To be sure, he was not a fair creature, but my shame is that I encouraged him. I was willing.'

Reading my expression she said, 'Let me speak, but do not tell any of this to Fey. She will take on my sin as her own and I will never hear the end of it.'

Mea and Fat Val joined me on the edge of the pallet. Gretchen wiped her face with the edge of the bedclothes, and attempted a smile.

'I have been curious about the union between man and

woman. About how they are joined. In bed. How it might feel, and whether I could incline myself to the marriage bed and, if so, to give up my vows. I feel shame telling you this but it is the truth.'

I could not believe her words. She had never spoken of this before.

'How long has this been in your thoughts?' I asked. I was careful with my voice, so she wouldn't think that I thought ill of her. But I did. She had gone against our teaching, and our vows. How could I feel differently?

'Since Mother Elena told us of Abbess Heloise and Abbot Abelard.'

'Mother was imparting a lesson in compassion,' I reminded her, a slight scold in my tone. 'She wasn't encouraging adultery.'

She shook her head. 'I had no feeling for the man; it was pure curiosity.'

This did not make it better.

'But your vow of chastity. Your pledge to Holy virginity.' What I really wanted to say was, I love you; you're my sister, but what has become of your mind? Why this attraction to the profane?

'You think me careless, and of contrary nature to what you know of me, but do not be so surprised,' she said. 'What we hold in our hearts as women is not the same as what we held in them as children. Our bodies have grown and developed new appetites. What did Abbess Heloise assert? "It is not the deed itself but the intention of the doer that makes the sin."'

'That was Abbot Abelard,' said Fat Val. 'And he was excommunicated for it. And...' She made a cutting gesture with her fingers. We made the sign of the Holy Cross.

Gretchen took my hands. Her eyes pleaded. 'God is not harsh. He is loving and forgiving. I am still innocent.'

My mind returned to the day previous when I had stumbled on the street into the performance of the Magdalene's story. It had stirred to remembrance a conversation I had overheard at Saint Agatha's between two priests and Mother Clothilde, all three referring to Mary of Magdala not as the saint we knew her as, but as a sinner. Why this sudden reversal? If the Magdalene was not a saint but a sinner, did it hold that Gretchen was no sinner but a saint? We had been formed to be virtuous and righteous, but what separates the virtuous from the wicked when a saint is abruptly deemed a sinner? I watched Gretchen's face as she spoke. It felt as if I had never known her.

'Consider Saint Bartholomew, whose feast day, by the way, has newly passed,' she continued. 'He travelled far, and preached virtue and love until he was crucified and flayed alive for it. Those who slayed the Apostle thought they were being righteous. Bartholomew thought he was being righteous. Who then would you say was righteous? Or were they both?'

I was out of words, shocked by her admission.

'Religious life was not my choice. It was not yours, either, Lucia; nor yours, Valentina. We did not choose Holy virginity; it was chosen for us. We have been beholden to a vocation that tethered us against our will, our nature. My love for God has not altered. But the same cannot be said of my sentiments for the life chosen for me. And this interlude, this time between religious houses, is a chance for us to explore our womanhood.'

Poor Gretchen. She had been beaten so often at Saint Agatha's that I feared it had deranged her mind.

'Lucia, you say you are in thrall of Abbess Hildegard and her freedom, yet you would not permit me freedom, or rather you would judge my freedom differently.'

'The Abbess did not lie with a man to sate her curiosity,' I said.

'Ah, you don't know that for certain. But be that as it may, she embraces her curiosity, you have to agree. Why then is her curiosity accepted but not mine? Why is freedom extolled for one woman and not for another? I was not tempted by lust but by curiosity. Now it is sated. By the way, the act is not as bad as I heard tell, but neither is it as wondrous. In case you wanted to know.'

No, I did not want to know.

'Does this mean you will relinquish your vows?' asked Fat Val.

'It is something I must ponder.' Gretchen grabbed my arm again. 'Are we not, all of us, at this moment, of two minds? We fled terror, and are doomed to travel through an unknown wilderness to an unknown place. Be truthful, Lucia: Have you yourself not felt doubts about your vocation? Now that we are free we must not be afraid what we discover about ourselves. My actions have offended you; I see it on your face. I beg you not to judge harshly. Remember what Blessèd Benedict says: "Listen with the ear of your heart." Your head wants to respond like the skittish herd in the field when they hear the dog bark. But pray, think deeper.'

Of course I too had questioned my vocation, but not the way she had. My vocation had constructed a palisade about me within whose precincts I was safe, unbothered. I knew, however, during our flight that I was unwise, naïve even, wondering if, by shielding myself within this self-made palisade, I had made myself ignorant, refused knowledge that God sought to instil in me. Was I more sheep than shepherd?

She got up. 'Come. I must wash. We will talk more of this. But not around Fey.'

We helped her into her clothes, and walked across the short corridor to our rooms.

Mea and Fat Val opened the door and entered first, but then stopped abruptly.

I peered around them.

There was Little Fey, covered in blood.

X

The Feast of Saint Susanna of Rome

Botzen to the Via Imperii

She faced us, palms upturned, arms stretched like the Crucifixion. Blood on her hands, on the front of her habit, a small pool on the floorboards at her feet. I could not imagine the innkeeper being pleased with this.

I pushed past Mea and Fat Val; Gretchen's unapologetic fornication far from thought.

Little Fey cried as if she had been visited by a ghost.

'My hands began to bleed, and when I stood up to attend them there was a sudden release within me and blood appeared beneath my tunic. Oh woe! I am dying! I must prepare to meet God.'

She spoke in gulps, frantic and frightened.

The rest of us stood before her like a tribe of elders. I felt older than Sarah the Matriarch.

'*Cara*, you are not dying,' I said. 'It is nothing and it is everything. God has made you as fruitful as woman can be.'

'It is your monthly courses,' snapped Mea. She looked at the work before her, pushed up the sleeves of her tunic, and sighed. 'It comes to all of us. Do not think yourself special.'

I threw her a bewildered look: What happened to the tenderness she had shown to Gretchen moments ago? Her body jerked at my furrowed brow. Though strained with impatience, she added in a gentler voice, 'Were you not prepared for this day?'

'What day?' Little Fey was hysterical.

I smiled to allay her fears, but she took umbrage.

'You mock me, Lucia?'

'I am not mocking you, Little Fey. There is no need to be in a dither.'

'I can't help it. It was the way God made me. And stop calling me *Little* Fey as if I'm a fairy.'

Never had she spoken to me with such sharpness. And she had never before minded me calling her Little Fey. It was part of our love-language.

'Lucia does not mock you,' said Gretchen. With a bare arm around Little Fey's shoulder, she proceeded to expound in unnecessary detail about the arrival of womanhood. 'The monthly courses are God's flowers to women. Like trees that do not bring forth fruit without flowers, so are women unable to be fruitful in childbirth without the regular flowering of blood.'

'But I do not want…'

'There is no choice,' said Fat Val. 'You may never have a child but you will always have your courses. It is the sin cast on Eve for defying God in the Garden. The mark of our sex.'

A Flight of Saints

Mea planted her hands on her hips. 'A sin for which you will always be reminded. Now that you have your courses, men will find all manner of ways to hold you to account for the failures and catastrophes of the world; for lost crops, for twattle, for their supper being too hot or too cold. They will say there is no birdsong and blame a woman with her menses for that, and when they hear a profusion of birdsong, they will blame the woman for that, too. Anything and everything. You have been cloistered so long that you do not know of such things outside the convent, but mark this: When we women have our natural bleed, we are deemed unclean, rushed into hiding, forbidden to attend church. Yet, a man who shits in the morning can stride into chapel still pulling up his hose and no one says otherwise.'

Her loose hair shook like black snakes from Medusa's head. Fat Val and I risked a glance at one another: *What brought on this cloudburst?*

Only Gretchen was unperturbed. 'I do not always have my courses each month. I did worry I might be with child,' she said in her sing-song voice.

'You cannot be with child unless you have been with a man,' said Mea. Her eyes burned knowingly into Gretchen. 'Excuse us if we do not consider you the Virgin Mary.'

The reminder of Gretchen's spoiling sent a prayer into my breath: *Please God, do not let her be with child. What will we do then?*

Mea reached for her headscarf to use as a shawl around her shoulders. '*Allora*. I will seek the innkeeper and ask for extra linens.'

'You can't tell a man of my condition!' cried Little Fey. 'It will dishonour me.'

'I will most definitely speak of it to a man,' huffed Mea. 'He has a wife. He has daughters. If he has no knowledge of menses, he is either blind or ignorant, and our plain speech will absolve him of both.'

'I shall fetch water to wash her and her habit,' said Fat Val. 'And the floor.'

'Ask the innkeeper's wife if she has sphagnum,' I said. To Little Fey I said, 'Lie down. I will fetch lemon balm and make you a tea.'

Little Fey crawled onto a pallet, curled into a ball and began to rock.

'And I will distract you from your belly pain and tell the story of Saint Susanna,' said Gretchen.

She sat on the pallet beside Little Fey and stroked her back. 'Susanna was the beautiful daughter of a noble family in Rome. It was the time of the wicked Diocletian, who wanted her to marry his son, Galerius, but she refused. Then Maximian, who was the army commander and who ruled with Diocletian, wooed Susanna. But she did not want him, either. In a rage, Diocletian murdered her family, and when she was exposed by Maximian as a Christian, he chopped off her head.'

Gretchen was not always wise in the ways of providing solace to others.

'Susanna is safe now,' she went on as if this would give further succour to Little Fey. 'They have built a church for her in Santiago de Compostela and taken her relics there.'

A Flight of Saints

I left them and went to look for lemon balm.

By midday, the floor was clean, and Little Fey was bathed. The scent of sunshine and lemon surrounded us. The warm breezes and sunbeams that came through the windows dried her habit.

We instructed her, our youngest sister, how to use moss to staunch her flow. She was not pleased by this abrupt siege on her body. Curled on the bed, wrapped in a sheepskin, she continued to hold her belly against the spasms. I placed a hot cloth on her to ease them.

The church bell rang for Sext, and the rest of us, unthinkingly, fell to our knees and recited the Office. The litany came easily now, all words remembered, and we were comforted by its drone of familiarity.

In the afternoon, I stood at the window, and absently picked at splinters around the frame. My eyes were alert for bounty hunters on the road below.

Mea, of calmer temper now, pulled me away. 'Let us avoid windows.' She closed one of the shutters.

'All these men,' I said. 'They frighten me. We must leave on the morrow. I know our direction.'

I spoke truthfully. Earlier, when I had gone out for the lemon balm, I had met a young woman. Her little boy, in playful exuberance, had run full into me, nearly knocked me down, though he ended up falling down himself. I had knelt to make sure he had not hurt himself. His mother, distraught by his behaviour, apologised, but I made light of it. She chatted kindly and asked from whence I came. I only told her where I was going.

'To the shrine of Saint Giacomo in Santiago de Compostela.'

She begged me to pray for her once I was in the Apostle's presence. I said I would, privately vowing to find some other shrine on our journey to say prayers for her. When I asked if she knew the way to the Via Imperii, her directions were abundant.

'But it is a dangerous road, especially for our sex,' she had said. 'My husband has travelled it and even he has feared for his safety. The dangers do not come only from other travellers but from the ground itself, for I am told that the path in places is treacherous.'

Fearing she might obtain the wider counsel of passers-by to vouch for her concern, and thus bring unwanted notice to me, I told another lie: that I had the companionship and protection of brothers and uncles for the journey. Still, she advised me to be wary, and finally bid me God's speed.

As I relayed this to Mea, I used a splinter to etch the route on the dusty sill.

'Here in Botzen two rivers meet, the Adige and the Isarco. If we go west and follow the Adige, we will find a more travelled but longer pass into Germania. If we go east, and follow the Isarco, we will come to the Via Imperii, a shorter route over the Alpes, but one with more dangers. My heart for some reason prefers this shorter route. Others have travelled it and survived; why not us? When we leave here, we will enter a long valley that leads into a gorge. Beyond that is another town also with two rivers, the Isarco and the Rienz. The Bavarians call the town Brixen. It has a cathedral. It will take three days to reach. From there, to the Brenner Pass on

A Flight of Saints

the Via Imperii, another three days. On the other side of the Alpes is the town of the Inn Bridge. I do not know how long it is from the Pass to the Inn Bridge; perhaps another three days. By my reckoning we will be over the mountains by the next half-moon.'

I had been hesitant about revealing our plan to her. I knew she wouldn't betray us, but she had not made clear her motives. She said she was fleeing her family, Mother Clothilde, and a wronged and one-handed fiancé, but to what or to whom was she fleeing? I doubted it was to Bingen. She didn't seem the type who would be at home in a cloister. I felt my pockets to make sure the jewels were still there. And yet, I needed to bring her into my confidence because she alone among us knew how to shift in this strange world.

I looked across the room at Gretchen. Days ago, I fretted over whether she might turn heel and return to Saint Agatha's; now I had to keep her away from men and hope that she did not have a child in her belly.

I turned to the other problem that vexed me, the one Fat Val and I had heard that day; the one she was now relaying to the others.

'When Lucia and I were at the well to fetch water, we learned of another enemy. Ghibellines.'

'What are Ghibellines?' asked Gretchen.

More men, I said to myself.

'They are the savage followers of Emperor Barbarossa and of the puppet pope Callixtus, both of them sworn enemies of His Holiness Alexander,' said Fat Val. 'They roam the countryside and slay those who revere our true pope. It is said the emperor has made peace with Alexander but many say it is a false peace.'

'We are on the side of the Guelphs,' I said. 'If a town hoists the banner of crossed keys, we are among friends of Alexander; but a flag that ripples with a red cross means it is the territory of the Ghibelline and the pretender Callixtus.'

'I cannot believe you are only now aware of this,' said the world-weary Mea. 'You in your safe little cloister do not know the half of it: Bishops at war with podestas; fathers at war with sons; bakers at war with farmers; mothers against daughters; house against house. Even convents are at war with other convents. Spies everywhere. I would wager your beloved Mother Elena fell afoul somewhere in this mess.'

Our journey was hard, but it also revealed the beauty of the world. Was there no sanctuary left in it? I did not seek fight or argument; I only wanted to cross the Alps and return to a life of prayer in Bingen. But with so many dangers and enemies, our chances of success grew dimmer by the day.

We had agreed we would leave early the next morning, but when I awoke everyone was still asleep except Mea, who was slumped over a bowl, sick. The rest of us drank weak ale, but she preferred wine, and had procured a fair quantity from the innkeeper the night before.

She turned her head, and without meeting my eye said she was unable to continue on.

Finally, a chance to upbraid her. There was no shortage

of arrows in that quiver: She was selfish for holding us up with her puking; her delay might cause another run-in with the bounty hunters; she was given to sloth and finery, traits unbecoming to one who had taken monastic vows; and by association she callously impugned our virtue; she should know better being the eldest among us; she was a disgrace to her noble birth; she was a murderess. Truly, there were many words I wished to hurl at her.

Instead, I kept my tongue. I rubbed her back while she retched, and brought her damp cloths to clean her mouth. My kindness must have prompted a change of heart for she promised to gather her wits and wherewithal, and be ready to leave with the others.

Whatever prayers she summoned to liberate her from her violent suffering were effective; by the time the rest of us were dressed and our bundles girded about our waists, she was ready. I said nothing more of it.

There were many things I learned during our time in Botzen. I learned the way to the Via Imperii. I learned about the profane thoughts that roamed in Gretchen's head. I learned about Mea's fondness for drink. I learned about Ghibellines and Guelphs, and that the world was full of war. I learned, too, the faces of those who were sent to capture us. It was new wisdom; not the wisdom of the scholarly, but of the frightened, anxious pupil.

I also learned that rest is a trickster. Food, comfort, unguents, and idleness had healed our feet and bodies, but had also made us soft and unfit for the demands of the labour ahead.

We left Botzen under conditions so contrary to those that

had greeted us that I wondered if it had been a dream. Gone were the stalls teeming with colourful spices, cloth of gold, skeins of wool. Gone were the beautiful men, the bejewelled women, the carts and chickens, the noisy throng. Now, no one was about. Not a goose, not a pig. Not the lecherous sentry. Not even the sun. Instead, there was rain.

It began gently, droplets bouncing on the earth and vanishing in the heat, but it grew more plentiful until it assailed us from every angle, like stones hurled in punishment. It drove into our faces and legs; it ran into our shoes. Rivulets streamed through our clean hair and down our newly washed faces and bodies. Through the mist and trees, I spied a scribble of smoke curl from a chimney and I longed for its dry warmth.

Beyond the gates of Botzen, the land rose steadily and put labour in my breath. We climbed higher. My limbs ached anew. Though we walked in the woods to avoid the worst of the rain, the damage was done: I yearned for hot water and dry hair.

I tried for brighter, happier thoughts; imagined our sunny arrival in Bingen and being welcomed by Abbess Hildegard who ordered a feast in our honour. My belly fluttered each time I thought of it. I also thought of Mea's green shoes and what it would be like to walk in them. Then my mind returned to our real situation, that I was walking with a murderess and being hunted by wicked men.

I shook my head to change my thinking. I thought of how I might talk my way out of an encounter with a Ghibelline, but this was a short-lived daydream because my mind jumped to the possibility that Gretchen would flatter and flirt with the enemy. And what would the outcome be from that? *Men. I must keep her away from them.* I tried not to think of Mother Clothilde, but she was always there, buzzing like an angry fly against the wall of my head.

So much was I in my head that it wasn't until we stopped to eat that I was aware that my shoes had dried hard and muddy, and had rubbed against my skin causing my feet to bleed. I looked at my sisters' feet: They had carried their shoes.

We had at least left Botzen well supplied. The innkeeper's wife, who had tended to Little Fey's courses, saw the marks on her hand, and having been duped by them had laden us with provisions of cheese, bread, salted fish, honey, almonds, plums, and greens. She also gave us a small pot in which to make tea. These were welcome gifts but they made our bundles heavier, and added to the strain of walking.

At midday, the sun and the heat had returned, and we found a clearing where we could sup and sleep. Fat Val had become proficient with the flint and set about making a fire. Mea had collected rainwater in the pot so we could have nettle tea. Little Fey and Gretchen went off to collect sphagnum.

'So much?' I said when they returned. It was enough to build a small island.

'For my courses,' sniffed Little Fey. As if the affliction, like her stigmata, was hers alone. She was becoming as obstreperous as Gretchen and as haughty as Mea.

'You do not need so much. Your bleeding will end in a day or two. When and where your next courses arrive, there will be moss aplenty. The world shall not run out of it.'

'Then I shall collect for you and the others.'

'Please do not. We manage according to our needs. My courses started this morning, as they have for Mea and Valentina, and see, we are not clearing the land of sphagnum. It is how it is with women: We tend to our private care, as Hildegard herself instructs.'

Gretchen had also collected spines of aloe and snails. 'Your shoulders are red from the sun, Lucia, and the slime will soothe the burn.'

We drank our tea and ate our food. Darkness descended like a soundless bell, and as if led by inner instruction I lay down in a pool of ferns, knees to my chest, and pretended it was a pallet of linen and skins.

The next day, with the sun at its zenith, we crossed an arid valley to the shady cover of a forest.

We found a small church. It had been some time since human worshippers had knelt in it. A congregation of pigeons now assumed a regular presence.

Four slender pillars held up the roof of the nave, their capitals spreading fan-like across the vault. Behind the altar stone was a window of coloured glass shards arranged in the shape of a lamb. It could have been a lovely place had it been given attention and swept clean of bird shit. A momentary urge came over me to take up its care and restore the place, perhaps occupying it as an anchoress, but I was absolved of the impulse when my eyes landed on an image of Christ that had been painted on one of the walls.

A Flight of Saints

It was vulgar. Christ with a tonsure? Sans beard or brow? What fool had drawn this?

A small mound of ash from another's fire lay at my feet. I dipped my finger in it and proceeded to improve on the invisible brows, the mournful countenance. I drew the corners of the lips slightly upward—I have never held that Jesus was constantly dour—and then applied strokes of ash around His jaw to give him a soft beard.

I stepped back to admire my work. At Saint Agatha's, I had worked within an aura of prayer in the scriptorium, and now I suddenly missed it, the ink, the variety of quills, the colourful drawings made by the senior sisters who taught me their skill. I missed my stained fingers that singled me out as one in their guild.

'Not bad,' said Gretchen, who joined me and appraised my work. 'Especially the beard; it gives a comely shape to the face.'

'I did good work at Saint Agatha's,' I said loftily. 'I am grateful to God for allowing me to use my skill again.'

She snorted. 'Don't be so sure. One of the sisters complained about your work. She said it was like watching a babe draw.'

I rolled my eyes. There was no end to Gretchen's envy.

Fat Val and Little Fey stood behind us.

'His hair could use some ash to rid him of that tonsure,' said Little Fey, tilting her head this way and that to assess the improvements.

When it was done and all had approved, I dipped my finger in the ash once more and, at the bottom corner of the painting, wrote 'Sister Lucia, AD 1179.'

Mea had remained outside all this time; her guts having required more heaving.

'I think that is the end of it,' she said, cleaning herself off, the others having disappeared into the bushes to relieve themselves.

'Then let it be the end, too, of your fondness for drink.'

XI

The Feast of Saint Mechtildis
Toward Brixen

We awoke surrounded by a wall of thick fog. It was clear amid the trees where we slept, but beyond the woods, the world had vanished into impenetrable cloud. There was no choice but to walk into it.

One by one we filed toward it, and I watched each sister fade into the whiteness. All that I could hear of them was the scuff of their footsteps on the rocky ground, or a cough or yawn. But when the cloud cleared, it hardly mattered: Where were we? It could be Francia or Jerusalem for all I knew.

I had not been diligent with my prayers of late, and so I first asked God to forgive my lapse, justifying it by saying I hadn't wanted to bother Him, for surely His labours were greater than ours. But once my prayer began: *Merciful Father, who guides our footsteps and keeps watch...* I stopped and began to wonder at all these words: Why must prayers begin with long, extravagant preambles? Is this a rule? Did

He decree it? I had never come across it in Scripture, and if it wasn't there, if the Apostles and Prophets had not made mention of it, then why the mumble-jumble? Why make a flowery poem out of a humble, necessary plea? If I faced danger, by the time I loaded my cry with twenty words of extravagant praise, the need for help or solace or even my very breath would have passed. If I were to call out, 'Heavenly Father, send Michael the Archangel!' would God still hear me? Or are His ears attuned only to loquacious petitions in perfect Latin? I began my prayer again—privately, for I did not want argument from my sisters—with a simpler summons: *God, please lead us to Bingen.*

I turned to Gretchen who was wiping damp from her face. 'What feast day is it?'

'Well, it is five days since Saint Bartholomew so it would be the Feast of Saint Augustine, or maybe it is the Feast of the Beheading of John the Baptist. I am no longer certain.'

'So much violence surrounds these saints. I have lost my appetite for it.'

'Oh, do not turn from them,' she said. 'Saints and martyrs are our guides. Besides, we are honouring female saints, remember? And today I shall tell of Saint Mechtildis. She is from these parts, and she did not die at the hands of men.'

We gathered close. Gretchen's vitas were brief but they were a reprieve from the punishment of walking on stone-riddled ground. In addition, the lives she spoke of were almost always of greater endurance than ours.

'The parents of Mechtildis were wealthy and devout. They built a monastery on their land, and in it they placed their daughter Mechtildis. She was only five winters old, but full of mystic wisdom. Like you, Sister Fey. Mechtildis performed many miracles. When she was older, the bishop made her the abbess of Edelstetten Abbey. She died seven winters later. They say she is buried in a glass shrine for all to see.'

'What were her miracles?' asked Little Fey.

'I do not know,' said Gretchen.

'Why did she die?' asked Fat Val.

'I do not know.'

'Was the monastery her parents built a double house or for women only?' asked Mea.

'*Nescio!*' Gretchen became furious. 'Why do you pester me with questions? Is it not enough that I tell their names and stories? If you desire more of their lives, seek it yourself.'

'We are grateful for your vitas, Gretchen.' I tried to becalm her. 'They give us much to think of on our long journey.'

I was no longer concerned that she would run from us, but then, what did I know of her mind? She might find a man and run off with him.

We walked through yet another meadow between yet another wall of undulating hills. The land never seemed to change.

A breeze rippled the grass. I looked up and there was a cloud, wispy as a dream, in the shape of a dove. It drifted to earth before suddenly changing shape and direction, so that the dove was soaring Heavenward. I wondered what it meant, but I did not share it with my sisters.

'I need to rest,' said Little Fey. Her face was wet.

Mea shielded her eyes as she placed the sun. 'It is midday. We will stop and eat. The grass is high enough that no one will see us. Find a place. I must go into the woods.'

She waded through the grass toward a stand of trees on a hill. I patted my pockets to make sure I still had the jewels. Would my mistrust of her ever change?

I found a slight rise, to better see the approach of the bounty hunters, my senses keened to their possible presence, but Fat Val was already flattening the grass on a lower area.

'It is not good to sit so high, Lucia.'

I scooted down to where she and the others had started to unpack our food when a voice called out, *'Bonjour!'*

We instantly slumped into the grass.

'I see you,' a teasing voice called out.

I peeked above the grass. A man—young, slim, shabby clothes—had doffed his hat.

Courage and violence rushed into my veins. 'Stay away,' I shouted. 'I have the Sweat.'

'And I have a stiletto,' Fat Val called.

The man moved closer as if he hadn't heard.

'Please,' he begged. His hands twisted his hat. 'I promise no harm. I only seek direction to find my way home.'

He came closer until he was standing directly in front of us. The stiletto in Fat Val's hand and my claim of having the Sweat were of no obvious deterrent. An aroma of amber and vanilla emanated from him; strange from one who walked all day.

I stared hard at him. 'Did you not hear me? I said I have the Sweat.'

'You do not look ill,' he said solicitously. 'And you are out on this fine day so it cannot be the Sweat. Perhaps a cold or ague? I have leaves of sweet marjerome. Here, let me give you some to make a tea.' He knelt on the ground and reached into his satchel. 'Where are you going?'

Thrown by his presence and nonchalance, we answered all at once without concord.

'Santiago,' I said.

'Bingen,' said Gretchen, who clamped her mouth immediately.

'Rome,' squeaked Little Fey.

'Nowhere,' said Fat Val.

He laughed. 'You are going the wrong way for Rome. But no matter. It is fair that you wish not to parley with a stranger. My name is Guillaume.' He placed a hand on his heart, and bowed to us. 'I only wish to know if this is the correct way to Provence.'

I had heard of the place but did not know where it was. He handed me a pouch of marjerome.

At that moment, I glanced up the hill where Mea, having spied the intruder, had launched herself toward Guillaume. He was in for it now.

'How dare you approach us. We have a stiletto and are not afraid to use it.'

Guillaume got up quickly and bowed again, terrified.

'Spare me, good lady. One of your companions has already brandished the stiletto and I do not doubt you would use it. But truly I mean no harm. I am unsure of my direction, and seek only to know the way home.'

But Mea did not hear him. She heard something else. Hooves.

'Down!' she ordered, and grabbed Guillaume by the hair, pushing him to the ground. A man! She touched and wrestled a man to the ground! And so easily performed! But praise God she had for the hooves grew louder, nearer. Voices, too.

'The three from the taverna,' whispered Fat Val.

'Do nothing,' I said crossly, and held her arm to keep her down.

Guillaume's face winced from Mea's tight grip of his hair.

The riders came nearer, nearer. Fear was ready to gush from me in a cry. But their sounds began to abate until we heard them no more.

Fat Val peeked above the grass. 'They are gone, but let us stay down a while longer to be certain.'

Mea released Guillaume's hair; he rubbed his head.

'You are fleeing them?' he asked.

'We do not wish any encounter,' I said.

A few moments later, still wary of being seen by those who sought us, we stretched out on our bellies, shielded by tall grass, and opened the remains of the food from the innkeeper's wife. We had eaten the salted fish the night before, but we still had almonds, honey, a few plums, and a heel of bread.

Mea glowered at Guillaume. She looked ready to rebuke him.

I said quickly, 'This is Guillaume.'

To him I said: 'You may help yourself to what little we have.'

Mea turned her glower on me. I looked away. I had been taught to offer hospitality to others; she had been taught only to accept it. True, the youth was a stranger, but I did not sense danger from him.

He frowned. 'I only have this, but you are welcome to it.'

He spread open his bundle: a large chunk of creamy cheese, a loaf of seed bread, and a fat cluster of purple grapes. A feast.

I am ashamed to say we set upon it like rats.

Resigned to his company (though Mea remained perturbed by it) we shared food and conversation.

'You said your home is in Provence?' I asked. 'Is that north?'

He tore off a piece of bread. 'South. A small town in the south. Grasse. On the great sea. I was on my way to Jerusalem when I was suddenly overcome with a change of heart and was desperate to return home.'

'Why Jerusalem?' Normally quiet, Little Fey had become chatty of late.

He held his hand over his mouth as he chewed. 'My father wanted me to join his business but I wanted to see the world. I do not care for the world now.'

'It would be a long way to Jerusalem,' she said.

His head bobbed. 'I got as far as Heraclea, in Byzantium, and there my journey ended.'

His eyes had filled, and tears looked ready to breach the rims.

'For two years I yearned for Jerusalem and for God. For two years I tried to leave home, but each time some disaster prevented me. This last time, I left my sister with her three young children. Her husband was a Breton who died in the revolt at Brittany. Now I ask myself whether my journey belonged there.'

'How can it be a journey if you stay in the same place?' I asked.

'Ah, but one can stand still and still be on a journey, *n'est-ce pas?*'

I thought back to Saint Agatha's, to the time I was held there terrified, and my mind had travelled to places of greater safety though my body could not.

He tore another piece of bread. 'I yearned for new people, new purpose, to live my ambition. Perhaps God's purpose for me is to care for my sister's family, and His ambition for me is to join my father's business.'

Drops slid over his downy cheeks. Gretchen shifted closer to him.

'What business is your father's?' asked Mea, easing into his company. She spread the hem of her tunic and smoothed its creases.

'Perfume.'

That explained his aroma. To him, we must smell like a lavatorium.

'We trade with the Persian merchants in ambergris and musk. Sometimes a knight returning from the East will sell us what he has brought back. Knights are canny traders. They fight not so much for God as for commerce.'

'I suppose they must make a living when they are not warring,' said Gretchen. Her head was tipped shyly to one side and she fluttered her eyes.

'Aye, they must, though I have seen many who possess the arrogance of a priest. One cannot be both priest and pirate.'

A Flight of Saints

We were silent awhile until Little Fey blurted: 'We are sisters.'

I gave her a steely look. *What are you doing?* She pretended not to understand it.

Guillaume's brow furrowed. 'I do not see much resemblance among you. Did you have different fathers?'

I laughed to deflect the truth; nudged Little Fey to play along.

Gretchen shifted closer to Guillaume.

When will her carnal desires end?

'Tell us more about the perfume trade,' I said. To Gretchen I said, 'Would you please pass me my bundle?' When she crawled across to get it, I moved into her place beside Guillaume.

'Ah, well, the Persians are the masters. Their recipes are ancient and they are not keen to share them. Who can blame them? But my father is an honest man and does not seek to steal from them. He has invited some of them to join our business and teach us their ways in return for a share in our profits. The Persians are ingenious in their methods and their ingredients. Rose, almonds, olives, frankincense, cedar; the list is endless. In Gallia and Germania, some are trying to make perfume, too. An abbess near Worms experiments with such potions.'

'Is it Abbess Hildegard of Bingen?' asked Gretchen. As she leaned across to speak to Guillaume, she stuck out her tongue at me.

'Why, yes, that is the one.'

Little Fey blurted again: 'We are all…'

I grabbed her hand and spoke over her, '... very interested in perfume.'

He turned to Mea.

'Forgive my impertinence, but I must say that you have a most elegant scent.'

I could tell by the lift of her eyes that he had stoked her vanity.

'Your scent reminds me of my sister. Rose, cinnamon, and labdanum?'

Mea brightened. 'It is exactly that.'

He tapped the side of his nose. 'God has given me a rare gift. Permit me to recommend an infusion of myrrh with rose, sweet rush, and black pepper. I believe it would suit you.'

'Pepper?' she said.

'I know!' he agreed. 'It seems wrong, doesn't it? But trust me, pepper lifts the aroma of the rose.'

With this he gathered the remnants of his repast and stood up.

'I must away, fair ladies, and continue my long way home.' He bowed. 'Fare thee well.'

I pointed in the direction from which we had come. 'Botzen will be the next town.'

'And Brixen is the next one ahead,' he said. 'There is a shorter route through a forest further on, but it unnerved me, so I avoided it.' He looked ready to say more but reconsidered.

As we waved him down the track, I thought of his words about wanting to go home. How fortunate he was to have a home. I hoped mine would be in Bingen. Botzen, Brixen,

A Flight of Saints

Bingen. *All these towns that begin with B. Another sign?*

We returned to the goat path. A long row of beech trees gave us dappled shelter from the sun. My leg brushed against a clump of lavender and tossed up a cloud of scent, and I thought how much it would have delighted Guillaume. Majestic mountains surrounded us, and I saw two springs, like silky filaments, unspool from a great, green height. Beauty was everywhere I turned.

At the bend in the path, we came to a large boulder with markings on it.

'It is a map carved by some ancient hand is my guess,' said Mea.

We made out figures—men with large sticks, and fearsome animals with bared teeth—and fields, rivers, dwellings, farms, and forests. But it held nothing to assist us on our way.

'In olden times,' I said, for I knew about art, 'people were not learned in the ways of drawing like we are today. See, the animals and man are rendered in a childish way.'

'Made by a man's hand,' said Gretchen. Her arms were crossed in sullenness and quiet fury. She was still angry at me for separating her from Guillaume. 'A woman would have drawn women and flowers, and marked wells for water, and would have shown the south direction for the growth of plants. There is no use to this map.'

'Maybe it was useful to the one who drew it,' said Little Fey.

Gretchen harrumphed. 'Must you always speak kindly? What is wrong with you?'

'I have no reason to be otherwise.' She smiled back. 'I was

raised alongside you so my character has been shaped by you. If anyone is to blame for my kindness, it is you.'

We chuckled at her wit.

Gretchen stomped off aggrieved.

'Perhaps she is about to get her courses,' giggled Little Fey.

XII

The Feast of Saint Minervus and Saint Eleazar

Into the Woods, near Brixen

We arrived where the path forked at the edge of a dark, dense wood, just as Guillaume said it would. I was unsure whether we should enter the woods or take a more-travelled road that led to Brixen. I could see the settlement ahead braced against thick forests of pine. I remembered hearing someone at Saint Agatha's tell of a fire that almost destroyed Brixen. The evidence was before me: the scarred, scorched land and ghostly swathes of blackened buildings; but there were signs of rebirth in the fresh frames of buildings being erected, and the sounds of hammer and anvil announcing restoration. Stacks of golden hewed timbers were waiting to be planted to remake the palisade.

I did not want to go into Brixen. I had no patience for another place of busyness and suspicious folk. The bounty hunters were likely there. My sisters did not voice opposition when I suggested we steer clear of the place, except Gretchen who complained of pains in her belly and wanted the comfort of a pallet.

On the other hand, the forest ahead of us looked scary.

We normally liked forests because they were dark and dense, easy places to hide among the weft of branches, but this one made my flesh tingle.

I could tell my sisters felt the same, for they loitered and paced back and forth and looked for the slightest occupation that would stall them from entering it: Fat Val took off her shoe and plucked a pine needle from it; Mea untied and re-tied her bundle; Little Fey decided that now was a good time to pray; Gretchen stared at the ground and spoke sparingly about her chosen saint for the day.

'I do not have much to say about Saint Minervus and Saint Eleazar so do not annoy me with your questions. All I know is this: They were husband and wife and they had eight children. And all of them were murdered long ago in Lyons, in Gallia, because they were Christian.'

'At least we can pray for them,' said Little Fey.

Her prayers could be as thick as treacle, but at that moment they were the right consistency to dull and divert our minds.

We huddled together, bowed heads, and… well, I could not keep my thoughts on poor Minervus and Eleazar and their babes. Instead, I looked at the blazing sky. I was parched and tired; the sun burned my skin. The forest suddenly looked favourable.

Fat Val eventually made up our minds. She parted the tangle of low branches, mused, 'The ground is trod upon. It must be where the path continues.'

'Come,' said Mea with her tone of impatience. 'The forest cannot go on forever. We always come out the other side sooner than we expect.'

'Yes, all will be well,' said Fat Val with a complete lack of conviction.

As soon as we entered, the sense of foreboding mounted. I tried to talk myself out of my fear: *These woods are no different from the countless others we have walked through—same dried pine needles strewn on the ground, same leafy canopy. And look, open meadow not far ahead.*

'Food!' cried Gretchen.

A small clearing held a cultivated patch of abundance. Aubergine, zucchini, dandelion, onions. Gretchen hastily filled her bundle.

I watched her, and then the eeriness, the unnaturalness of the forest suddenly fell upon me: There was no birdsong, no scurrying creatures, no flutter of leaves. I listened for the sound of a bee or fly. Nothing. But the air wasn't entirely without sound. *Was that singing? Humming?* I said nothing to the others in case it was a trick of my own hearing, but it continued, sweet and ethereal, drifting in and out of my ears.

'Let us hurry,' I said, anxiety growing.

I walked on, and then I saw her, a woman, bathed in light at the edge of the glade, waving. We moved to her like a murmuration. Unblinking.

I awoke on hard earth. Smoke clogged my throat and stung my eyes.

My head felt cold like stone until I realised it was lying on one. I sought my sisters but could only make out their groans and shapes. There was a stench that I couldn't place.

I began to cough.

The woman who had beckoned us in the glade stood before a kettle of billowing steam that added to the fog and fug.

'Oh, I hope you are alright, my dear. Sometimes the heat and the smoke are enough to drive me out of my own place. It happens on occasion when I cook. But I'm so very glad you are here. You all look so worn.'

A cheery, heart-shaped face came into view. She had round, wistful but eager-to-please eyes that also held some private anguish. Her pale, dishevelled hair, white as parchment, was gathered into two unequal halves, each tied with a strand of wool. In stark relief against the hair, her brows were thick and dark. Her thin lips were quivering things that offered a tentative smile. She was dressed in layers of colourful shawls tied at her waist, around her middle, and around her shoulders, while her neck and wrists were wrapped with ropes of metal links, and agates and other gemstones, berries, and beads.

'Would you care for some walnut bread?'

She held out a plank on which were several chunks. I was starved for bread.

'*Grazie.*' I stuffed my mouth.

Only when my mouth was empty did I ask, 'How did we get here?'

'Oh my, well, you looked distressed and weary, and you all seemed to just walk toward me. I asked if you'd like to come into my home for a drink, and once inside—it was most worrying—you all just fell to the floor. I didn't quite know what to do but felt it best to let you rest. You poor things. Are you lost?'

I took another chunk of bread and wolfed it. My senses adjusted to the dim interior and its stench: I hoped it wasn't from me.

'Ah, your friends have roused.'

She shuffled over to each and offered her bread. I sat up and took in the place. It was hewn from the earth; roots and fibrous tendrils hung from the ceiling and came out of the walls so that I wondered whether we were under a tree. A long dark shape was at the back of the hovel but it was too hazy to make out. A door, open, and a small shutter-less window beside it were the sole sources of light. Behind me, a black iron kettle hung in the grate where a small fire blazed. Something was on the boil. A long table next to the grate held a dusty collection of vials, pouches, gnarled roots, and birds' nests.

'Who are you?' I asked.

'Oh, forgive me! My name is Mathilde. Would you like tea?'

'Yes,' we chimed.

My sisters and I crawled toward one another and we sat in a group. None of us were quite sure what to make of it.

'Look at you. All so adorable.'

Politely, I made introductions. 'I am Lucia, and this is Gretchen, Valentina, Mea, and Fey.'

She smiled, and handed us bowls of tea ladled from a smaller kettle. Good tea. Mint.

She sat and sipped with us. Then, in an eager, conspiratorial whisper: 'Are you the five who fled Saint Agatha's?'

Mid-sip, I sputtered into my bowl. I was afraid to meet my sisters' eyes.

'What makes you think that?' said Mea. 'We are pilgrims on the road to Santiago de Compostela.'

'Ah, you prefer not to say. And yet I can tell you are not who you pretend to be. This one here, as pale as the Holy Ghost, is a sister. The rest of you—except you'— she nodded to Mea—'have remade your habits. No one wears tow except the poor and the religious. You will need to do better with your disguise. Perhaps I can help.'

I didn't know what to say. I felt uneasy but I tried to show I was not. 'I like your clothing. The colours.'

'Not as fine as what your *duchessa* here once wore, though I see you have salvaged a garment from your earlier life.'

We all lowered our bowls and looked at Mea. How did this creature know of her?

'Are you a hedgewitch?' ventured Gretchen.

I gasped at her brazenness.

'Yes, I am that,' said Mathilde without a trace of shame.

I gripped my bowl. I had heard of these women who beguile and bewitch, heal and harm; who straddle this world and the next, armed with their potions and charms of good and malefic intent.

'It is why I live among the trees and rocks and grass. Folk are wary of my kind.' She looked at the ground, and fussed with one of her shawls. 'But I mean well, and I do no harm.'

I angled myself toward the door, and gauged our chances of escape. But I steadied myself, too, not wanting to make too hasty a judgement. I had never met a hedgewitch.

'You live in the woods, alone?'

'I do. Or rather now I do.' Sadness fell across her face. Then, she brightened. 'But you are here now, and I praise God for your company. Please, stay and rest your bones. I will cook supper.'

I was ready to offer our regrets—*What was that awful smell?*—when the hedgewitch clapped her hands and added: 'By the stars that light Heaven, I was gifted a hide of lamb by a charitable soul the other day. That is what I shall cook!'

I immediately withdrew my protest. *Meat.* Roast lamb had not passed our lips since Mother Clothilde took charge of Saint Agatha's.

We offered our assistance and she sent us outside for onions, carrots, zucchini, and herbs from her garden. It was like being back at the convent.

'What putrid smell pollutes her home?' said Fat Val once we were outside.

'Should we ask?' said Little Fey.

'Well, that would be rude,' said Mea.

'I am so hungry for meat I will simply ignore it,' I said.

'Imagine,' said Gretchen. 'Lamb!'

We returned to the hovel, and no sooner did we enter than the skies opened and it began to pour. Smell or not, we were stuck here now. I edged closer to the fire in the hope that the roasting meat would fragrance the air.

At supper, we gave thanks to Mathilde and to God for our feast. As nubs of old candles and the fire in the grate cast an amber light on everything, we ate heartily and drank her ale.

Conversation was lively and cheerful: We asked Mathilde many questions and she asked many about our time at Saint Agatha's. She had a habit of tilting her head when we answered her. I liked the mannerism; it gave a sense of deep listening, and I decided I would adopt the affectation for myself.

She was breathless when we told of our escape.

'How brave you are, Lucia. You not only saved yourself but you saved your sisters.'

'Brave or foolhardy, I can no longer tell the difference.' I felt myself redden from the attention; more at ease with praise over gaze.

She looked at me, head tilted a bit more. 'You would do well to think more highly of yourself. There is much good in that busy brain of yours. Don't fall into the pit of doubt. Uncertainty is the great unraveller of dreams and desires.'

'I'm afraid we live with all manner of doubt and uncertainty. Our vile Mother has sent bounty hunters to find us,' said Little Fey.

'And we can't understand why,' I added. 'If she hates us, why would she want us back? We posed no threat to her.'

'Control,' said the hedgewitch. 'Hate alone is flaccid, thrusts in its moment of passion, and shudders when sated, like lovers.' My face flushed again, this time at the unseemly analogy. 'But control, ah, that is a deeper hate. It shapeshifts, and imparts steady ruin on its victims; pain so grave that it scores its victims with everlasting damage. Shall I cast a spell on Mother Clothilde? Turn her into a stoat?'

We laughed and clapped approval. It seemed as good a punishment as anything.

But that smell.

We asked about how she had come to live in this place.

'I am one who, for whatever reason God has bestowed, is guided by instinct rather than intelligence. My brothers and sisters all found good work and marriages, lives of relative ease. I am happy for them. But that has not been my way. I did find work at the start. A merchant family in our town asked if I would help care for their children. When the family moved for reasons of business, I moved with them, first to Montpellier and then Genoa. After a few years I set out on my own. My wanderings led me to this forest. Like you, I was near collapse. A hedgewitch took me in, and I never left. She taught me her art.'

The smell seemed to worsen.

Midway through our meal Gretchen put down her fork.

'Dear Mathilde, you have been so kind to us. We are grateful for your hospitality and cheer. I beg you not to take offence when I tell you that there is a most dreadful odour in your home. Because you live among the wild creatures, perhaps one has strayed in here to die and its body lies somewhere in a state of putrefaction.'

'Forgive me!' Mathilde broke apart. She who had been gentle and sweet was convulsed with desperate tears. I put an arm around her shoulder.

'I didn't know what to do,' she blabbered. 'I, I…'

'Didn't know what to do about what?' Fat Val sat on the other side of our host and took up her hand in comfort.

'She died.' Mathilde's shoulders heaved as she wailed. 'Alas, she died!'

'Who died?' I asked gently.

'Ursula,' said Mathilde.

We looked at one another. *Ursula?*

'The hedgewitch who took me in. My teacher. My friend. That's her. Over there.'

Our heads turned slowly from Mathilde and looked toward the back of the hovel—the long shape wrapped in hemp was Ursula—and slowly turned back to Mathilde.

Roast lamb glistened on my plate but I suddenly had no appetite.

'Mathilde,' Little Fey said as if addressing a child. 'How long ago did she die?'

'On the Feast of the Nine Hundred Martyrs,' she said through sobs.

'That's in the month of Martius,' said Gretchen. Much time had passed since.

Mathilde got up and wandered into her kitchen, whimpering and blowing her nose.

We had all stopped eating. Even the rain had stopped as if the shock of Mathilde's confession had been too much for Heaven. My sisters looked at me.

'We find ourselves in somewhat delicate and unusual circumstances.' Their eyes widened. 'It would be cruel to leave her like this. Not after she's fed us. I say'— I took a steadying breath—'that we offer to bury her friend. It is the right thing to do. Indeed, it is our duty.'

They were about to launch into me but Mathilde returned to table.

'I am full of shame and grief...'

'Mathilde,' I said. 'God has brought us to you for reasons we cannot fathom. As we are here, let us help you give Ursula her dignity, and return her to the earth.'

'Would you?' she gasped. Her appreciation nearly broke my heart. She did not wear distress and loneliness lightly.

'And since Sister Mea is professed, she will say prayers at the burial. For this is what we do, is it not, Sister Mea?'

Mea did not argue. She nodded and smiled pleasantly, but beneath the table her fingers found my thigh and dug their nails into it.

I stifled my pain. 'Now that the rain has stopped and loosened the ground, why not go now and seek a place of burial while there is still light.'

She hurried away, and left us with the long-departed Ursula.

'Let's make a run for it! I'm not touching that body,' said Gretchen.

'Yes, you are,' I said.

'No, I'm not, and you can't make me.'

'If I'm doing it, so are you.' Mea gave Gretchen the evil eye.

'This is madness,' said Gretchen. 'It would be kinder to burn that thing.'

'That "thing" once breathed and lived,' said Little Fey. 'That "thing" is a child of God. Where is your compassion, Gretchen?'

'Why do you quarrel?' I said with weariness. This tribe was always looking for argument. 'We'll do what we must and then leave.'

'But there is no need to do this at all,' said Gretchen.

'And yet, we're doing it, as penance for our sins.' I looked pointedly at Gretchen and lowered my voice. 'And you, of all of us, have much to atone for. Or have you forgotten?'

Mathilde returned. She had found a place worthy of her friend, and took us to see it.

We welcomed the chance to breathe clean air again. The site was in a small clearing surrounded by pine trees; a place where many dead things had gathered and been returned to the earth. We dug with what implements we could find but mainly used our hands. The ground, being humus, made light our labour.

It was full dark by the time we returned to the hovel; no way to do the burial that night. We had to suffer the stench of Ursula until morning. But at first light, we readied ourselves for the dreadful task ahead.

I told Little Fey to keep Mathilde distracted. 'Take her for a walk for this will be no sight for her.'

When they left, we found a shawl and rolled Ursula's body onto it. The intention was to drag it to the grave. But when we rolled the carcass, what covered it fell away. Sight and smell drove us back. A miasma of liquid had pooled and dried around the body. Maggots, having feasted upon the flesh, scurried from our disturbance. Gretchen threw a cloth on the corpse's face.

Even now, bile rushes into my throat when I think of the

grisly work. When we shifted the body, the skin of one of Ursula's arms slid off as cleanly as meat from a boiled chicken. I used a stick to prod it back with the rest of the body.

'Like I said,' Gretchen tutted, 'kinder to burn her.'

'Shift it, Gretchen,' snapped Fat Val.

As we dragged the body out of the hovel and toward the grave, a leg and then the other arm slipped off. By the time we reached the clearing, Ursula was more slop than body.

Seeing us approach and gauging the horror on our faces, Little Fey covered her mouth and quickly turned Mathilde in the opposite direction toward some distant distraction.

The rest of us dropped the burden into the hole and pushed earth over it, leaving enough of Ursula visible for Mathilde to know it was her. Putrid air permeated everything around us.

Gretchen scavenged an armload of pine boughs. 'These might help.'

We tossed several onto Ursula, and held the others to our noses and inhaled the resin.

'She was my family when I had none,' Mathilde wailed once we were all gathered at the edge of the grave.

Mea, the murderess, said prayers of consolation. We recited the Shepherd psalm.

'Was that alright?' Mea whispered on our way back to the hovel. 'I did not know what to say.'

'It was fine.' I said, surprised that she would seek my approval. I still didn't trust her, but if truth be told she was at least quicker than the others when it came to helping.

Once back, and without asking our host, we set to clean the hovel. We propped open the front door and beckoned cool breezes to blow out the stink. I swept the floor and washed the area on which Ursula's body had lain, then scattered the area with rose petals and pine needles. Fat Val, who I had never known to arrange anything in orderly fashion, helped Mathilde organise her herbs, tinctures, and potions. Gretchen and Little Fey picked wildflowers and ivy from the woods and placed them in a small broken ewer on the windowsill. Mea brought in water from a stream to wash implements and pots. Then we boiled more water and washed Mathilde and her clothes.

We were up with the sun, anxious to leave but careful not to appear in too much haste.

Mathilde, revived in spirit and in cleanliness, was up before us. She had made bread and tea. It was as if a spell had lifted from her.

'You have restored my sanity,' she said. 'I am grateful.'

She gave us some clothing to improve our disguise—a few shawls, a linen chemise, two necklaces of polished glass beads that did not impress Mea, judging by her expression, but that looked fine to me, and two kirtles, a veil, and two wimples.

I glanced around the hovel. Sun dappled the floor; a fresh fire burned cheerily in the grate. For a moment I imagined that I could make a life here with Mathilde. She was as crazy as a bag of frogs, but her heart was good, and she would be a fine teacher.

'You look as if you want to stay.' She stood beside me with her bowl of tea, head tilted as if discerning my thoughts.

'You have a life of your own, and answer to no one,' I said. 'Many would envy you.'

'Ah, women envy me, yes, but not men. Men mock my liberty, and jeer at the very oddity that you praise. They are fearful of a woman who lives unbeholden. I am content, but this life is not for everyone, in the same way that your life in community is not for all. But I will admit'— she leaned close to my ear—'being alone can sometimes turn you a little crazy.'

She chortled.

I smiled. *Surely not just 'a little.'*

'Besides, you must go. You are meant for Bingen.'

'It is a hard and dangerous road.'

'All of life is a hard, dangerous road. If your soul isn't ready for that then neither will your body or your heart. And you have already proven your fortitude.'

'At times I think God has thrown me into the fire.'

'You have not been thrown into the fire, Lucia. You *are* the fire.'

She reached into her pocket.

'Here… a token to remember me. It may come into use on your journey.'

She put into my hand a small shard of looking glass. A ray caught the glass and blinded me momentarily.

'You can see yourself in it, or you can observe what is behind you without turning around,' she said. 'Or it can be used to start a fire by slanting it toward the sun.'

I bit my trembling lip. I had never been given anything by anyone.

We tarried no longer with our farewell. Mathilde gave us a bundle of bread and cold lamb for our journey, then wishing us Godspeed she waved us off.

XIII

The Feast of Saint Anne
Toward the Valle d'Isarco

'That was a harsh lesson about being wary of accepting charity from strangers,' said Fat Val.

'And to never enter a place without first checking for dead people,' said Gretchen. 'It is the last time I bury someone. The stench!' She made a face at Mea.

'You'd think a hedgewitch could summon a better smell for her home,' said Little Fey. 'Shame she did not meet Guillaume. He might have set her right.'

'Guillaume would have fainted at the first whiff,' said Mea.

I was glad to be free again. It didn't take long before I had laid aside my earlier desire to have a life like Mathilde's. Still, I was glad of a happy conclusion to our encounter, and hoped God would reward my charity.

The land rolled out into a vast stretch of green, and far off, far beyond a distance I could fathom, was a long shadowy blue line of mountains folding one upon the other. Such sights goaded me into playing a game with God: Get me across that meadow and I'll say a prayer; get me up that hill and I'll say two prayers; get me across that valley without being accosted by Ghibellines, bounty hunters, or hedgewitches and their dead companions, and I will give you a whole day of Pater Nosters.

'I do feel sad for Mathilde,' said Little Fey. 'I know she was strange, but somehow, I don't know… Do you think we should have asked her to join us?'

Mea sputtered. 'Bring her along? With us? To Bingen? She wasn't strange; she was deranged.'

'She might have helped us against the bounty hunters,' Fat Val reasoned. 'You know, casting spells.'

Mea's head shook frantically; she threw her arms into the air. 'One who lives with the dead for half a year is not one with whom we want to forge companionship. I can't believe I have to tell you that.'

'Well, we have forged companionship with you, and you murdered someone,' countered Gretchen.

'I'm different.'

'Are you sure?'

'You are too kind to people, Lucia,' said Mea, swiftly turning the attention back to me. 'From now on, we make decisions as one.'

Her accusation made me hot. 'I was being kind because that's what we've been taught. I did not see any of you using your wiles and wits to get us out of there.'

'That's unfair, Lucia,' said Gretchen. 'We did our part. We did your bidding with that disgusting body.'

'We dug the grave…' said Fat Val.

'We cleaned the hovel,' pouted Little Fey.

'And you were all quick to accept her food,' I said. 'Let's not forget that we avoided spending a night in the rain. Anyway, what is done is done.'

I blew air from my cheeks and looked around to get my bearings.

'There is Brixen. Let us move swiftly before we encounter more danger or distraction.'

We set off through the wildflowers, thoughts of our recent ordeal in stark contrast to the surroundings.

Gradually, the landscape shifted from fair to desolate, from green to dust. Instead of soft grass and flowers there were boulders and fallen trees. We descended into a desiccated valley, like a forest that had stopped breathing. It was all hard rock and granular soil, a place that had learned to survive without the grace of rain. Dry branches, limbs and stumps, like white bones stripped of flesh, poked from earth and rock at odd angles; hollowed trunks looked like the decayed remains of warriors after battle. Deeper and deeper into the earth we went, so deep that soon we lost sight of the sky altogether.

A wide cleft opened up in front of us. It could only have been the work of the Devil for it was too terrifying to be the work of God. On one side of the chasm, the ground sheared away into a watery abyss. On the side we were on, a towering wall of bulbous rock crowded our steps as we followed a narrow ridge. Below us, the violent Isarco River, roaring and thundering like a drunken man barging into a tavern, watery arms thrashing as if deflecting insult, mouth spewing upon the stony walls. I missed the gentle Adige, its grassy riverbanks, easy slopes, and lush trees. There was nothing peaceful about this place.

We crept nervously along the rock ledge above the angry torrent. When I looked down, my head felt light; I feared losing both footing and nerve. When I looked up, the rocks seemed ready to topple. Around us, large birds flew in majestic circles. I hoped that Ghibellines did not prowl these parts.

'We must have taken a wrong path,' I said. 'There is barely room for a cart to travel.'

'Should we retrace our steps and find where we went awry?' asked Little Fey. She was twisting her prayer beads, looking nervously at the prison of rock that surrounded us.

'Thyrus the wyvern lives in these parts,' said Gretchen. 'Perhaps he is watching us, assessing us for his supper. He is flexing his great wings, ready to swoop on us.'

'Stop it,' wailed Fat Val. 'I am fearful of dragons.'

'Then perhaps you prefer kobolds: The likes of Allerünken or Galgenmännlein hide among these rocks. Or a werewolf.'

'Stop, Gretchen! You are being cruel,' she scolded again. 'Why must you frighten us? Such things were not spoken of at Saint Agatha's.'

'They weren't,' agreed Gretchen. 'But my grandmother told me tales about our village in Bavaria. It was a wool village and everyone had to keep watch for the werewolf.'

'Well, I am from Bavaria, too,' said Fat Val indignantly, 'and no such tales were told to me.'

'Because your family kept it from you and quietly placed charms around their home in secret places or slipped them into your bed while you slept.'

Fat Val turned angrily toward Gretchen. 'My family were gentle Christian folk. They did not vex themselves with childish tales.'

'It is precisely the soft Christian heart that the wyvern feeds upon,' taunted Gretchen.

Deus, quomodo finiam cum istis amentibus?

I steered the conversation away from monsters. 'Since both of you are from Bavaria, you can help us with the language once we cross into the north country.'

'I remember only a few words,' grumbled Fat Val. 'I had no cause to keep it up.'

'As with me,' said Gretchen. 'But I have remembered stories of the werewolf, the wyvern, and the kobold, all of whom have eyes upon us ready to eat us!'

She grabbed Little Fey around the waist, which caused her to shriek.

'If you do not stop this talk, I shall be so full of terror that I will fall to my death.'

'Then we will blindfold you,' said Gretchen. 'I have heard tell that some are so fearful of evil on this crossing that they blind themselves until safely on the other side. If not wyverns, then other demons, wicked magi, beasts that lick clean the bones of children.'

'For the love of God and His angels, Gretchen, why did you bring this conversation upon us?' I yelled. 'We have enough fear without you adding to it. Look how you have terrified Sister Fey. Give us a saint, Gretchen, for I am done with your whinges and pranks.'

Little Fey shivered against the rock and scratched her palms.

'I only do it to ward off the spirits,' said Gretchen. 'To speak aloud our fear lessens it.'

'Not for me,' said Fat Val. 'And mark that when you cause us to scream, our voices carry in the gorge and give us away to those who hunt us. So much for your protection.'

Little Fey began to sob.

I glared at Gretchen as I took my sash and bound it around her eyes. 'Always full of help, aren't you?'

She gave a shrug and changed the topic: 'Do you think Mother Clothilde still seeks us? She cannot hunt us forever.'

'Speaking of wyverns…' muttered Mea. She immediately clapped her hand over her mouth and looked at me with apology.

'Even a wyvern with seven heads?'

We stopped and gave Gretchen the evil eye.

'What?' she said, her face full of innocence. 'She brought it up.'

'If you keep frightening us, God will punish you,' Little Fey said from behind her blind. 'He might cause *you* to slip into the abyss.'

After a period of quiet Gretchen returned to her saints.

'Today we will remember Saint Anne, mother of our Queen of Heaven.'

'Do you think Saint Anne ever had to scold the child Mary?' said Fat Val.

'I don't think it is right that we speak like this,' Little Fey cried out. 'We blaspheme both Saint Anne and the Virgin.'

'I like your question, Valentina,' said Gretchen, ignoring Little Fey. 'Do you suppose Saint Anne became pure when her daughter was made pure by the Angel, or was Saint Anne pure before Our Lady was conceived? And if so, might she have been a Virgin before her daughter?'

'That is too complicated to consider on this treacherous path,' said Fat Val.

As we picked our way along the ledge, our backs to the gorge and our hands clinging to the rock wall, I dared not look down, not even at my feet. Rocks the size of giant heads loomed above us; others, broad and jagged, elbowed our advance or forced us to bend to a crawl.

Little Fey whimpered. I was glad she was blindfolded and could not see the ibexes that stared at us from the other side of the chasm, or the vultures that swooped so close that I felt the gust from their feathers.

'What was that?' she cried.

'Only the wind,' I said.

We came across a cave. Its mouth was canopied with dry, dusty ivy, but there was a small spring that burbled and pooled near its entrance. Without discussion we went inside.

'Never have I held my breath for so long,' cried Mea. She untied the bundle from her waist and collapsed on the rock floor. I did likewise. 'I hate heights. I don't know how we will continue…'

'… or how much further we must go to get out of this gorge,' said Fat Val. She and the others ventured further into the cave to be as far from the cliff edge as possible.

'Do not bed down at the back,' Mea called. 'We will use that as our privy. I refuse to relieve myself outside this cave while we are so close to the ledge.'

Suddenly, a voice, weak and raspy, cried from the dark depths. 'I beg you, do not use this place as a privy.'

Our screams boomed off the cave walls and soared out across the gorge.

XIV

The Feast of Saint Monica
Valle d'Isarco

If wyverns and kebolds stalked the gorge, then our screams had surely awakened them from their lairs. We scooped up our bundles and made for the cave entrance.

A man's voice cried out again: 'Pray do not leave. I mean no harm. On my word, I can do no harm as I myself am harmed.'

We stopped. I wrung my hands. Outside the cave, the light was draining. Should we return to a perilous path and risk plunging into the abyss, or engage with the one who spoke from the back of the cave?

'Who are you?' Fat Val said. She deepened her voice to make herself sound fierce. The stiletto was already in her hand.

'Let's leave!' hissed Mea.

Another cry came from the back: 'I am one who should be your protector but am myself unprotected.'

I thought of the foul men we had encountered so far. Why trust this one? Maybe he was one of the bounty hunters.

'Show yourself,' I said, now brave of voice myself.

'If only I could. I am injured and trapped.'

Metal scraped against stone. A howl of pain followed.

'Where are you?' shouted Mea, face gritted with impatience as she squinted at the darkness.

'I have fallen into a hole. My leg is caught in a crevice.'

'Are you alone?' called Gretchen.

'If you saw where I am, you would pray I was alone.'

'I will go to him,' I said. I did not want to go. My frantic mind considered the obvious danger, but it was overruled by what Mother Elena had taught me—that it was our duty to help those in need. I bent low, and all but crawled toward the back of the cave.

The air was foul. I pulled my coif from my pocket, held it over my nose and mouth. A shard of light appeared in the corner and I directed myself toward it. Something rested against the wall: a helmet with a red cross painted on it.

I peered into the hole. A distressing sight! A knight, in mail and armour, was wedged in a cleft of rock, and he hung over a long, unbroken drop into the thrashing Isarco. An errant movement would send him to his death. His bloodied, terrified face looked up at me. Part of a red emblem was visible on his upper garment.

'Oh! It is a Templar.'

My sisters rushed to join me.

Our arms quickly plunged into the hole. All five of us had our hands on him.

'Let me remove your coif. You will be more comfortable,' said Fat Val.

She eased the links of mail off his head. Fear breathed from him in ragged gulps.

'What prevents you from freeing yourself?' asked Little Fey, studying his predicament.

'My arm is gashed; my leg…' He let loose a wail that could be heard all the way to the Holy Land.

A tree limb that appeared to have been supporting one of his feet suddenly snapped and fell into the river. The knight slipped further down, as did our arms.

'Good sisters, there is no help for me. Pray for my soul.'

Fat Val and I were on our stomachs. We threaded our hands between the stony walls that held him in place and found the hairy hollows under his arms. Gretchen reached down his back and finding his belt, gripped it. Mea held the rim of his breastplate. We tried to pull him up but he would not move. His arm, wedged between body and rock, could provide no purchase.

Little Fey gave the orders.

'Sir, move your foot to the side. No, to the other. There is a niche where your foot can rest. Yes, there. When we pull, try to launch from it.'

We yanked again. He rose a little.

Little Fey counted us into our next heave, '*Uno, due, tre.*'

He rose a bit more.

My hands were slick and damp but I didn't dare let go.

We gave another great pull and this time we were able to drag him from the hole entirely.

A Flight of Saints

We cheered our effort.

The knight beached on the ground, gasped wildly. Mea tipped the gourd toward him and he gulped greedily until sobs got the better of him.

'Fair sisters,' he blubbered. 'Christ has blessed you with the strength to save a man.'

Each of us rested a hand on him to calm him. When his composure was gathered, we eased him into better light.

His body was in great distress. I imagined his mind was likewise. To dangle high above a river knowing a moment or a movement could send you to your death was too terrifying to contemplate.

We lifted off his mail, his black tunic on which was sewn the red cross, his gorget of brass, his hauberk of mail, his elbow pieces, brassards, wrist guards. His body reeked. Blood dripped from gashes on his head and upper arm. One of his legs was twisted awkwardly.

He was tall, broad of chest, and looked to be twenty winters old. He continued to weep.

'Handsome. I like his hair,' cooed Gretchen.

'You always know the right thing to say at the right time, don't you?' I hissed. I saw my next challenge, to keep her away from him.

His armour removed, I asked the knight, 'How long have you been there?'

'This would have been my third night.'

We worked silently, deftly, around him. Fat Val made a fire; Mea crushed lemon balm for tea; Gretchen opened her bag for the stalks of aloe she had plucked earlier; Little Fey knelt beside him and held his hand. Using my wetted coif, I daubed grit and blood from his wounds; Gretchen pressed the cool paste of the aloe into each one. His face was creased with pain. He howled again when we tied a stick to his injured leg with one of Mea's veils in the hope it would reset itself.

'We are like Saint Monica, administering to Augustine,' said Gretchen. I didn't trust for one instant that her mind was on her beloved saints and not on this knight.

'How did you fall in the hole?' asked Little Fey.

'I came here to rest, as you yourselves have done. It was near dark when I arrived, and soon after I heard voices. I crawled to the back of the cave for I did not want any encounter. I found the hole and, there being little light, decided to crouch in it. The lack of light, however, caused me to misjudge what I was getting into, and I became stuck. By then the men—I guessed there to be three of them—were in the cave. I did not call for their assistance for I sensed that no good would come of it. When I heard their speech and their manner, I was glad of my silence. They did not stay long. I thought them foolish to leave for it was full night, and no one with any wisdom should walk on that narrow ledge in the dark. I heard the river below me, but it was not until first light that I fully saw my situation. There was nothing to do but accept my fate and say my prayers.'

We went about our ministrations. I tended to his wounds without looking at his eyes.

'But praise God for you sisters. Had you not happened by…'

'Sir,' I slid easily into my lie, 'you see one sister among us; the rest of us are not in Holy orders. We are pilgrims on our way to Santiago de Compostela.'

'Oh, but you are sisters of Christ. I can tell by your hands and from the wordless way you work. You have been well trained, and your trust in one another is plain to see.'

Trust? If you only knew you were in the company of a murderess and a fornicator.

'The men who came to this cave seek you.' He frowned and slowed his words. 'They spoke of five who fled the Convent of Saint Agatha.'

I kept my eyes down.

'Truly, do not fear me,' he continued. 'I am in your debt. You saved my life; I shall do everything to save yours. I will not betray you.'

'What is your name?' asked Fat Val. The fire she lit crackled, and its shadows licked the walls of the cave. She knelt at his side, beside me, and across from Little Fey.

'I am Clovis, a sergeant knight. Please dispel yourselves of any vestige of valour you may associate with that rank. I am a better carpenter than a knight. I have not deserted my Order, but of late I have required long examination of my soul. Like the Son of God, I came to the wilderness to ponder my duty and also to beg release from it.'

'If you are a knight, where is your horse?' asked Little Fey.

'My palfrey is above this cave, lashed to a tree. I pray he has not perished. I only intended brief respite here. The more-travelled road is higher up. Having been this way before, I remembered the cave. I hid Vento in the woods and climbed down to get here.'

'Your horse is named Vento?' she prodded.

He smiled; soft lines fanned around his mouth. 'Fast as the wind, and black as night.'

Fat Val took the cloth from me and resumed washing the knight's face. 'You said your soul was troubled.'

He nodded, but the smile was gone. 'I have done no ill, cheated no man. I am true to my vows. But sadness wanders in me, as heavy as the hand of God and as cold as the Devil. I am like that lizard upon the rock behind you.'

I looked nervously behind Fat Val.

'He will not harm. But see how he is, as pale as the rock on which he rests. If you beheld him on a tree branch, he would be another colour, and if on a leaf his colour would alter again. He befits his place. I, too, once befit my place. I was charm when needed, brave when needed, benevolent when needed, severe when needed. We are all of many dispositions, but when alone with ourselves what is our true nature? I no longer know the answer.'

Fat Val wept; her tears fell onto him. He tried to sit up and give comfort but was thrown back by his wounds.

'I meant no distress to you, Sister. But you asked, and I answered.'

'Forgive me; your words speak of a suffering shared by many.'

'I do not agree,' he said. 'I have travelled far, to the Holy Land in the East, and to Santiago de Compostela in the West, and met many who showed ease in their character and manner. I am not reconciled to mine, not even among my own

A Flight of Saints

Templar brothers. I am recently returned from Damascus where I served in the Battle of Montgisard. There were fewer than four hundred of us; we were greatly outnumbered. By the grace of God, we surprised the enemy, but it was a narrow and brutal victory. My brothers, most of whom I knew to be kind men, behaved in ways contrary to our code, like animals; like men I had never met. In battle, natures change, and they acted as though it was their right to do as they did, that their oaths and emblems, their fraternity, even God, permitted it. The slaughter, the indignities to women and children; I am haunted by what I witnessed. We claim to fight in the name of Christ but He would die a second death to see such destruction. I myself fled when I saw it.'

'Surely that is what soldiers and knights do,' I said.

He closed his eyes as if to shut out the memory. 'It is one thing to fight; another to destroy. Saladin will avenge this desecration, and show no mercy. Meanwhile, my brothers are building a castle at Jacob's Ford, a boastful monument to their hollow victory. But it will not hold: I would not be surprised if Saladin destroys it and those who made it.'

Who was Saladin? What was Jacob's Ford?

Clovis bowed his head. 'In any event…' He did not finish his sentence, and I guessed he wanted to say no more about his spiritual wounds. Instead, he turned to Fat Val. 'What is the nature of your suffering, Sister?'

She pretended to not hear the question. 'Sir, we have a bit of soap. Permit me to wash you so that it may hasten your healing.'

She looked at Mea, who had the soap. I waited for her

protest, but she took the soap from her bundle and handed it over quietly. Then she said: 'I shall fetch clean water.'

What mischief was this? This was not Mea's manner. Gretchen looked at me with the same sense of wariness.

Four of us prepared supper while Fat Val lingered an immodest amount of time washing Clovis's hair and body. His sighs of satisfaction made their interaction too intimate, and I was about to chide Fat Val when Mea touched my arm.

'Leave her be,' she whispered. 'He is a valiant man who is troubled. Let her show him tenderness.'

She was definitely up to something. If anyone was like the changeable lizard upon the rock it was the murderess.

Not so, Gretchen, who was still admiring his hair: 'Look how it shines.'

Fat Val emptied her bundle and made a pillow of it for Clovis. He smiled his thanks, and despite the low light in the cave I saw a blush bloom on her face. We helped her ease him into a sitting position against the wall, and then she fed him tea and bread that Mathilde the hedgewitch had made for us.

Clovis, much revived by her ministrations, told stories of his family in Siena: his parents, two sisters, and a brother. He told us some of his adventures but made light of his heroics; in fact, he looked more ashamed than proud of them.

His talk grew quiet and serious.

'The men I overheard, the ones who seek you, are driven by reward. A bounty is upon you.'

So, he knew about the reward. My mind tumbled. Was he, too, tempted by reward?

A Flight of Saints

I stared into the fire, my mind sputtering like the flames before me. On the one hand, I, who did not know how to cope outside the convent, would be foolish not to accept his offer of protection. Perhaps he would see us safely to Bingen. A knight would be a worthy ally: Not only a protector, but a shield of propriety; a cover for our ruse. His skill with bow and arrow would ensure we had food on our journey. As well, one who had travelled throughout Christendom would know the way to Bingen.

On the other hand, did the bounty on our heads make us attractive to him? Would he flatter us into submission and reap his reward? And what of the damage he suffered during the Crusade? Might that make him a millstone, or a danger to us?

The psalmist asks: 'In whom do I place my trust?' I did not know whether to put my trust in Clovis. If he proved unworthy or dishonest, well, there were five of us against one lame knight. We could take him, though I'm not sure where Fat Val's loyalties would land. She seemed taken with him, and was flirting. Still, even four could wrestle him out of the cave and roll him over the edge. It was not a kind thought, but the bounty hunters had heightened my caution. I wanted to believe that Clovis was good and true. Hadn't Mother Elena taught us that love is the soil that makes honesty flourish?

I took a breath. 'Fair Clovis, my name is Lucia. We are indeed the sisters the men seek.'

The eyes of my sisters spun toward me, wide with alarm and remonstrance. I continued undeterred: 'We encountered them in Botzen, but'—I did not look at Gretchen as I said this—'we were quick to deceive them.'

Despite their disapproval, my declaration relieved my sisters of the burden of our secret. How swiftly they joined in! Complaint burst from them like flour from a split bag. Words tumbled over words. Fat Val told Clovis about how Mother Clothilde silenced us, and how her cruelty forced us to flee Saint Agatha's. Little Fey told him about the bounty hunters. Gretchen told him how she would kill Mother Clothilde if she saw her. I told him about the hedgewitch. Mea merely smiled at it all, as if watching young children in the throes of excitement.

Clovis listened with grave attendance, furrows deep across his brow. When we told him of being beaten and sheared, his body flinched, as if he himself had experienced the abuse; or perhaps his was the flinch of revenge.

I told him everything. 'We say we are pilgrims travelling to the shrine of Saint James, but in truth we are going to Bingen to join the community of Abbess Hildegard.'

Clovis's face brightened. 'Ah, the one who scolds churchmen for their vanity and corruption. May God continue to bless her work. Then it will be my honour and duty to see you safely to the door of Bingen Abbey. You saved my life; I shall save yours. I have an affection for the community. I once knew a monk-priest who recorded Hildegard's visions and sermons.'

'Was his name Father Volmar?' I asked eagerly.

'The very same. A good man if ever there was one. I met him on the pilgrim road. He prayed with me and encouraged my vocation. It was long ago, some seven years.'

Clovis winced as he tried to make the sign of the Holy Cross with his sore arm.

How fortuitous to meet one who knew the same monk-priest who had guided me. I told him of my own encounter with Father Volmar not long ago.

'He came to Saint Agatha's and saw my suffering, my bruises and wounds. He bade me leave the wretched place. He said I would find welcome at Bingen Abbey.'

Clovis's eyes clouded with surprise and doubt.

'You say you met him not long past? It could not have been him.'

'It was,' I assured him. 'We spoke at length; he held my hands.'

'Dear Lucia. You say he visited you on the Feast of John the Baptist, just gone; but that cannot be true. Father Volmar has been dead these three years.'

I could not sleep. It was as if the foundation of my life had broken apart. How was it that Father Volmar was dead when I saw him, spoke to him, barely three full moons ago? How could my memory be wrong? That chance encounter had given me courage and purpose to escape Saint Agatha's. It was impossible that I would have imagined it.

I sat up. My sisters were in slumber. Clovis was also awake.

'I am vexed,' I confided to him. 'By what you said about Father Volmar. I no longer trust my mind. Yet, the meeting is so clear to me. Can it be that you are mistaken of his death?'

'I was told of it by one who is like a brother to me, whose word I trust. But let us consider for a moment that what you say is true. You are certain it was on the Feast of John the Baptist just past?'

'As I said.'

'Then suppose this. Could he have visited Saint Agatha's before? Might you have confused his visits?'

'Father Volmar had come to Saint Agatha's many times, but I had never spoken to him. We had a different mother then. Mother Elena. She was good to us, and loved the monks from Saint Disibod as much as she loved Abbess Hildegard. I had no desire to leave the convent.'

I went over every detail from the night of the storm, to the knock on the convent door, to my conversation with Father Volmar: All that I had heard and had seen.

Clovis pondered my words.

'Lucia, I believe all you have said. I wish with all my heart that it was as real as you say. But perhaps there is a way to explain it. Those who endure cruelty as you and your sisters have suffered often seek relief through hope, through wishful thinking. It is possible that your mind, burdened with worry, grief, unspeakable fear, became disordered; that your conversation with Father Volmar came to you as a vision.'

'But it was real,' I said. 'I felt his hands.'

'And do you not feel God in your heart? Do you not feel the Devil tempting you?'

What he said didn't make me feel better. And yet, it should have. After all, my sisters and I were bound for Bingen to commit ourselves to an abbess whose visions were revered by churchmen and kings. Why should I not have had a vision to compel our journey?

'It could be that Father Volmar visited you but not in the way you perceived,' said Clovis. 'Do not be ashamed. To see beyond the world in front of us, to receive word from those who have left this world, is in many ways a greater gift. Look how it has set you free. Your vision saved you and your sisters.'

I nodded, but privately I did not agree. I was certain of my memory.

XV

The Feast of Saint Hild

Valle d'Isarco

We stayed in the cave with Clovis the Templar. His strength slowly returned, but the injury to his leg was great and made him limp. But instead of complaint he shed tears of gratitude, and repeated his promise to us of protection and service. He was brotherly in concern and advice, and such was his pleasant nature that it was as if we had known him all our lives.

I was surprised how relaxed I was in his presence. Save for the murderess, and Gretchen's imprudence with the bounty hunter, the rest of us had not spent much time in the company of a man, let alone full days and nights with one.

Valentina rarely left his side. She continued to wash his wounds and soothe them with Gretchen's aloe spines; she combed his hair, and asked after his comfort. She cleaned his tunic and his boots. Yes, that's right: She was Valentina now, not Fat Val. I had woken up one morning no longer able to think of her as Fat Val. There was a shift in her, welcome of course but also unexpected. She had become duty itself. Although her care was largely of one person, she also cared for all of us. She made tea for all not just for Clovis; she kept our small fire alive; she began to fuss over us: Were we well? Were we comfortable? She hummed during the course of the day. She was so pleasant in diligence and manner that it forced a change of heart in me and I found that I could no longer think of her as Fat Val. Indeed, she seemed a different person entirely. She was brave, bold, and caring, yes, but in appearance, too, she was changed. Scant food and long days of walking had whittled her shape. I could not call her Fat Val even if I wanted. She seemed aware of this herself because she began asking Mea or me if her tunic was straight, or if her hair, which had grown curly and fell over her shoulders, was sufficiently tidy. Clovis's presence had no doubt wrought some of this change.

Clovis blessed us in other ways. His fair humour sloughed our petty complaints with one another and smoothed our words. He brought forth our considerate and compassionate natures, which had been shaped by Mother Elena but undone by Mother Clothilde. He helped restore our gentle friendship with one another. The only thing he stole from us was sleep, for he snored like a bear through the night.

In the morning, he led us in Lauds:
Oh Lord, open thou our lips
and our mouth shall shew forth thy praise
In the evening, he led us in Compline:
Keep watch, dear Lord, with those who work, or watch, or weep this night, and give your angels charge over those who sleep.

In our prayers, we gave thanks for fair weather, for our safety, for the shelter of the cave, but mostly we gave thanks for Clovis. Life felt easier in his company. Privately, I reasoned that if we were captured it would stand us in good stead to say that we had saved the life of a Templar.

Gretchen, who was as fond of animals as she was of saints, clambered up the rocks each day to the place where Clovis said he had left Vento to make sure the beast had water.

Between Lauds and Compline, we six plotted our journey.

Clovis suggested we make a small adjustment to our ruse.

'We shall say that I am pledged to Casa Siena where the *duca* has bid me accompany his daughter and her ladies on pilgrimage to Santiago de Compostela. Word is likely out already that Casa Vicenza seeks Mea so we must change her origin. As I am from Siena, it will make our story more believable.'

We agreed.

He knew the land where we were, had travelled over the Alpes often. He told us some of the difficulties ahead while reminding us that there were things that couldn't be foreseen. He said he thought the bounty hunters were four days ahead of us.

'But do not be lulled by pretty thinking. One of them might have become ill and required rest for a day or more, or they divined that women could not have travelled with speed over dangerous terrain and hence they have slowed their progress and are lying in wait ahead. Or they have become lost, or set upon by others. All manner of misfortune befalls those who travel this way.'

While he spoke, my mind took its familiar walk back to my days at Saint Agatha's, not to ruminations on Mother Clothilde but to my meeting on that thundery night with Father Volmar. Had our flight truly been sparked by a spirit? I picked at different moments of that night. Surely I had not conjured Mother Clothilde's presence or her words that evening. But upon closer examination, when my mind considered the morning after the monk-priest's visit, I could not recall having seen him, nor witnessing any indication of his visit. Sister Bettina would have made comment because she fussed over guests and the food she made for them, yet she had said nothing of it. Had my memory gone astray? Was I like older folk whose minds grow hazy, who can no longer tell truth from dream?

I returned to the present, to the talk of crossing the Alpes. My sisters, freed from their previous hesitation to speak, nattered about everything except Father Volmar. They talked about dangers, about what to do if other travellers came to the cave. 'We will say we have the Sweat,' or 'If the interlopers look to have ill intent, we will use our weapons.' Would we kill if necessary?

This sent them into full squabble:

'What of *Thou shalt not kill?*' said Little Fey.

'Is it kinder to let them murder us?' asked Mea.

'I am only reminding you of our vows.'

'What do you believe, Sister Fey? I should very much like to know,' Gretchen pressed. She looked at Clovis for support, but he said nothing. 'You are foolish to cling to piety while we wander through a godless land, living by wits alone, and being pursued by those who would harm us.'

'I believe all that the Creed and the Commandments teach,' said Little Fey. 'I never doubt or waver from them. They are my rule.'

I glanced at her hands. None of my sisters had mentioned her stigmata to Clovis.

'An answer as dry as sand,' said Gretchen. 'Are you governed by your soul or by your stigmata?'

Here we go.

Little Fey was unperturbed. 'My wounds keep me ever-present in God.'

Clovis's head jerked. He looked at all of us, startled, as if to say, *What stigmata?* But the conversation charged ahead.

'Well, I, too, believe in the Creed but my wits are my divining rod when it comes to the Commandments,' huffed Mea, entering the fray. 'For example, I agree that we should not steal, but what are the hungry to do? Are they to be damned for their affliction? I do not damn Valentina for stealing the jewels and the stiletto. Or the bag of salt. Our plight is desperate. And what of coveting? I have seen Gretchen giving my shoes the eye.'

'I covet them, too,' I confessed, resigned to join in and ease Clovis's glare off Little Fey.

'As do I,' admitted Valentina.

'I like them, too,' mumbled Little Fey.

'What shoes?' burst Clovis. 'What stigmata?'

Mea laughed. 'So many feet yearning for my shoes! Still, I do not think it wrong. To covet is to desire, and what is wrong with desire so long as it does not turn you into a thief? How can we not desire when all manner of things that God has bestowed or that human toil has created are put before us? I covet—there, I said it—but I do not think myself damned. Clovis, here are my shoes'— she took them from her bundle—'but there is no chance they will fit you and therefore you will not covet them.'

'Yet you made vows contrary to what you have now spoken,' said Gretchen. She had turned mean, though I could not account for her anger.

Mea faced her with calm: 'We make many vows and oaths to one another out of passion, duty, want, to seek favour. But when circumstances change, the oath may no longer serve, and we must bend to the wind of change. I have too many questions for God. Perhaps I am not meant for a nun's life.'

My thoughts precisely. I watched Mea. She fidgeted with the ties of her bundle. I wondered if she felt she had said too much.

'You speak of one who has acquaintance with broken vows,' Clovis said, handing back the shoes. More to my surprise, he didn't ask about the stigmata.

Would this be the time Mea would confess to murder, or would one of the others raise it? But again, she did not and we did not. Poor Clovis saw goodness and piety in us; how long before he realised we possessed neither of those virtues.

'It is true. But do you not agree that a vow unfulfilled or broken might not be so bad? In my experience, a broken vow has been a welcome release, though I did not see it that way at the time. Now, it feels more gift than grief. And you, Clovis. What does your Templar faith believe?'

How smoothly she turned interest away from herself.

'I hold to the Creed, to all it teaches, but I also hold beyond the Creed. I believe in love, that to love all as our Saviour taught is more important than any creed.'

'Is that not blasphemy?' Valentina sat next to Clovis. Their knees were touching. 'To say that anything is more important than the Creed is to dishonour the teachings.'

'To believe any teaching is easy, but I would rather parley with a man who loves all and is truthful and kind than one who adheres solely to the Creed. Too many hypocrites spout the Creed but do not adhere to it. What of you?'

'I believe the Creed, like Sister Fey. But in truth I do not give it much thought. It is part of me, as much as breath is part of me. I am settled to that.'

'Your faith humbles me.' He smiled sadly. 'Since all of you have been truthful with me, I must be so about another matter. I have decided to seek dispensation from my vows. It will not be easy. The Order desires more and more recruits, and once ordained a knight, only Death can release you. But if I were to find a priest…' He shook his head, blew air through his lips. 'This cave has brought injury upon me, but perhaps the hand of Providence was in it. If a priest or a fellow Templar can vouch for my lameness it might aid my plight. Strange how misfortune can also answer prayers.'

He read our silence.

'I swear this will not alter my promise to you. My bond to you is true.'

'What will you do after you are freed from your oath?' said Valentina.

'I shall see what God has in mind.'

A look passed between them, but given my false experience with Father Volmar, I no longer trusted my eyes.

I turned to Gretchen. She was sullen so I asked, 'What do you believe?'

'My soul and I have been in conversation about that very question since we left Saint Agatha's. I do not believe much of what we are told. I do not believe God put bad things in our midst to tempt us. I think He wanted us to be merry. Nor am I vexed by my lack of belief. When Mother Elena looked after us, I was content and unquestioning, but when the hag Clothilde arrived something changed in me. I cannot name it, only to say that something once learned and valued was lifted out of me and may never return.'

'You speak of the sin of acedia,' said Little Fey. 'It plagues one's soul, heart, and head, yet many overcome it.'

'Why must everything be a sin? Maybe it shows that God has loosened His care of me. Maybe He has enough souls in Heaven.'

'Every soul is a gift, Gretchen. We must preserve it for that day when God redeems us.' She took Gretchen's hand. 'Be not disillusioned. None of us know if the soul survives death. But to lose it while you breathe is worse than death.'

'All of us bear wounds of varying kinds,' said Clovis. 'Who but God would love us?'

I hoped no one would turn the question on me, and force me to admit that fear and doubt made little room in me for prayer and faith. At first, I took it as a sign that I was without belief, without God. But I shook away the thought. I knew who I was and what I was: a child of God who desired to consecrate her life to Him. And yet, how strange that He had lately been absent from my thoughts. If I was betrothed to another, my first thought upon rising and my last before sleeping would be to my betrothed. But I no longer felt this way toward God, and I was ashamed to tell it to my sisters.

We were in the cave three days.

On the morning of our leaving, we stood in a circle and listened to Gretchen's vita of Saint Hild, a saint with whom none of us had familiarity. Gretchen said it was because Saint Hild was from the far-off kingdom of Britannia.

'She lived in the north lands, long ago. An abbess who ruled over a double house. She was held as a leader of the Church. When she summoned bishops and priests from all the lands to meet, they came. That meeting decided the date we honour the Resurrection.'

Easter. *Would we be in Bingen by then?*

We gave thanks to the cave for its shelter, and commenced our way over the rocks to the path above, helping Clovis, whose injuries still plagued him. His face brightened when he saw Vento.

We insisted he ride, but he refused, and suggested we take turns so that each might benefit from a rest.

I looked back down into the gorge; the Isarco still thrashed with fury.

'I forgot to mention that Saint Hild was not loved by all,' said Gretchen. 'Many disagreed with the way she calculated the date for Easter. But she stood firm. By a miracle—and this shall make you happy, Lucia—none of the men killed her.'

A Flight of Saints

'Thank you, Gretchen,' Little Fey said. 'I shall say a prayer for Saint Hild, but right now I cannot think of anything except my footing. When we are free of these rocks, when I no longer have sight of that gorge, I shall be of stronger mind.'

'Should we put the blind on you again?' asked Gretchen.

'No, and do not taunt me with your foolish tales of wyverns.'

XVI

The Feast of the Holy Innocents

Beyond the Valle d'Isarco

By now it was the dregs of Augustus. The full moon told me we had been gone a month from Saint Agatha's. It felt as if more time had passed, that I had not known any other life but this itinerant one. At once I felt weary. My body had been so long in a posture of fear that it creaked when I stretched. My mind could not remember a time when I wasn't frightened. Even with Clovis girded in armour and sword, Fear gripped me.

I watched him, considered his fair face and nature; his sad limp. Would he be more burden than help? He was surely the weakest among us. Worse, though, was that his presence might enfeeble us, cause us to be simpletons waiting on his word when thus far we had been mistresses of our own decisions.

As we treaded through the barren gorge, devoid of leaf and petal, I thought of winter, and of the changing seasons, and that made me think of my sisters, for they had shed their season of play and entered the season of knowledge: Gretchen the Jester was now Gretchen the Fornicator; Valentina the Clumsy was now Valentina the Brave and Caring; Mea the Haughty was now Mea the Murderess. Fey the Pious was now Fey the Fraud. And me? I once saw myself as Lucia the Clever, but now I was Lucia the Unreliable, or Lucia the One Without a Plan. Or perhaps Lucia the Dreamer. For all I knew, this crossing, this angry river, these sisters, this knight, were a mirage. I might still be slumbering in my straw at Saint Agatha's, dreaming it all.

Dream-thinking made my footing careless. I chided myself for not giving full attention to our dangerous progress; an errant step could send me down the stony cliffside and into the raging Isarco. I was grateful to the sister behind me who, when my feet wandered too close to the edge, put a restraining hand on my shoulder and guided me away from it. A few times of this and I was moved to thank her, but when I turned to do so, there was no one. I was the last in line. *Another angel?*

It was all upward now, through forests of skeletal trees and gorse. I kept behind Little Fey in case she stumbled and I could arrest her fall. The scrub and brush scratched my skin. I had come to expect nothing less each day than raw and bloodied hands and feet.

But soon dry rock gave way to green ground, and gloom to sun. It was a relief to be out of the gorge and to see hills as round and gentle as a mother's breast. But my cry of joy was quickly stilled: What beasts were these that stared at us with jagged teeth and thick white patches like sparse hair on their craggy faces?

'The great Alpes,' said Clovis.

We stood, slack of jaw, in fearsome awe.

'We will not climb those.' My words were more prayer than murmur. If Gretchen thought wyverns and werewolves inhabited the gorge, she would redouble her folly with the creatures that lived in those mountains. And Little Fey, fearful of falling: I did not know how I would get her across.

'We will indeed climb those,' said Clovis. His arms were crossed as if taking the measure of his opponent. I looked at his straight nose, the sharp planes of his cheeks; eyes like a sparrow hawk. He seemed chiselled from the very rock that loomed in our midst.

I was glad the Templar was with us. I was not sure I alone had the confidence to push myself onward let alone push my sisters. Clovis had taken from me the burden of leading them, of providing the ready answer, the quick direction. My sisters showed more charity and deference to him than to me. It was easier for me to be one of them than to be herding them, or to listen to their constant mutter and murmur. They would not behave so with Clovis.

But those icy mountains. What madness had made me believe we could cross them?

I looked down at my feet shod in torn leather, and at my thin tunic. The obstacles were too great; the mountains too high; the gorges too deep; the meadows too long; the way too unknown; the world too strange; my imperfections too many; my sisters too ill-prepared.

That morning, we had cast lots for who would ride Vento. Mea had drawn the long stick, and as if it were something to celebrate, she wore her pretty shoes.

I looked at her, astride Vento, green silk ribbons fluttering carelessly about her ankles.

I looked at Little Fey, eyes closed in prayer.

I looked at Valentina, flirting and laughing with Clovis.

I looked at Gretchen, arms spread wide and twirling like a fool.

I breathed a prayer to the Holy Innocents, but the words that passed my lips were simply, 'Here. Now.' Because this was the moment I knew with the wisdom of my near-fifteen winters that no God or saint would get us to Bingen. All hope of seeing the place I so desperately yearned to reach floated away on a cloud. Restless in my skin, I felt the hand of desperation, teasing at my itch to leave my tribe.

For days we followed a stony path that climbed back and forth like the letter Z; higher and higher. The air was fragrant with pine rather than lavender; the ground harder, sparser, with boulders and pebbles; the water pooled in small lakes colder. The billowy grasses and flowers from past days had given way to windswept plains of short grass and flowers that shied back to the earth. No more butterflies, no dragonflies. Birds were still with us but they were not as effusive with their twitter, preoccupied now with their winter preparations. Rabbit and squirrel, too, gathered their hoard.

I sniffed the air: Surely it was too early for snow.

The land was a wolf that stalked us, hungry and desperate, waiting for us to falter so it could pounce and devour. I wished it would. The vigilance was constant and it exhausted me more than the endless walking.

'We are at the height of the pass,' Clovis announced. His face was red, his breathing hard. 'Ahead is Lengmoos. There is a hostelry. Those who sought you in Botzen may be there. Let us be on our guard and remember our story.'

The bounty hunters were not at the hostelry, but they had been.

'They were here two nights ago,' said the innkeeper. He had the look of one who had been whipped by the wind. Great folds of skin sagged beneath his eyes: a done old man. 'I hope they be not friends of yours for never have I lodged fouler men.'

'Be sure they are not friends, good man,' said Clovis. 'We have met them before and wish not to do so again. Did they give hint to their route?'

'Aye. One said they were travelling to the Inn Bridge. There was another with them, a lad they kept outside tied to the horse. Oh, they were an awful bunch. Said they were seeking five nuns who fled their house. I do not condone runaways but I pray God they do not run into the arms of this lot. It would be an unkind capture.'

The innkeeper, who had been wiping his serving bench, was suddenly alert to the entirety of our group. His head bobbed as he counted us.

'I see where your mind is,' Clovis said, breaking into a nervous laugh, 'but it is no more than coincidence that they are five and those being sought are five. This good lady is the Duchessa di Siena.' Mea gave a curt nod. 'Her father has charged me to provide safe passage for her and her companions to Santiago de Compostela.'

'It is a strange route you have chosen, quite out of the way. Why did you not travel by way of Francia?'

We hadn't anticipated such a question.

'I chose this route,' said Mea, with a haughty lift of her chin, 'for its length and difficulty for I knew it would give greater hardship and therefore greater expiation of my sins.'

So cool a liar.

The innkeeper nodded slowly, weighing the truth of her words. Judging it unwise to delve further into the matter—Mea had fixed him with one of her imperious glares—he changed topic and asked if we required chambers.

'No, sir, we have stopped only for refreshment,' said Clovis. He removed his gloves and proceeded with the business of men. 'The last time I was this way two bridges had been washed out.'

'Indeed,' said the innkeeper. 'Last year, with all the rain, one was washed away and the other had its footings ripped out by a rockslide. Some good soul laid down planks at one of the crossings only to have a bad soul make off with them.'

'Where does one cross now?'

'Nowhere. The Isarco is too swift for ferry or fording; it would swallow you before you could fight it. Best to continue to the path yonder. At the dead bear, turn toward the mountains and it will see you to the Brenner Pass. What will you have?'

'Is the Dead Bear the name of a hostelry?' I thought it a most peculiar name.

'No.' The innkeeper set six cups on his bench. 'Just a dead bear. It is said winter will come early. You don't want to be in the mountains then. Make haste while you can.'

XVII

The Feast of Saint Gretchen

In the Alpes

'Are we there yet?'
Gretchen's courses had resumed along with her tetchy nature. Mea and I exchanged looks of relief: We no longer had to worry that she might be with child. All we had to do now was keep her far from men until we reached Bingen. She had shown little interest in Clovis, for which I was both surprised and gratified. She had no doubt seen that his eye was taken by Valentina. Her nature had returned to surly form.

'I cannot tell how far to Bingen.' I kept my manner calm and bright for I knew that if my temper stirred, she would take delight in pouncing on me, and rag me for being uncharitable. So, with as much indifference as I could muster, I said, 'Ask Clovis.'

She walked with me on the mule track. A brittle, caustic tone always accompanied her monthly bleed. I fortified myself for the added spur of insult.

'I have a secret,' she said. The sly, silky prelude to her attack. 'It is not one I wish to tell but I do so as your dearest friend, Lucia. You may not have noticed, but not everyone likes you.'

Here it comes.

'Pray what?' I imagined my body encased in all the armour that Clovis wore.

'They think you prickly and pushy. That you will abandon us if we don't do your bidding. That you only care about getting to Bingen.'

I stopped and stared at her. 'I *do* only care about getting to Bingen. What else is there for us? That we become dancers, lubbers, palmers? Besides, I am not leading or bidding, as you may have noticed. We are all following Clovis.'

'Be that as it may, I merely relay to you that you are not favoured by the others.'

'I don't believe you.'

I wanted to be careful with my words. I was always holding them around Gretchen, but I wanted no argument with her. Besides, how else to be with a friend? We were all brittle and out of humours; to say the wrong thing would snap us, break us open, and risk letting loose our demon natures.

She drew breath between her teeth to effect her greater knowledge over my ignorance. She loved to stoke conflict to enliven drudgery. It often worked. Now, her charge pierced the lone chink in my armour. My defences scrambled into position on the parapet of my pride.

'You forget that I am the chosen one,' I said. 'I was the one the angels visited, not you. We all prayed for a miracle to be released, and we—or rather I—received it. So, I am in God's favour, and that is all I care about. If you or the others don't think me worthy, take it up with God.'

With a dramatic gasp and titter, she strode ahead to whisper with Valentina, looking back at me with a mocking sneer.

What had I done wrong? Did the others really despise me? It was reason enough to flee them if that were the case. I slowed my pace and waited for Little Fey to catch up.

'Do you think me prickly and without heart?'

'Why do you ask?'

'Why do you not answer me plainly?'

She rolled her eyes. *Little Fey! Rolling her eyes at me! When had this begun?* 'No, Lucia, you are not prickly and without heart.'

'Have I ever offended you?'

'Was Gretchen needling you?'

'She said everyone dislikes me and thinks me sharp.'

'She says that about everyone, especially when she knows she has done something wrong and tries to make it someone else's fault.'

It ate at me, this charge of being thorny. I had been kindness itself to Gretchen, extending my hand to her more than I had to the others. But then, I had also interrupted her play for Guillaume the perfumer, which must explain her animus. There was her copulation with the bounty hunter too. Perhaps she regretted confiding in us about it.

I was suddenly fatigued. The labour of our journey had pushed me to the end of patience, and now this charge against my manner. Sometimes I hated them.

'How much farther to Bingen?' asked Little Fey.

'Much. Ask Clovis.'

'Now you are being spikey.'

A day later, my bleed commenced, as did Valentina's and Mea's. Little Fey was not yet in harmony with our timing. I told Clovis that we needed to stop for a few days. I had never had to confess my womanly needs to a man, but I didn't care. Modesty had left me. I was more animal than sister.

We made our camp, and I went off to collect wood for our fire. I came across a pool of watercress, and I tore bunches of it and stuffed them in my mouth. I didn't take any back to the others.

When night fell, I stared at the small fires that flared across plain and hill marking the places where other travellers had bedded down. Were there bounty hunters among them?

By day we huddled in the shelter Clovis built, watching the slow parade of travellers: a grand lady of ancient years carried in a litter by four men; embassies and messengers, their colourful flags snapping in the wind, court robes flying; nobles in litters trailed by lesser litters bearing attendants, servants, and priests; merchants who cracked the whip on weary horses lugging carts of salt, timber, and unknown wares and provisions tied up in sacking. Among this salmagundi was a contingent of self-flagellating monks. Not Benedictine, I deduced, but an unfamiliar band of religious of more severe practice. I saw no Ghibellines or bounty hunters, but then I'd only recognise them if they looked like wyverns.

Two days on, we resumed our journey.

'What is our saint today?' asked Valentina.

Gretchen shook her head. 'I am disordered. I cannot think of any saint. So, instead, I will give the vita of one who is not dead, who lives in your midst.'

We gathered close.

'Saint Gretchen was born…'

'Gretchen,' Valentina chided loudly, 'it is blasphemy to call yourself a saint.'

'It is not blasphemy,' she snapped. 'Besides, I do not care. I want to give account of my life.'

Mea's arms flew above her head in exasperation. 'What makes *you* a saint?'

Gretchen bowed her head. 'I am a saint because I have suffered.'

'Why does she get to tell her story…'

'This is not right.'

Warring again, this troublesome tribe. I searched for an oath beneath my breath, something to shock them to silence, but I knew no such language. *Mary's apron?* It barely held the heat of my anger.

'Hush,' I said. Then, remembering how Gretchen had told me that the others thought me prickly and above myself, I thought: *I'll show her.* 'You would stifle your sister when all she desires is to confide her story? Speak, Gretchen. Tell it as you wish.'

Gretchen straightened her shoulders.

'Saint Gretchen was born in Riva del Garda…'

'You said you were from Bavaria,' Valentina interrupted again.

'I did not say I was born in Bavaria; I said my mother and

her mother were from Bavaria. If you heeded my words, you would know this.' She waved her arms the way Mea had done, and continued her tale.

'Riva del Garda was a settlement of great beauty and prestige. Many noble and religious families lived there. Saint Gretchen herself did not belong to any great lineages, but her mother Gudrun did, in a fashion. She was from Bavaria, and was a dancer of exotic and tempting style. When a noble gentleman fell in love with her, he brought her and her mother—for Gudrun insisted her widowed mother named Rosa accompany her—to Riva del Garda. Sadly, the gentleman died or was killed, or was lost, I am not sure which. Nevertheless, Gudrun and her mother found themselves alone in Riva del Garda. But Gudrun was clever and quick, and soon she was dancing for many gentlemen. One day, she captured the heart of a great man. This man was torn with desire for Gudrun. He could not live without her, but he could not live with her, either, for he was a Holy man, an abbot. His name was Giovanni, and he presided over the Vallombrosians. So strict is this Order that its monks cannot leave their abbey even if their mission is one of mercy. But Abbot Giovanni could leave because he was the abbot, and he made many journeys to Riva del Garda to visit his beautiful Gudrun. The moment he arrived, they fell into one another's arms and stayed that way until he departed a few days later. In time, Gudrun grew great with his child. Giovanni continued to visit her, and soon they welcomed their baby, who they named Gretchen, which means pearl. Giovanni visited his secret family whenever he could but suddenly the visits ceased. He had been elected antipope, and had taken the name Callixtus.'

We stopped in our tracks. Even Vento turned his head to her.

'You are the child of the antipope?' said Mea.

Gretchen folded her arms. 'As I said. Are you not paying attention?'

She continued. 'Abbot Giovanni made one last visit to Gudrun to tell her that he had to live in Rome and could not see her anymore. Gudrun was broken-hearted. She promised to love him forever. But once he left, she became angry. She yearned to dance again and to enjoy the company of men. She took little Gretchen to her mother, Rosa, and asked her to look after Gretchen for a few days. Gudrun never returned.

'Rosa was good to Gretchen and loved her, but she no longer loved her daughter. Rosa said Gudrun had abandoned Gretchen and had abandoned God. She said Abbot Giovanni had done the same thing, and that pretending to be pope was no excuse for leaving a child. Gretchen did not mind. She was happy with Rosa. She did not ask for her mother, or her father. All Gretchen wanted was to make her nonna Rosa laugh so that she would forget Gudrun and Abbot Giovanni. She would sit at her nonna's feet while her nonna sewed for other people, and she would make her laugh. Nonna Rosa loved Gretchen, and Gretchen loved Nonna Rosa. One morning, Gretchen woke up beside her nonna. She played with her and laughed for her, but her nonna did not wake up. For three days little Gretchen sat on the bed hoping her nonna would wake up. In time, someone came to the house to fetch their sewing and saw the terrible sight. Unwanted by her father or her mother, unwanted by anyone in Riva del Garda —they claimed Gretchen's red hair was the mark of the Devil—Gretchen was sent to Trento. She was given to the sisters at Saint Agatha's to bring them laughter and merriment. And that is the story of Saint Gretchen.'

Gretchen sobbed. We all sobbed, even Clovis. Her hair was damp from our tears as we embraced her.

Her story clawed at something deep in me, something that I knew to be there but could not reach. But as the claws dug, it struck a kernel and from that kernel emotions flew from me like frightened birds. A truth uncovered that I had not considered: Gretchen was abandoned by her mother. Little Fey was left naked by her family on Saint Agatha's doorstep. Mea was deceived by her betrothed and denied succour by her family. My father brought me to a place I did not know to live with people I did not know and to live a life I did not know. I used to comfort myself by thinking it had been kind of him, but I no longer felt that way. All of us had been abandoned. All of us were broken. Valentina had yet to tell her story but how could it be any different from ours?

I was softer toward Gretchen, having heard her story. At Saint Agatha's, she had always twirled and made jests in serious moments. She was frequently chided by Mother Elena to control herself, and she would correct herself but never for long. She moved with an airy manner, deflecting reprimand by drawing attention to how a breeze rustled the leaves or how water tinkled when it spilled over a stone, or she would surprise us with some story about the saints. Now I saw that her manner was and had always been her mask. She had been in disguise longer than we had been aware.

This was the true nature of our origins: We were all scourged by the loss of home and family. None of us belonged to any place or to anyone. And I realised that, broken as we were, they were all I had, and I was all they had. We were all saints because we had suffered.

XVIII

The Feast of Saint Agnes
Onward to the Inn Bridge

The air turned cold. Wind cut through gullies and passes, sometimes bearing whirls of snow as if to make more wretched our journey, if that were possible. The land made great demands on me. Though I walked all day it did not seem as if I moved closer to Bingen. All around were mountains, and behind them more mountains, and behind them more still; a ceaseless stretch.

Where were we in the year? In the day? Was it Terce? Prime? Sext? I was weightless without the mooring of the Hours, existing but not belonging, lost to God and the angels. At sunrise I knew it was morning; at sunset I knew night approached, but between these points I had no tether; a horse without reins, a novice deaf to the call to prayer.

I heard a wolf howl. Beyond the trees? Beyond the mountains? I couldn't say in what direction danger was coming for me. It surrounded me. The sky filled with ravens, circling, screeching, scrounging from above as we did likewise below. I glared at them. *You will not find enough flesh on our bones to give you another day of life.*

I did not like this wild world. Its smells and sounds, its unpredictable nature and raw edges. Oh, it could be fair and pretty when the days were warm and bright, when flowers and bees danced in the meadows, but this was its seduction, for its beauty had delivered us into harsh arms. The wild world was the Devil's. Were we living in the woods or wandering in the wilderness? Frequently, my mind returned to the hedgewitch. I had considered Mathilde brave and poor, but now, compared with my present state, I thought her rich and settled while I was becoming something other, something I did not like.

My entire life had been spent in the service of perfection: the tidy tunic, the even stitch, the careful lettering, the correct words for prayer, the right note for chant, the proper manner in greeting a visitor. I thought all of life was measured in its careful, neat details, because it was the details, the minutiae of Creation, that you offered God to prove you were attentive to the small and humble, and that He would be well pleased by this.

But it was a lie. At least in this wild world it was. Learning and manners were for naught. The wilderness did not need my perfect Latin, my skill to read, my talent to illuminate parchment, or my ability to calculate upon the abacus. It did not need our pouch of jewels or clean nails. I looked at my murdered feet. I could not remember what day it was or when I had last bathed.

I wrenched my mind away from foul thinking and forced it into a fairer mood, away from my filth. I looked Heavenward and gave thanks for the vast clear blue and the warmth of its golden orb. And then a cloud wandered in, like an innocent, followed by another and another, until what had been blue a moment ago was now white like ash.

Suddenly, Heaven gave a tremendous roar and shriek; arrows of rain assailed us while claws of lightening ripped the sky into potshards. I clutched my hands and held them, like a singular fist, to my throat, and bent myself into the quickening squall.

'Over here!' Clovis's muffled call broke through the chaos.

The wind whipped his cloak over his head so that only a bare hand was visible, pointing toward a cleft that disappeared into some rocks. We six stumbled in as wind sheared across the plain, howling its rage. Clovis hunkered in the opening and held tight to Vento's rein lest the beast be blown away.

I shivered in our cramped, stony nest while the storm raged. *Where was God?* Had we been abandoned anew? My face fell into my hands. He would not be out here. The God of our cloister was not the same God who oversaw the mountains. We were under the rule of a harsher force.

What saint could Gretchen summon to lift us from this wretched state? I thought of Saint Agnes, protector of virgins, and with face buried in rough, dirty hands to hide my tears I breathed: *You who could not be saved from the vengeance of the terrible Diocletian, have mercy on us. I beg you, get us off this mountain.*

I was still hunched when morning arrived. The sun was out; the ground and the fir trees were sugared with frost. It was beautiful, like the threshold of Heaven. For a moment, I was heedless of my uncooperative bones.

We continued on until we found ourselves behind the strange group of ragged monks I had seen before. Still self-flagellating; all moan and chant in indiscernible tongue. Their habits were dusty; their cingula of sisal hung loose around their hips. Two of them scourged themselves with boughs; the other two clung to stripped branches that they used as staffs. No one dared approach them—not even the palmers—for a foulness surrounded them, which drew much comment from other travellers.

Presently, a cart pulled up alongside them. Without a word the monks climbed in.

Mea saw this and linked her arm through mine. She had been more friendly of late, but my trust in her continued to waver.

'A curious lot, are they not? If they are in Holy orders, and hold to strict asceticism, why are they in a cart?'

'Perhaps their Order makes concession for travel,' I said.

'We are pilgrims on the way to Santiago. I am a *duchessa* and you are my ladies. Why are we without transport when those monks are given it?'

Always after your comfort.

'You may be a *duchessa* but may I remind you that we are only pretending to be on a pilgrimage, and I am not your lady. Or have you forgotten that we are sisters who have fled our convent and a bounty is upon our heads?'

'I am only saying that a litter would improve our disguise.' She straightened her shoulders and sniffed the air as if to restore her lofty status.

I looked at her. Once so immaculate and fastidious in appearance, she no more resembled a *duchessa* than I resembled a butterfly.

'We have no coin for food. We have been brewing nettles for tea, eating berries and leaves that we forage, and flesh that Clovis kills. When we reach the Inn Bridge you can buy a litter with the jewels.'

She threw back her head like one deranged.

'Ah! When we get to the Inn Bridge we will have a big feast, no? And a bath. And new clothes.' She lifted her arms up to the sky as if greeting victory. There was hair in her arm hollows this time.

We walked on, and I studied her refined profile: the upward tilt of the chin, lips closed and slightly pursed, the graceful shape of her eyes, and I thought, *Murderess*. Though she no longer frightened me, I was perplexed as to why she remained with us. Each morning, I half expected her to be gone. This was not her world. And yet, in spite of the mystery she presented, I had grown fond of her.

She leaned into me in the manner of one who yearns to share a confidence, though there was no one remotely near to hear us.

'I am sure I smell like Vento.'

'Sorry to say, but you smell worse than the horse.'

Her shoulders jerked at the offence, but then she sighed, 'Alas, we all smell worse than the horse.'

I shrugged. I had stopped paying her deference long ago. My speech had grown blunt and coarse.

'When we began our journey, you had no hair under your arms. Now I see there is hair.'

'That is true. I was in the habit of removing it.'

'How?'

'Pumice stone. It was in my bundle but I lost it along the way.'

'Why remove the hair?'

'Why have it? I am not a beast. Though I am as unkempt as a goat's beard now. I could not face a looking glass.'

I patted my bundle, felt the sharp edge.

'I have one. The hedgewitch gave it to me.'

I reached in to get it, but she stopped me. 'No. It would depress me to see myself. It has been nice not to worry about how I look. Growing up, it was all that mattered: my face, my gowns, my bearing, my silence. I will worry about those things again no doubt, but for now, it is a nice freedom.'

'Why not leave it be? The hair.'

She looked at me as if it was the most obvious reason. 'Because it is unsightly. Unclean. And you know what Abbess Hildegard says of cleanliness.'

'I can't imagine the Abbess removes hair from under her arms. She doesn't write of it.'

'Well, she is free to do as she pleases. I am free to do as I please, which is the habit among fashionable women.'

This easy independence of hers. I despised it as much as I envied it. Was this the way of all women outside the cloister, or only those to whom Fortune has bestowed the birth right of fearlessness and the shield of constant comfort.

'We speak of our foulness, but look ahead,' she said. The fetid monks were bent almost double in their cart. 'Something snaggles about that group, and I mean to find out.'

At midday, when the caravan of peasants, palmers, salt merchants, and farmers stopped for rest, so did we. So did the cart of odoriferous monks. We watched them leave the cart, confer with one another. Two of them walked into the woods.

Mea grabbed Gretchen by the hand. 'Come,' and off they went after them.

By the time our rest was done, we were in the cart with the monks. Their smell was awful though it was not half as bad as that which had emanated from dead Ursula. Valentina rode with Clovis on Vento.

Gretchen's legs juddered with the excitement of twaddle. Poor Gretchen. She knew twaddle was a sin but could not help herself.

'We figured they were going to tend to their relief,' she said behind her hand. 'But when they squatted Mea sprang upon them. The monks are not men, but women! As are the other two. We bartered our silence for this ride.'

'Why are they disguised?' Little Fey squinted against the sun.

'Like us, they have fled their convent,' she whispered.

Mea patted Gretchen's knee to silence her. We were all more tolerant of Gretchen since she had told her tale. 'They will tell all once darkness comes. They are afraid to speak with so many around. In the spirit of fair exchange, I told

A Flight of Saints

them we are bound for Santiago de Compostela, and that Sister Fey was a nun'— she held up a hand to stop my protest—'I did not mention the stigmata.' What I was going to ask was whether they believed we were religious sisters. We looked as if we had never had a home.

That night, under a ghostly moon, when the night creatures began to rouse, the nun-monks crept to our fire. Close up, their skin was dark and their eyes sunken.

We laid cedar boughs across our bare legs to keep them warm but also to somewhat lessen their smell. They weren't as bad as I had thought earlier, and I assumed this to be because we smelled worse.

Clovis had caught a hare, and it hung skinned and impaled on his sword, sizzling over the embers until it was brown and crisp. He tore it in pieces and handed these to the nun-monks. They pressed together their skeletal hands and bowed their thanks. They ate gratefully but sparingly. After we had supped, we stared at the fire, divining the direction of the sparks, the shapes of the flames; willing it to offer a good portent. I divined nothing.

One of the women began to speak. Her voice was soft and low like a murmur. She gave her name as Sister Miriam and said they had travelled from the monastery of Saint Giulia in Brescia, three days' journey from Trento.

'We come from the city of Baghdad in the Caliphate of Persia. We left our Christian families to become scholars and religious in the Christian Empire. During our travels we heard of the double monastery at Brescia and directed our journey there. We were welcomed warmly by its superior,

Mother Tekla, and she urged us to enter the novitiate. She wanted to make hers a place of scholars.

'We were happy there, and completed our lessons, and were duly professed. There was urgency in her desire for us to be professed, but we excused it as Mother Tekla's enthusiasm. But once professed, she sent us to the monastery's guest house. At first, we did not mind, but soon we were working endless days and nights in its upkeep, cleaning and cooking.'

'We were given no time to pray or contemplate the Scriptures, or continue our studies,' another sister said. Her mouth quivered with anger. 'Instead, we were whipped and made to work harder. We were not allowed to leave. We were kept like slaves.'

Another sister, who looked to be the youngest, chewed ferociously on her thumb. Sister Miriam took her hand and stroked it.

'Things worsened,' Sister Miriam continued. 'We grew weak; Mother Tekla gave us less and less food and more and more work. One day, I was sent to the infirmarian to seek help for wounds that would not heal. The monk immediately saw our suffering, and vowed to help. Everyone was terrified of Mother Tekla, so what he did was an act of courage. He gave us these weeds, and we were able to walk out of our monastery without suspicion. Mother Tekla sent people to find us. For days we hid in a tunnel beneath the city that was served by an underground river. We had shelter and water. From there, we moved at night outside and took refuge in caves. By chance, we came across the same infirmarian, who was on his way to a town near Lake Garda. He hid us in his cart and moved us further away from Brescia.'

She continued to stroke the hand of the young sister. 'Our distress is great. We started out as seven, but one was eaten by a bear, and another died from her wounds while trying to save the one who was eaten. A third sister wandered into the woods and never returned.'

Sister Miriam's companions wrung their hands and stifled their anguish.

'The horror we have endured is a great sorrow,' she said. 'Though we are far away we still do not feel safe. Some of us have been sacrificed on this journey.'

Her breath was ragged; she closed her eyes. When she opened them, she turned to me and asked: 'And you? Who among you have you lost?'

Shame streaked through me, but so did pride. 'No one; we are as we set out. Aside from the knight who we met and accompanies us.'

She shook her head. 'There is no glory, no success, without sacrifice.'

'That is the Inn Bridge,' said Clovis. He pointed to a distant glow, like a sphere of gold.

'It is so close,' I said. I wished to leave immediately, but it was decided we would spend a final night on the mountain and make our descent at first light.

'Some forge ahead in the dark,' he said, 'but it is foolish. I have bid farewell to many who did not heed the wisdom to wait, only to come across their bodies, frozen or wolf-eaten, by morning.'

'I wonder what they are celebrating,' said Gretchen, eyes fixed on the Inn Bridge. 'Maybe it is the feast of Lazarus. He is honoured in these parts.'

'You have remembered your saints' days,' I said.

'I have not remembered. One of the nun-monks told me. But as we are following our scheme to honour only those of our sex, we shall call today the Feast of Saint Verena. I shall tell you of her tomorrow. I am too tired to tell it now.'

I thought of what Sister Miriam had said about there being no glory without sacrifice. Did she think her journey more worthy because of their tragedy and suffering? Was our suffering not laudable? We had walked all this way and had passed dangers as if through a cloud without losing one of us. It was a miracle. Wasn't that enough? Many times I had wanted to die as we travelled, had even wished to die to avoid the travails. With the Inn Bridge in sight, almost within reach, my hope was restored.

I did not know why, but I suddenly wished for snow. Snow softened the world, covered its sharp edges and mess, and made everything clean and bright. Snow made you forget the cruel, harsh corners of the world, made it dream-like. The cover of snow was as if Creation had been put to bed. And I wanted desperately to forget what we had endured.

Heaven heard my wish. The next morning, the pines under which we slept had formed a white roof. We stepped into the clearing. All around was a radiance of white. I stuck my finger into it to get its measure, and it nearly swallowed my hand. I scooped up the snow and ate it.

Our thin shoes were no match for the icy descent. In my impatience to rid myself of this wretched mountain I slipped and went head over feet, again and again, tumbling over rocks and uncertain depths of snow. Down, down.

'Lucia!' screamed Little Fey.

My arms flew out to grab onto branch or root and stop my hurtling body, until I flipped onto my belly, and suddenly came to a stop, face planted into the snow. I couldn't bear to look at the distance I had fallen, but when I looked up, Little Fey was sliding toward me on her backside, and then dug her heels into the snow to stop beside me. She looked at me, and laughed.

'It's not funny,' I said. 'My leg grazed against a rock.' I looked down at it and saw that it bled.

Still, Little Fey laughed. 'Your face!' She could barely get out her words for her mirth. 'You look like an old man!'

I did not know what was so funny about that. I wiped the snow from my face.

Then, righting myself, I took her hand and continued on. We limped and slid the rest of the way through swaths of forest, clung to tree trunks and stray branches to stop our fall. In some places, drifts came up to our knees. My hands were so cold I could not feel them; my feet were blocks of ice.

From time to time my eyes glanced across the broad valley toward a ribbon of green river—the Inn, Clovis had called it—to gauge our distance. When I could see neither river nor town, I knew we were no longer above them, but level with them. We had crossed the Alpes and reached the bottom.

We should have danced and laughed, showed glad hearts for our feat. It was something I never dreamed possible. But not for us the hoop and cheer; we were done in. All I wanted was hot water, food, and warm shelter.

Clovis, Valentina, and Vento rode up to us. We embraced without words.

The cart carrying the nun-monks clattered past. We bade them Godspeed, and they vanished into the twitter-light. I wondered where they were bound.

We stood in the road like those who had forgotten way and purpose, dumb with bewilderment. I could not believe we had made the crossing, had come this far, and still more road ahead.

'Can we please go? I'm cold,' said Little Fey, stamping her feet.

We limped toward the town. Sounds of revelry came toward us and soon we saw its source. Throngs of noisy merry-makers had taken to their cups with vigour. Torches blazed in the streets so that it looked more like day than night.

We were in no mood to revel, and the folk of the Inn Bridge were in no mood for us. They knocked into us, called out to us, staggered between us, an unsavoury assortment of skewed hair and dress, red faces and bleary eyes. They pushed us like a great wave, and snarled at us for the hindrance of our presence. They looked askance at our tattered clothes, ripped shoes, and loosened knotty hair. I did not care. To live close to death for so long is to forget how to behave among the living.

We staggered through the door of a taverna named the Bär, fulsome in apology for our ragged state. My eyes flickered around the room, warily assessing the other patrons who were chatting happily in a side room. I hoped the thugs that Mother Clothilde had sent were not in this town, but a part of me knew it was a vain hope.

The innkeeper of the Bär, tall and lean, like the letter I, stood importantly behind a high desk, quill in hand. Flesh swayed from the bones of his cheeks.

Clovis gave our practised ruse and said, 'We require two chambers, if you please.'

The innkeeper acknowledged Clovis's Templar insignia with reverence, but shrugged in helpless resignation.

'I am sorry, but we have none left. It is the Eve of the Feast of Bishop Lazarus, and all our chambers…'

My ears closed; my eyes roamed the entrance of the inn: Low ceiling, polished beams, walls of stone and wood. Two chairs flanked a wooden chest on which were carved small flowers that looked like the edelweiss on the great mountains. Fire crackled in the grate and warmth wreathed across the room. Cleanliness, order, stability, and beauty were here. I desired it more than anything I had ever desired. I wanted hot water to clean myself, to scrub every vestige of filth from my body, to rid myself of the foul rags that hung in tatters from my bones. My hair was matted like that of the hedgewitch. I looked at my poor sisters, their hollow gazes and faces smeared with dirty streaks where their tears had run dry. They could not spend one more night in the wilderness.

My eyes returned to the innkeeper who wished us away. Desperation filled the emptiness of my stomach. The interminable days of walking through foul and fair had hardened me, had made me wiser to the world, canny to the ways in which it favoured not the devout and needy but the wily and cunning; how those who want what they desire get it by parleying as if in a joust. I hefted the lance. This man would give us a room if I had to kill him for it.

I seized Little Fey's hand and flung it, palm up, on the innkeeper's desk. I hissed with a voice that was not my own, indeed it almost sounded like that of the Evil One.

'You deny a room for one who Christ has blessed with the mark of His wounds?'

From the corner of my eye, I saw Clovis's mouth fall. All this time, we had kept Little Fey's secret from him, not out of malice but because we didn't think to speak of it, and I for one did not want to explain it. All my lies and secrets were piling up and I couldn't bear to add another.

The innkeeper's mouth dropped as well; his eyes grew wide. He sputtered incoherently as if the Devil had his tongue. He ran his hand through his black hair.

'There are rooms above the stable but it is not our custom to give them to guests, and certainly not to ladies.'

His eyes moved momentarily from Little Fey's palm to Mea's haughty countenance.

'We would be grateful for them.' She said it with measured imperviousness.

I was not done. I regained the innkeeper's eye and kept Little Fey's palm open. 'Food, hot water. Bring them to our chambers with haste.'

I did not let my authority waver. This power, this firm spine; this was me. This is what the Isarco gorge and the

A Flight of Saints

Alpes had made. There had been change in my sisters; this was my change.

The innkeeper summoned a boy to take us to the stable. As we filed behind him, Mea leaned into me.

'Well, well, Lucia. That is not a side of you I expected. *Brava.*'

'I had a good teacher.'

We climbed the steps above the stable; Clovis led Vento to a stall and made provision for him.

The loft chambers were large and dry; the floorboards strewn with soft hay. The beds were pallets but the mattresses were stuffed with down. There was a basin for washing. It was entirely comfortable. The boy returned with an armload of wood and laid it in the grate. We would soon be warm.

My anxiety shook loose. Relief blew through me. I turned from the others and dropped my face into my hands. *Thank you, God. Thank you, Blessèd Virgin. Thank you, dear sisters.*

When our bodies were warm, when we had washed the worst from us, when we had fed on bread and cheese, we went to the church. I could not stop weeping.

XIX

The Feast of Saint Verena
The Inn Bridge

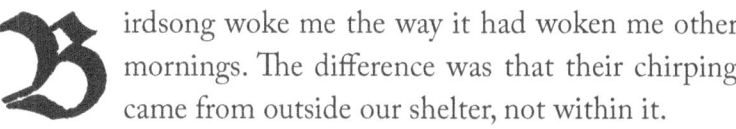irdsong woke me the way it had woken me other mornings. The difference was that their chirping came from outside our shelter, not within it.

Tears sprang onto my cheeks. Little Fey, who slept next to me, turned her face to mine.

'We are on the other side of the Alpes,' I whispered. Rivulets streamed into my mouth. I needed to say those words again and again to convince myself of what we had done, of where we were. It was difficult to believe. 'We never have to cross them again.'

'Touch wood.' She held out the cross of olive wood that hung from her neck.

I pressed my finger on it.

She did not admonish me for my abuse of her, for the violence with which I had revealed her false stigmata to the innkeeper. Instead, she took my hand, gave a gentle grip, and said: '*Ti amo per sempre.*'

We fell back to sleep.

Our second waking was not so peaceful.

'*Allora.* The cock has crowed. The hens have given up their eggs.' Mea stood above us, hands on hips. 'We must get new clothes. I cannot believe I have to put on this filthy tunic again. And we need cloaks, for the weather is turning.'

Orders. I had forgotten the sound of it.

'We have no coin,' I said. I stretched my arms and legs under the sheepskin. Sheepskin. We slept in sheepskins now.

'Clovis met another Templar. I gave him the ruby to exchange for coin. We have more than enough.'

She went into the pouch without asking?

'Where is he now?' said Valentina. She rubbed her eyes and looked around the room. 'Must we all go?'

'He bought bread after he saw the Templar,' said Mea. 'And yes, we must all go; to be measured for new tunics.'

'What about bounty hunters?'

'They are drinkers,' she said. How was she so sure? 'If they are here, they are sleeping off their indulgence.'

She would know that.

I had wondered whether our arrival in the Inn Bridge might give her cause to seek wine, but it hadn't. After attending church, she hadn't gone for a bottle, but had returned to the inn with us.

I turned to Little Fey. 'Stay in bed, *cara*. I will find a suitable tunic for you.'

She held on to my hand and whispered: 'I must speak to

you.' Her eyes blinked tears.

Mea's foot tapped on the floorboards.

'When I return, we will talk. For now, just rest.'

Outside, the streets were a-bustle. Some people appeared not to have left the drinking tables from the night gone past, but most were respectable, engaged in purpose and business that befitted a town of rising consequence.

Mea led Valentina, Gretchen, and me into the labyrinth of stalls. She dragged us from one to another. She scrutinised and dismissed many items. She perused coifs and cloaks. She examined fabric and stitching. She queried merchants. She instructed us to be measured. She purchased a tabard lined in squirrel for Clovis. Her eyes roamed stalls of leather satchels and purses. No sooner did she settle on a choice when she demurred, then agreed, then changed her mind again. We left it to her to haggle over tunics and chemises for we had no intelligence for this. Eager for her custom and coin, the merchants mustered the fortitude of Job as they countenanced her to-ing and fro-ing. Decisions finally made, purchases agreed, Valentina, Gretchen, and I breathed relief behind Mea's back.

We turned to head back to the inn when Mea said: 'Now to the cobbler.'

We looked to Heaven and beseeched God to spare us. He had spared us crossing the Alpes; He would not spare us going to market with Mea.

The cobbler's stall with its leathery aroma threw me back to my father's bench, its resins, dyes, skins, and tools. I thought of my father, but not in a kindly way. Would he care now for the brave daughter he chose to abandon?

The cobbler was amiable and solicitous but was much less so by the time Mea finished with him. Again, the wrangle of shall-we-choose-this-shall-we-choose-that, and the inevitable dance of bargaining.

By the end of the morning, we all had new chemises, coifs, and cloaks; tunics and shoes would be ready in a few days, though Mea insisted we each buy one of the already-made lesser-quality tunics to wear until the finer versions were made.

'Two tunics each, then,' said Gretchen. 'Aren't we rich.'

None of us had ever owned more than one tunic.

'There is more than sufficient coin and jewels in the pouch for the rest of our journey,' reasoned Mea. 'We can afford it.'

'I did not think the day would come when I would thank someone for thieving, but I thank you now, Valentina,' I said. 'Had you not stolen the pouch, how would we pay for this?'

'Pfft,' said Mea. 'Giacomo has more jewels than he knows what to do with. He would not miss them.'

I could not imagine having so many jewels that I would not miss the loss of some.

On the way to our lodgings through the piazza, we passed the well and overheard two women—each with a basket in one hand and a water bucket in the other—mention 'Abbess Hildegard.' I slowed my pace and loitered nearby.

'*Ja*,' said one, all breast and little trunk. 'A good and a brave woman, I daresay, but not a fair one, for she doth not welcome all God's women to her convent. My daughter yearns to join her community but the Abbess only receives those from the nobility. Doth she help the poor and disdain them also? Are poorer families not virtuous?'

'Maybe 'tis for the better,' said the other, baber-lipped and stout. 'I hear that girls who join her abbey are worked like slaves. They clean, plant, harvest, cook, and serve the older sisters, travellers, and guests. They clean the stables and hoe the garden. Barely do they have time to attend their prayers. Yet the noble sisters glide through the cloister with their white hands...'

'And gold crowns atop their veils!' interjected the first. 'Imagine, gold crowns! No wonder she has angered the pope...'

'And brought shame upon her community since the Holy Father has silenced her singing and preaching...'

'And withholds even the Sacraments from her and her sisters.'

Gold crowns? Hildegard under papal interdict? Had I brought my sisters all this way, over the perilous Alpes, only to be shunned at the Bingen door I had said would be open to us?

'Do not believe what is said in the road,' said Mea, rearranging her bags and bundles. She had heard the conversation; the others had gone on ahead. 'Hark the adage, "Man walks; rumour runs."'

'But you heard them; they said young girls do all the labour with barely time to pray. And crowns?'

'Put it from your mind. We will see these things with our own eyes and make conclusion then. Given what we have been through, will you put your trust in a couple of old women who brabble in the piazza? All will be well. I will make sure of it.'

But how? Who was she, against the power and influence of Abbess Hildegard, and even the pope? I thought of the nun-monks, and their story of toil and servitude. If what was said at the well about Bingen was true, we would find ourselves under a yoke similar to the one we had fled. How different life had been under Mother Elena, where chores were shared among all. Even she had cleaned the grates and privy.

We caught up with Valentina and Gretchen.

'I forgot to give the vita of Saint Verena yesterday,' said Gretchen. 'Shall I give it now?'

We nodded. We knew about Saint Verena but if it kept Gretchen's mind off wyverns and menfolk we could bear it. I had seen her make eyes at a few men in the market.

'Saint Verena travelled from Egypt to these parts,' she began. 'She was searching for her lover who was a soldier. But upon learning of his death, she became an anchoress. She lived in a cave and fed the sick and washed their hair. Like you have done, Valentina, with Clovis.'

Valentina gave her a stern look. Gretchen paid no heed. 'All came to admire and love Verena, and her good works planted the seed of service in young girls who yearned to follow her. The end. I would like to be like her, and have girl children who loved me so much that they desired to follow my good work.'

'So spaketh the saint,' said Mea, and rolled her eyes.

'It is good to strive for that, Gretchen,' I said. 'You have a playful soul, and children naturally favour you. Perhaps Abbess Hildegard will bestow such a duty on you.'

'I shall pray for it,' said Gretchen with quiet resolve.

At the Bär Inn, Clovis was in conversation with the innkeeper. He smiled when he saw us. He had washed and cleaned his clothes, and looked fresh and handsome. His hair shone and fell in gentle waves upon his shoulders.

My sisters returned to our chambers with our purchases; I stayed with Clovis and the innkeeper because I wanted to know how to get to Bingen.

'Good sir, how far to Bingen?'

The innkeeper did not reply, as if I had not spoken at all.

Clovis repeated my words: 'Good sir, how far to Bingen?'

The innkeeper answered him forthright, and the two conferred as if I was not present.

I set my hands on the oak ledge that separated Clovis and me from the innkeeper. A fly crept toward my fingers. I waited, and brought my hand down swiftly and loudly over the creature. The men stopped speaking, looked at me, then resumed their conversation. I was as inconsequential as the fly that buzzed in the cave of my palm.

When I had forced my voice and used Little Fey's stigmata to secure our chambers, the innkeeper had heard me. He had paid me attention. Now, I was little more than a ghost. Not accorded so much as a *'Guten Tag.'* In private, Clovis often sought my counsel. Why did he not now? My sisters and I had proven our worth: *We* escaped Saint Agatha's. *We* found our way from Trento to Botzen to Brixen. *We* shifted for ourselves, procured necessities ourselves. *We* found Clovis in peril, saved him, and returned him to robust health. On a ledger, our deeds were far from trivial. But under Clovis's care, in this world of men, our seigniorage was whittled away. We had bartered our independence for his protection and though glad of it, the arrangement had rendered us as mute as we had been under the heel of Mother Clothilde.

If someone had asked, I would have admitted that I would have wished to continue to Bingen with my sisters, as we had before we met Clovis. It was a selfish wish: I wanted my sisters to myself. And yet, the more I learned of the world the more I knew it was a fool's dream. He was necessary to us. Even with his limp, which had only marginally improved since we pulled him from the hole in the cave, we needed him. I needed him. I had no faith in my confidence or charm. Besides, how could I turn away he who had grown as dear to me as a brother; one who had fallen for Valentina? I did not begrudge them; I was happy for them, but I had grown to understand how someone's happiness could be another's regret. Their love felt like my loss. I wanted us to be as we had been when we fled Saint Agatha's, despite the fact that none of us were as we had been when we fled. Though we travelled as one, I was seeing the end of us, the loss of us.

And then I remembered that Little Fey had wanted to speak to me.

She led me to a small room above the stable rooms we occupied.

'It is more private to talk here,' she said.

She appeared anxious, and when she sat on the straw, she

leaned forward so that her face fell into her lap.

'What I have to say I can only say to you.'

'You know you can tell me anything in your heart. It will not be breathed to another.'

'My stigmata.' She held her hands out, palms up. The marks had darkened but there were no fresh wounds. 'I have not been truthful about them.'

I kept judgement off my face. She did not know that I was already wise to her deception.

'How did they come to be?' My voice rose a little; I hoped I didn't sound false.

'I made them myself. Scraped my palms with the end of a stick, a stone, whatever I could find. Tried to do it on the other side of my hands but it hurt too much.' She hung her head; her body shivered. 'I don't know why. I was young, and when people started to say it was the stigmata I didn't want to disappoint. Better to lie than disappoint. Soon enough, I myself believed it, and that it was necessary and good.'

'Your lie probably saved Saint Agatha's, but also the poor; be glad of that. The purser lied, too, about the amount that was collected so that it wouldn't all go to the bishop. You know how he and his priests would have spent it.'

She nodded.

'You had companions in your laugh. I think Mother Elena knew too.'

I didn't want to justify her fraud, so I asked, 'Why did you do it?'

'It must have begun when I was told how I came to be at Saint Agatha's. About being found at its door. Everyone,

A Flight of Saints

even Mother Elena, said it was Providence, but I saw it as shame. Shame that someone had discarded me.'

'You were a gift. We loved you.'

I knew my mouth would not bring solace. Nothing could make palatable the knowledge of being cast off by your family. I knew it myself; the ghost-ache of unspoken grief always seeking something touchable to mourn.

'I was not wanted, either,' I said. 'My father walked me up the steps of Saint Agatha's and didn't so much as bid me fare thee well.'

'That's cruel.'

We were quiet for a moment, and then she said: 'Do you think that is why we love God? That if we consecrate our life to Him, it gives us a Father, and the Virgin becomes our Mother, and the community to which we belong becomes our family?'

'If it means belonging to a family that includes Mother Clothilde it's a wonder there aren't more runaways.'

'But when it was good, when we had Mother Elena, it was the best family.'

'And yet it did not bring you comfort. You gouged your hands.'

'But it made me appear Holy to other people, and that made me greater than the mother and father who had no need of me. I was making myself better than them, more worthy, and in return I made them unworthy of me.'

Something rustled the straw. A mouse emerged, and behind her we glimpsed her nest of babes.

'Oh, precious things,' Little Fey squealed. She pressed together her hands, bent her head closer to them. When she sat up she looked chastened.

'I don't understand why I continue to do it. I am trying to stop.'

'Like Gretchen and her fingernails. You will be able to stop if you will it.'

'That is my hope. But it is a habit in me.'

'Then come to me when the thought pricks you. I will try to help. Perhaps you can keep your hands busy with something else, like the berries you string into prayer beads. I would very much like you to make one for me.'

I leaned over and embraced her. 'I love you. And I won't tell the others, but you must try and stop.'

'I will. I love you too.'

XX

The Feast of Saint Rosalia
Inn Bridge

We were two nights at the Inn Bridge. Two nights in which contented sleep found me. There were times when I jolted awake in the dark, in doubt of my surroundings, not knowing whether I was captive or free, inside or outside, but I was able to settle myself easily. Fear still lurked, but it was more stray dog than wolf.

I lay on my pallet on the third morning. Sunlight ebbed into the room and I watched the ceiling timbers lighten. I began to think about what would come after the Inn Bridge.

We were ten days from Bingen, by cart, not foot. There was no enthusiasm in any of us for more walking. Each time I broached our journey, they groaned, turned away, and feigned some great need to go to church or visit the market or sleep. Even the promise of getting a cart to take us onward was not enticement enough. They had found comfort in the stable's pallets of feathers and wool, and did not wish to give them up.

I was no different. Like them, I longed to remain wrapped in down and dream. Like them, I renewed my devotion to attending the Hours. Better on my knees than on my feet. But in church, my mind would not hold to prayer. It had been fixed too long to a state of anticipation, of starting each day in stealth and wariness and ending it in fear of being found. I could not account for my rambling thoughts, except to say that I was always fatigued, and that Bingen seemed still so far off that I was certain I would never see it except in a dream. Clovis had spouted place names yet to come—Kempten Abbey, Stuttgart, Heidelberg, Mannheim, Worms—names that sounded a world away.

Still, we had to leave the Inn Bridge. I crept from bed and into my clothes. I would surprise them with a litter and another horse. Vento couldn't alone be expected to pull all of us. It was an expense but I was certain they would approve. To travel by litter would get us on our way, save our feet, and perhaps allow us to reach Bingen before the bounty hunters caught us. What's more, I wanted my actions to make them see that, like Hildegard, I was pure action; that I was not one to dither or dally; that I could be as decisive as Mea. Maybe they would favour me more, if Gretchen's twaddle was true.

I said some words to Saint Rosalia: *Spare me but a portion of your conviction.* I reached into the pallet where I kept the pouch of jewels.

Gone!

I looked around.

So was Mea.

My stomach lurched. I grabbed a shawl and quickly slipped

from the room. At the bottom of the stable stairs, I looked down the road. *Where would a murderess go at this early hour?*

The day before, she had been friendly, laughing at us as she watched our unpractised hands roll stockings over the knobs of our knees.

'I cannot believe you have never worn hose.'

'Never,' I said.

'But in winter…?'

I hadn't forgotten the icy creep up my flanks. Mother Elena had given us blankets, but Mother Clothilde had let us grow stiff with cold and hunger. 'Never. We sat close to whatever fire was burning, and wrapped the hem of our tunics around our legs.'

To Mea, now partway restored to the lavish threads of her upbringing, the poverty of our wilderness lives was an aberration; to us, it was only moderately distant from how we had lived under Mother Clothilde.

One moment friendly, the next imperious: there were always two Meas, and neither could be trusted.

The sky was clear; the sting of snow from the mountains was in the air but thankfully not on the ground. Cocks from various parts of town erupted with their crow; brave Sun broke through the scudding clouds; a few people moved about, mostly merchants setting up their stalls. Then I saw her. Far end of the piazza, jinking around a corner. I flew after her.

My heart pounded with outrage. *I knew it. I knew she would take the jewels and leave us.* I worked up words to hurl at her; words to justify exactly what I thought of her. Murderess. Thief. Liar.

I rounded the corner. She was partway up the lane, talking to a man. Brazen as her so-called harlot cousin. The pouch was in her hands.

I hurried toward her, anger building in my mouth.

She turned. Saw me.

Waved.

She left the man and came toward me.

'I did not want to wake you,' she said excitedly before I could deliver my wrath. 'I took the pouch. I'm sorry. But I wanted to surprise you.'

Surprise?

'I wanted to buy a litter, so we could continue our journey. I know how much you long to get to Bingen. But, Lucia, I cannot continue on foot. The others, too. We are so weary and sore. But I know your desire, and I do not want you to be let down. A litter and horse will get us there faster. In days! Oh, I know you think me frivolous but…'

'No. It is fine.' My heart pounded. My mouth was dry. 'I was worried that you had gone.'

She gasped.

'You think I stole the jewels and left you?'

I tried to make my face look as though no such thought had crossed my mind. Had never entertained the idea.

I must have succeeded because she looped her arm through mine and said, 'Come. Let us return to the inn. The man I spoke to does not have a cart or horse to sell, but he is going to ask around.'

My heart still thumped violently. My mouth struggled to swallow the words that were about to pass my teeth and tried to form calmer, kinder words. 'Yes, a second horse. It is too much to expect Vento to pull us all.'

'Yes! My thoughts exactly! Oh, for a moment I thought you would chastise me.'

'Not at all.' I had become as cool a liar as she was. 'I cannot face walking, either. I was thinking of a litter, too.'

Back in our rooms, the others were in various stages of wakefulness. Little Fey was rubbing sleep from her eyes. Gretchen was washing her face. Valentina was seated in a corner, a bundle of leather strips on her lap. I hoped she had bought them. Her beloved would hardly countenance her penchant for thieving. She was braiding the strips, and I guessed she was making a belt for him. She avoided my eye.

'We must talk about leaving,' I said.

'I have asked around town and no one has seen the bounty hunters,' said Clovis. 'Still, that doesn't mean they aren't here. You won't be out of danger until we reach Bingen.'

'*We* reach Bingen?' I looked from him to Valentina.

A corner of my heart knew that Valentina would take up with him, and not join us at Bingen.

'My promise remains, to ensure your safe passage,' said Clovis.

His eyes slid toward Valentina. She lowered her head. Colour rose on her neck. She stopped braiding and set her work aside.

'I have resisted speaking of this,' she said, 'because I did not want you to think harshly of me. But I shall not join the Bingen community. I will marry Clovis.'

We rushed to them, and crowded them with embraces and blessings.

'Oh, Valentina, I knew this would happen,' I said. 'I shall miss you.' I held her close. 'But I am full of happiness for you. You have found good love.'

'You are not angry?'

'Of course not. Why would you think so?'

That my words surprised her showed that she, like Gretchen, saw in me a penchant for judgement, the arbiter of permission. As I embraced Clovis, the shame of my reputation stung. Earlier, I had misjudged Mea. Perhaps I was, as had been pointed out on our journey, guilty of swift judgement.

'How will you live?' Little Fey gazed up at Valentina with wonder.

'We have spoken only as dreamers,' Valentina laughed. 'Perhaps we shall have a bake house or offer lodgings to travellers. We will find a place to settle and let the needs of others determine what we might offer. Our only certainty is that we shall be together.'

'A wedding!' says Gretchen. She clapped her hands and danced about. 'What joy and excitement.' She stopped, tears suddenly spilling from her eyes. 'Please find work in Bingen; I cannot imagine not seeing you again.'

My eyes filled too. Clovis put his arm around my shoulder and pulled me to him.

'Do not weep, Lucia. We will be with you till Bingen. Maybe even after. Valentina does not want to desert her sisters, even in marriage.'

'Are you certain you can marry?' said Gretchen. 'Templars

are in Holy orders, so how can they breach their vows? Bernard of Clairvaux called his soldiers monks, which means you have taken vows, which means you cannot marry.'

'That is true,' said Clovis. 'As a monk I could not renounce my vows, and if I tried, I would be called a traitor, and jailed. What I have not told you is that I am a lay brother, a hired soldier bound to a term of service; still a Templar but one not under Holy orders. My service has not yet come to an end, but it will by the time I deliver you to Bingen. Although I am not yet free to marry, I will seek counsel from a priest to see if Valentina and I can be hand-fasted.'

He knelt before Valentina and clasped her hands. 'We shall marry, I promise. Your sisters are my witnesses.'

'*Allora.*' Mea stood up. She looked at me. 'Lucia. Come. We need bread. And we need to collect the tunics and shoes from the seamstress and the cobbler.'

She pulled me away from the others and out into the street toward the market stalls.

I shook away her grip. 'What's this about?'

She was surprised by the question. 'Bread. Of course. I am hungry. Plus, we need to get the clothes if we hope to leave tomorrow. Also, I want air.'

'I will not accompany you if it is your intention to shop.'

'There is nothing I need except bread.'

My doubts about Mea's honesty had been rattled by my near-harangue of her earlier, but in truth, I enjoyed her company. She had bravely weathered the same path and travails as the rest of us; unlike the others, largely without complaint. Still, I could not shake the portion of mistrust I held for her in reserve.

I linked my arm through hers. 'Have we changed, Mea? For I feel altered.'

We wandered among the stalls, picked up our garments and shoes. I tried not to be swayed by the aroma of spices and leather.

'I am definitely changed,' she said. 'In my home, I was coddled. Maids dressed me. Servants brought my food. If I went out, footmen and ladies accompanied me. Look at me now: I am holding a bag! I never would have been allowed to do that. My gait, too, has changed. I once walked serenely, like this.' She minced along the cobbles. 'But now, well, you have seen me. I clomp like a horse.'

I smiled.

'And you,' she said. 'You have changed.'

'Me?'

'Much. You are better this way. Stronger. You have the spirit of a mutineer, though it's taken you long enough to believe it. I am still impressed by how you got us rooms.'

'My vow of obedience has certainly diminished.'

'Obedience requires strength not submission. Don't confuse it with servitude.'

'I also feel angrier.'

'Good. It means you have erected a palisade around a wound to repel attack. Every day we women are wounded; every day we face an enemy; every day we are attacked. But look at us; we are warriors who have slayed the Alpes and foiled those who hunt us. We are remarkable.'

I steered her toward a stall that sold bread. I had the velvet pouch and was conscientious about not squandering its contents. There had been seven when Valentina snatched it from the rider Giacomo. There were now five, though I had been certain that I had counted only four the day before. Still, it was plenty to see us to Bingen.

Mea's scrutiny with wares proved to be the same when it came to bread. She examined each loaf, sniffed it, put it down, did the same with the next and the one next.

'To check for freshness,' she huffed in reply to my disdain.

I turned away and idly watched the folk who wandered among the stalls, admiring this, judging the weight and quality of that. I supposed this was the way for those acquainted with commerce. I still did not feel entirely comfortable in such places and yet I could be easily mesmerised by them.

As my eyes roamed the crowd, they fell on three men procuring arrows and knives. *Bounty hunters!*

I grabbed Mea's arm.

'Do not show alarm: The three from Botzen are here.'

She tossed the merchant a coin, grabbed the loaf, and we hurried away.

XXI

The Feast of Those Who Kill

Along the Inn River

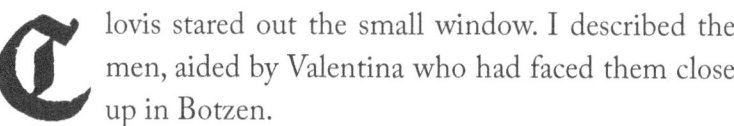lovis stared out the small window. I described the men, aided by Valentina who had faced them close up in Botzen.

My heart banged beneath my breast; my head filled with the thrumming chaos that had become a second nature. This time, the sensation was different. In the past, it was the calamity of fear that jangled me, made me breathless with terror; and now, transfigured into hate grown viscid, my blood ran cold. It frightened me. Against all I had been taught, against all the vows I had pledged, something had turned. There was no road back.

My sisters brabbled about where to hide, where next we must go, whether to separate our numbers to be less conspicuous, or improve our disguise and dress as old women; or whether to forget the road and use the river; find a boat to take us north, through Bavaria and into Germania. Scattered, frantic thinking. Since leaving Saint Agatha's our days had not held to the rhythm of the Hours but to the rhythm of running, lies, disguise, evading suspicion and capture. Was this to be our life? Was this what my prayers had led to? No. This would not continue. Patience had emptied. Wyverns and werewolves, send them to me, but these men who hunted us, I was done with them.

'No.' I cut sharply into the babble. 'We will stop running.'

'And be captured and killed?' said Gretchen.

'Do you mean to surrender?' said Little Fey. She dropped her beads.

'No. I mean that running will not end their pursuit of us. We must attack first. It is the only way. No longer the hunted, we will be the hunters.'

It was madness, and I knew it the moment the words left my mouth.

'Lucia, five sisters, and me, a lame knight? We would need to hire strength.'

'Can we use the jewels to gather more men?' said Valentina.

'Let righteous fury be our strength.'

The room fell quiet at my words. I hoped they would find their way into at least one of my sisters.

It was Mea. 'Lucia is right. We must end this our way, not theirs. I am done with being at the mercy of men. They steal our voices and our liberty; mock our wisdom. Let us be brave. Those who hunt us are not the world; they are thugs and ruffians.'

'I will stand with you,' said Clovis, but he did not look settled to it. 'I have witnessed your strength; indeed, I have been its beneficiary. If you want me to find men, I will, but if you want to do it alone, say how you aim to do it.'

Mea and Clovis were on my side. Valentina, too, because she would follow Clovis. Gretchen would agree, because she kindled the fire of defiance and recklessness. Little Fey? Would she hide among the folds of her piety?

'Killing is a sin,' she said.

'I said nothing about killing, Little Fey.'

'But won't they try to kill us?' said Gretchen.

'If they were buying knives and arrows, it means they have camped nearby,' said Clovis. 'The arrows for shooting prey, for food; the knives for skinning. After all, they seek five nuns, not five brutes. No reason to arm heavily.'

Oh, Clovis, if you knew my heart you would see that a breadth of a hair separates me from a brute.

'Mother Clothilde will want us back unharmed so she can take vengeance on us,' said Mea. 'If they threaten us, we will naturally defend ourselves. But if it comes to killing, I will kill, and if that makes me unfit for Heaven I will gladly burn in Hell.'

'These men do not know that you accompany us,' I said to Clovis. 'Can you ask in the town if anyone knows their camp?'

He reached for his cloak. When he was gone, we sat on the floor where the light was low, and spoke of matters closer to Hell than to Heaven.

Mea's finger circled in the dust as if the motion itself was a necessary prelude to divining a way to proceed. She was calm, eyes lit with the flint of one who had walked this road before, knew its contours and divots. The mind of a plotter, but also of a murderess. I decided to cast my lot with her. If she wanted to take the lead, she would get no argument from me.

I was useless as a leader. I had been able to get us out of Saint Agatha's, I had been able to shoulder the means to compose a route and a routine to practise it, but none of it had been due to skilful thinking or enterprise, simply nerve and desperation. My sisters had let me lead because there was no one else. Not until someone with more competence came along. Mea could have led—she had the bearing of a leader—but she had murdered and lied, and my sisters wouldn't countenance it, regardless of her apparent authority or her nobility. Maybe they would now, for compared to her, I was unworthy.

'We don't have to kill,' she said to the others. 'All we need do is maim them enough that injury affords us time to get far away from them.'

The others looked at me for approval.

I shook my head. 'My trust is in Mea and her plan.'

Clovis was soon back with news.

'They are not far; down the river a way, but still close to town. A man told me of their movements. They arrived the same night we did. How we have not seen them till now is a miracle.'

We figured them to be heavy drinkers, even the bishop's man. Especially the bishop's man. I knew the kind: oleaginous and pious with his master or when it suited; harsh and demanding at the gaming tables and brothels. His two companions were there for brawn, to keep clean their superior's hands and plush cloak.

And then Clovis surprised with words I did not expect: 'Should we consider reasoning with the men?'

I expected such limp talk from Little Fey, not from him. Not from a warrior. Love had made him soft as melted butter. I had more fire in me than this knight who had fought in the Crusades.

'What method of reasoning had you considered, my love?' asked Valentina. Even she could see the frailty of his approach.

'No.' Mea shut down further discussion. Her indignation flared. 'Men of ill repute do not reason except for money, and one bribe would only make them hungry for another.'

'I agree,' said Gretchen. 'We go straight to injury and bypass reason.'

Little Fey cleared her throat, which she did when she had lots to say. I thought, *Here she comes, brandishing her moral energy to change our minds. Well, let her make her sermon.* I shifted my legs to a more comfortable position, prepared for her pious words, prayers, and possibly an adage or two from some Testament prophet.

'Clovis, it is right to want to reason with our adversaries, but how receptive will these men be? We are young and fair, untried in battle. They can easily overpower us, bargain or not. Maybe the sight of us aiming to attack them will rattle their senses, make them laugh at our show of puny strength. But they do not know our strength, and they do not know that you, Clovis, are with us. They will think us easy prey. I say we use the trick of surprise, then beat them; as Gretchen says, go for injury over reason.'

I hadn't expected that, nor had the others.

'What do you propose?'

'That we sneak up and clobber them with sticks.'

I could feel the room smile; winced lips holding back the mirth that was yearning to burst from them but restrained for propriety's sake by their mistresses. My own lips stayed steady and sober, but my mind couldn't stop its chortle. She might be pious, but she was thick as a beam when it came to strategy.

Yet, as soon as my mind ceased its ridicule, it pondered anew the simplicity of her words until they struck me as rather brilliant. For here was the thing: No one expected shrewd thinking from us, let alone strength. The hunters had already formed their opinion of us just as Mother Clothilde had not expected her starved novices to mount an escape. We had fled and run and climbed mountains, and we had survived thus far. Surely six of us had enough wit to overpower three drunk men (for an inner feeling convinced me that they would be drunk). The more I thought of it, the more plausible it became.

Once I explained this, the others saw the sense of it. And so, we plotted: We would steal to their camp, sneak up on the inebriated foe, clobber them with wooden spears and iron rods, bind them, and drag their senseless bodies to a waiting barge, where Clovis would purchase passage for them and send them sailing west on the Inn River.

Well, that was the plan.

The bounty hunters' camp was a scrappy affair. Not that I had envisioned it much better, but given that a bishop's man was part of the group I figured a tent would at least be erected. Instead, we found a clearing littered with torn blankets, leather satchels, a small axe, and two rabbit pelts. A spit was set over the fire pit, anchored by a trestle of chopped tree limbs. There was nothing on the spit, but it appeared they had supped that day on rabbit based on the two discarded carcasses that rested at my feet where I now crouched behind a tree.

We had taken our places in a half-moon formation around the perimeter of the camp, armed with rocks, long sticks, whatever came to hand. I had found part of a spear, halfway eaten by rust; my other hand held a rock in case the spear failed me.

The toll for Vespers rang out; a breeze ruffled the air. The twisting, silvery undersides of the leaves augured a storm. Darkening clouds pushed against one another. Downriver, a barge bounced against the shore. Clovis had already talked to its owner.

The bounty hunters were in a taverna not far away. Their boastful carousing carried easily to us. I hoped they would drink well so that we could make light work of them.

As light dimmed, my senses pricked. My heart did not thump as it had previous times; it was cold and steady. There was little room for fear or blunder.

Little Fey was beside me; her pale hands clenched a chunk of root like a club.

'I was proud of how you came up with the plan, Little Fey,' I whispered.

A Flight of Saints

She did not acknowledge me with thanks, but said: 'I have asked you before to stop calling me Little Fey but you do not heed me. I'm not a child. Next time...'

Something stirred. The crunch of leaves. My tongue swept along my dry lips. I tightened my hold of the spear. A shadowy form crept through the woods on the other side of the camp, and ambled into the clearing.

Canis lupus.

A she-wolf, teats visible on a gaunt frame of grey fur. She pawed the ground around the fire pit, nosed the pelts and satchels.

I felt damp on my back; my body trembled, but at the same time I was moved by sympathy. I had not forgotten the weakness, the madness that hunger arouses, when reason flees. And she, with babes to feed.

The wolf sniffed the air. She looked around, and walked toward where I stood with Little Fey.

I didn't know what to do. To move would startle the beast and cause it to attack. To do nothing would mark me as easy prey. Either way, there was no good outcome. I did the only thing I knew: *Pater noster, qui es in caelis...*

My head was bowed, so was Little Fey's. My eyes slid toward the wolf and watched. She came close; her musk was leaves and rain. She lifted her head. The pale, impassive eyes. Did she sense a foe or a wild thing?

...fiat voluntas tua, sicut in caelo et in terra...

She bent her head, took the carcasses in her mouth, and rambled into the clearing.

Suddenly, a charge and shouts. I had been so captivated

by the wolf I had forgotten the bounty hunters. They had seen the she-wolf, and rushed to attack, knives raised. She dropped the food and lunged at them.

I leaped from the bushes into the fray with my spear and my rage. I did not care about myself, only about saving the she-wolf. I ran into one of the thugs and thrust my spear hard at him to shove him away from the beauty. Fur brushed my leg as she rose on hinds and bared her teeth while I hammered the spear with a frantic energy until blood flew back at me and the thug fell.

I spun round.

The she-wolf was gone; so were the rabbit carcasses.

Valentina and Clovis wrestled one of the other thugs to the ground while Little Fey—*Little Fey!*—swung her club at his head to knock him out.

Mea was pounding the bishop's man with a rock where an ugly wound had already bloomed. Gretchen's stick took aim at his knees. *Thwack!* He fell with a cry, and Mea continued to beat him violently until Gretchen pulled her away.

We panted over our prey, and surveyed the wreckage of victory. It had been quick, feral, and so utterly removed from our original plan that I scarce remembered the initial arrangement. *Seek to reason with them.* Was that it? Or was it *Clobber them senseless?*

I knelt beside the thug I had felled. I thought I had struck him with the blunt end of my spear, but the gashes refuted that. I shook him, to bring life back to him, until Valentina pulled me away: 'There is no use in it. He is gone.'

I ran into the bushes. My bowels emptied and piss gushed

out. My legs juddered; I breathed through my teeth, half mad, half ashamed.

'Quick, get these two to the barge,' called Clovis.

We dragged the men through the scrub toward the waiting barge. I looked back and saw Clovis and Little Fey roll the dead man to the river's edge, and heard the splash.

We hid in the trees while Clovis whistled for the boatman. They bound the battered men, and heaved them onto the deck. The business done, Clovis handed the boatman a purse, and they shook hands.

Returning to the clearing, the others collapsed on the ground; I stumbled to the river's edge to wash the blood and shit from me. I had killed a man. I was a murderess. There was his body in a tangle of reeds.

A band of townsfolk, made visible by their torches, came down the hill toward us, about fifteen in number, mostly men but also women. The men carried implements of wood and iron; one had a threshing flail. Metal glinted from the belts of a few of them.

'We heard a brawl,' said one, 'and have come to give assistance.'

'They tried to harm us,' said Mea, quickest with the lie. 'We were obliged to defend ourselves.'

'Are you hurt?' asked a woman, but she had already seen our blood-smeared faces and wounds. She beckoned two women, who immediately laid out their bundles of tonics, unguents, salves, charms, and linens. 'Come, let us do you up. Leave the men to sort out the violence.'

The men walked away with Clovis. We sat with the women on the ground. I felt like I had been in a dream. I wondered where the she-wolf was.

'I am Uta, a healer, and these are my daughters.'

They went about their work with skill and care.

'They were a sordid lot,' said Uta. She daubed unguent on a wound I didn't know I had. 'When we heard a howl, we hoped wolves had got those men, or at least chased them off.'

'You knew the men?' asked Little Fey.

'They have been skulking for days in our town. No one knew their business, but we could tell it was not of a pleasant nature. Had you killed them, we would have thanked you.'

The sky was now dark as death, save for the flicker of torchlight. I did not feel myself, and I wanted to ask the healers if they had something for it.

But one of the women who was wrapping linen around Little Fey's arm looked at me and surmised my state. 'You have suffered a shock. It will take your mind longer to heal from it than your body.'

We left the Inn Bridge before dawn had splayed her hand across the land.

I walked as if in a dream as the truth of what I had done seeped into my bones. I had not meant to kill the bounty hunter. Though I had spoken of violence while we made our plan, I had not believed such carnage would occur, not by us. My intent was to maim another in self-defence, not to bring the greatest sin upon myself. And yet, how easy it was to kill.

It hadn't taken more than an old weapon and the advantage of surprise. It amazed me there was not more murder in the world.

Murder. *I am a murderess.* I glanced at Mea. I had been impressed by the armour of self-possession she wore so lightly, and the air of self-righteousness she bore without apology. Hadn't I tried to emulate her, adopt her confidence, embrace her passion? I saw the danger of coveting an attribute of another, donning it as if it was a pretty new cloak without knowing what hid in the lining, or lurked up a sleeve, ready to slip unnoticed into your innocent soul. In desiring parts of her, I had caught her infection of revenge, and it had metastasised into a frenzied stain that now radiated like fire through me. I tasted the ash of shame and regret.

My sisters and Clovis urged me to banish my guilt, saying it was a necessary consequence. Even Little Fey refused my plea of forgiveness. If she was so changed, if she could brush off murder, then God help us.

XXII

The Feast of Saint Agatha
Toward Hirsau Abbey

On the road out of the Inn Bridge, we met a farmer who sold us his litter and horse. I felt the price high given that the horse looked worn by years of heavy work, and the litter was about as mean and dirty as one could be, but I said nothing. I handed the pouch to Mea and let her do the business.

'We will call her Apfel,' said Gretchen, stroking the horse's soft, sad face. She felt it necessary to name animals.

My head was not set to the demands of commerce or beasts. I had killed, and I saw only doom ahead. All I could think was, *I have murdered, and yet I am on my way to a convent to present myself as a worthy handmaiden of God.* How did Mea reconcile this? I wished to ask her, but at the same time I wished to distance myself from her and from whatever other pollutions she possessed that could latch on to me.

We clambered into the litter. How swift we moved; how

A Flight of Saints

different it was, like being taken to your execution.

Too soon, however, I learned that speed was not kin to comfort. By midday, the rocking motion that had soothed when we first set off had rattled my bones. We stopped to gather straw and fern fronds to pad the litter's floor; we stuffed our bundles with grass and sat on them, but it was little improvement. I could not think or doze. Gretchen began to tell us about Eugenia the Virgin when the wheel of the litter hit a deep rut and the jolt sent her teeth into her lips.

Valentina sat upfront with Clovis, her hand on his arm as much to steady her against the jerky ride as to make plain her standing as one who was to be hand-fasted. Her body swayed with the movement of the cart, and my mind moved to her and Clovis in the marriage bed. I pushed it from my mind: Like murder, it was an act I could not think about. She had yet to tell how she had come to be at Saint Agatha's, but what did it matter now? We were all so changed by what we had done the previous day that we no longer knew who we were. Our stories had been rewritten.

I barely took in the settlements through which we passed. When we had travelled on foot, we had relied on overheard conversations, keening to words of possible dangers ahead; we had hidden in lanes, and stolen food. Now we rolled through settlements without speaking to anyone or picking up chatter. We kept a wary eye out for Guelphs and Ghibellines, for we had heard that they fought in Bavaria as fiercely as they battled elsewhere in Barbarossa's kingdom. Everyone could be an enemy. As for bounty hunters, we could no longer depend on news or rumour unless we stopped and asked, which risked betraying ourselves.

We lodged that night at the abbey in Kempten. The day after, we crossed from Bavaria into Swabia, and bedded down outside Ulm in a rough hostelry beside the Danube River.

From Ulm to Stuttgart, and after to Hirsau Abbey, a monastery of shameful prosperity and decadence. Monks in double worsted; the abbot swathed in brocade. Rude, too. They treated us as lepers, and refused to let us join them in prayer or hear our confessions.

'Shall I?' Little Fey turned her scarred palms to me. 'It might move them to kinder treatment.'

'No,' I said. 'They would find a way to exploit you or turn us over to our enemies. These are not Benedictines. Besides, are you not letting your hands heal?'

'They are not healing as fast as I hoped, and I am prone to picking at the scabs.'

I could not chide her. Given what we had been through I, too, had begun to fidget. I tried to set my anxious mind on Bingen, to recommit to it like a faith lost and found by imagining its shapes and order, its smells of lavender and wild thyme, the sweetness of its conviviality (of which Father Volmar had spoken), but my mind kept leaping back to my sins.

In early light, we set off for Speyer. The morning was a fine one, and warm sun soothed my troubled soul. Other than a woman collecting eggs from her flock, no one was about. We clattered down the lane, pale fields and hills spread before us. All was peaceful. If not for the discomfort of the litter and my battle wounds, I might have fully relaxed.

Gretchen was about to give the vita of Saint Agatha when suddenly the thick bushes that lined the lane split apart, and our litter was overtaken by men. Two this time.

One was a giant and he jumped on Clovis and raised a knife.

Valentina screamed. She pulled the stiletto from her pocket and sunk it into the attacker's neck. The man flung around and struck Valentina with such force that she was thrown clear of the litter. Clovis was on him in an instant.

We fought with fists and feet.

Little Fey held up her palms to the face of one of the brutes—I suppose she thought her barely healed hands would give her power—but her assailant recoiled only momentarily before smiling and calling to his accomplice:

'You were right. These are the fugitives; I have the one with the stigmata. We are in for fat reward!'

'You are stupider than you look,' I sneered, and beat his face and pulled his hair.

Then darkness. A sack went over my head. My hands were bound so tight it burned my wrists. I struggled and snarled, and then something hard hit my head.

I awoke with a throbbing head. The hessian scratched my face and smelled of dead chickens. I could tell that I was on the ground, that there was straw beneath my legs, that I was propped against a wall. My hands were still bound. I tasted blood at the corner of my mouth. I sniffed the close air of my sack. Above the odour of dead chickens came the smell of aged wood. There was also another faint, peculiarly pleasant smell that I couldn't name.

Through the sack weave I could make out shapes that I hoped were my sisters. Someone groaned beside me. I turned toward it and made out legs—a man's—but not Clovis's. My belly lurched. *Did they kill him?*

Dread ate at me. Who was alive? Who was dead?

Abruptly, the hessian was yanked from my head.

Gretchen and Mea, faces bruised from one battle and newly marred from this one, held their fingers to their lips.

I gauged my surroundings: A small barn in a state of neglect; broken implements scattered about. Beside me, a man, thin, his clothes torn almost to nakedness. Wounds wept on his gaunt face. And yet I recognised him.

Guillaume?

I spoke with my eyes and breath to Gretchen and Mea. Yes, they inferred as they untied my hands, it appeared to be the young perfumer. He flinched at my touch, and when he turned his head, his eyes showed terror.

'Guillaume, it is I, Lucia. We met on the path between Brixen and Botzen. You shared your food with us.'

He nodded quickly, but his jaw quivered. I was not certain he truly remembered.

'Why are you here? You were going to Provence.'

'Don't talk,' said Mea. 'Guillaume, can you stand?'

His head bobbed timidly.

Little Fey and Valentina were still bound and hooded. Clovis was nowhere in sight.

'They are drinking outside,' said Mea. Her dark eyes relayed something that could not be said aloud. I understood. Once again, to the Devil with my faith and its Commandments.

'Here's what we must do,' I said. I might not have been swift when it came to directions without a map, but I could muster a plan for murder before you could recite the *Pater Noster*.

Gretchen crawled to Little Fey and Valentina, and whispered instruction while she untied them. I heard Valentina weep beneath her hessian as she gave Gretchen the flint from her pocket. I put my finger to my mouth as a signal to Gretchen to quiet Valentina.

The men were outside, lazy and loud. That is one thing I could rely on with men: their penchant for ale and boast. *Keep drinking.*

Gretchen, Mea, and I returned to our places, put the sacks over our heads and our hands behind our backs. And then we waited. Every so often, one of the men staggered in to check on us before returning to his cups. We waited some more.

I did not let Fear take hold of me. I refused its comforting hand. There had been times when I had been truly frightened on our long trek, when my familiarity with Fear had made it more friend than foe because I knew my sisters were frightened too. But I was done with Fear, just as Mea was done with men. If my heart renewed its acquaintance with Fear, it would slip into me so easily that the sinews that held my very bones together would melt like candle wax. I would be of no use to my sisters or to myself. But now, oh now, I felt invincible, inviolable. I was no knight; I was a warrior.

My soul was fiery, vicious. Moor or mountain, send them to me! I breathed through my teeth. Like an animal. When I sensed Fear slither toward me, I flung it off; sent its writhing tentacles to tangle with the fibres of the sacking. When the moment came to tear it off, I would be reborn to violence. I would be pure action.

It was well past midday when Mea nudged my leg.

For that which they are about to receive, O Lord, be merciful to us.

I lifted the sacking, nodded to Guillaume, who shivered like a newborn beside me. I crawled to the middle of the barn, struck the flint. It wouldn't ignite. I tried again. Nothing. I prayed to Saint Agatha, namesake of my former home, the one summoned by those facing fire. Nothing. I reached into my pocket for the shard of looking glass I had been given by the hedgewitch Mathilde. A sharp band of sun had found its way into the barn and I used the glass to catch it. It brought the straw to flame, and I heaped on more straw and bits of wood, anything to help it along. Two long stripped tree branches leaned against the wall near the entrance. I pushed some of the fiery chaff toward them. It smouldered and puffed. *Come on.* When it finally flared, I scurried back to my place and let the room fill with smoke. Sack on, hands behind my back. One by one we sputtered until we were at full gasp and hack. I heard one of the men get up from the table. Through the weave I saw the giant enter and cry out: 'What's this? Fire!'

The other oaf stumbled to join him.

'Never mind the fire,' said the smaller one. 'Get the fugitives. There is no reward if we return charred nuns.'

They seized those closest to the door—Little Fey and Valentina, as we predicted—and dragged them outside. They rushed back in for us. We were ready.

We threw off our hoods and leapt to our feet. Gretchen had a log; Mea had the stiletto with the giant's dried blood still on it. I found a long nail on the floor, and along with the hedgewitch's shard of silvered glass, these would have to serve me.

They were strong, these men; accustomed to the dodge and thrust of combat. My mind returned to the camp beside the Inn River, and to the she-wolf, and I let my wrath rise. One of the men tripped me and the nail cut my hand. I scrambled to my feet.

The idea of killing was easy in me now; it was the doing of it that wasn't. My first stab was weak in thrust and poor in aim. But on the second, my weapon found its target and slid into shoulder flesh as easily as knife into a ripe plum. It was not enough to fell him. He smiled with the assurance of one who knows he will survive—a scratch is all, he might say—and win. But he was drunk, and I was not.

Taking the shard from my pocket, I jabbed it into his knee. As he bent, I sent the nail first into the crease where forearm meets upper arm; and next into his neck. His thick arms flailed at me but being smaller and quicker, I pulled the nail across his throat, dodging the red spray, something learned from the last outing. I had felt remorse at killing the thug at the Inn Bridge, but this time I gave no thought to mercy.

Flames licked the rafters of the barn. Guillaume, unsteady

on his feet, grabbed the end of a pole and jabbed at the giant, who continued to tangle with me, and drove him backward until the ogre staggered in his bloody, drunken state into smoke and flame. I grabbed the pole from Guillaume and pressed it hard into the giant's chest to keep him down, and let the flames do the rest.

Little Fey and Valentina had re-entered the burning barn with flame-tipped sticks, and ran them into the back of the oaf who was straddling Gretchen and choking her, while Mea tore at his hair. His one arm spun round and grabbed her leg, slamming her onto the floor. He was stocky but nimble.

I grabbed a flail from the wall and whipped him until Mea, wobbly on her knees, drove the stiletto under his arm and into his heart. He fell on Gretchen. Valentina, whose fury had given her the strength of an ox, lifted him and threw him into the flames.

By now, the barn was fully aflame. We helped Guillaume, who limped on feet that had, he would later tell us, been beaten by the thugs to prevent his escape.

There was a small gathering of folk outside the barn.

'Some clothes and food for our friend,' I gasped as they approached us.

A couple led us to their home. They fetched water and cloths.

We daubed our wounds while Valentina wailed into her hands.

I explained her sorrow to our hosts.

The woman's husband said, 'I drove through those parts this afternoon and saw no one. Someone has moved your friend. Or he got up under his own will and found safety.'

A Flight of Saints

He looked sadly on Valentina.

'I will rally some men,' he said. 'We will search for him as long as there is light.'

He went outside and called to the menfolk in his language.

The wife laid blankets and sheepskin on the floor for us. We had no words. I could only think of Clovis, whether he would be found; and if he wasn't alive, how our journey to Bingen could continue without him.

Darkness descended. The fire in the hearth lit the room. I could no longer see my damage, but I could see the flicker-light of flames that continued to burn the barn, and hear the villagers who tried to douse them.

Another commotion erupted outside. Voices called: '*Wir haben ihn gefunden.*'

The door opened, and the husband came in with a bloodied, battered Clovis.

Wounds forgotten, we staggered to our feet and ran to him. Valentina sobbed louder.

With the couple's help, we bandaged Clovis's midsection where he had been stabbed.

Valentina tended him with cloth and water. 'All I seem to do is clean your wounds, my love,' she chided through tears. 'You must take better care.'

'We are a small village,' said the wife as she embraced each of us the next morning. 'If someone asks, we will say those men had much to drink and set fire to the barn themselves and burned to death. It is all anyone needs to know.'

Vento and Apfel were found unhurt, and our already-ragged litter no worse for wear.

We rode off toward Speyer. There was no confidence in any of us. How many more bounty hunters were there? We were numb to all of life, dazed by fighting and killing. We were raised in a convent amid roses and orderly routine. Our only foe had been the Devil. Now everything was the enemy. Each line of bushes, each rise in the road, each corner we approached; nothing was safe.

XXIII

The Feast of Eugenia the Virgin

Toward Speyer

We were all murderesses, even Little Fey. Murderesses on our way to an abbey to present ourselves as sisters of Christ.

As the litter clattered over dry, lumpy earth, each jolt delivered a surge of pain. Arms, faces, legs showed both fire and fight. Mea's hair was singed, and a bubbled swath of skin ran up one side of her leg. Valentina, who drove the litter so that Clovis could rest in the back with us, had a frightening patch of purple, blue, and yellow on one side of her face where she had been struck. One of Gretchen's hands was burned. The woman who had tended us had treated it with a salve of garlic, honey, and milk, and wrapped it in linen. Little Fey had not been spared. Like Mea, her yellow hair was singed, and there was no hope of anyone detecting her stigmata because both palms bore burns and welts. Worse, her normally sunny face shocked me with its glower of hate. She looked much older than her years.

My own hands were raw and cut; a gash ran along the top of my arm, and there were marks of harm on my arms, legs, as well as on my face, but I did not think them as bad as what my sisters had received. I had checked my face in the glass shard and found myself staring back at eyes that were black and hard.

Clovis, propped against the side of the litter, tried not to let his injuries worry us but we knew that the jostle and jump of our transport exacerbated the pain.

'I have had the knife before,' he said. 'In Constantinople, and again in the Holy Land.' We had noticed the ropey scars on his chest the day we rescued him in the cave. 'There is nothing for it but rest. I will recover.'

Well, we have had the knife, too, and have fought with our bare hands, but whereas you have been trained for battle, we have been trained only for peace, and look at us now.

Our tunics, so newly made, were tattered but we had our cloaks, which had been spared having been stowed in a trunk in the litter that the bounty hunters had not inspected. I wore mine as much to conceal my wounds as to hide from the world's gaze. The shiver of horror had yet to run out of me. I never believed murder was in me, but then, who does until their breath is challenged?

Back in our shrouds of silence, grim-faced, alert to the next attack, we held the crude sacred trappings of our new faith: Rocks and thick sticks, the stiletto, and I thanked God for them. Each time a litter or a rider approached, we clutched

A Flight of Saints

them anew, braced for attack, and kept eyes on them until they were out of sight.

On we went, up stony hills, through valleys of trees whose green leaves had dulled to yellow. We stopped when needed, for water, for relief, and to give Vento and Apfel a rest, and continued resolutely on our way. Life and towns went past in a slurry of haste.

Guillaume was with us, face constantly buried in his hands. His poor feet had been rubbed with the same salve used on Gretchen's wounds, and were bandaged.

There had been no time to speak to him until now about how he came to be captured by the brutes. I put a hand on his back, stroked it.

'After I saw you that day, I walked toward Botzen, as you had directed,' he said. 'The men accosted me in the road.'

'But they were not the same bounty hunters we had seen earlier.'

'The three we saw that day had gone on to Brixen. There are many looking for you.'

'Why did they seize you?'

'When they saw me on the road they asked if I had seen five nuns. I remembered that one of you had said you were sisters. I had not understood at the time, but suddenly I did. They took my prevarication as proof that I had parleyed with you. When they learned I was from Provence, they bound and dragged me everywhere, claiming me as their prisoner. They intended to use me against you, as one uses a small fish to catch a bigger fish.'

I was going to mention the forest he had warned us about,

the one that had taken us to the hedgewitch, but it seemed so long in the past that I felt it unnecessary to bother him with it. Gretchen would have been only too keen to wax lyrical about the details of that gruesome misadventure and I couldn't bear to hear it.

'When we reach Speyer, we will buy you transport to Provence,' said Clovis. 'The Rhein will take you as far as Chur, and from there, a litter to Nice or Cimiez, and then you will be almost home.'

'And there I shall remain,' said Guillaume. 'Never will I wish for distant lands again.'

He looked at me. 'I owe my life to you.'

There was that. We had saved Guillaume. We had saved Clovis. And we had saved the she-wolf. But we had also murdered three. How does that weigh on God's scales?

XXIV

The Feast of The Innocents

Speyer

The Rhein was broad and blue, thick with boats and rafts laden with timber, grain, and shouting men. We followed its wide curve to a stone bridge that crossed to Speyer.

It looked a prosperous town with many tall towers, but its dark gates stirred unease in me. I prepared to suggest we continue on to a smaller town, but I knew my sisters would protest. Their bodies, sore with their wounds, wanted the comfort of lodgings and to be done with the litter for the day.

We went over the bridge, rode up to the main gate, and joined the long procession waiting to be admitted into the town.

'Guillaume,' said Clovis. He pointed to the river. 'There is a boat that bears your country's flag. Let's see if it will give you passage home.'

We bid our hurried fare-thee-wells and embraced Guillaume.

It was so hasty a farewell I barely took stock of it happening. I couldn't have imagined when we met him near our journey's beginning, that he would become part of its miserable ending. His awful tribulations and suffering vied with our own. I didn't know whether to be glad to have met him or sad that his association with us had brought him such trouble. But he was on his way home and I was happy for him.

Clovis and Guillaume, both wounded, helped one another to the wharf to speak to the boat's captain.

My attention turned to the busyness on the wharf. Cogs and small galleys bobbed as their contents were unloaded. Crate after crate was taken off boats and loaded onto other boats, or into litters, or onto tanned, damp shoulders. White gulls strutted proprietarily on pink legs and screeched their opprobrium while merchants, sailors, and men-at-arms shouted orders, chatted with one another, or paused to stretch their backs and stare at us. Valentina flung on her cloak to conceal her sex and her wounds while she held the reins.

I became aware that one of the shoremen had moved closer to our cart. My hand tightened around the stick in my hand. His hair was so black it shone blue. A sleeveless tunic, dirty and torn, revealed arms that were thick and bulging. His hands were large, raw. A scar on his cheek ran almost to his eye. I felt no sympathy.

He saw me watching him, and stopped his work. His hooded eyes regarded me shyly.

'*Buona sera, ragazza.*' He bowed. '*Come sta?*'

It was a surprise to hear my language spoken. I was softened by the comfort of its familiarity, and wanted to return the greeting, but I stiffened and turned my head. *Trust no one.*

Clovis was back from the wharf. We saw the boat's sails lift and billow like the letter D. Guillaume, on board, waved to us, and soon both the ship and our friend were gone. Our tribe felt suddenly empty without Guillaume.

With a jolt, our litter passed through the gates of Speyer. Upon the recommendation of a merchant, we headed for the Ziege Inn.

It was a clean and comfortable hostelry. I was glad to be off the road, out of the gaze of others, where I could be myself, wash my wounds, and wash the earth and its stains from my ragged tunic.

I was tired of travel in all its forms. I longed to bed down for more than a night in one place; to be safe and unmolested behind cloistered walls; to return to the simple pace of life. We were nearer to Bingen though, and the ordeal would soon be behind me.

In the evening, we sat at a table by the fire in the inn's main room and waited for supper. Murder had made me hungry.

We had mentioned Santiago de Compostela so often I had almost convinced myself that it was our true destination. The lie slipped easily off our lips. We told it to the innkeeper, who believed us, though it would not have surprised me if he hadn't. Judging by the state of us, we looked unlikely to make it out of Speyer, let alone Germania, alive. But he was nonetheless convivial, and told us he himself had not long returned from the same pilgrimage.

A goose was brought to our table with carrots and cabbage, along with ale and wine. We ate well.

After supper, Valentina and Clovis excused themselves, and we bade them goodnight.

'*Allora*, we shall not talk about yesterday or the day before that,' Mea said. None of us had an appetite for slaughter. 'They were brutes. It is done. Let us rinse ourselves of remorse and guilt, and celebrate our victory.'

She closed her eyes, and her hand made a sweeping motion over her face. 'There,' she smiled. 'Much better.' As if that was all it took to absolve and forget.

She leaned across the table. 'Now, Clovis. Is he not a fine man? And a handsome one. I am glad he will wed Valentina. They will care for one another.'

She was much in her cups. Having filled her tankard three times during the meal, she was now drinking wine. 'Not all men are bad. But marriage is not for me. Look at us. Free as the birds. If we married, we would be washing, birthing, cooking, cleaning, caring, mending.'

'We did all that at Saint Agatha's,' said Gretchen.

'Except for the birthing,' I said.

'Or the coupling,' giggled Gretchen. Little Fey looked away.

'Maybe, at this moment, Clovis and Valentina are making a baby,' Mea sniggered.

I glared. She was as bad as Gretchen. I changed the subject.

'I cannot believe we have come all this way on our own. To be so near the end of it.'

'Clovis says we will be in Bingen in three days,' said Little Fey. Her smile was bright for a change. Bless her. She had helped kill men and yet there she was, as clean and innocent as the Jesus babe.

'There were times I worried you would not be strong enough for it,' I said. 'It has been a wretched journey.'

'I am surprised myself,' she said. 'But the further we went the stronger I grew.'

Gretchen turned to Mea, who was unsteadily refilling her goblet. The ruby liquid splashed from the bottle onto the table. It reminded me of blood.

'Since you are already professed, will you need to renew your vows at Bingen?'

'What silliness!' Mea slurred. She threw back her goblet. 'Me? A nun?'

'But you are a nun.' I put down my cup. Her manner and words were not like her.

She laughed and called for more wine. 'Not for long.'

'When did you decide?'

'Long before we left Saint Agatha's.'

'You took the veil for convenience?'

'Would you not have done likewise?' She leaned toward me, prepared to challenge any disagreement. 'I bought the veil to save my life.'

I felt betrayed. Confused, too. Had there been any faith in her? She had bribed Mother Clothilde into professing her, but she had never mentioned during our time together of casting aside her vows.

'Oh, I did once think of marrying the Church, but I am not one for rules and restraints. Besides, the Church hates women, especially women who forge an independent path.'

'How can you say that?' I said, 'What of Hildegard, and the Virgin, and Eve in the Garden?'

'Ha, Eve in the Garden.' She smirked. 'Such a story. Why do men accept it? It makes a mockery of them. Adam wasn't bewitched by Eve. It was he who seduced Eve. He didn't protect her; he lured her with his ignorance and false concern.'

'And the serpent?'

She stabbed the table. 'Don't you see? Adam was the serpent!'

What warped theology was this? In a different place I could argue with her, but I was tired and so was my faith.

So tired, in fact, that I had begun to consider the type of life that Mea desired, or that Mathilde lived. I, who had murdered, could take one of the jewels and that would see me through. I had played the notion back and forth, but each time felt like an evasion of my calling. I wanted the comfort of the cloister, its companionship and protection; to be among prayerful people. And I also wanted to be free. And then there was this stain of murder. Perhaps I was better suited to live alone.

I didn't have the will to fight with Mea; I wanted to love her despite my mistrust of her. My feelings were complicated. But what was clear in that moment as she swayed in her seat was that she was not fit to reason. The look in her eyes told me she was ready to spar in a loud voice.

I looked out the window. Townsfolk were enjoying the cool of evening. I stood up from the table.

'I'm in need of some air. I shall not be long.' To Gretchen I murmured, 'Look after her. She is drunk. I think it is from trying to forget what we have done.'

The day's final shards had dipped onto Speyer's narrow, cobbled lanes. I covered my head with a veil to conceal my face, and kept my wounded hands hidden in my sleeves. *Slough off your ire*, I chided myself. *Don't dwell on Mea.* When her mind was clear again, all would be well, just as my mind and soul would return to their purpose and vocation. We were almost in Bingen. Almost at the place of my dreams. I was safe; my sisters were safe. For the first time, I believed that we were.

I walked along the crowded lanes, brushing against the townsfolk, listening to their happy chatter. Did they know a murderess walked among them?

All around me was evidence of Speyer's wealth. Minters, blacksmiths, armourers, bakers, goldsmiths, glaziers. Beneath broad stone arches, men and women plied the treadle. I wanted to turn back and tell Mea because she was fond of cloth, but she was too drunk, and I needed to be away from her for a spell.

A glassblower had drawn a small crowd to his forge. I joined them, and watched him fix molten glass to the end of an iron rod and blow it into a bubble, and then perform a kind of dance in which the bubble was rolled and swung and shaped with pincers into a vessel to hold flowers. It made me wistful for the work I had done in the scriptorium, and I wondered whether the language and concentration of art was a means to restore me to what I had once been.

I was so mesmerised by the glass and the fire that when I turned around, I saw that the bright fire in the glassblower's furnace had given a false sense of light. The crowd had vanished. The sky was almost dark.

I looked for the road back to the inn, but dusk had altered

the scene, and all the laneways that fanned out before me seemed similar. Which was I meant to take?

Fewer people were about, no one to ask. Shadows moved beneath me like fish on a river bed. I felt a chill and looked behind. It felt as if someone was close by. I gathered my wits and chose a lane to take, when a man stepped from behind a pillar.

'*Ah, ragazza.*'

It was the young man from the wharf who had spoken to me earlier in my tongue.

'You are lost?' His smile showed gaps between his teeth. The dark hair that had gleamed earlier under the sun was now so black that it vanished on his head. The scar on his cheek was more pronounced.

I felt uncertain, looked around, and back at him.

'I will see you back to your lodgings,' he offered. 'The Ziege, is it not? At night, these roads can confuse.'

I did not want him to sense my fear so I feigned nonchalance. After all, I had killed. Shown bravery. Perhaps because of my sin, which weighing so heavily, I was keen to show that I was not hard, that I was not bad; that I was of decent, proper stock. Besides, what harm could come from him walking me to the inn? It could not be far.

He did not say much, only words of direction as we hurried down a lane. 'Turn here. Up at that corner we turn to the right.'

Soon we were at the large iron gates of Speyer. He had taken me the wrong way. In a few steps we would be outside the town entirely.

'No,' I protested.

A sentry, roused by my voice, wandered toward us.

'Help me,' I cried.

But the brute gave quick assurance to the guard. 'Nothing to worry about. She is always like this. It is our private game.'

The sentry chuckled and walked back to his post.

I pulled away, but he grabbed my arm and squeezed it. Terror weakened me. He wrenched me so close I could smell him. The hooded eyes that had given him a sleepy, shy appearance, were hard as pellets, as cold as the Alpes.

He pushed me down another lane, and another, each narrower than the one before. I tried to scream but there was no voice in me. I was scared. I hit him, struggled to break free. I had murdered a man; this one would not best me. But he was unperturbed by my struggle, as if it was an expected inconvenience.

He dragged me to the end of a lane, to a yard scattered with straw, axes, and piles of stone; threw me to the ground. Straddling me with a knee on my chest, he stuffed straw in my mouth. I pushed it out with my tongue but there was too much of it.

Many things happened at once. I wanted to save myself but I lacked the strength to take him on. Where was the power, the violence that I'd had at the Inn Bridge, or yesterday with the bounty hunters at the barn? I turned my head in search of a weapon but there was nothing in reach, and the man was fully on top of me, pinning me against the cold ground, huffing, violent.

Make me wild, God. Make me a she-wolf. Make me a she-wolf on fire!

I beat at him with one fist, while the other pulled my tunic away from him as his hand forced its way under it. Viciousness was not my first tongue, and he sensed it. With deftness, he took both my wrists and held them above my head.

He licked my neck. Next, the awful violation as pain drove into me.

Breath left. Agony reared again. And again. Each thrust more searing than the last. He rutted and panted; straw in my throat; throbbing panic in my ears. *How can I make this stop?*

When he was done, when he collapsed, I thought I would suffocate under his weight, under the foul smell, the shame, the hurt.

In his lust-fury his grip loosened. A gasp of breath returned to me. I pushed my knee against his side so that he slid off me, and I rolled to my feet.

My bruised legs, unsteady as a newborn calf, staggered down the lane. I gained purchase with each step. My fingers dug at the straw in my mouth; damp pieces flew back at me. Something trickled down my leg. I looked back; the creature was up.

I ran.

Out of the lane and the shadows, I reached the crossroads. To the right, the town gates. A watchman ambled toward me with his torch. I spun left and slipped on the cobbles, landing on my knee. I got up, and loped like a wounded animal. Past the glassblower's ovens, past the silent looms, until I saw the inn.

I pushed on the door, and threw myself sobbing onto the cold, stone flags.

XXV

The Feast of the Exaltation of the Holy Cross

Speyer

A wake and not. Dead and not. A shadow-self rendered mute, impassive, living in a shadow world of heavy mist. I was like one who had been drawn and quartered, and did not know how to put myself back together. My ears rang as if bells were set in them. My heart marked onward time when I wished for time to turn back so that what had happened had not happened. But what was done could not be altered. What was left undone only time could finish.

Where were you, God, who promised never to abandon me? You have put me through enough. Is this my penance for murder?

I sat by the windowsill, arms wrapped tight across my belly, a pale protection. My gaze swam over the townsfolk who passed beneath me. A few looked up, saw me, looked away. I didn't care. I only watched for one. If he appeared I was to say, 'There,' and Clovis would spring to my side, fix his sights on the brute, and fly into the street to kill him. Death would be small compensation.

It was the innkeeper who had found me the night before, and had carried me to my sisters. Clovis sought the watchman; my sisters sought a healer. I did not want anyone to touch me or come near, but then I reasoned, *Why not? Come, touch me. One has already spoiled me; what is another?*

I could not think beyond my wrath. I heard Gretchen tell the others that the commotion over what had befallen me had caused us to stray from our daily honour of the saints; we had missed the Feast of Eugenia the Virgin.

'But no matter,' she said with elaborate piety. 'Today is the Feast of the Holy Cross, so we shall pray for both Eugenia and the Cross.'

My jaw clenched in outrage, yet no breath in me to scream, *Why pray for Eugenia and the Holy Cross, for the dead and decayed? Look what has been done to me! Do not pray for them; pray for me.* I had hoped the flight from Saint Agatha's would be a cleansing balm for me, to rinse me of rancour and dare I say hatred; to allow me to make a wholesome new start at Bingen. And now I was spoiled, broken, and filled to the brim with fathomless rage.

A stool scraped across the floor toward me. Someone took my hand. Little Fey.

She bowed her head. 'I am broken-hearted. I don't know what to do or how to be with you. I want to restore you but I don't know how.'

'Everything irritates me,' I said. 'It is best to stay clear.'

'That is not like you, Sister. Do not let this break you. It will change you, yes; how can it not? But every event, good and bad, changes us. To endure our adversity we must swim into the dark to find light.'

She drew me from the window and back to my pallet.

'Come, lie down,' she whispered. 'Evil hands have been laid upon you. Let our good hands take over and heal you.'

My sisters washed me and blotted my welts and scratches, put poultices on my bruised knee, and wrapped linen around my wounds. I hurt everywhere, inside and out, in places where I had always thought no hands but mine would ever touch. I had injury upon injury from all the battles fought and won, and yet victory had eluded me this last one. I wished he had killed me.

Gretchen tried to cheer me with tea and memories of the times when we were little and played hiding games in the cloister at Saint Agatha's. She said my wounds already showed much improvement, but when I saw Valentina's face gather into a wince when she applied ointment around my eyes, I did not need the looking glass to know the damage.

Mea was quiet, busy with tasks that required her fussy attention—the shopping, cleaning, fetching new towels, asking for food to be brought to our rooms. She had been avoiding me, no doubt ashamed of her drunken words.

'Let me wash your hair,' she said.

'No.'

She ignored my terse reply. She was deaf to the word 'no,' when it did not suit her. She went to fetch bowl, soap, and comb.

My anger needed someone to blame. In the absence of the creature who bore my hatred, there had to be one to bear it in his stead, or at least share it, and that person was Mea. My mind flared with words that would bite her: *If not for your manner this would not have happened. Had you not spoken as you had, drunk with self-righteousness and lies, I would not have ventured out for air. I would not have met with disaster.*

To blame her gave me comfort. Kept at bay the blame on myself that was building. If I hadn't gone out alone; if I hadn't trusted; if I hadn't wanted to prove I was better than a murderess to assuage my guilt, this wouldn't have happened. He had said he wanted to help me; I decided to be gracious, and because of it my prudency looked like recklessness.

No, there was no balm in any of it. My life was cracked, hewed, and all but destroyed.

Mea returned with the wash bowl. Empty.

'I remember him, the one with the scar. By the wharf. I will kill him with my bare hands.'

I closed my eyes. *So dramatic. All passion and promise. Just like a murderess.*

'You would be no match for him.' I rolled my head away from her. *Then again, perhaps she would.*

My eyes saw poor Clovis. He who had pledged himself to our protection berated his failure. He had taken shield and sword, and rallied local men to scour the wharf to find the swine, but there had been no sighting. Still, one cannot hide forever. The desire for goodness eventually forces all of us from our fetid dens.

Clovis's jaw twitched. Anger and revenge had scored a

groove on his forehead between his eyes. He still had wounds that required rest. I did not know what to say to make him feel better, but nor did I want to make him feel better. It was not my duty to salve anyone. I needed his outrage to feed mine.

'What if we offer reward?' said Gretchen. 'We can use one of the diamonds.'

'It would be a fine idea if you were not being sought,' said Clovis. 'We must think of the attention we bring upon ourselves. Remember, you are not safe until you are through the doors of Bingen Abbey.'

'We let down our guard too soon and it undid us,' said Valentina.

Us? She had let down her guard and fell in love and was now hand-fasted. I had let down my guard and was now spoiled.

'We must do something,' Gretchen insisted. 'It is a day to Worms, and after that less than a day to Bingen. I asked in the market.'

'So close,' said Little Fey.

'Close, yes, but we must stay here a while longer,' said Mea. 'We cannot leave until Lucia is healed.'

She looked at Clovis, who nodded. The two of them must have decided this earlier. We were back to the days when we spoke with our eyes behind the backs of others.

She picked up the wash bowl then set it down and took up her shawl.

'I must go to the apothecary. Lucia will need tansy and pennyroyal. Gretchen, did you see aloe in the market?'

'Yes. I will come with you.'

When they were gone, I sat up, but Little Fey gently pressed on my shoulder, and bade me to lie down. She cupped her palms around the scratched and bruised parts of my hands and pressed against them.

'I have heard that you can touch a person to wellness,' she said. 'Maybe it will help.'

And then she wept. 'I am ashamed of my unholy lie. I have wondered if what happened to you was because you held my secret.'

'If God sought punishment, he would deliver it to you not me. But do not fret or feel guilt. God welcomes a repentant sinner.'

Tears dribbled onto her habit.

'I haven't told the others. But I will.'

'And when you do, they will understand, and they will still love you as I love you. You don't need the stigmata to make you a saint.'

Clovis and Valentina sat in a corner speaking in low voices. Clovis got up and came to me. He clutched his side where the knife had gone. Poor Clovis. He had fled one Crusade and found himself in another. He rubbed his face. How worn he looked.

'I shall go to the wharf again. To see if there has been news or a sighting of…'

We did not know how to speak of the beast. Brute, monster, swine, criminal.

The agony that raged through my body turned me away from all charity, and from food, consolation, sleep, kindness, prayer. I was as bitter as a child whose toy has been withheld, and as riddled with pain as a shot boar charging through thicket and brush.

When Valentina closed the door behind him, she came over. 'This might help,' she said softly. She lifted a piece of wet linen that had been warmed by the fire, and stretched it across my face, over the welts, bruises, and scratches, and smoothed it with her fingers. Behind it, tears began to pool.

What hands. What love. In that quiet, unremarkable moment, I realised that I had looked in the wrong places for the saints. I had listened too much to Gretchen who carried their lives in her heart. They were the saints of their time. What of the saints of our time? They were everywhere and yet nowhere. They were not the departed; they were the ones who walked the Earth—who healed, shared, fed, farmed, cared for the poor, the neglected; the ones who wandered without kin or home, the ones like me who cried out to be healed and made clean.

I had a sudden wish for Mother Elena, to comfort me with her reassuring embrace, to impart her gentle wisdom that would relieve my sorrow and shame. What had become of her after she had been taken from us? Was she still alive? Had she been exiled? Fate arrives to us as a bundle of disasters and triumphs, and doles out its random gifts without our say in the matter.

I blew a prayer to her, and imagined her, upon receiving it, blowing it back.

And then I sobbed. Not for me, but for her.

XXVI

The Feast of Saint Nonita

Speyer

'Tomorrow is your name day,' whispered Gretchen. Her hands cupped a small bowl filled to the rim. 'Betony. For your headache.'

I had fallen asleep; I couldn't remember anything after Valentina had placed the linen on my face.

'You slept long,' said Gretchen. 'It is a new day.'

The busy chirrup of morning birdsong filled the room along with bright sun. The sound hurt my ears; the sun stung my eyes. My senses returned to the soreness of my body, and with it the rage, the shame.

I took the bowl from her. Heat curled from it as I tipped it to my lips, and radiated into my hands. I lowered the bowl, regarded its plain but useful purpose. I thought how alike we were to things that have no breath. A bowl has no heart, yet it breaks like one. Stone can be cut. Glass shatters. The glassblower's forge flew into mind. Like his fragile creation,

A Flight of Saints

I, too, had been plunged into fire. Unlike it, I desired to burn the world.

'Did you know your name means light?'

I said nothing. I was all out of charity for the likes of Mea and Gretchen. She would try to leech out my grief and anger with silly stories or, God forbid, another martyred saint.

Undeterred, she flopped on my pallet.

I turned my head away.

Blithely—*how indomitable were my sisters!*—she launched into the story of Saint Lucia.

My mind was having none of it, and ran off like a screaming child into a crowd of thoughts. But something drew it back for though I knew the vita well enough, I wanted to see if there was common ground between the two Lucias, one sainted, one stained.

'She was betrayed by her fiancé for her faith. Thrown to cruel Diocletian, who ordered her to be sent to be used by men, but they were unable to move her. They brought oxen to shift her, but still she prevailed. So they built a fire around her, and do you know what she did? She sang and cried out her faith!'

I looked at Gretchen.

'And then a soldier speared her in the throat, but she refused to recant.'

I set my jaw.

'And then gouged her eyes.'

Why did she think this would make me feel better?

'And finally they had to chop off her head.'

She picked up my hands.

'Don't you see? Your namesake suffered greatly, but would not be daunted.'

'Yet she was destroyed by men.'

'But you have not been, Lucia. You are here, with us. You were too strong to be sacrificed.'

'Thanks for the cheery story. I feel marvellously better for it.'

I'm not sure she read my rue. What did she or anyone expect? For me to draw power from each trial? To become inviolable? No, I could not be like Saint Lucia. It was not in me. Each trial put more violence in me; fuel to my heat.

I put down the bowl. Gretchen began to rub my back.

'I cannot stop thinking of it,' I said. 'The memory stalks me like the bounty hunters.'

'But one day it won't. You will wake up and the memory will no longer haunt you. It will vanish—*poof!*—and you will know that what was done to you has given you the power to forget.'

She took a breath. 'Remember—though it pains me to say it—he too is a child of God.'

I did not want to hear it.

She shifted into a more comfortable position.

'I'm going to give you another saint today,' she said, taking my hand.

Heaven help me!

'Saint Nonita was a Holy woman from Breton who travelled across the seas to the land beyond Britannia known as Dyfed. When she arrived, she was violently seized by one of its kings, and the seed of a child was planted in her. When a priest found himself unable to preach in the presence of the unborn child—he feared it, thinking the unborn would grow into a greater preacher than he, and so he plotted to kill the child once born. But on the day of Nonita's labour, a terrible storm whipped up, and scuttled the priest's plot. Nonita gave birth to David, who like his mother, grew into sainthood. Nonita was revered for her wisdom and fearlessness, and is prayed to as the saviour of raped women.'

My clenched expression caused Gretchen to add: 'I am not telling you this because I think you will bear a child—Mea has been feeding you too much pennyroyal for that to happen—but because the virgins of our teaching, Eugenia, Ursula, Cecilia, Agnes, even your namesake Lucia, endured the same crime that was used against you. They perished. But Nonita survived. And you survived.'

A knock. I lifted my head and looked toward the door. But it wasn't the door. A gust had blown open the window, and its frame banged against the wall. A hand rested on my back. I knew that hand. By now I could tell the hands of each of my sisters without looking.

I turned to give a weak smile to Valentina, but pain lurched in my ribs and threw me back.

'Gretchen has gone to find some chamomile. Let me help you.'

Her large hands scooped my torso and gently rolled me. 'Mea has gone to find another healer. You were screaming in your sleep.'

'It is no use. Nothing can be done for me. Nothing is broken, but everything is sore. And soreness is injury not disease. My body will heal.' *But maybe not my spirit.*

The room was empty but for us.

'Where is Fey?'

'She was on her knees all night, praying at your side. I do not know how she does it. She has gone to wash.'

'And Clovis?'

'He is in the other room. Praying.' She glanced worriedly toward the door. 'He cannot quell his anger.'

'May it be satisfied soon. I want revenge, too. I want the evil creature brought to me so that I might inflict greater agony on him than he has on me.'

I was not ashamed of my words. My namesake would not have said such things, but she was not me.

'He has spoiled me. The Abbess will not want me.'

The room gradually refilled with its tenants: Little Fey returned from her ablutions and lay down beside me. Gretchen and Mea returned with herbs but not a healer.

Valentina fussed and wrung her hands. Several times she looked out the window.

'You said he was praying in the next room,' I said.

'Was praying. He went out again. I do not know where.'

I eased into a sitting position. My sisters' faces did not meet mine. They held the expressions of those who have much to say but are afraid to bring themselves to say it. I myself had much to say but was not ready to give it voice.

'I would like my hair washed,' I said, if only to disturb the quiet and give them something to do.

Mea and Valentina fought over who would do it. Valentina won, but Mea satisfied herself with another chore.

'While we were out, I remembered another remedy that may help you,' she said. She dropped a length of towelling into the cauldron of water hanging in the inglenook. She poked it a few times with a stick, drew it out, and squeezed the excess water. 'To wrap around your belly. The heat will soothe it.'

It was hot against my skin but I used my breath to adjust to it, and once in place its heat soothed.

When Valentina finished washing my hair and had wrapped it in towelling—I was swathed in towelling from head to foot—I returned to my pallet.

'I must speak of things that...'

'Please, Lucia, no. Rest...' said Gretchen. The others rushed to concur. They cooed for me not to fret, to only think of healing.

'Pray, let me say what I must. I have thought of what has happened. It is difficult to speak of, and indeed, it is something that will remain with me all my days. You have seen the wounds on my body. You have not seen the wounds in my heart. I am soiled, though you have done your best to clean me. I am ruined, though you assure me I did no wrong. Indeed, I know that to be true, and I must look at what was done to me as another trial set before us. The pig will be caught and butchered, but I cannot sit here and wait for that day to come. Every part of me is on fire but the flame that burns strongest is the desire to reach Bingen. That is where I will heal.'

'But you have been violated,' said Gretchen. 'You must lay a charge.'

The word made my body jerk. I held up a hand to still her. 'Hear me before your anger makes worse our situation. First, we cannot lay a charge or make a claim, nor do we have the means…'

'We have the means,' said Gretchen. 'We have jewels…'

I raised my hand again. 'Let us be sober. Consider what will happen if the beast is found and brought before a judge. While he stands in silence, smug in denial, impugning my dignity, I will be forced to recount events to the lawmakers. Even now, to speak of it is more than I can bear. I will be asked for proof as to what was done to me. They will want to see the tears in my clothes, blood on my garments and skin. They will ask me to reveal my wounds, the bruises and scratches on my body. Would you yourselves allow examination this way?'

'We would stay with you,' said Mea. 'We would not let anyone touch you.'

I shook my head. 'That is but a small portion of what I would endure. Here is the nub of it: They will ask all manner of questions, and in some way, by some account, I will betray myself as a religious. The judge will say, 'Oh, so you are a nun. What is your Order? Who and where is your superior? Why are you so far afield? Who are these with whom you travel? Ah, you fled a convent? You said before that you were a pilgrim bound for the shrine in Compostela. So, what is the truth? If you have been untruthful about that, and if you have escaped your convent—if that be true, how are we to believe what you tell us this man did to you? Did you call out for help? Did you resist or was your aim to seduce him? Did you fight against he whom you accuse? Who is witness to this?'

I did not know from whence this wisdom had come. What did I know of rape or the laws around it? Yet, I felt some inner ken, as if the knowledge was bred into me. Perhaps by Saint Lucia herself.

My sisters stared at the floor.

'Do you see? If I tell what befell me, I risk condemning myself and you also. What's more, my wounds speak of other attacks, and by some establishment of fact or witness, our murderous deeds will be revealed, and we will be hanged.'

They murmured agreement.

'Any search by us is fruitless. Let others take it on while we continue to our destination. There is nothing more for us here, and every hour we remain makes me suffer more. Every hour brings another set of bounty hunters closer. And were they to attack us, I would not have the strength to resist. Indeed, I might well surrender. We must go to Bingen.'

It was dark when Clovis returned. The innkeeper, conscientious in asking after my health and whether he could do more for fellow pilgrims, brought food to our chamber. I had told my sisters that I could not face leaving the room, and so we stayed together.

Beyond our rooms, a new moon was out, fresh of face and strong of promise, while bruised, shredded clouds passed over its confidence.

A sudden, invisible disturbance shifted the air. I opened

the window as if doing so would permit a better gauge of things, but all I received was a mysterious drone, like a cloud of bees.

'Something terrible will happen,' I said.

'How can it be worse than our present woes?' said Mea.

'I do not know what it is, but it's out there, like a dark cloud, but whether it is one that will storm or pass quietly I cannot tell. Or whether it augurs well or ill for us or someone else, that, too, I do not know. Whatever it is feels close at hand. Do any of you feel it?'

'I have felt it,' said Little Fey. 'It is like a persistent feeling of doom.'

'Might it be the weather?' said Valentina. She joined me at the window. 'But, no, I do not feel anything.'

'It is beyond weather.' Little Fey looked at me as if to say, *For you, too?*

I nodded. 'It is a disruption, a flux.'

'Like a death.' She shuddered. She turned over her hands, looked at her palms and folded them together. The balm that had been applied after the barn fire had healed them well. There was barely evidence of her original wounds.

Clovis was at one of the other windows watching the street, face drawn; skin raw from constant rubbing. His linen shirt was unlaced. We were all casual now.

I wanted to get him back. Indeed, I needed his cheer to lift and embolden me.

'I am glad we have decided to leave tomorrow.' I said it in a louder voice to jolt Clovis from his brooding. The sky was red; it would be fair in the morning. 'We shall make an early start.'

'Clovis says we are next bound for Worms,' said Valentina.
'An ancient city,' he said.
'Does it have a cathedral?'
'Still being built,' he said.
'I should like to see it.'
There was false gaiety in my voice, but it was necessary. If I was gay, others would be. And if they showed gaiety, I might feel it myself.
'I have meant to ask what you and Valentina will do once we are at Bingen. After you marry. What industry you will take up?'
His heart was not in the answer and I did not pursue it.
Gretchen moved closer to the fire, near Valentina.
'On our journey, we have all told our stories, but we have not heard yours, Valentina. Has she told you it, Clovis?'
'No.' He moved from the window to the settle and sat beside his love. 'I did not think to ask, for I was smitten by her from the moment she laid her hands on me. What more could be told beyond what I see in that face and feel in her presence? Goodness shines from her.'
He gave her a teasing nudge with his elbow. A smile from him, finally. 'What is your story, my love? I am ashamed that I never asked.'
Her cheeks flushed. She looked down at her needlework.
'What is there to tell? And why tell it? It was so long ago…'
'Do not play the shy one,' teased Mea. 'It is surely laden with intrigue and mystery.'
Valentina fanned her face. 'Ah, nothing can best your story, Mea. To be sure.'

I couldn't recall when Clovis had learned of the murderess's story, but he knew it. But given that we had all killed in the last few days, what of it? She was hardly special now.

The lighter mood in the room brought relief, and I welcomed the shift of everyone's gaze. I covered my bruised wrists so they would not distract.

Valentina was quiet for a moment, eyes fixed on the rafter to draw the past back to her. For a moment, I wondered whether she would feign forgetfulness about her beginnings.

'Well'—she returned to her needlework—'I was born in Bavaria. Many of the places we passed once we crossed the Alpes reminded me of my birth home. I remember much snow but also the tiny flowers, and the green hills which I used to roll down with my sisters.

'I was the middle of five girls. They were all tall and as slender as cathedral pillars, with hair as dark as yours, Mea. They were beauties, and my mother and father dressed them in ways that made folk stop and stare and marvel at their loveliness.

'I was not like my sisters. Far from it. My hair was pale and curly, my face freckled like the pox. My gait was clumsy. I was not slender.' She paused. 'I was called the ugly sister.'

Her voice caught.

Clovis, brow furrowed, stared at her.

'My parents wanted everything to be neat and lovely. They tried to mould me to my sisters. They fed me less so I would be slender. They darkened my hair with madder. They had me lie on the floor with the blanket box atop my hair to press out the curl. Nothing worked. I was to be forever different from the rest.

'Four betrothals were made for my sisters. No one asked for my hand. My parents took this as an affront, so they decided to make a story of it, to turn my birth into a blessing rather than a curse. They told people that my appearance was a favour bestowed by God, that I had been made different so as to make obvious which of their daughters was to be given to the Church. I was to be a Holy tithe like Abbess Hildegard was made a Holy tithe by her family.

'I don't know why they chose to send me to Saint Agatha's, perhaps because it was far enough away that I wouldn't return. They did not bring me to the convent; they sent me off with a farmer's son. I never saw them or heard from them again. That is my story.'

She lowered her head.

We were startled by this. Mea was the fairest among us, but Valentina was next, and if given more thought I would have said that her courage and kindness made her more of a beauty than Mea.

'I find it difficult to understand what your parents did,' said Clovis. 'At the same time, I am grateful for what they did, for we would not have met had they not sent you away. It was my good fortune to fall into the cave hole so you could rescue me.'

Tears dripped off her nose onto her needlework.

Clovis took her hand. 'I had never been shown such care and love by another.'

We chimed our praise for her.

'If your family saw you now, they would be in awe of your fairness and bravery,' said Gretchen. 'Do not forget all the times you saved us, when you faced danger alone.'

'You stole bread from the convent for us,' said Little Fey.

'And salt from the Botzen market,' I added.

'And what about your talent for fashion that day in the forest?' said Mea. 'Clovis, you should have seen how she altered her dress and hair and played the part of our mistress to ward off the bounty hunters. She upbraided them as if she was queen of the forest.'

We laughed until we remembered what befell those bounty hunters.

The mood in the room fell.

'Let us leave this place in the morning,' I said with blunt determination. 'As early as we can. My whole heart desires to be in Bingen.'

XXVII

The Feast of Saint Lucia of Syracusa

Bingen

We were in Worms by next midday. Never was I so grateful to get out of the litter. The road, though flat, placed much hardship on my body. I held tight to the cart edge but each rumble and jostle sent spikes of searing pain through me.

We visited the cathedral to say our prayers. There was much building work apace, but I saw that it would be an enormous, commanding place of worship when completed.

Beneath the shade of an apple tree, we ate our cheese and bread. The grass was cool and soft, and it made me want to lie down. But a thought suddenly seized me: We were not far from Bingen. Half a day's journey at most.

'Why do we tarry in Worms when we could be in Bingen before supper?'

We were off. My body was sore but the thrill of knowing

our journey was nearly, finally, at an end overtook any thought of pain or discomfort. We were almost there.

Before the Vesper bell tolled, our litter clattered into Bingen. The town had been in my dreams for so long that at first it seemed impossible that we had truly arrived. It was different from how my imagination had created it, but now that it was real, I took in every home, every forge, every church and market stall, as if we were riding down the road of Heaven itself. We were here. All that way. All that terrible way.

I was exhausted, but having held itself together for so long, my body would not give in to collapse. Not yet. It was not enough to be in Bingen; I had to be inside Bingen Abbey with my sisters. I pushed away thoughts of being shunned at the Abbey doors. I had learned how to lie, and if that's what it took to be brought inside, so be it. This journey was not over until we were through its doors and assigned our cells.

We found a hostelry. I prayed it was our last. The transient life had lost all appeal; I would not have made a good mendicant or desert mother. I was happy to be put to work, be it garden or grate, if it meant safe shelter, food, and a ewer of hot water to wash.

One by one, we filed out of the litter. Mea put a hand under my arm and helped me off. She looked full into my face.

'Is it all right with you?'

'Yes,' I said, because we were in Bingen now, and that was all that mattered.

In our chambers at the inn, my sisters and I were quiet. Clovis had gone to settle the horses, but I think he had really left to give us privacy.

We fussed with our bundles while we waited our turn at the basin. Warm water was the first thing Mea ordered whenever we arrived anywhere. We took off our ripped clothes and brushed off the earth and washed off the blood. Then, we washed the same from our bodies.

The end of our journey. Excitement gained in me, and I sensed it in the others. The promising life we had travelled toward was now around the corner and up a hill.

'We are finally here,' I whispered, and my words ignited the room. We became like birds twittering in a barn, unable to cease our noisy chatter. Would we ever give ourselves to silence again?

'I am fearful about meeting the Abbess,' said Gretchen. She was smoothing the creases in her tunic, to give herself a better appearance. 'I hope she will show compassion.'

'What if she turns us away?' said Little Fey. 'What if God has told her of our sins?'

I wondered whether Fey had confessed her fraud to Our Lord or even to her sisters. Then again, when would there have been time? Our full attention had been taken with our survival, and we had fallen into muteness as we comprehended how it had all come to this.

'I am almost envious of you,' said Valentina. With Clovis out of the room, we were five again.

'You must promise to visit us,' said Gretchen.

None of us asked Mea what she would do, or where she would go.

'What shall we do with our bundles?' I asked. 'There is nothing of worth in mine.'

'Nor mine. It is quite useless,' said Gretchen. 'See how it hangs by only a few threads.'

The only bundle with anything of value belonged to Mea.

I watched her by the window combing her singed hair. She looked back at me.

'You have the dagger and should keep the jewels,' she said. 'Make them a dowry to the Abbey.'

'What will you live on?'

She turned back to the window, shrugged. 'I will be fine.'

She also declined to make the short walk from the inn to the abbey with us after supper.

I trod carefully on the cobbles, not wanting to do further damage to my body. I also did not want to ruin my shoes. Like my sisters, we had cleaned them and smeared them with dubbin that Clovis kept for his boots. They were the best part of us.

At the end of the lane, we turned a corner; there was Bingen Abbey.

It was smaller than I expected, about the size of Saint Agatha's. Part of it was made of stone and had a tower, but another section was of wood. A rambling, humble building. It did not look like the home of a great abbess. Across from it, on the other side of the river they call the Nahe, was a more impressive building, chiselled from the crag on which it rested. Towers and turrets sprouted from roofs of different shapes and heights.

'That must be Saint Rupertsberg,' said Little Fey. 'It looks like a castle.'

Father Volmar's words trickled back, that the Abbess had

A Flight of Saints

first built Rupertsberg, and when it was filled with sisters, she had built the more modest Bingen Abbey. The two houses were connected by a long stone bridge that spanned the river. In which convent did Hildegard live? Did she spend time in both? Such useless questions. All my dreams placed me where she lived and breathed, but now I saw that she could easily be in both places. Perhaps she was at one in the morning, and the other after midday.

We walked alongside the walls, pressing our hands against it as if to draw strength from it. We were about to turn back toward the inn when Little Fey gasped and pointed to a tower.

'Look. On the balcony.'

We followed the direction of her finger.

There she was. She who we had come so far to see and to serve.

She stood facing the Rhein River and the range of sun-dried hills and blue mountains on its opposite shore. Her hands rested on the parapet. Even from a distance, I could see that she was aged: the rounded shoulders, the slight body. I did not know why I had imagined her as being young.

Her eyes were lifted Heavenward. A ray had pierced a dark cloud and caught her in its light. Her veil fluttered as though wind or breath were upon her, yet the air around us was still. Suddenly, she threw open her arms, not in welcome but in a gesture of argument, and waved her arms about, much like Mea did when she was agitated. I heard the Abbess call out to the ether. What was her quarrel with Heaven?

The Abbess seemed to exhaust herself, because her arms fell resignedly to her sides. Her mien changed and she became contrite. Hands clasped in front of her, she looked to be begging, pleading. Then her palms came together and she bowed her head—the posture of one reluctant to accept what was being pressed on her. As she turned to go inside the tower, she saw us.

We waved like madwomen, giggling and calling greetings. She leaned forward and peered, as if to convince herself that we were not an illusion but a deranged cluster of novices.

Tentatively, Abbess Hildegard raised her arm and made the sign of the Cross. And then she was gone.

Our mouths went slack, and then we jumped and screamed.

'We saw her!'

'She saw us!'

'She blessed us!'

'Let's return to the inn,' I said. 'We shall sleep well, and tomorrow we'll come back and present ourselves. After that, we will truly be free.'

XXVIII

The Feast of Saint Mathilda

Bingen

Settembre's dawn woke me next morning, thick rafters burnished gold. The air was cool and fresh, yet no sooner had my eyes opened than the same ominous feeling from the previous night in Speyer rushed back.

I got up from my pallet, hoping movement and a new posture would scatter doom and doubt. After all, we were here. We were in Bingen. By day's end we'd be abed in Abbey cells. Perhaps.

Warm sun streaked my feet while the rest of my body tensed as if preparing for an oncoming storm.

It didn't help that this feeling, this flux, was doing battle with my change of heart. During the night, plagued by doubt and misery, I had come to a terrible reckoning: I decided I would not join the Bingen community. Instead, I would throw my lot in with Mea or Valentina and Clovis, or if necessary, find my own way in the world. I, who had travelled over mountains and through gorges, who had suffered all I had suffered with the single ambition to reach Bingen and to make my home in the community of the august abbess, now wanted none of it. The life of a nun is a busy one, every hour taken up with prayer and chant along with dull duties of washing, cleaning, hoeing, learning. Routine keeps us fixed at all times and in all ways to God. But not being tethered to such routine was something I had grown to enjoy. I saw merit in freedom and the solitary life and I believed I could adapt to it. Like Mea, I had grown accustomed to not being bothered by orders and direction.

As my slumber-head cleared, I knew I could not say those words to my sisters, to let them think me mean of spirit, and lazy of faith. I could tell them that I did not have the courage for the convent, but that wasn't true; it was that the convent had no courage for me. My sins of murder and of spoilage weighed too heavily. In my soul I knew they were no fault of mine, but God would see it differently, and others would see it differently; they would regard me unfit for the veil, and their knowing glances and relentless, persecuting whispers would undo me. There was of course the cover of not breathing a word of these transgressions to anyone, and I was certain my sisters would keep our secret, but holding secrets was no way to begin life in a Holy house. I could make a good case for myself, prostrate myself before the Abbess, confess all and beg forgiveness, but now, after all the leagues I had walked, there was no energy left in me for it. What's more, the greater fear was that she wouldn't forgive me, and wouldn't admit me as a sister, and that would have been a shame too harsh for me to bear. No, it was better, safer, for me not to seek admission to the community. I would make sure that Gretchen and Little Fey were given a home there, but once they were settled, I would take my leave and seek some other vocation.

I walked to the window. Cold rain had fallen overnight, but the growing heat of morning dried the cobbles and rooftops, and sent up wraith-like plumes akin to souls rising on Judgement Day. Unusually, many people milled about in the street—odd given the hour. They appeared caught in the grip of some quiet commotion, a local disagreement or gossip no doubt. Above the town's crowded rooftops, I spied the top of one of the Abbey's towers. All the words I had silently rehearsed to tell the Abbess of our terrible journey were unnecessary. There was no need to tell any of it.

It was strange to be of a new mind, so quickly reconciled to a new direction. I could scarce believe it. Then again, what purpose is there to our desires or dreams when Heaven can intervene in an instant and blow them out as if they held the consequence of a candle flame. I had been wholly unprepared for the world, for this flight to a decent, merciful life. And the result? I had behaved without decency, without kindness or mercy. I was guilty of the gravest sin, and in justifying it, almost forgiving myself, indeed—dare I admit—feeling valiant and mighty, a crime was dealt back to me. Did the animal justify his violent rutting? Granted, I had survived but I was also destroyed. Inside me, a smouldering ruin. Did my sisters feel likewise for their deeds? Does everyone who fights and scrapes through this harsh life feel spent and cheated? Where is the glory, the love of God, in any of this. We are born sinners and we die sinners. There is no health in us.

My sisters. How to tell any of this to them without spitting it out. My stomach clenched at the thought of their reaction, especially Little Fey.

Who was suddenly beside me. She could be as noisy as a rolling barrel or as quiet as a draught slipping through a window.

'You slept well?'

She obviously hadn't. Her elflocked hair, normally tidy and shiny, looked like an unravelled ball of wool that had been left in the rain.

I kept my counsel; I couldn't reveal my heart now, indeed I could only bear to do so once, to all of them at the same time. I had yet to work out the correct words.

She didn't answer. Her face showed distress.

'Are you ill?'

She was paler than usual; eyes frightened and rimmed with the purple of peevish sleep. Mine surely looked the same.

'What is it?'

'I had a dream.'

'Tell me.' I held her tiny hands.

'I was falling from a great height, but something unexpectedly drew me up.'

'Your mind is playing a game. It thinks you are still walking above the Isarco. Or perhaps it is the anxiety of the day ahead that nibbles you. We are in Bingen, safe. All will be well, as you yourself have said many times.'

She shook her head. 'It feels like something bad will happen.'

She sensed things before others did; I wondered if she surmised what I had yet to tell.

The others roused, and the chamber soon filled with the hum of excitement and preparation. I joined it. We spoke of the astonishing sight of Hildegard on her balcony, and her blessing to us. I could tell that Mea wished she had been with us. Maybe it would have given her cause to change her mind about joining the community. Then again, I didn't want her to join; I needed her to abet my new creation.

'Saint Mathilda today,' said Gretchen, rubbing linen over her teeth. 'Queen of the Saxons and revered in these parts. Since Germania is now our homeland, it is fitting we honour her. Was pious, generous to the poor, founded many monasteries. Blah, blah, blah. She is the last saint I will have to summon. We will be back to the calendar of men; Festus and Desiderius will be next. I have much preferred our own assembly of saints.'

We plaited one another's hair. We washed, dressed, and made ourselves tidy and worthy to the Abbess's eyes.

We were ready. We left our room, and all of us, including Valentina, Clovis, and Mea, set off for the Abbey. I decided I would take Mea aside and tell her of my change of plan, to seek her encouragement.

Across from the inn, people were gathered quietly on the piazza. For such a bright day, the mood was strangely sombre.

'Why is everyone so glum-struck?' said Gretchen.

Guards and sentries wandered back and forth like dogs waiting to be fed. Some stood alone, heads bowed, barely acknowledging those who entered the town. I exchanged concerned glances with my sisters.

Like the guards, folk wandered without purpose, spoke in reverential voices, or wept. Worn hands twisted the hems of aprons in private anguish. When the Terce bell tolled, some hurried into the small church. Others dropped to their knees on the cobbles and prayed.

'Maybe the Pope died.'

My eyes raked across the grey cobbles, the wooden houses, market stalls, the barns and hay stores searching for something that might give reason to this grief.

'I shall ask someone,' I said, but impulsive Gretchen was ahead of me, wandering among the folk in the square, looking for someone to bother. She approached a man who was praying. I turned my head away, ashamed of her intrusion. Until I heard her gasp.

I looked back. She had dropped to her knees beside the man, and was crossing herself. The rest of us remained planted and perplexed. When she got up and came running to us, her face white and wet.

'Abbess Hildegard is dead.'

We stared, waiting for her to say it was a jest because that was Gretchen's way.

'It is true,' she implored. Her body quivered.

'The great woman died in the night, the night of a new moon,' wailed a woman who passed by. 'This world will not be the same without her. The Jewel of Bingen has died.'

'But we saw her yesterday,' I said. 'How can this be?'

'We must go to the Abbey. Now.' Little Fey pushed past,

A Flight of Saints

and not gently.

I seized her arm. 'Why the rush? Are you getting your courses?'

She looked insulted by my words, and I thought she might rebuke me, but her look quickly vanished and was replaced by one of awe, a look not unlike the one she had the day Mother Elena had explained the stigmata to her. The wonder-calm of epiphany.

'Tell me,' I said.

'We must go,' is all she said. To the others she said, 'Please,' and pressed her palms together in an urgent beseech. And then she was off, hurrying toward the Abbey.

'Where must we go? Why?' Valentina looked at Clovis. He shrugged, took her hand and followed Sister Fey.

Hildegard dead!

What were we to do?

'We have come all this way, and now she is no more?' I was ashamed of my petulance before the words left my mouth.

Mea's arm circled my waist. My wounds still hurt when I walked so I did not resist her help.

'Lucia,' she said. 'The Abbess has died but her home has not. Another abbess will take her place, and you will present yourself to her.'

'No, I won't...'

But she interrupted me. 'Yes, you will. You must keep going.'

Carts clattered into the road. Folk and beasts crowded us. A noisy, weeping crowd stood at the door of Bingen Abbey. I was still coming to terms with the news. How could this happen? Was it an omen?

The door opened, and a nun came out.

'The soul of our glorious Abbess has returned to the Father. What remains of her has been taken to the Rupertsberg chapel. She will receive you there.'

The throng turned as one, and trudged back down the hill toward the bridge that crossed the Nahe to the other convent. My sisters and I fell in among them.

The sun was high and hot. Sadness and exhaustion increased my pain. I had not anticipated so long and crowded a walk. Then again, there had been many things on this journey that I had not anticipated. I surrendered to the swell, and allowed myself to be borne on the listless wave of mourners.

Little Fey and I held hands. She was more anxious than I had ever seen her before. Most times I was able to assuage her worries, but this time nothing I said soothed her.

I tried to be light. 'Imagine how mad Mother Clothilde will be when she learns we are here?'

I tried to be sober. 'Shall we say a prayer, perhaps a chant?'

I tried to be direct. 'What is wrong?'

But she gave no satisfaction. Her mind was elsewhere. And because of it I didn't dare tell her what I wanted to tell her about not joining her at Bingen.

Her hand slipped from mine and she melted into the throng.

Mea was back alongside me. 'This crowd. So many people. All of Germania seems to have come to pay tribute.'

'I hope the new abbess is kind.' This from Gretchen who was behind me.

'If we have learned anything from the religious it is that they do not wait upon death to name a successor,' said Mea. 'They will have settled on one well before the Abbess died, or she would have chosen one before her death.'

'Something has come over Sister Fey,' I said. I raised my head above the horde to see if I could find her. I saw Valentina and Clovis, but not Little Fey.

Mea inclined her head. 'I must speak to you about that night in Speyer before I lose you completely to the Abbey.'

'I must speak to you too. I have decided not to join the community.'

'What?'

I hushed her. 'Speak softly for I have not told the others.'

'This is nonsense talk, Lucia. What has come over you?'

People jostled us. My irritation rose. 'Tell me what you were going to say to me before I tell you more of my decision.'

'Very well. First, I am sorry that I was so sloppy in my drinking. What I was trying to say that night was that the crossing of the Alpes, and everything that happened to us changed me, as it changed all of us. I said that I had decided before I left Saint Agatha's not to seek admittance to the Bingen community, but that is not entirely true. I had not shut out the possibility of continuing in religious life, but the longer and further we walked, the stronger independence grew in me until I knew I could live by myself. I am not in want of marriage, or husband, or children. I want freedom but purpose. It is complicated. Do you understand?'

'I feel likewise,' I said. 'Once we fled Saint Agatha's my singular thought was to reach Bingen, but overnight I was changed. I realised that...'

We were suddenly shoved violently. The crowd, thick and unruly, roared. I noticed that we were no longer walking on earth but on stone. The bridge. We were crossing the Nahe. The masses had funnelled onto the bridge and surged like a singular beast. We were twelve abreast on a bridge more suitable for six. I looked down between the stone gaps. A fair drop. My eyes searched again for Little Fey. Her fear of heights needed me to steady her.

'We should have tied ourselves together with Mea's sashes so as not to lose one another,' said Gretchen, squeezing away from people. 'Everyone is touching me. I hate it.'

Mea gritted her teeth and pushed back against the crowd with her elbows. 'These people... so fat and foul... without manner... pushing. Argh!'

A square oaf, his body like the letter H, thrusted himself through the crowd heedless of injury to those around him. He was thick of neck, the type who could knock down a door with his head. His arm struck Mea, and she swung at him and pounded him on the back. The oaf looked as if more insult had been done to him than he had done to her.

'Mad woman! Mad woman!' he cried, and pushed forward with more urgency, displacing more folk and causing many to stumble.

Ahead I saw a small figure among the crowd. At first, I thought it was a child until I recognised Little Fey. She was midway across the bridge.

'Fey...' but the rest did not come. My parched throat refused loudness in my voice.

A Flight of Saints

I waved to gain her attention, but she was not looking in my direction. She will be trampled, I thought.

I surged through the throng, ignored the protests of those who pushed against me like a wave, who trod on my feet and jabbed me with their shoulders.

I was almost in reach of her when the same square oaf launched himself again through the crowd and caused several folk to push into Little Fey. The sides of the bridge were low. She tried to back away from the mob but got pushed further to the side until she was teetering on the edge of the bridge. Panic lit her eyes. Her arms flailed for someone to grab her. It should have been me. I lurched forward, but, alas, too late.

She saw me before she dropped over.

Reaching the side of the bridge, I threw myself after her.

Down, down. Air rushed into my ears through the emptiness. I plunged into the river and the water closed over me like a seal. Then all was silent. A great peace filled me, like one that I imagined arrives at the time of death, and I yearned to surrender to the watery womb, and live unknown and unfettered in its cool haze. But my eyes were open, and through the flickery light I saw her, and swam to her.

She was suspended in the deep blue; gold hair lifted by the water into a corona, arms swept up on either side so she looked like the letter W. Her eyes were closed, her mouth slack; I knew she was gone. And then in astonishment I saw her shadow-self in cloud-like form peel away and proceed up through the water like a plume. I followed it with my eyes until it whispered through the skim without breaking it.

I turned back to where her body hung lifeless, weightless. I grabbed her arm and pulled her up, up, through the cold river toward the surface. Watery faces and shapes peered down at us. Arms plunged into the water and thrashed like a hundred eels until I was hauled back to land, to the shrill sound of life. My hand slipped from hers.

I gulped for air but my breath would not calm, uncertain whether I was convulsed by grief or relief. *Little Fey gone. No, it cannot be.* I screamed but I think it was only in my head.

A voice, alarmed, cried, 'Sister Lucia!' and then gave brisk orders: 'Quick. Take them to the infirmarium.' A hand—smooth, tender—grasped mine; its owner babbled, 'Lucia. Lucia.'

I drifted in and out of awareness, felt myself carried up the banks of the river, and thereafter into a room where I was laid on a table. The bitter scent of tonics and tinctures filled my nose, my head. The river was still in my throat. The rushed patter of footsteps, back and forth, all around me. No longer a rabble, but hushed voices, practised hands rolling me this way and that. Then that voice again, the one from the riverbank. Giving urgent instructions for my treatment, calling for towelling and blankets, for this tonic, that balm, a spoon.

The voice drew closer until I sensed its owner looking down at me.

My eyes fluttered open, and I beheld the last face I saw before awareness left me.

Mother Elena.

XXIX

The Feast of Saint Scholastica
Bingen/Rupertsberg
1180

The view from the tower is far and wide. I have the sight of a bird. Stubborn patches of snow that have resisted surrender to spring streak the broad hills across the river. Soon the torn skies of winter will disappear, and there will be flowers and warmth again. Spring will be victorious. It always is. God has planned it so.

The mighty Rhein collars a land of endless pines. I think of the creatures that shelter amongst them. I was once like them, foraging, hiding, sleeping, howling, surviving. I do not miss that life.

My eyes dip and roam across rooftops of thatch, clay, slate, and rock that harbour lives of both hardship and contentment. It moves upward to fathomless Heaven, but I cannot bring myself to look at it too long.

Six full moons have come and gone since God took Abbess

Hildegard into His arms. Our community is in prayerful reflection today for its esteemed Mother. I can see a few of the sisters in their solitary perambulation around the physick garden. Long white veils trail them like the wake of a boat. The sight reminds me of when my sisters and I ran through vast meadows, parting green grass like the sea. Free and wild.

Soon enough I crumple into a chair with grief sobs. This is her day too. Dear, gentle Little Fey. I miss her like breath.

The day she left us returns like pieces of ripped parchment, edges frayed, surfaces crinkled and in need of smoothing. Not all the pieces are there; not all that are there are assembled in the correct places. It will come. Or it may not. I must accept the memories I am granted in whatever form they arrive.

I turn toward the small desk, pick up the quill.

The day that our litter rumbled into Bingen returns to me. This is the way with my thinking nowadays; jinking from memory to memory with no coherence. I was heavy with fatigue that day, faint with the pain of my battered womb and bruised confidence. I remembered thinking how it was possible to bear the pain of the attack that was made against me and to yet feel numb to it; to crave un-Christian revenge that would reap more suffering while at the same time desiring to commit myself to Christian community. A Devil within God's House. Even now, be it day or night, I fall into a trance or dream that finds me brawling, clawing my invisible enemy with a ferocious hatred. I have awakened my sisters many times with my cries and thrashing, so I am told.

The Abbess has instructed me to let these memories come:

'Welcome the visions, good and bad, and spill them onto parchment.'

And so, each morning after Lauds, I climb the tunnelled archway to this tower, to this room with its desk, chair, and stool, and its three windows facing West, North, and South, and I sit with the love and the hate, and record my journey. I seek no pardon from God.

My mind rears back often to that night when angels visited me and prodded me to flee. In the place that least deserved their presence, at a time when I least expected it, grace and mercy were granted. But with grace came grief, and it arrived in such swift abundance that it could only have been a lesson from God concerning life's permutations. And here I sit in leisurely ponderance to make sense of it. I'm not sure we ever neatly arrive at the end of grief, just as we are never neatly prepared for its beginning.

I don't need a looking glass to know that all of this has aged me. Strands of white mingle with the dark that fall upon my shoulders. I am as bleak as winter, though spring has announced itself outside. Yet, my sad state has strangely brought calm to my soul. Mine is not an agitated sadness, but one of acceptance. I feel I have a talent for sadness. Some, like Gretchen, are blessed with a gift for happiness; others, like me, have been built for grief. Perhaps I am and always will be a winter person.

A rap on the door brings me to my feet. I brush my tears away.

Mother Elena enters with tea of chamomile and bread. I must adjust to her new name; I am forever forgetting it. She is now Abbess Elisa of Rupertsberg and Bingen, elected by the sisters to continue Hildegard's work.

She sets down the tray and embraces me.

The remarkable story of how she came here is as strange and remarkable as my own.

After she was wrestled from Saint Agatha's, she was brought to the bishop's palace to work in the laundry. No reason was given as to why she was removed from Saint Agatha's, only that she would face a tribunal for her crimes. She suspects it was her fervour for the Abbess's pronouncements that brought disagreement from the Bishop of Trento. 'It seems the Church can tolerate one woman rebel, but not two,' she has said. Outwardly, she accepted her punishment and her fate; but inwardly she wasted no time devising escape. She, too, heeded Hildegard's advice of 'pure action.' She has told how, early one morning, a cart arrived with goods for the palace. Unseen, she climbed in and hid under its thick cover of straw. She didn't know where the cart was headed, but she had already plotted her destination. When the cart stopped in Bergamo she slipped out. For days she ran and walked, and made her way up into the Alpes and across the San Bernardino Pass to Chur and down into Swabia. Like us, she sheltered in caves or among the boughs and hollowed trunks of the forests. The miracle of her journey is that she never came to harm. She was protected by peasant and princess alike, she said. Along the way she adapted her name to suit the land through which she travelled, and became Elisa. She arrived at Bingen Abbey and presented herself to Hildegard, with whom she had corresponded many times.

A Flight of Saints

She told her all that had happened. Hildegard held her secret, and gradually bestowed her with greater responsibility within the community.

She hands me the warm cup. I take it, wrap my fingers around it; let the heat enter my hands, my arms, through my body.

She beckons me to sit, and takes the stool next to me.

'How is it coming?' She nods toward the parchment on my desk. It is she who has directed me to write the story of our crossing, as a way to remember, to heal, and to come to understand all that happened. Writing will purge the anger and grief that cling to me, she says. My story is for no one's eyes but hers and mine. I can afford to be honest.

'Memory rushes away from me at times,' I say. 'I get lost in remembrance and forget to write it down, so I must go back, seek the memory again and make sure my quill records it.'

What I do not say is that days go by when words refuse to come; when all I do is stare at the parchment.

'And how is your soul today?'

She is gentle with me. I reply with truth.

'It grieves.'

Other days I answer: 'It is heavy,' or 'It yearns to run,' or 'It is empty.'

She nods. We spend as much time in conversation as we do in silence. When she speaks it is to prod my memory of all I have been through, about the journey, about my sisters, about all that happened. To bring me back to the living. When she is silent it allows what has been spoken to permeate my heart. At times, the silence says more than the speech.

On the days that I am without words, she speaks with the quiet excitement I remember so well when we were at Saint Agatha's. It is enough for me to simply be with her.

Although she has much responsibility in her new position, and has ensured that the sisters in both the Bingen and Rupertsberg houses are in complete accord with her—'Such prickly creatures these nuns; one never knows their mind'—she sits with me every day, even on feast days like today, the Feast of Blessèd Benedict, the father of our Rule. She takes her time to unravel her memory and stitch it to mine, gathering me into the fabric of our shared past and of this new life that we also share.

She has only recently begun to speak to me about the great abbess. She did not want to muddle my head with stories. Her concern was for my recovery and my mourning.

'I spent much time with her,' she says of the old abbess. 'She was like all the stories told of her. Tall, erect, full of purpose, but also restless. Restless for God's word. Restless for change. She always looked like one whose ear is attuned to the summons of another. Distracted. Yes, that was it: distracted and restless. Did you know, she suffered greatly with head pains. They often brought on the visions she so eagerly awaited, but sometimes they were nothing more than searing headache. There wasn't enough betony in the world to cure them.'

The sound of laughter interrupts us. It is unseemly given the sombre time of remembrance we are in, and yet we can't help but smile. We get up from our seats and move to the window that overlooks the cloister.

A Flight of Saints

Below us, Sister Gretchen is frolicking with the children who appear each morning like a gaggle of geese at the Abbey door. With Abbess Elisa's blessing, she has been given care of them. She greets them, gives them food, teaches them their Pater Noster, and plays with them. Dressing up is a favourite activity. Sometimes she bathes the children and washes their clothes. Always, she makes them laugh. They never leave her side, but huddle close like chicks, even when their mothers arrive to fetch them. She has been granted her wish to be one like Saint Verena.

'Sister Gretchen was always blessed with high spirits. The children adore her.'

I am about to ask if she knows Sister Gretchen's birth story, but I stop. It is not mine to tell. I will ask Gretchen if she has told her, and to not be ashamed of it. No story is shameful. Our creation is the work of others and of God. The rest is life, and life brings what life brings.

'Do you remember when she left a small vial of ink in her pocket and it found its way into the wash?' The Abbess turns to me; her smiling-sad eyes search mine for the glimmer of recollection.

I stare at the pitted stone sill of the window as if it holds the memory. How much it resembles my mind: divots of memory, some deep, some shallow. Ah, there it is, far back in the vault of remembrance. I lift my head and laugh. 'Yes, and the surprise on Sister Bettina's face when everything in the wash turned blue. She thought it was a miracle wrought by the Virgin.'

Our laughter relaxes me.

'I confess that all my thoughts of Saint Agatha's come from a time as distant, as ancient, as Our Lord's first days in the stable.' I turn from the window and walk, eyes on the flags. 'A time when I was a child and thought as a child. I feel so changed now, more kin to the widow in the street than to the children who dance with Sister Gretchen. Little more than half a year has passed since we left Saint Agatha's, yet it seems I have lived a lifetime since.'

'Well, haven't you? Think of what you accomplished. You dreamed of being here, and here you are.'

The bitterness of ambition sits in my mouth. Perhaps this is what holds me back from reconciliation with myself. Was our journey sparked by dreaming of something better, or was it a need to prove my worth after being abandoned by my father and mother? Early memories are never done with us. Or was it purely for survival, to escape Mother Clothilde? Was it done for me or for my sisters? I am haunted by the words of Sister Miriam about there being no glory without sacrifice. Does the price of liberation justify sacrifice? If someone perishes during the pursuit of freedom, is the achievement rendered hollow? I want to feel that it is. For to survive at the cost of sweet Fey's life does not feel like survival at all.

Abbess Elisa pulls me into an embrace. It shocks me that I am as tall as her.

'I know that you are not thinking so much of Abbess Hildegard, that your heart trembles for another. It is her anniversary too.'

I have seen emotion prick her eyes when we mention Little Fey; have heard the ragged breath of grief in her voice.

A Flight of Saints

Or maybe it is the sound of my own voice: I am barely able to speak or think of my lost sister without weeping.

'I should have stayed closer to her.' This has become my refrain. I wish it would take its leave, but guilt is determined to live in me forever.

The day we were pulled from the river and taken to the infirmarium, they tried to revive Little Fey. My head had rolled toward those who worked to bring life back to her. I wanted to tell them to not bother, that I had already witnessed the departure of her soul. At the same time, I wanted them to keep trying, to claw her back from God; that He would be merciful, change His mind and send her back. When I saw the face of Mother Elena, nothing mattered after that. I knew we were all safe. Dead or alive, we were entirely safe and free.

It was many days before I came back to the world. I was told that my sisters kept vigil constantly. They said prayers. They chanted. When I eventually woke, they fed me meat broth. They spoke but did not expect answer, knowing my head was still in a watery state. When it cleared, when strength returned, that's when I began to sleep the sleep of the broken-hearted.

During the time that I was not in the world, my sisters washed and prepared Little Fey. They refused to put her in the ground until I was better and could witness her burial. Mother Elena stood firm with them. By then she had been declared abbess, and any argument from the community, if indeed any existed, never occurred. The Bingen sisters were too busy mourning the old abbess, not Little Fey. It wasn't until the new moon, on the Feast of Saint Luke, that we carried Little Fey, her body uncorrupted, to her grave. She is buried on Abbey land. Always with me.

Mother Elena—I mean to say Abbess Elisa; will I ever get it right?—holds me by my shoulders.

'Do not torment yourself. You did more for her than anyone. You cannot protect a person forever. You must give thanks to God, for He called her back, and she is with Him. She is with Hildegard too. I hold a vision of the old abbess holding her hand, questioning her with such energy that Sister Fey strains to hold her temper.'

That makes me smile. 'Sister Fey came into womanhood during our journey. It made her bold; she was no longer meek as her piety suggested. There was humour and playfulness in her, but also wisdom and a lot of fight. I was glad to see it.'

'Her soul had ripened and was ready to be reclaimed by God.' She leads me back to the desk. 'She was born wise, beyond all understanding. It should be no surprise that she was taken from us so soon. The wise always depart before the fools.'

She pauses. A curious look appears on her face. 'Did you believe her stigmata?'

Oh dear. Here we are.

'No,' I say. 'I knew it was a fraud because I saw her begin it. She scratched her palms to the point of bleeding. She herself knew it was not genuine, but some part of her convinced her that it was. Or others convinced her of it. It surprised me that no one questioned it.'

The heat of guilt rushes into my face. My throat tightens. Although I have said that I can afford to be honest in my writ-

A Flight of Saints

ing, there are some things I cannot bring myself to confess. In truth, I encouraged Fey's fraud. I often goaded her to make herself more holy, told her to claim that she'd had visions, or to suddenly stand up in chapel and babble in tongues, saying that it was the words of one of the prophets. I told her that doing so would make Mother Elena admire her, and favour her even more. Fey was all about favour: She sought the halo of pride. And I was jealous of Mother Elena's concern and protection of Fey. I wanted Mother to protect and concern herself with me, and me only. I wanted her to see me, not Little Fey. I had seen her look of scepticism at Fey's stigmata, and I worked quietly to further that scepticism. I urged Fey to flaunt her piety in order to sew Mother's disfavour. We practised her faux rapture, and when she displayed it, I saw how the other nuns, including Mother Elena, turned away in embarrassment. Fey never knew the shame she was cultivating because I encouraged her, and she trusted me. Soon enough, Mother Elena began to steer Fey's piety to more practical uses, such as cleaning the grates and washing the dishes like the rest of us. No one knew I had abetted the deception. Not even Little Fey. As she reckoned with the shame of her deceit, she did not for one moment assign blame to me. I had never let on that I knew her stigmata was self-inflicted, and thus she judged me innocent. Oh, Little Fey, forgive me.

'Well, you saw the coin it brought us,' the Abbess says now. 'I was not proud of that, but we can only survive with what we are given, and I have absolved myself of my part in it, knowing that we used it to help the poor. As for Sister Fey, hers was a sad affliction. It is difficult to know how to help one so deep in the grip of inner pain.'

My head snaps up.

'What inner pain?'

The Abbess sits down, and gestures for me to do likewise. 'Fey did not come to Saint Agatha's by chance.'

'I know. I was the one who found her at the front door. She had been abandoned.'

She smiles. 'That is partly true, but there's more to her story. There was a young farmer who lived near Saint Agatha's whose wife had recently died. This farmer brought vegetables and meat to us as a way to honour her life. In time, he caught the eye of one of our sisters, who fell in love with him, as he had for her. Such is the way of God, is it not? When she came to be with child, I urged her to leave the convent and make a home with the farmer and raise their child together. He was a good, honest man, and he would have cared for her and the child. But the sister was adamant; she said the child was her sin made manifest, and she refused to tell the farmer, and vowed never to see him again. The farmer was distraught, but the sister would not be turned. Only I was privy to all this. And when her time came, she delivered the child in silence at Saint Agatha's. Her child was Fey. After a brief weaning, she gave the infant to me. I kept my sister's secret, and placed the babe at the front door, where I knew she would be quickly found. When Fey learned that she had been abandoned, she felt the pain deeply, and began to harm herself. When that old sister claimed it to be the stigmata—oh, how I wish I had spoken up—well, once something is planted it is hard to convince others that it is not there.'

A Flight of Saints

I am astonished.

'The two of you were so close, and I worried that she would bring grief to you so I kept a close eye on her. I wanted to shield you but you were so self-assured, and any interference from me might have made things worse.'

But they might also have made things easier and better.

I don't want her to read my doubts or misgivings so I say, 'She was overwrought the morning we crossed the bridge to pay homage to the old abbess. She'd had a dream the night before of falling. I had put it down to the weight of the day, of the entire journey, of presenting ourselves at the Abbey. Do you think she foresaw her death?'

'Perhaps. She had a sixth sense about some things, and when her thoughts were proven correct it gave her the confidence to believe herself special and deserving of stigmata, even while knowing the falsity of it.'

'Why did Fey never tell me about her birth? We were the closest of sisters. It was not as if I would have held it against her.'

'Even the closest of friends hold secrets from one another, not out of malice or furtiveness, but because it is simply too painful to relate. What you need to know is that her death was an accident. And yet, a miraculous one.'

Again, her words surprise.

'How so?'

'Her death brought us together. I have told no one about this, but I will tell you: That morning, I was preparing to flee this place. Although Hildegard made clear that she wished me to be her successor, the other sisters were not in favour of it. They saw me as an outsider, and I knew that once the Abbess was cold, they would do everything to prevent me from assuming authority. I chose not to fight it; I couldn't face another challenge. I entered religious life for peace, not for war. I decided that when Hildegard died, I would go to Francia or to Britannia and join an Order there. On the day she returned to God, I was going to use the distraction of the throng of mourners as a cover to slip away. I was all set to leave when the commotion on the bridge reached my ears, and I ran to the river to offer help. When they pulled you from the water, and I saw it was you, my plans changed in a heartbeat. I made it my sole purpose to restore you to wellness. You will not believe this, but you worked a miracle that day: Those sisters who had been hostile to me were impressed by my quickness and my healing work, and their hearts turned toward me rather than against me. They concurred with Hildegard's wishes and made me Abbess.'

I am thoroughly dumbstruck. So much so that she places a finger under my chin to close my mouth.

She draws away from me.

'I must go and tend to my work and to the others, my dear. I will come again tomorrow. Is there anything you need?'

I look at my hands. I have not had to partake in the community's work because Abbess Elisa does not want strain put upon me until I am fully healed. My hands are white and without blemish. You wouldn't know they had fought their way through gorge and over range; through a wilderness of good and evil, that they had murdered. Clean through idleness, not so clean of sin.

I have been truthful with Abbess Elisa about most of what has happened; the light and the dark, and she has waved away my concern, as I knew she would, and justified my deeds as defending myself and my sisters. 'Doubts and recriminations will rise to the surface from time to time, but it is only the natural way the soul purges its distress. Release all to God.'

She sees me looking at my hands.

'You could return to your manuscript work,' she offers. 'You had a gift for it. Sister Marta would welcome more hands in the scriptorium.'

As soon as she says it, I notice how she stands like the letter R, head tilted forward in anticipation of an answer, leg slightly extended, arm curved toward her hip. Suddenly, I am rampant with the joyful memory of creation, inks, colours, the smell of hides and brush hairs. I can draw the great variety of flora and fauna I observed on our journey. I can draw Little Fey as the letter W, as I saw her under water.

'I would like that very much.'

'As you write your story you can practise your art in the empty spaces. The heart can be more disposed to describing an experience in a picture than in words. Just a thought.'

It's a good one.

At the door, she turns and says, 'I almost forgot. A letter arrived for you. I meant to bring it with me, but I shall do so tomorrow. From Grasse. A man writing to say he arrived home safely. Does it mean anything to you?'

She leaves, and I am alone again. I go to the window and face the land from whence I came. The air is hazy, and I can only see so far. Perhaps for the best.

My eyes return to the smaller of the two rivers below me. The Nahe. I wonder if it joins at some point with the Adige. I watch the current's rhythmic lap, and it makes me think of walking the riverbank in bare feet, mud-streaked legs, dirty tunics. My hands glide down the sides of my habit, black and smooth as silk. No tow now. My grief spares a moment to give thanks. I am here. I am safe. I am warm. I am home.

In the depth of my soul, as fathomless and dark as the seas, many emotions and anxieties fight among themselves, like children over a plaything, leaving me to mediate them from time to time. Some of them are things I have not yet spoken about to the Abbess. I have yet to ask her about Father Volmar, and my encounter with him. Or have I already done so? The mind is still a soggy, mushy field. Then again, what import would it have? I am here, regardless of whether the monk-priest was alive or a ghost. Counsel, miracles, visions, they arrive in many forms and I must respond to the form that is real to me.

And there is the other question—about the mother who birthed me, the one Father Volmar said was in this place. I am certain of the answer though: Mother Elena. I think it was she who was betrothed to my father and forsook him for the Church. I have not forgotten the way she looked at me when he brought me to Saint Agatha's: the quiet gasp, the quivering chin; and afterwards, how she seemed to favour me over the others. Now that she described how deftly and secretly she handled Little Fey's birth, it makes me more certain: This is one who had prior experience with such things. Even in her daily visits to me now, I regard the way she looks at me, the

A Flight of Saints

way she has been attending me. Our features are similar—same chestnut hair, same shaped mouth, the same restless eyes, the small, swift hands. When she stands like the letter R, I recognise it as a pose I strike too. One day I will ask her. It will have to be soon.

A knock at the door jolts me. My shoulders drop. There is no end of interruptions in a convent. How can one contemplate anything here in this constant state of busyness?

'Come.'

The door swings open; my face suddenly brightens.

'*Allora*. Do they feed you here? Is this a prison? Look at you, so thin.'

I fly into her arms.

'If it is a prison, it is a nice one. I recommend it.'

'In that case, I bid you blessings on Saint Scholastica's day.'

My puzzled expression earns one of opprobrium from Mea. (If ever there is a face to prompt the mind to speedy recollection it is Mea's.)

'Ah, of course,' I say. It is the Feast of Blessèd Benedict, but in keeping with the feminine liturgical calendar devised by Sister Gretchen during our escape, Mea honours Blessèd Benedict's twin sister Scholastica. Ever the rebel.

'Come,' I say. 'Look who I can see from here.'

She glides to the window that overlooks the cloister.

'Is that Gretchen? Ah, it is!' She waves wildly to her and blows kisses.

Mea is much changed. She is as dear to me as a friend can be. And to think she was once my enemy.

I was surprised to see her during my recovery in the infirmarium. I had thought she would have left, gone to her life of liberation. But that was not the case. She has told me that she is more like me than I realise: No plan. She simply wanted to flee Saint Agatha's and figured that the details of where she ended up would take care of themselves.

She sets down her basket and we unpack it.

'The Abbess let me in. Such kindness. She embraces me like one of her own. I still cannot believe she was at Saint Agatha's. I thought the place only housed witches. But her…'

She sees my baffled face.

'Do you remember?' asks Mea. 'She was gone from Saint Agatha's by the time I arrived.'

My mind takes longer to piece together the past. Yes, of course.

She has brought so much food.

'I cannot eat it all!'

'Nor will you,' she says. 'I told the Abbess I was bringing you only a small amount. Most of it is for the convent larder.'

She places my writing tools and parchment on the windowsill, then sweeps the table clean with her hand. She lays a rough cloth over it, smooths it out.

She is Mea now. Not Sister Mea, though she might as well be; I am told that some in the town refer to her that way. Others call her *Duchessa*. They like the sound of royalty in their midst. Everyone knows her. She is the lady with the fine clothes and the finer heart. She hires them to help her around her home and pays well; she patronises their businesses, and gives money to send their children away to be educated.

A Flight of Saints

After I was pulled from the river, she, too, helped nurse me back to life. Day and night, she never left my side, I was told. When I recovered, and we had buried Little Fey, she went to the Abbess, made her confession and asked for release from her vows. In return—Mea is always about quid pro quo—she became a tertiary of the Order of Mount Saint Rupert. She is a blessing in every way possible. She gives time and riches to both our houses, and is here most days to attend Sext and to share the midday meal with us, or to supply it.

I also know, though Mea denies it, that during our journey she added more jewels to the velvet pouch. No wonder I struggled to keep the number of gems straight. Before we fled Saint Agatha's she had sewn some into her bundle and used them to refill the pouch. 'It was full to the brim,' Abbess Elisa gushed later, saying that Mea had given her the pouch when the community admitted us. She has also helped Clovis and Valentina set up home and business.

'All is well?'

'Yes, Sister Lucia, I am well. Alone and well. You know me; I cannot follow the rules of others, so I am best on my own. Besides, my true family is here.'

'Is that new?' Her tunic reminds me of the pines that gird the mountains.

'A woman in the town had this cloth. She needed money for food, so we exchanged. Of course, I had to have it made into something.'

'They will match your pretty shoes.'

'Ha! You remember the shoes. Well, they are pretty to look at, but I do not wear them.'

'If I did not live here, I would wear them.'

'Then my suspicions are correct: You are fonder of finery than me. Not the right thinking of a nun.' She wags her finger, and we laugh.

We haven't spoken of that day when we crossed the crowded bridge, when I almost confided to her that I was not going to enter the Bingen community but instead lead a life of my own choosing. My mind then was disordered, overwrought. This is where I belong.

'When do you receive the little gold crown the others wear?'

'When I am professed, which will be soon.'

'I cannot say I like it, do you?'

'I am indifferent to it. But 'tis the custom.'

I bite into the bread, soft as a down pillow. A few sunflower seeds stick to my teeth.

'What news of Valentina and Clovis?'

'This bread is from their bakery. Business is good. The baby will arrive by the next full moon.'

My arms fold across my belly. She does not notice, having closed her eyes and raised her hand in anticipation of my question.

'Don't worry. The Abbess has instructed Valentina to come here when her time is due. The infirmarian and the Abbess will tend to the birth themselves.'

Like Mea, Valentina and Clovis live and work nearby. Their bread supplies the Abbey and the town, and they visit when time and work allow.

'Everything is fine, Lucia. You no longer have to control the world. You are not Sarah the Matriarch, though you would have made a good mother.'

The remark pierces me, rolls me back to the where and the when. One hand strokes my belly, where another secret leaps in my womb; where movement exists in the place it once felt hunger and anger. Six full moons have passed since the night I was defiled and spoiled. But Mea cannot know of this. Her ministrations of tansy and pennyroyal did not have the desired effect. She would feel terrible about it.

'I am sorry. I did not…'

'It is alright. The memory torments from time to time but there is nothing to be done of it. It arrives and leaves. The Abbess counsels me well. It is good to be with her again. And to have all my sisters near.' I pause. 'I am told he was hanged. I feel better for it.'

'Clovis and I went to Speyer to see it. To make certain it happened.'

A long sigh leaves me, unbidden. Even I am surprised by it.

'The attack made upon you is now part of your wisdom,' she says. 'Embedded in you. Don't lose the anger, but at the same time make peace with it. For yourself.'

'I feel old.'

She smiles. 'No, you feel new. Trials make us weary, but so does change. It's not burden you feel but alteration. Not everyone knows the difference.'

'You should be a nun with wisdom like that.'

We are silent for a while.

'The Abbess has asked me to work in the scriptorium. I am agreed to the idea.'

'This is monsterful news, Lucia. All that you dreamed is

yours. I am happy for you.'

Tears suddenly collect in her eyes and she pretends to resume interest in her food. She knows I do not have all I dreamed. She misses Fey, too, but we are not ready to speak of it.

When Mea leaves, my world falls silent again.

A white feather drifts past the window. It is so large that I am compelled to lean out and look toward Heaven to see what creature has shed it. Ah, I know.

'Hello, dear Fey,' I call out. *'Ti amo per semper.'*

The sun casts its afternoon portion of glitter upon the Rhein and the Nahe. Something Little Fey once said rises from the glare: 'To find light, you must first dive into the dark. It is the only way to endure adversity.'

I have found light, though I do not yet feel light. Still, I know that I am alive and that my soul is awake. And that I carry another within me. When I tell the Abbess, she will know what to do. Perhaps she and I—mother and daughter—are destined, for whatever reason, to breed beyond convention.

To take the veil is to relinquish possession and ownership and take the oath of obedience and chastity. That is what the world outside the cloister has been told; it is not the one that exists inside it. We are the broken, the scorned, the abandoned. We wrestle in lonely silence with the dark and the light, with the angels and demons of our nature. Like Sister Gretchen says, we are all saints because we have suffered.

It is almost time for Nones. Down in the yard, the black and white wake of sisters moves toward chapel. I must join them.

A Flight of Saints

I tidy my desk and prepare to leave when my eyes are drawn to the other side of the Rhein, where the land is greening. I spy a shepherdess guiding her flock along the hillside and I pause to watch her. But what is this? A dark shape hunkers in the grass. The shepherdess sees it. A wolf. She waves her crook at the creature while the sheep skitter-skatter behind her. The wolf lunges, but the shepherdess stomps forward, crook raised to strike. The wolf retreats, but from time to time it looks back to gauge its chances. The shepherdess, meanwhile, gathers the flock and herds it up, up the steep hill until they are over it, and out of sight and danger.

THE END

AUTHOR'S NOTE

The genesis for this novel began a few years ago when I read a newspaper article about a group of nuns who fled their European convent alleging abuse and overwork. Their mother superior took them to court for breach of vows. The story astonished me. Cloistered women escaping into the secular world, a place with which they had little facility and few contacts, takes guts. Did this happen often? If it happens in this century, it surely must have in previous ones.

Interest piqued and merged with my love of all things medieval, I planted the scenario in twelfth-century Italy, a time when nuns were revered, and convents were the safest places for females; where they acquired power, responsibility, education and skills. We owe a lot to nuns for advances in science, medicine, hygiene, and health, not forgetting their considerable impact on music, art, and literature.

As my idea germinated, Hildegard of Bingen (1098–1179) elbowed in. Talk about an iconoclast: This brilliant abbess refused to be silenced, and spoke her mind to popes and emperors. Attaining rock-star status, she attracted legions of medieval fan-girls eager to emulate her.

In this work of fiction, a few real-life characters appear. In addition to Hildegard is the priest-monk Father Volmar. Prior and confessor to the nuns at the Disibodenberg monastery where Hildegard was raised, he was her spiritual advisor, and recorded her visions. Their friendship lasted more than sixty years until his death in 1173. Hildegard's death on September 17, 1179, has been kept by the Church as her feast day. As a coincidental aside, her successor was Domina Elisa, of whom I was unaware until after I had written my novel and I had already named the character Elena/Elisa. As far as can be determined, Domina Elisa's story is unknown; what I've presented is entirely from my imagination.

I wish to acknowledge Joanne W. Anderson's research into the cult of Mary Magdalene: The Magdalen Frescos Cycle in Trentino, Tyrol, and Swiss Grisons 1300–1500 (PhD Diss: University of Warwick, 2009). For literary purposes, I have brought these beliefs into the late twelfth century, a good 150 years before the cult's time.

The saints and feast days in this novel conform, where possible, to a twelfth-century Benedictine missal from southern Italy, now housed in the Biblioteca Apostolica Vaticana (Vat. lat. 6082). When the Roman Catholic Church revised the General Roman Calendar in 1970, many feast days were reorganised. For example, the Feast Day of Saint Lucia was moved from September 16 to December 13. In my novel, however, our rebellious novices devise an all-female calendar of their own design and date.

ACKNOWLEDGEMENTS

We all create our own sisterhood, that necessary community (of men and women) that brings constancy and faith to life and work. I am grateful for my core team: Colin, my children and their partners, and friends Jeannette, Nancy, Allan, Trudi, Paul, Robert, Kim, Georgina, and Jimmy.

My Faber posse has been equally indispensable. Tamsin Barrett, Sacha Bonsor, Santanu Chakrabarti, Amanda Ford, Jan Holland-Hayes, Clare Lynas, Trevor Steel, and Shelley Weiner were first readers and invaluable critics. They continue to be my literary-life support.

My agent Judith Murray and her team at Greene & Heaton provided valuable input and encouragement which was much appreciated.

Rev. Elisabeth Lakey has for the last decade included me in her monthly email of saints, obscure and not. Some of them have found their way into Sister Gretchen's knowledge.

The Sisterhood of Saint John the Divine, Toronto, continues to sustain me spiritually, and has encouraged my knowledge and interest in monastic life, past and present. Deo gratias.

A heap of thanks to Sarah Dronfield for proofreading; Dinah Drazin for formatting; Stephanie Hofmann for the map and technical design; and Haychley Webb for the cover art.

Is it weird to thank one's imaginary characters? Well, I don't care if it is: I am truly grateful to Lucia, Bartolomea, Valentina, Gretchen and Little Fey for living in my head these last few years with their sorrow, humour, nascent courage, and enduring friendship. I'm in awe of their perilous journey, one that was no doubt endured by real women in centuries past.

EB
2025

Made in United States
Cleveland, OH
21 March 2025